Killer by Candlelight

ALSO BY LIS HOWELL

SUZY SPENCER MYSTERY SERIES
Book 1: The Flower Arranger at All Saints
Book 2: The Chorister at the Abbey
Book 3: The Death of a Teacher
Book 4: The Judge at St Jane's
Book 5: The Gardener in the Graveyard
Book 6: Killer by Candlelight

KILLER BY CANDLELIGHT

LIS HOWELL

Suzy Spencer Mystery Series Book 6

JOFFE BOOKS

Joffe Books, London
www.joffebooks.com

First published in Great Britain in 2025

© Lis Howell

This book is a work of fiction. Names, characters, businesses, organizations, places and events are either the product of the author's imagination or are used fictitiously. Any resemblance to actual persons, living or dead, events or locales is entirely coincidental. The spelling used is British English except where fidelity to the author's rendering of accent or dialect supersedes this. The right of Lis Howell to be identified as author of this work has been asserted in accordance with the Copyright, Designs and Patents Act 1988.

No part of this book may be used or reproduced in any manner for the purpose of training artificial intelligence technologies or systems. In accordance with Article 4(3) of the Digital Single Market Directive 2019/790, Joffe Books expressly reserves this work from the text and data mining exception.

Cover art by Dee Dee Book Covers

ISBN: 978-1-80573-116-0

CHAPTER ONE

And they had no child, because that Elizabeth was barren, and they both were now well stricken in years. Luke 1:7

The summer sun shone through the trees. There was a sense of drowsy peace. But Suzy Spencer sat up suddenly in her garden chair. She was overwhelmed by a vivid memory of winter, caused by sunlight on the thick white roses draped over the wall. For a second, it looked like snow, and she was transported back to the day when it all began . . .

* * *

The weather wasn't too bad as she was about to set off from Tarnfield, the village where she lived in Mid-Cumbria. The snow was light and wet, but it wasn't sticking. There had been heavier snowfalls on the coast, but travelling was still possible.

'I'm not sure about this job,' she said, standing outside her front door and looking up the lane. She ran her fingers through her spiky blonde hair, puffing out her cheeks against the cold. She was going away on an assignment, something she didn't do as much these days.

She turned to her husband, Robert, who had come out to see her off, and jumped. 'What the heck is that, Rob?'

'It's my old mac. I found it in the back of the cupboard. It's got this useful hood . . .'

'I can see that. You look like a mad monk! It's ancient.'

'I've only had it for thirty years.'

'Is that all? Look, I want to kiss you goodbye but I'm not venturing into that hood.'

Robert laughed, and kissed Suzy enthusiastically on the lips.

'Yuk!' she said. 'It's like being embraced by Rasputin.' But he looked all right now she could see him properly. The fine snow was melting on his greying hair and the cold brought brightness to his eyes.

'I'll miss you,' she said, seriously.

'You'd better go, before I persuade you to change your mind.'

* * *

Suzy was a TV producer based in Manchester, but lately she had been working more in Norbridge, on her Cumbrian podcasts. She had agonized about taking this latest job.

But it had been too good to pass up. Just after Christmas she'd had an email from a woman in New York called Eva Delmondo.

Eva was the Communications Director for the Caldfell Chorus music project. It was an intensive choral singing course, to be held at Caldfell Hall in West Cumbria, privately financed by a wealthy US couple with Cumbrian connections. They would be recruiting amateur singers to take part in a new composition.

The email led to a transatlantic Zoom. Eva Delmondo explained that she was representing 'two individuals of high net worth'.

Suzy laughed. 'You mean the Scott-Broughtons.'

Everyone in the county knew all about them. Gervase Scott-Broughton was a fabulously rich music streamer who had returned to his ancestral home in West Cumbria with his American wife. They'd employed local builders to refurb the place, so word had spread like wildfire.

Eva Delmondo said portentously, 'My clients are re-imagining a beautiful home and concert venue.'

'Yes. I know. In Caldfell.'

'You seem well informed, Mrs Spencer.'

'Just call me Suzy. And I hate to seem rude, but I need to cook supper. What is it you really want?'

'OK, I'll cut to the chase.' Apparently, the Scott-Broughtons wanted to involve the whole community in their music project. *Hmm*, Suzy thought. *Nothing like sucking up to the locals.*

'We're performing in the family chapel at the stunning Caldfell Hall, which of course Gervase and Lauren run sustainably,' Eva gushed. 'There'll be a livestream of the premiere of a new exciting piece of choral music, free to access, at the end of the week. We're recruiting local singers and I'm looking for a new singing talent. A little choirboy perhaps . . .'

'Or girl?'

'Oh yes. Of course.'

But Suzy could sense it was a cute little boy treble she was looking for. Eva Delmondo had a ruthless marketing brain under her breathless voice. Eva went on to reiterate the project was sustainable and eco-friendly. Caldfell Hall was miles from a town. When Gervase Scott-Broughton's ancestors had built it, it had been completely self-sufficient. Gervase was restoring that ethos. What was there not to like?

Clever. But to Suzy it all sounded a bit contrived.

'They're pushing the Cumbrian connection and their eco-friendliness,' she told Robert later. 'They're obsessed with their image as local heroes, rather than landed gentry.'

'And that sort of thing plays well these days.'

'Yes. I'm not saying they're being cynical, but they're definitely thinking about their image. It's opportunist. They want me to do a podcast, building up to the performance. They've got a studio the BBC would die for, in an eighteenth-century Gothic folly in the grounds of the Hall. They call it the chapel. I'm supposed to do interviews and get the sense of what it's like being at home with the Scott-Broughtons — making crazily rich people seem nice and normal.'

'Nice and normal like us?' Robert paused. 'Me anyway...'

'Some people think you're nice, Robert, but you've got a nasty sense of humour.'

'And some people think you're normal, Suzy, but we all know you're bonkers.'

She stood up and smacked him lightly over the head with the shiny hard copy of the Caldfell Chorus prospectus.

Robert laughed. 'Would you drive there and back every day?'

'No. I'd have to stay.'

'Pity.'

They smiled at each other. Suzy had always commuted to Manchester or Newcastle for her work, even when her children were young. But now Jake and Molly were independent and living away, and she and Robert were enjoying life on their own for the first time.

'I'd only be at Caldfell Hall for the last few days of the course. And the money is good.'

That mattered. Their old house, The Briars, gobbled up funds. But Suzy loved it. The house had been a refuge after her first husband had left her. He'd uprooted Suzy and the children to Tarnfield in search of a rural idyll. But he'd found that village life cramped his style, and in the first wet winter he hightailed it back to Newcastle and his glamorous PA. Suzy had coped alone for a while until she and Robert met. They'd been an unlikely couple. But Robert enjoyed his ready-made family. The Spencers had come as a tightly wrapped package, but that was fine. He loved them all.

Suzy outlined the dates. 'The Caldfell choral singing course lasts a week, and I don't need to be there at the start. The premiere performance is on Candlemas, February the second. And the clincher is that the music's by Edwin Armstrong.'

'Edwin! Really? Well, that's different . . .'

Suzy and Robert had met Edwin and Alex Armstrong at the time of the chorister murders at Norbridge, and became friends. Then international fame had taken the Armstrongs abroad and they'd lost touch. Edwin was now a well-known composer.

'What's he writing?' Robert asked, with more interest.

'It's a setting of the *Nunc Dimittis*, the Candlemas canticle about Jesus as a baby being presented in the temple.'

'Yes, and old Simeon sang about departing in peace now he'd seen the Lord's anointed. Lovely stuff.' Robert sang in the choir at All Saints Church in Tarnfield. He'd convinced Suzy to go to church with him, though she still insisted she was sceptical. 'Maybe you should do this job, Suzy. It sounds interesting.'

And so it was agreed that Suzy would go to the Caldfell Chorus. But as she climbed into the car, wet sleet spattering her face, she still wondered if it was the right thing to do. She pulled away from the spot where she had crashed her car into Robert's fence all those years ago, leading to their meeting and romance. Back then, he had been the local stuffy widower, while she was a controversial daytime TV producer — and suddenly she felt a sense of loss. Robert was older than she was. She didn't want them to be apart.

'Oh, don't be ridiculous,' she said to her image in the driving mirror, as a flurry of grey wetness hit the windscreen head on. Robert wasn't yet seventy and fit as a flea. Wasn't he?

She pushed that thought away. She needed to concentrate if she was to get to Caldfell before nightfall.

* * *

As Suzy drove west, her old friend Alexandra Armstrong was sneaking quietly towards the door at the back of the beautiful seventeenth-century Caldfell Hall. Behind her, Alex could hear loud voices around the log fire in the huge open sitting room, all competing to entertain Gervase Scott-Broughton.

Alex hated the sycophantic atmosphere, but her husband Edwin hardly noticed. He was wrapped up in his work as a composer, creating a new piece of music which he thought might be his best yet.

'Where's Parry?' Gervase Scott-Broughton brayed. 'We need Parry to make us all laugh. Is he off chatting up one of the little sopranos? Horny beast!' He laughed too forcefully, and a rumble of male voices followed. Most people on the course disliked the choral director, Parry Palmer, but were too scared to say so. Palmer was court jester to the all-powerful Gervase Scott-Broughton. Now, after lunch, and before the afternoon rehearsal, Gervase and his cronies were hitting the decanter. Chief among them was Gervase's poor relation, local folksinger Brigham Broughton. The two men had bonded again after forty years — the super-smooth businessman and the busking crusty cousin. They were an unlikely combination.

As Alex Armstrong walked by, she heard Gervase call, 'Edwin deserted you again, Alex? Come on, join us for a snorter and a bit of banter. No? Spoilsport!'

She pretended not to hear, pushing open the back door to be met by a wall of freezing air. She gasped, taking a deep breath; then she ventured out, rounding the house to the front, looking at the white magical view sweeping down to the Irish Sea. For a few seconds, being at Caldfell Hall was almost worth it.

The air had the metallic smell of new snow. It crunched under her feet as she walked. Despite being Cumbrian, she had never been to Caldfell before. For the last ten years she and her husband had spent their time between London, Philadelphia and their base in Frankfurt.

Then Edwin had told her that billionaire Gervase Scott-Broughton and his American wife, Lauren, were considering commissioning a new choral work and had approached him.

The Scott-Broughtons had made a fortune through their music streaming service. Now they were siphoning massive funds into their new project. It seemed to Alex and Edwin like a wonderful opportunity to come home for a while. They had friends in the Norbridge area, and Alex particularly wanted to see Suzy Spencer again.

But now it was already day four of a ten-day trip. Alex and Edwin had been trapped at the Hall since arriving, first by the intensity of the work and then by the weather. There were fifty people involved in the project, staying at the Hall and in the surrounding buildings, and storms were coming in from the sea. Alex could see the sky was thick with the heavy yellow-grey that meant more bad weather on the way. They would be snowed in by evening.

The atmosphere inside the Hall was equally heavy.

Gervase Scott-Broughton had made it clear that he wanted to encourage gifted amateurs from the area. It was a carefully designed marketing ploy, presenting the Scott-Broughtons as community-orientated and yet capable of producing a world-class product. Each member of the chorus had been selected after sending an audio file for the audition. They had arrived full of excitement and enthusiasm.

But the choral director treated the locals with contempt. Parry Palmer, brought in from London and supremely metropolitan, mocked northern accents and couldn't hide his contempt. And, thanks to the weather, there was no escape.

In the coffee break that morning, Alex overheard two of the male singers.

'Poor old Dave Oldcastle. He's got a bit of vibrato on the high notes, but his mid-range is fine.'

'It's nerves. The more Palmer goads him the worse he gets.'

'Yeah. Dave's talented, but you could see he was cracking. Palmer's vicious.'

'But Palmer is Gervase's choice. And he does teach at the Academy of Voice.'

'True. Top place. So how has Palmer survived?'

'Maybe he knows where the bodies are buried.'

'Got you. 'Cos Palmer's hardly world class, is he? Mind you, Armstrong's music is. He's excellent.'

Alex had breathed a sigh of relief. At least her husband's reputation was intact.

She silently agreed that Parry Palmer had been a strange choice as musical director for the Scott-Broughtons. She'd listened to the gossip. Not only was Palmer a bully and a snob, but he was also rumoured to survive by appropriating his students' work for his own musical arrangements. These days rearranging music was a big deal. The popularity of community choirs had given a boost to musicians who could adapt classics for enthusiastic amateurs. That was Parry Palmer's speciality — along with making people miserable.

Alex stood looking down at the grey sea beyond the rolling white farmland. She could smell the woodsmoke. For a moment the scene seemed idyllic. But they were all stuck here until the premiere of Edwin's work. The road was gritted, up to a point, but the steep drive to the house was like a glacier. The caterers were living in, and lavish supplies had arrived earlier by truck, so at least they could eat. And drink, though that had its downside.

Now Alex had to decide where to go for her walk while the weak daylight remained. There was a path ahead which had been cleared, leading to a fork. One way went upwards to the ancient graves and pillars of stone perched above the Hall on the fell, one of many prehistoric sites in Cumbria. The other way led down to the weird building where Edwin's music would be performed.

Alex turned downhill to the Gothic folly. If the door was locked, she would walk back slowly in the hope that Edwin might take a break from his work. Then they could have tea in their spacious bedroom, which she had to admit was lovely. It had a huge fireplace and four-poster bed. A big window looked out at the back of the Hall, over the fells to where the Neolithic graves stood against the horizon with the stark standing stones. But she doubted Edwin had noticed the view. When Edwin was working, he was aware of nothing else.

Standing in the heavy stillness, Alex heard a fabulous voice in the distance. It was the sixteen-year-old Lily Martin. There were a lot of unhappy singers at Caldfell, but Alex felt most for Lily, the teenage find, shipped in from Norbridge for local colour. The project's comms director, Eva Delmondo, had wanted a cute choirboy, but Edwin as composer had overridden her once he'd heard Lily's voice at the auditions. Eva had sulked momentarily, but she was a realist.

And musically it had turned out very well. Lily Martin wasn't just a gimmick: she had a wonderful voice and was perfect for Edwin's composition. But Alex thought Lily was out of her depth. She may have been sixteen, but she should have been protected by a professional chaperone, or a parent at least.

In the still air, the girl's voice rose above everything, singing the haunting words of the *Magnificat*. It was the song of the Virgin Mary to her older cousin Elizabeth, celebrating her pregnancy. Elizabeth was an older woman, barren for years. But now she too was pregnant like Mary.

Alex had warmed to Lily, not just because she had a gorgeous voice but because she was so young and so lost at Caldfell Hall. If Alex had a daughter like Lily, she wouldn't let her near this poisonous atmosphere.

But Alex hadn't any children. She was in her late forties. Like Elizabeth in the Bible story, she was an older woman, unable to conceive without a miracle. Alex's last cycle of IVF treatment had been two months earlier. Now there was evidence it hadn't worked. She needed somewhere to be by herself and come to terms with it.

Setting off down the path, she slipped slightly but regained her footing, making progress towards the folly. She pushed the door, which was newly oiled and varnished; it swung silently open. What had once been a fanciful family chapel had been stripped and turned into a state-of-the-art recording studio with space for a choir of two dozen, plus the soloists and the small chamber orchestra Edwin needed.

There were candles burning on the table where an altar would have been, and on the window ledges. The light flickered in the draught from the open door. Her eye caught the strange patterns of muddied snow on the tiled floor. She looked up and saw the back of a seated figure, who seemed to be praying. The place was so quiet, she could almost hear the candles guttering.

'Parry?' she said in disbelief. Then louder: 'Parry?' Her voice seemed to disturb the man in the seat, as, slowly, he fell sideways and crumpled to the floor.

There was a penknife in his neck. Lurid scratches on his face. And a lot of blood.

Parry Palmer, musical director of the Caldfell Chorus, was dead.

CHAPTER TWO

Sing to the Lord a new song, and his praise from the end of the earth. Isaiah 42:10

Robert Clark watched Suzy's car bump unsteadily up the lane, on her way to her assignment in West Cumbria. It was Wednesday afternoon, and she would be home on Sunday. Five days. But it felt like an age.

He remembered the day they met, when she drove into his fence. Suzy had been dropping the kids off at the station to visit their dad in Newcastle. Jake had been in his teens and Molly was six. Suzy was a good driver and had been mortified by the accident. Robert's wife, Mary, who had died the year before, had already made sure everyone in Tarnfield thought Suzy was a mess, a crazy outsider. But Mary had had her own reasons.

Robert sighed. It was all so long ago and seemed like a different world. Correction. It *was* a different world. He went back into the house and upstairs to his study.

If you could call it a study. It was the small single bedroom with its window over the front door. For years he had used this room for his work as a lecturer in English at the local college. But last year he'd retired.

The Briars was an attractive house. He'd been rattling around on his own when he met Suzy, and they'd been caught up in a murder in the village, to do with secrets and lies in a rigid old-fashioned community where you hid your faults.

But these days, village life had changed. People 'vented' more — and the problems in Cumbria were like everywhere else. Poverty, drugs, mental health, homelessness. He was finding that out, volunteering at the Norbridge Advice Centre.

'You wouldn't believe how remote Cumbria was when I first came here as a kid on holiday,' Robert had told Christopher Murray, the founder of the Centre. 'The M6 only went to Penrith, and you couldn't get Radio One.'

'Not all bad then,' Christopher had laughed.

'Oh, don't get me wrong, there were some wonderful aspects to it. But people could be very judgemental.' Christopher nodded. He was a pillar of the local LGBTQ+ group and made no secret of his homosexuality. But that wouldn't have played well in rural Cumbria in the seventies.

'Even a few years ago, when Suzy's husband left her and she was a single mum in Tarnfield, there were people who snubbed her,' Robert had said. 'Of course, it's different now.'

'I would hope so!'

Robert liked Christopher Murray. He was a calm, competent presence at the Advice Centre, infinitely patient with the clients, and with the paperwork. He had his quirks — always wanting to be called Christopher rather than Chris, and in Robert's view, occasionally being a bit too bureaucratic. But the Centre was well run. These days, safeguarding and respect for the individual were paramount. Not like in the bad old days when conformity was everything. *How things have changed*, Robert thought.

* * *

Eva Delmondo, the communications director for the Caldfell Chorus, was thinking the exact opposite. This place was stuck in a time warp, and she was stuck here with it. She lay on her bed at Caldfell Hall sipping a very strong vodka martini made from her private stash.

The year before, Eva had come to Britain for the first time, to a very different village in Gloucestershire. She'd been hired to arrange the media coverage for a glitzy wedding. There she'd met the urbane Scott-Broughtons, who invited her back to England six months later to lead the comms strategy for the Caldfell Chorus, their vanity music project. She jumped at it. Gervase Scott-Broughton was paying way over the odds. And she would be staying in a stately home. History! Awesome! That was something she could work with.

Eva was sharp. She had imagination and an eye for trends. She'd thought up the hedgehog theme for the little bridesmaids at the Gloucestershire wedding, carrying dinky posies with eyes and little ears. So eco-friendly that everyone forgot the airmiles!

Eva had gone into comms after finding journalism at Columbia a tough call. And she'd discovered her vocation: creative marketing. She didn't work for an agency. She was solo, cheaper, more responsive, more exciting. Her work was on sideline projects. She specialized in one-offs. Hit and run.

And the English were a new market.

Except these weren't the English she recognized — those were smart, leggy and blond with cut-glass accents. And that was just the men! No, up here in the boonies you couldn't tell who had money, which left Eva without her social compass. For a start, there was Brigham Broughton, Gervase's so-called cousin. Why was he so important? He dressed like a hobo.

But what's new? He wasn't the only one.

Two days ago, before the big snow dump, she'd gone into the dinky grocery store in Norbridge for Sevillano olives. They didn't have them, natch, so she'd bought the green ones. Despite all the fabulous food and drink at the Hall there was no call for cocktails, so she made her own. Sigh.

Ahead of her in the queue had been an old man in a raincoat tied with a piece of string. He took an age at the till. Eva wanted them to call the cops and move him on. She hopped from one freezing Dior ankle boot to the other.

The woman behind her said, 'Don't mind 'im, luv. 'E's one o' t'richest gadgies round 'ere.'

Eva understood only the word 'rich'. But that was enough. She was stunned.

The old man gave them a broad smile. ''Ow do, Betty,' he'd said to the woman.

''Ow do, Fred.'

As he shuffled out, the woman said to Eva, 'Old Fred Lamplugh's family's been 'ere since Adam were a lad. Lamplugh owns all that land where them ancient graves are.'

So he was a neighbour. Whaddya know. Eva had smiled coldly at the woman, bought her olives and left.

Now, from her small, utilitarian bedroom at the back of Caldfell Hall, she looked out on those graves and shivered. She had never come across anywhere like this place. Or dealt with people like this.

They just didn't get it. For a start, her big idea had misfired. The cute choirboy. She'd seen little choristers on the TV coverage of the British Coronation. Watched by *four hundred million people*! Caldfell Chorus's target audience for the streamed premier was aged fifty-plus, all classical music lovers, who would have adored a choirboy, especially in the States. It would have been perfect — if it hadn't been for Edwin Armstrong, the composer. Preferring a teenage girl just because she had a beautiful voice! Some people had no sense of what would play well on social.

But Eva was pragmatic. OK. Whatever rocked his boat.

Though Lily Martin, the girl prodigy, was a pain. Once the snow started and it looked as if she might have to stay overnight, she'd wanted her mom with her at Caldfell. Eva needed the girl's mom like a hole in the head. The woman was a flake, from all accounts, so Eva had squished the idea of mommy staying over and getting in the way. Eva had sorted Lily a nice bedroom in the Hall with wi-fi and an Xbox.

What more could a kid need? But the girl still mooched around with a face like a slapped ass.

Yawn. Eva didn't do kids.

But hey, there were only a few days to go. Within a week she'd be back in NY, working on her next pitch. A boy band B-lister promoting a male fragrance. Eva had a brilliant idea for a TikTok launch, featuring a fierce-looking cat who loved the smell of the loser's armpits — after the scent had been applied, of course. Miaow . . . easy, tiger. It would be a big hit.

* * *

Christopher Murray locked the side door of the Norbridge Advice Centre. As a solicitor he dealt with most of the issues that came to the centre. But he had several volunteers with their own specialisms. Robert Clark had been a quick learner when it came to problems with schools and education, and he was generally a source of wisdom.

It was dark as Christopher walked home through the backstreets of the town. He liked Norbridge with its solid sandstone abbey, the glass and concrete university building, the remnants of a castle, the standard shopping centre and the outdoor market every Thursday. He felt the frosty cheer in the cold air. The Christmas lights were on until Candlemas. Of course, the council didn't call it Candlemas. But having fairy lights till the first week in February meant the town was brighter for longer, for the winter visitors.

Christopher was a Londoner who'd discovered the Lakes when he'd been at Durham University forty years earlier. It was one of several of his discoveries at the time, like his sexuality, his appreciation of the great outdoors and his interest in church music. But after graduating he went back to London to work in a major law firm and stayed for over thirty years. He'd relished the vibrancy of the gay scene in the capital. At that time, the worst of the AIDS era was coming to an end but Christopher had known people who'd died. It had brought the gay community together. He'd made good friends, with gay women as well as men. He'd been a key figure in the politics of the time, but never in the limelight, always working behind the scenes for equality.

But when he decided to retire, he wanted a complete change and decided to come to Cumbria. A chocolate box cottage in the Lake District was well within his budget — Christopher had made a lot of money — but he wanted something useful to do, with people he could help, and that meant being in a larger community. So he chose the market town of Norbridge.

It was snowing more heavily now. Christopher pulled up his anorak hood as he turned into a ginnel running between two tall buildings. It was dark after the lights in the market square. A figure came the other way, blocking the alley.

The woman in front of him was an Advice Centre regular. She was skimpily dressed in a thin bomber jacket, skinny leggings, shabby trainers with no socks, and a baseball cap. She should have been freezing. But she hopped, elated, from foot to foot and shouted, 'Ay, I've been looking for you, Chris. Can we talk?'

Christopher's heart sank. It was Carly Martin, mother of the singing discovery Lily. She was the last person he wanted to see.

'Aw, please, Christopher. I need to talk to you. It's a secret. I've been trying to keep it to myself but now I want to share.'

'OK, Carly. Let's go to the Crown and Thistle. But just orange juice.'

'Sure. You know I'm off the sauce.'

No I don't, Christopher thought wearily. Carly was always promising to give up drink and drugs, but it never happened. She was a bag of nerves at the best of times, and her edginess infected him. She turned in a pirouette and headed up the passageway. She always wanted something, even if it was just attention. He felt ambushed. Once they were inside the pub, Carly had an odd, suppressed excitement about her, wriggling in her seat. As far as Christopher could tell, she wasn't wired with any of the usual substances. It was pure adrenaline making her so twitchy. She sat there expectantly.

'How's Lily getting on? Up at Caldfell Hall?' Christopher asked. Like everyone else in Norbridge, Christopher knew that Carly's daughter, Lily, had been accepted for a starring role on the Scott-Broughtons' project.

Carly smiled. 'She's all right. She's missin' school. She's staying up there 'cos of the snow.'

'Really?'

Carly nodded, smiling more broadly. Christopher had assumed Lily would be coming home at night to keep her usual rein on her mother's activities. But of course . . . the bad weather. So Carly was home alone, without her daughter. That was bad news. She would probably be off on a binge with her dubious mates as soon as she'd told him whatever her so-called secret was.

But Carly surprised him. 'Yeah. So, after I dropped Lily off, I decided I'd go away for a night. That's why you haven't seen me. I've been to London. Came back today.'

'London? But how did you afford that, Carly?' Her trips to the Advice Centre were usually about money. Or the lack of it. Then he twigged. 'Did Lily lend you any money before she left?'

'Yeah well, not exactly, but she won't mind. She left some dosh in her knicker drawer. She knows her mum needs to get a few things. I went on the coach from Newcastle.'

'In this weather?'

'Yeah. It ain't so bad over there.'

'Where did you stay in London?'

'Oh . . .' Carly's eyes slipped shiftily sideways. 'Wiv one of me old mates. Just one night. I needed to think things over. Because you won't believe what I'm going to tell you, Chris.'

Carly leaned forward, locking his eyes and drinking in the drama. 'I saw him. When I took Lily up to Caldfell in the taxi.'

Carly rarely took Lily anywhere. The girl was usually left to fend for herself. But this was different. Carly would certainly have gone with her daughter to the Hall, hoping to be invited in, to hobnob with the rich and famous.

'I saw him,' she said again, smiling, enjoying Christopher's attention.

'Who, Carly?' Christopher was getting irritated.

Carly paused, milking the moment. 'I saw Lily's father. It was him, I knew it was.'

The effect on Christopher was even more staggering than Carly had expected. Watching him turn white and shake his head, she forgot to smile.

'You all right, Chris?'

'Yeah . . . yeah. Go on.'

'Well, if I'm going to tell you everything, I think I deserve a nice sparkling white wine.'

For once Christopher didn't insist on orange juice. He got up and stumbled to the bar, hoping Carly was too self-absorbed to realize how shocked he was. He ordered a Prosecco for her and a whisky for himself, took the drinks in trembling hands and made his way back to the table.

'You'd better go on,' he said, harshly for once. Startled by his tone, Carly took a deep breath and started talking. Christopher hardly took it in, feeling dazed.

All he could think about was that Carly couldn't have seen Lily's father at Caldfell two days ago.

Because *he* was Lily's father.

But she was gabbling on. 'I went back to Caldfell Hall. And I did for him. That bastard who screwed me all those years ago.'

'But I thought you were gay?'

'Yeah, well. It was all the same to me. My girlfriend wanted a baby and picked some bloke and got a sample in a turkey baster or something. But it didn't work. I got this bloke off the internet. But he wanted a shag. So that's what he got.' Carly went on in lurid detail. Christopher was disgusted but transfixed. Then she got to the best bit.

'But I got my own back, Chris,' she said excitedly. 'I killed him. Today. I want you to know that. I don't care if they lock me up and throw away the key. He got what he deserved.'

Now Christopher was doubly gobsmacked. Carly watched his reaction with satisfaction. That had given him something to think about. And then, job done, she sprang up and danced out of the pub and away.

CHAPTER THREE

The father shall be divided against the son, and the son against the father; the mother against the daughter, and the daughter against the mother. Luke 12:53

At the same time, Suzy Spencer was driving through grey sleet around Norbridge. At first the going was easy. But as she passed Workhaven on the coast and took the country roads up to Caldfell, she hit a white-out and slowed to walking pace. The satnav seemed as confused as she was.

As she stared through the windscreen trying to make out the horizon, the snow dwindled away, the sky lightened, and she could see ahead. She crawled along the slippery road, aiming for the gritted bits, skidding once or twice. The road curved slightly to the right as she glimpsed the sea down below, steel grey like the blade of a knife on a fresh white tablecloth. Caldfell was ten miles further on.

An hour later, stiff with concentration, she dropped into the village. The Hall was half a mile more. It was a bit trickier going uphill in the twilight but, just when she was struggling with the visibility, she turned a corner into an astonishing lightshow. Blue flashing beams cut across the snow. A four-by-four police car with tyre chains had forged its way into the drive. Suzy fell into its tracks and pulled up behind. A figure in uniform came towards her.

'Suzy!'

'Ro. What are you doing here?'

'I should be asking you that!' Ro Watson, Police Community Support Officer, was a good friend of Suzy's. Ro was a veteran PCSO, based at the tiny police station in Workhaven, where she worked alongside Detective Inspector Jed Jackson in an unusual partnership just about tolerated by the local chief.

'I'm here for work,' Suzy said. 'I'm doing a podcast about the Caldfell Chorus.'

'Are they expecting you?'

'Yes.'

'They never said. You'd better get out and walk up to the front door. Jed's inside.'

Suzy picked up her overnight bag from the back seat. She knew better than to ask Ro anything else when she was on duty. She trekked up the frozen path to the open front door. The PC on guard nodded her in.

The Hall was stunning — the massive front door led straight into a large open room with a huge old fireplace. It was toasty warm, with underfloor heating as well as the smouldering log fire.

Suzy looked around, trying to make sense of the scene. DI Jackson was talking to a man and woman slumped on a massive sofa. Their faces had the waxy look of people in shock. The man, well upholstered, was dressed in an immaculate tweed suit with a velvet collar. The woman wore something silky and black, her arms crossed in front of her whip-thin body. She was hunched forward, with a curtain of the smoothest, shiniest grey hair Suzy had ever seen, draped over one side of her face. The other side of her head was shorn to reveal an ear encrusted with silver and diamond earrings.

Gervase and Lauren Scott-Broughton. Married late in life, childless. Both rich and important individually, and formidable as a couple. Gervase was pale under a suspiciously even tan, overlaid with a mass of red, broken veins. Lauren was a strange off-white colour with a thin gash of blackcurrant lipstick. Her eyes were scrunched up. DI Jed Jackson was talking softly to them.

Gervase looked over, saw Suzy and barked, 'Hey, there's a woman here. Do something . . .' Then he turned his head away, uninterested.

A short, curvy woman in a tight-fitting dress, with waves of dark hair and perfect makeup, came shimmying over from the other side of the room.

'Hey,' she said in a suspicious voice. 'And you are . . . ?'

'I'm Suzy Spencer. Podcaster.'

The woman's face crumbled. She shut her eyes. 'Shit.'

Suzy leaned forward confidentially, not wanting to make a fuss. 'You're Eva Delmondo, aren't you? Communications director for the Caldfell Chorus. OK, something's happened and you've forgotten all about me, Suzy Spencer. The community podcaster. Right?'

The woman raised her perfect eyebrows and nodded slowly, her black hair rippling with balayage.

'I'm sorry,' Suzy whispered. 'I'd leave if I could, but I can't go now. It's getting dark, and there's the snow. But I don't want to cause any difficulties.'

The woman's sharp black eyes, fringed with lashes like tarantulas, reappraised Suzy. She nodded again and cocked her head, indicating that Suzy should follow her. At the back of the big hall, in the oak panelling, a door led to another hallway with a massive staircase. They went through, out of sight and earshot.

Eva said softly, 'Thank you so much for that. Not alerting him. Gervase, I mean.' She spoke gratefully, and Suzy knew this wasn't marketing speak. Eva meant it. 'Suzy, I'm going to ask you to go to your room and wait till things have calmed down. I can't tell you any more at this stage, but I'll brief you fully in about half an hour.'

A sudden noise on the open landing above them interrupted their conversation. Suzy looked up to see Alex

Armstrong. She was thinner and taller than Suzy remembered but still statuesque. Her auburn hair glowed. She looked elegant, beautiful even. But her face was white and drained, her features fixed in pain.

'Suzy!' Alex hurtled down the stairs and took her friend in her arms. 'Thank goodness it's you. We're in a nightmare here. Come up to our room.' She turned to the comms director. 'Don't worry, Eva, I know Suzy. I want her with me. She's someone we can absolutely trust. Suzy, there's been a murder, and we can't find Edwin.'

* * *

Christopher Murray sat opposite Robert Clark in the cosy living room at The Briars. After his terrible shock at the pub, he'd called Robert in desperation, saying he urgently needed to talk to someone, and then driven through the snow to Tarnfield.

'Thanks so much for inviting me over, Robert. And so late.'

'Well, it's only nine o'clock. And I'm by myself. Suzy's at Caldfell Hall, doing a podcast.'

Christopher looked up sharply.

Robert waited. He'd been surprised when Christopher had phoned him, an hour earlier, to ask if he could come over for a chat. It was too late for a casual visit. Christopher had always been cool, unfazed by any of the dramas which unfolded at the Advice Centre. But for once he'd sounded tense and in need of a friend.

Finally, Robert said, 'So what's this really about, Christopher?'

Christopher said nothing for a minute, but his features were working, He had a pleasant, handsome face and a thatch of thick dark hair. He usually appeared younger than his age, but tonight he looked haggard and old.

'How much do you know about the gay scene?' he asked with sudden, angry brusqueness.

'Not as much as you, obviously.'

'Of course. Forgive me for being so touchy.' Christopher paused. 'But you'd be surprised how much insensitivity there still is. Even these days it isn't always easy, Robert, especially when it comes to parenting.'

Robert nodded, wondering where this was going. Christopher had never shown anything other than a professional interest in family matters.

Christopher went on, 'The last hurdle to equality was the idea of gay couples having babies. It's not that long since the first same-sex couple were named as parents on a birth certificate. And those of us who were in the vanguard became very close to each other.'

'Yes, I can appreciate that.'

'We all stuck together. Men and women. Gays and lesbians.'

Robert nodded sympathetically but said nothing.

'I became quite close to several lesbian couples. And then one friend introduced me to another, and I got to know her. We all sang in a gay chamber choir. I used to be into music myself. But I don't sing much now.' He sighed. Robert waited.

'Anyway, this woman confided in me that she wanted a child. For the women it was easier but . . .'

'. . . they had to find a way of conceiving?'

'Exactly.'

Robert waited, thinking about it. 'And so you offered to help?' he said eventually.

Christopher looked up sharply. 'You make it sound casual. Unimportant . . .'

'I'm trying to understand. Though actually it's not that difficult. They wanted a baby, and you could provide one. I assume you did it by artificial insemination.'

'Yes. A lot of blokes would treat that information with a bit of a dirty laugh. Or contempt. You know, the idea of some queen trying to get it up with a dyke. It wasn't like that. It was very organized. Scientific.'

'So you provided your sample, and that was that?'

'Well, not exactly. My idea was that I'd be part of the story. You know, allowed to see the child, be part of its life. This was seventeen years ago. But it turned out that the sample wasn't for the woman I knew, it was for her partner. My so-called friend couldn't have children — she'd had an early menopause and was desperate for a child. But the night she took my sperm sample was the last night I saw Renee. I never met her partner, and I never saw her again.'

'So you felt betrayed?'

'Yes, of course I did. But I had no rights over a sperm sample. Still, she misled me.'

Robert poured Christopher another drink. 'So what happened?'

'Oh, later on I did a bit of digging. I found out the partner was a younger woman called Carol from the North. Not well educated. Very different from Renee. Renee was the woman I *thought* I knew, and very much the dominant partner. I assumed when Renee disappeared that the pregnancy had never happened. But a year or two later I heard on the grapevine that Renee had left the scene altogether and the girlfriend had gone home to Norbridge — and had a baby girl.'

'Did you try to locate her?'

'No, I really didn't have enough to go on. And by then I'd met my partner, Simon. Simon didn't want children, and it wasn't an issue for us. We were very happy for years until he died. Cancer.'

'I'm sorry.'

'Thank you. But maybe, after Simon passed and I was alone, the idea of a child of my own was at the back of my mind. Perhaps that's part of why I chose Norbridge for my retirement.'

Robert nodded. He could imagine what it was like, nursing a remote possibility and building it up into a dream.

'Anyway, I started the Advice Centre. And Carly Martin came for help. At first, I thought she was a pain. A narcissist, probably. Quite damaged. And then she became increasingly dependent on me, mainly to sort out her finances. That's how I found out her real name was Carol. She'd changed it to be like Carly Simon the singer. And I started to wonder . . .'

Robert nodded, waiting.

'I didn't stop her coming to me for advice, although perhaps I should have done. I knew she had a teenage daughter, but I never met the child. Then one day a few months ago she brought Lily to the Centre, and I just thought, well . . . I know it sounds crazy, Robert, but she had the look of my mother. That red hair . . .'

People see what they want to see, Robert thought.

'There was nothing I could do to find out,' Christopher went on. 'But I became more and more convinced. Carly never mentioned a father for Lily, which was significant — because she mined every other source of income. She'd talked about being in a gay relationship back in the past, in London, but I thought that was just to get my sympathy because I'm gay myself. But then I saw Lily and it all just seemed to fit. I didn't say anything. It was just a sort of private consolation, for me, to know Lily might have been my daughter.'

Robert nodded again.

'You won't tell anyone, will you? It would make me look stupid. Sad and indulgent.'

'Why?'

'Because Carly told me tonight how Lily was conceived, and it certainly had nothing to do with me.'

'So Carly isn't the woman you thought she was?'

'Oh, she most definitely is. No doubt about it. She told me everything. She even told me the name of her partner, Renee. It's not a common name. They had to be the same couple.'

'So what happened?'

'Carly told me that they tried for a baby with artificial insemination, but it didn't work. That must have been my sample. So, shortly afterwards, Carly contacted a man who was offering his services online as a sperm donor. Using a false name, of course. Apparently, he was a real shit who turned up and then suggested they do it "the natural way". Carly was desperate and went along with it.'

'And what happened?'

'She fell pregnant. But Renee found out about it and was furious. She had wanted to pick the child's father herself. She didn't want just any baby, and certainly not the child of a sex predator. And she was disgusted with Carly. So she left Carly with no money or support, and Carly came crawling back to Norbridge.'

'So why has this all come to a head now?'

'Because Carly says that on Monday she saw Lily's father. Her natural father. The man she slept with.'

'Good heavens!' Robert was astonished. He hadn't expected this. 'Really? Did she tell you who it was?'

'No — she couldn't remember the name he gave her. I know that sounds crazy, but you know what Carly's like. Anyway, it wouldn't have been his real name. But she recognized him, all right.'

'So where did she see him. In Norbridge?'

'No. Caldfell. She went up there with Lily earlier this week, before the snow got bad. He was someone to do with the Caldfell Chorus.'

'So what did she do . . . ?'

'She was vitriolic about him, Robert. With reason. Carly blames all her problems on Lily's father. If she hadn't been seduced by him, she would still be with her partner and kept in clover. Of course, without him she wouldn't have Lily either, but you know what Carly's like.' Christopher stopped and his breathing quickened. 'She's not rational, she has no self-control and she can be very aggressive. I've told you this long, involved story about Renee and the past, but that's just the background.'

'The background? What do you mean?'

'Because tonight Carly sat there in the Crown and Thistle, looking like the cat who got the cream, and told me she'd killed Lily's father.'

'Killed him? You mean murdered him?'

'Yes.' Christopher put his head in his hands. 'Robert, what am I going to do?'

Robert paused before responding. It sounded completely mad. He took a deep breath. 'Look, Christopher, you're going to go to bed and get some sleep. We both know Carly majors in self-dramatization. And delusion. You've no evidence that she's done anything. She could easily be fantasizing. Have a whisky and conk out. You're in shock. Caldfell Hall is snowed in and cut off. If there's been an incident there, we'll find out and deal with it in the morning.'

And in the meantime, I can call Suzy, Robert thought. If he could reach her. There was nothing else they could do. The snow had reached Mid-Cumbria and was falling heavily. And Christopher needed to think very carefully about what he said to people about this. The chances were that there was no murder, just another one of Carly's fantasies, but if not there were serious implications.

They would just have to wait for news from Caldfell Hall. Robert shook his head and concentrated on trying to get Christoper up to bed. He was surprised not to have heard from Suzy. As soon as his friend was settled, he would call her. If there had been a murder at Caldfell Hall, Suzy of all people was bound to know about it.

CHAPTER FOUR

Sanctify unto me all the firstborn, whatsoever openeth the womb among the children of Israel. Exodus 13:2

Suzy followed Alex into her four-poster bedroom. It was stunning, to say the least. A small wood fire burned in an open grate. There was a floor-to-ceiling sash window with wooden shutters still open. The rise of the snow-clad fells was clearly visible, along with the humps of the Neolithic graves and the broken teeth of the standing stones. A lamp gave a soft pink glow.

Alex collapsed onto a sofa. 'Oh, Suzy, I'm worried sick . . .'

Suzy dropped her bag on the floor and went to sit by her friend. 'Has Edwin been away long? He can't have driven off from here, can he? I'd have passed him on the road.'

'He's on foot, Suzy. The car's still here.' Alex paused, looking dazed, and remembered that Suzy had only just arrived. 'Oh, I'm sorry. You must have had a hell of a journey. I've got tea and coffee here and I suppose the kitchen can send up some sandwiches.'

'That would be good but, for now, tell me what's going on. I've just blundered in here. I've no idea what's happening.' She waited. Alex fixed her large dark eyes on Suzy.

'Well, for a start this place is a nightmare. Oh, Edwin's music is going well enough. Very well in some ways. He's discovered this wonderful girl singer . . .'

'Yes, Lily Martin. She's become a local celeb.'

'And no one expected a teenage girl to get the gig. Everyone here wanted a little choirboy for the solos. But you know what Edwin's like when he sees a talent he wants.'

Alex looked away towards the window. Suzy restrained herself from asking more.

Then Alex looked wildly at Suzy and stirred to get up. Suzy placed a comforting hand on her arm, and Alex suddenly relaxed back into the sofa. She continued, her voice shaking. 'I found the body, Suzy.'

'You did? Whose body?'

'Parry Palmer. The choral director. Horrible man. It was in that weird Gothic folly where the concert was going to be. I just walked in. I thought he was praying. Then he slumped over with a knife in his neck, blood everywhere, terrible scratches on his face. So I just took off and came back here. I went straight to Eva . . .'

'Eva — the communications director?'

'Yes, the one who looks like an extra from *West Side Story*.' For a moment, Alex's usual wry tone had come back. Then her voice started to tremble again. 'I didn't lose my nerve about the body. But now I'm in bits because of Edwin going missing. Eva and Gervase kept giving me coffee and brandy and pills, and asking questions. Then the police seemed to be here in no time in that tank of a car, though I guess it must have been over an hour.'

'So how long has Edwin been gone?'

'I don't know. I last saw him when I put my head round the door of his workroom and told him I was going for a walk. Then I found Parry Palmer's body and rushed back. But Edwin had gone.'

'Could he have just gone for a walk?'

'You must be joking. It would take an atom bomb to dislodge him from his work. I just can't understand what's happened.'

There was a knock on the door. Eva Delmondo swayed into the room without asking.

'Alex, Edwin is back,' she said. 'He's with the police. Don't—'

Alex leaped up and made for the door. Eva stood in her way. 'I said he's with the police, Alex. There's been a homicide, remember? You need to know that Edwin came back covered in blood.'

Then Alex was unstoppable, forcing her way past the diminutive Eva. Eva raced after her, clip-clopping in a pair of ridiculous bootees. Suzy followed cautiously.

Edwin Amstrong was standing in the huge entrance hall cum sitting room, talking to DI Jed Jackson. Suzy and Edwin had met years before, but Edwin looked quite different now. For a start there was blood all over his face and hands, and down his coat.

'Oh my God! Edwin!' Alex ran towards him, but DI Jackson put out his arm.

'Stop, Alex.'

'It's OK, Alex,' said Edwin. 'Don't worry. This blood isn't mine. They need to know if it's Palmer's, and if I was attacked by Palmer's killer. I'm OK. Well, a bit nauseous. All I did was go outside, and then I got hit on the head. Up by the graves.'

'What? You idiot! Why did you go up there?' Alex's relief was turning to anger.

'I was worried about you,' Edwin said.

'*You* were worried about *me*?'

'Yes. You said you'd try going for a walk as the snow had stopped. I was a bit absorbed; it took a few minutes to sink in and then I thought I'd follow you.'

'Oh, Edwin.' Alex moved towards him, but Ro Watson, the PCSO, held up her hand.

Edwin went on, 'But I didn't go to the chapel, I set off up towards the graves. I thought you might have gone that way. And then I got hit on the back of the head and knocked out. When I came round, I was frozen. I crawled back here to find blues and twos and goodness knows what else going on.'

Ro Watson said quickly, 'Alex, why don't you go back upstairs with Suzy? Get some tea and maybe a drink. Edwin will be OK, but we need to question him and to check out this blood and his injuries. Gervase has a resident doctor here.'

At that moment, Gervase Scott-Broughton appeared through the panelling doorway, and everyone stopped. Behind him was a man with a bag and a harassed look.

Gervase addressed the room. 'This is my personal physician. Obviously we have medical personnel to hand. Let him get to Edwin.'

'Let's go and sit down over there,' Suzy said to Alex, indicating another sofa at the other side of the room. 'Let the doctor do his stuff.'

Alex nodded, moving over with Suzy. They sank down into a deep, overstuffed sofa. The room was so big, they could hear only the doctor's reassuring murmur from where they were sitting.

Then Gervase Scott-Broughton came across, bending over Alex. 'Don't worry, Alex. We have a scan machine here,' he said. 'Lauren and I want full medical support wherever we are. We love the remoteness of Cumbria but fortunately we can afford to look after ourselves properly.' He gave a loud booming laugh. Laughter was out of place, but then again, Gervase ruled here.

'Go to your room,' he said. 'You have your friend with you and Eva will join you.'

To Suzy's surprise, Alex didn't argue. She just said, 'Please come and get me as soon as Edwin's been examined.'

'Of course. We have all the medical support he could need. Much better than the local hospital. Don't fuss.'

Suzy had never seen wealth like this in action.

As Gervase walked away, Alex stared after him, resentment on her elegant features.

'Come on, Alex,' Suzy said. 'Let's go up to your room and I'll get you a drink.'

Alex knew when she was being sidelined. Her dislike of the Scott-Broughtons and the whole Caldfell set-up was written all over her face. Suzy couldn't help shuddering. Parry Palmer's murder seemed like the tip of a toxic iceberg.

Outside, the snow started to fall again.

* * *

Parry Palmer had been found dead by Alex Armstrong just after four o'clock on Wednesday afternoon. By six, the Scott-Broughtons had arranged a business meeting in their suite.

Before this, Gervase had met with the security firm he employed. For a very generous sum, the four guards had agreed to work longer shifts and stay on site, not that they would have had much option with the incoming snow. But they flattered themselves they had driven a hard bargain. Gervase Scott-Broughton laughed behind his hand. He was paying peanuts, relatively speaking. It was well worth it to have a few heavies around, twenty-four seven. Not so much to protect the singers as to keep them under control.

The second snowfall of the day, at dusk, had finished. The countryside looked like a white plumped cushion dotted with lights from remote farms and clusters of cottages. There were no headlights from cars on the cross-hatching of lanes. It was utterly silent.

But the Scott-Broughtons weren't looking out. With them, seated on three sofas around a huge coffee table, were Eva Delmondo, a shifty-looking, weaselly man called Trent who was Gervase's lawyer, and a dumpy woman called Pearl who was Lauren's personal all-round assistant. Waiting by a distant sideboard were two servers wearing black trousers and white blouses, ready to pour coffee or champagne.

Lauren Scott-Broughton was hunched into herself. Pearl put her hand on her boss's arm and said softly, 'Mrs S-B, we need to make our position clear.'

Lauren's head shot up and her curtain of steel-grey hair swept back to reveal her gaunt but striking face. Her voice was in soft contrast to her husband's loud British accent. Lauren spoke like an American aristocrat. Brought up on the Hamptons, educated at Vassar, with a degree in law from Harvard and a spell at Oxford on an international scholarship, Lauren had become a rising-star media lawyer, and then one of the earliest investors in streaming technology.

Keen on classical music, she had launched a software product which attracted the attention of pop producer Gervase Scott-Broughton. He had admired her calm, detached intellect and obvious class. She had admired his financial acumen. Together they were a huge force in the music streaming business, and she also helped him rediscover classical music.

They weren't in the league of Bill Gates or Elon Musk, but they weren't short of a bob or two.

In fact, it had been hard to know what to do with all their wealth. Gervase's brainwave of a music festival in an obscure part of Britain was perfect. It bought them prestige in the music world, reputation among world-class philanthropists, and praise from fans of community and sustainability. The Caldfell Chorus had it all. Lauren had had virtually no idea where Cumbria was, but she had been hugely enthusiastic when Gervase suggested it.

But now they were contending with murder.

'I think we should go on with the music, in some form,' Lauren said softly.

'You do?' Gervase sounded irritated. Lauren had always been the silent partner. He hadn't expected her to speak at the meeting.

'Yes, I think we should carry on,' whispered Lauren again. Gervase stifled his irritation with his wife. Any rift between them could be commercially sensitive. The partnership between the Scott-Broughtons was a Nasdaq legend.

Trent, the lawyer and sidekick, read his boss's mind. 'This could have implications for the business. Murder is unpleasant. Our shares might take a hit.'

'So how can we spin it?' Gervase demanded.

Lauren Scott-Broughton's voice became even quieter. 'Parry Palmer has been murdered, probably by someone with a specific grudge. Goodness knows, he upset a lot of people.

I had no idea that he was so disliked. I do so wonder why you employed him, Gervase. You did the due diligence, I presume . . .'

'He was bloody good at whipping amateur choirs into shape. You were very keen on the amateur gimmick. You were the one who bought into Eva's pitch, Lauren. But it meant we still had a product to make with too few professionals and a limited timeframe. And you didn't object to Parry, which you could have done if you had doubts.'

Pearl, Mrs Scott-Broughton's assistant, said soothingly, 'Parry Palmer was a good choice on the face of it. Mrs S-B acknowledges that she supported his appointment, but wants it made clear that she wasn't in full possession of the facts.'

'So, whose fault was that?' Gervase said nastily. 'You're her adviser.' But Pearl was impervious.

'The point now is what we do to proceed,' Trent said. 'Mrs S-B obviously thinks we should go right on. And given the weather, we may have no option. It's actually to our advantage. With all the course participants stuck here, it gives us some control over the narrative.'

Gervase stood and strode to the window, his bulky presence causing a draught. Everyone waited. Gervase was the boss. He turned round into the room.

'In truth,' he said conclusively, 'Lauren is right.' He bowed graciously in the direction of his wife. 'As she so often is.' Lauren nodded back at him. Everyone breathed a sigh of relief. Gervase's rare meltdowns were terrifying and to be avoided.

Gervase went on, 'We need to continue with rehearsals and stay on site. The weather will be like this for another two days, or so Trent tells me. And we don't want people leaving. We can offer to help anyone who's desperate to go, maybe suggesting a chopper, or tyre chains on a four-by-four. But we should stress that they won't get out without a lot of trouble and personal expense.'

Trent said, 'And there's the police, of course. They want everyone to stay.'

Gervase flexed his shoulders. 'Absolutely. Yes. We don't want anyone to leave until we have all this tied up. It shouldn't take long to find out who did this terrible thing.' He thought for a moment before continuing. 'We need to make staying here seem both responsible and attractive to the chorus. We don't want them to panic. So we need to set up counselling services online for anyone here who needs support. We don't want legal cases around PTSD.'

Trent nodded furiously. Lauren murmured, 'Of course.'

Gervase continued, 'I'll appoint a deputy chorus director from the ranks, and we'll carry on working on a new programme. The orchestra aren't here yet, thank goodness. They'll be cancelled but paid in full.'

He paused but no one spoke. He waited just long enough for questions which didn't come. 'We'll put out a statement and press release tonight. Trent, you and Eva draft something together, saying we're continuing in a limited form, without a streamed performance — but make it clear that we're only doing so owing to the weather situation and police procedure. There will be a concert in-house but there must be no suggestion that we're insensitive to this dreadful death. Is that clear? And if necessary, we'll pay the singers to stay. Throw money at them. All agreed?'

Of course. They had money to throw.

'And Trent, it might be an idea to check the wi-fi.'

Trent nodded. He knew what Gervase meant. He would be checking the wi-fi, all right. He had already taken out some of the boosters and unplugged the connections into the various buildings. The S-Bs, of course, had satellite phones.

Gervase waved at the two servers waiting at the edge of the room. 'Perhaps we'll have the champagne now. Oh, and one more thing. I want Brigham to join us.'

Just fleetingly, Pearl and Trent caught each other's eyes. There was one thing on which they silently agreed. Brigham Broughton, the poor relation, was a tiresome irrelevance upsetting the carefully nurtured ecology of the Scott-Broughton household. They both wanted rid of him. For good.

CHAPTER FIVE

The elders have ceased from the gate, the young men from their music. The joy of our heart is ceased; our dance is turned into mourning. Lamentations 5:14–15

Earlier, the scruffy and slightly smelly Brigham Broughton had been sitting in his favourite part of the vast entrance hall. He had pulled his chair up to the fire, blocking it for others.

'Poor old Davy boy,' he said to the middle-aged man sitting opposite him. 'Are you chief suspect then, lad? Eh? You got it in the neck from Parry Palmer this morning, then he got it in the neck this afternoon!'

Brigham roared with laughter at his own joke. One thing Brigham had in common with Gervase was a loud voice. Dave Oldcastle squirmed. Being mercilessly picked on by the choral director had wounded him, and he didn't want to be reminded of it.

But Dave was prepared to put up with jibes from Brigham because he needed to talk to him. Dave was deeply worried. Brigham was one of those people who always knew what was going on and repeated it noisily. Dave needed to know what Brigham knew.

Brigham told Dave he'd been thinking of going out for a quick spliff that afternoon, but he couldn't find his coat in the cloakroom. So he'd been looking for any old anorak to grab when Mrs Armstrong came stumbling into the Hall, calling for help. Brigham gave Dave all the details, in full. Parry had been stabbed in the neck with a penknife. His face had been scratched raw. He'd been dead a few hours when Mrs Armstrong turned up. No one had seen him since before lunch.

'I know you shouldn't speak ill and all that, but Parry Palmer was a bastard,' said Dave, fishing a bit.

'True enough. Aye, well, don't fret. You're a good musician, Dave. Everyone has duff moments, and we all know Parry's a sod. *Was* a sod. I mean, I get it. My stuff is different. Solo work. I have to get the crowd onside. But I know what it's like to have bad days.'

Dave smiled and nodded acknowledgement. But he thought Brigham's howling renditions of folk and rock classics outside Bargain Stores in the Norbridge marketplace were hardly performances. No one ever stopped to listen. It was sad, really. Brigham Broughton had been good at music when they were at school together. Dave and Brigham had both sung in the abbey choir back in the day.

'So why did ya fuck up at the rehearsal then, Dave?' Brigham seemed genuinely curious. Dave was a fine singer. But that morning he had made mistakes, and his baritone voice had been tremulous.

'I was worried about something, Brig. My mind wasn't on the music, which was my bad, so I do take some responsibility. But Parry was disgusting. I've never been so humiliated.'

'But ya didn't murder 'im?'

'No. This afternoon I was in my room, practising. Of course, I can't say I'm sorry he's dead. And I bet there's no shortage of suspects. But I'm not one of them.' *Though I know someone who might be*, Dave thought. And the worry was agonizing. Was he betraying his anxiety?

But Brigham's short attention span meant he wasn't listening anymore. He was relaxing back into his super-comfy chair and sipping his Super Blend. Not the most expensive whisky in the Hall, but his personal favourite. He had his own bottles behind the bar, with his name on. It was so lovely and warm by the fire; his big feet in his smelly socks on the stone flags assured him of the underfloor heating. He had a berth here with lots of food and drink. When he'd heard about Gervase coming back to Cumbria, he'd made contact through one of the builders at Caldfell. And when he and Gervase had met again, they'd got on famously, against the odds.

It had been a bit of luck for Brigham. He had an axe to grind with old Gervase. But it was all going surprisingly well. Brigham yawned and snuggled into his chair.

Dave saw that Brigham had fallen asleep, dribbling. Not a pretty sight. He stood up quietly and left, grabbing his anorak from the cloakroom. Heading out and down the path, Dave desperately wanted to make a phone call. The wi-fi had been down for the last few hours, but he would give it a go. His conversation with Brigham had made him more worried than ever.

The suspicion was gnawing at him now. He had to make that call.

* * *

After Carly Martin had left Christopher Murray in the pub in Norbridge, she'd taken a taxi using Lily's cash. She directed it to her latest boyfriend's dilapidated cottage on the outskirts of Pelliter, near Norbridge.

To say he was her boyfriend was a bit of an exaggeration. 'Fuck buddy' was a better description. Carly was bi, although in middle age it had been mainly guys. Most of them weren't up to it anyway.

She said 'Ta' and took the spliff. They slouched on the battered, stained sofa. She inhaled deeply. Skunk. It was strong stuff, not like the weed she'd used back in the day. She hardly ever thought of those times now. She never talked to Lily about them either. She was blessed with a daughter who had common sense, as well as brains and a phenomenal singing voice. No point in worrying her about the past.

Lily's voice had always been good, but post-puberty it had developed a special quality, higher and brighter than Adele, more like Carrie Underwood meets Sarah Brightman.

Oh yeah, Carly knew her music. It was Carly who'd spotted Lily's voice and taken her along to the abbey — the only place she could think of where Lily could get free singing tuition. Lily had joined the abbey choir when she was nine, and her voice had become bigger, warmer and more wonderful every year. She'd passed exams too, and then this amazing chance came along, to sing for Edwin Armstrong at Caldfell Hall.

But then, who would have thought it? Unbelievable. After seventeen years. Up there at Caldfell Hall, Carly had seen him. Lily's dad. Or maybe it wasn't so surprising. Her and Renee, and their mates, had all been in the music scene one way or another. What a lying shit that man had been. Before he came along, her bossy partner had already found some dupe who'd thought he was going to be a daddy through a turkey baster. But two weeks after that, Carly had come on, a bit early. A dud. No baby on the way. Carly had never mentioned it to Renee. Renee could be pretty difficult and might have blamed Carly for getting the wrong ovulation date or messing up the process.

Instead Carly immediately found a man on the internet who sounded OK and was willing to offer his sperm. She invited him around when Renee was away and planned to use the same kit. But the arrogant sod with his cocksure walk was hardly inside the door when he started pawing her and, frankly, it was just easier to let him do it. Three times. That had to work better than a plastic plunger. And Carly didn't really mind men. It was all the same to her.

When she realized that she was pregnant, she never meant Renee to find out it wasn't the turkey baster man. But then the real daddy had turned up a month later. He thought Carly might need another 'seeing to', as he called it. It took seven months on average, he said, for it to work. This time, Renee was at home. She didn't give him seven minutes before kicking him out. Then she went to town on Carly.

'I was only doing it for the best, for you,' Carly had whimpered. She really couldn't see that it mattered that much. Sperm was sperm. But Renee was disgusted.

After a few days of screaming recriminations, Renee left. She wasn't going to raise that man's child. And she was disgusted with Carly for being unfaithful. He may well have thrust himself on her, but she had gone along with it. That was unforgivable. Renee was tough like that.

Carly went home to Norbridge. She had nowhere else to go. Eventually she was just another single mum.

And then at Caldfell Hall, seventeen years later, she had seen the scumbag responsible through the cab window, strolling with his cocky walk up the lane.

When the penny dropped, her first feeling was a raging desire to get the funds that she deserved. She'd brought up Lily by herself, hadn't she? But then she thought, *Could he make a claim on my daughter? And my daughter's future fame and fortune?* That mustn't happen. She would do anything to stop it.

Now she sat back on the sofa and took another drag before passing on the spliff. It had been a hell of a day, but she was sleepy and warm and happy. The snowy fells, the old graves, the lamplit Hall, all flickered behind her closed lids. Somewhere in her heart, Bonnie Tyler was singing . . . yes, Lily was even better than Bonnie. That girl was going places and taking her mother with her, and no one would get in the way. Whatever it took.

* * *

Dave Oldcastle had been unable to get a phone signal in his room and he was desperate. Even before the snow, the wi-fi had been temperamental in the modernized block of outbuildings which housed the men of the chorus. They were now having supper. But Dave wasn't hungry. He just wanted a connection.

He didn't know what was going to happen next on the course. There were to be announcements in the morning. The general gossip was that Parry Palmer had been killed by someone who had come to Caldfell for that purpose, taking advantage of a brief period of clear weather. It was a convenient theory.

And the Scott-Broughtons were impressively organized. Eva Delmondo had addressed all the singers before supper. There would be a full briefing in the morning. Until then, she was very reassuring, particularly about the renewed security. The unlimited drinks and fantastic buffet helped too.

Dave hoped his roommates wouldn't return the worse for wear and keep him up that night. Not that he was sleeping well anyway. He remembered how excited he'd been at getting a place on this course. Sharing a room and working ten hours a day had seemed part of the challenge. He'd had no idea how wretched the whole set-up would make him.

Now he was the only person around in the men's quarters. He tried his phone again. Nothing.

* * *

In the empty hallway to Dave's block, Trent was kneeling on the floor, fiddling with the broadband connection. He'd unplugged it an hour earlier but now thought better of it. The loose connection was too visible. He wanted to tread on the end so it would be unusable. In a reflex action he plugged it back in. As he'd feared, it was too easy to do. He was about to unplug it for good and damage it beyond repair when he heard footsteps coming down the stairs. He shrank into the corner behind a convenient coat rack.

Dave Oldcastle walked past just feet away, suddenly saying, 'Yesss!'

Trent froze behind the coat rack as Dave began speaking on his phone. He couldn't afford to be seen. But he didn't want Dave talking for long. As soon as Dave shifted his position, Trent pulled out the connection. Dave's phone call came to a sudden end. He swore and left the building.

Trent stamped on the wi-fi lead. There was no way that was going to work again. Dave's call would be the last one to leave Caldfell Hall until the Scott-Broughtons had everything under control. Now, the chorus was completely cut off.

CHAPTER SIX

And pray ye that your flight be not in the winter. For in those days shall be affliction such as was not from the beginning of the creation. Mark 13:18–19

It was seven o'clock that evening when Dave's short phone call reached the landline on Professor Irene Przybylski's desk. She was still at work at the Academy of Voice in Islington, London. She had been sitting, thinking, looking down at her smart tailored suit. She was always chic and composed on the outside. But inside was different. Now she jerked her head up and stared at the phone. A dozen possibilities, mostly unpleasant, flashed through her mind.

Irene Przybylski was principal of the Academy. It was a prestigious job fraught with problems. This year was already the worst she'd experienced, thanks to one person — Parry Palmer. And now he'd buggered off to Cumbria and she was left with the mess he'd made. Irene was furious.

Parry Palmer had been at the Academy for over thirty years. Irene had been there for a decade. She had always distrusted him, but he was a fixture. In fairness, in the past he had headed up some successful amateur choirs in the outer London boroughs. But he had a reputation for bullying his singers and students. Yet Palmer was one of those people who seemed fireproof however badly he behaved. He had a knack for ingratiating himself with the great and the good, particularly the men, making them laugh and bolstering their egos.

This time, though, he'd gone too far. He'd disappeared in term time to moonlight at a prestigious choral course. It was worse when she realized what it was. Irene was well known to the Scott-Broughtons, who were lavish donors to the Academy. She couldn't understand why they hadn't invited her to be choral director of the Caldfell Chorus. Parry Palmer had never conducted at a major venue. He had no international standing. He wasn't popular. His compositions and arrangements for choirs were gimmicky. Just being a bloke's bloke was surely not enough.

Worst of all he was also the subject of a bitter student complaint. He had a reputation for claiming students' achievements as his own. Irene was pretty sure he was guilty, but he'd put up a big, noisy defence. She didn't believe him. If it were up to Irene, he would be on a warning at least. But she had to contend with her own board of trustees — who didn't like trouble — and with the giant HR apparatus of the larger university.

The phone was still ringing. She picked it up.

'Irene Przybylski.'

'Thank goodness. My name's David Oldcastle. I'm sorry to bother you but . . .'

Oldcastle. The name rang a bell at once.

'. . . my son is on your master's course . . .'

Irene drew breath. 'I'm afraid I can't discuss your son with you without his permission, Mr Oldcastle. Callum is an adult. It's a question of confidentiality . . .'

'Wait! All I want to know is if you've seen Callum. I'm begging you. If you've seen him, tell me. That's not breaking any confidence, is it? I just want to know if Callum's in London.'

'Might I ask why?'

The line was crackly. The man's voice was shaking. 'Please. Just tell me. Have you seen Callum?'

'I'm afraid not. Callum has been missing classes, which doesn't help his case. But that's all I can say.'

'Oh my God. Are you sure?'

'Of course I'm sure. What's this about?'

'Professor Przybylski, I know Callum was incandescent and threatening to get Palmer sacked—'

'I really can't discuss that with you, Mr Oldcastle.'

Irene squirmed. This was the issue which had kept her in the office till seven o'clock at night. The complaint against Parry Palmer. The board was dragging its feet about it. And she knew that Callum Oldcastle and his friend and collaborator Freddie Lamplugh were getting increasingly angry.

'Goodbye, Mr Oldcastle.'

'Listen! Palmer has been murdered. The news isn't out yet because we're all snowed in up here at Caldfell Hall. It's a miracle that I managed to make this call. Palmer is dead and I can't get hold of Callum. That's why I called you. I needed to know—'

The line went silent. Irene stared at the handset, then slowly put it back in its cradle. Callum Oldcastle and Freddie Lamplugh had accused Parry Palmer of stealing their work. They'd had no satisfaction from the Academy.

Now they were both missing. And Palmer was dead. Murdered.

No wonder Callum's father was worried. She was worried too. Very worried.

* * *

At Caldfell Hall that evening, Suzy put down her half-eaten sandwich. She was full and warm, dozy now, sitting by the log fire in Alex's bedroom having enjoyed a glass of red wine.

She and Alex had walked over in the snow to see Edwin in a cottage which had been converted to a medical centre. He would spend the night there under supervision. The portable CT scan showed no injury. He'd been walloped with something and slipped, banging his head. The assailant could have done more harm but seemed to have made off. It would be a day or two before they managed to identify the blood on Edwin, but he had no other wounds himself. He'd been given a sedative and the two nursing assistants employed by the Scott-Broughtons would be watching him all night, on shifts.

'I doubt I'll sleep,' Alex had said to Suzy as they walked back up the path, now cleared of snow.

'You'll be surprised,' said Suzy. 'You're probably exhausted.'

'But I'm feeling uptight right now. Come back to my room, please, Suzy. I can order some food, and we can talk. I don't want to be alone.'

'That's fine by me. You can give me the heads-up on the whole situation here.'

The log fire burned brightly in the antique grate. The huge window looked out to the back of the Hall up the fell. Alex hadn't closed the curtains: the snow softened the darkness and reflected the starlight. The Neolithic graves were now dark blue shadows.

Suzy sat next to Alex and could feel her tension.

'My kids send their love,' Suzy said softly. 'You were around at a pretty important time of their lives, Alex.'

'Of course. Jake and Molly. I should have asked before. How are they? Is Jake still playing the sax?'

'Off and on, I think. He has a serious girlfriend now. She's French, very cool. A little older than him. And Molly is at university in York.'

Alex relaxed a little. 'And that was the time when we found out who murdered the awful Morris Little. And I met Edwin . . .'

Alex smiled. She finally sipped at her glass.

'We can talk about this murder, if you like,' said Suzy. 'Why don't you explain what's going on here to me.'

'OK,' Alex answered slowly. 'Firstly, there are about two dozen amateur singers staying in the outbuildings.'

'Are you singing with them?' Alex had a lovely contralto voice and was an accomplished singer.

'Not likely! Not when it's Edwin's music. Too close to home. All the singers were auditioned online. They're from all over Cumbria. They have to be top class. The best of the bunch is Dave Oldcastle. He's from Norbridge and sings in the abbey choir.'

'I think Robert knows Dave Oldcastle.'

'Dave's a well-known local baritone. But he was being picked on relentlessly by the musical director, Parry Palmer, and seemed to be going to pieces.'

'Anyone else I might have heard of?'

'Well, there's Brigham Broughton. He's Gervase's second cousin or something. He plays and sings in the marketplace in Norbridge, apparently.'

Strange, Suzy thought. *Why would someone like Gervase Scott-Broughton want to dig up a poor relation?* There were probably dozens of people in Cumbria distantly related to the billionaire. But Gervase had picked Brigham Broughton, busker. Suzy was curious but put the thought to one side.

'OK. What about the others?'

'Well, then there's team USA. Gervase's wife Lauren is blue-chip Ivy League. Then there's the staff. Gervase has an aide, an American lawyer called Trent. Lauren has a devoted assistant called Pearl, who has been with her forever and doesn't say much. But they're just Trent and Pearl, the factotums. And you've met Eva, of course, the publicist. I didn't like her at first. She swans around like a miniature Jennifer Lopez. She's effective, though I suspect she's about as Puerto Rican as I am. But that makes for a good look.'

Suzy laughed. 'Is there anyone else I should know about?'

'Well, there's a secret only Edwin and the Scott-Broughtons know. They've engaged Marcus Sotheby to sing the bass part in Edwin's *Candlemas Oratorio*.'

'Marcus Sotheby! Wow. That's a big name.' Even people who didn't like reality TV shows liked Marcus Sotheby, the famous singer and panellist on *Vocal Vote*. Suzy was seriously impressed.

'Yes,' said Alex. 'A good call. But of course, he won't be coming now.'

Alex shut her eyes. She was flagging. It had been a dreadful afternoon for her. Suzy looked into the fire and thought about Marcus Sotheby, a super A-lister. Would he have heard about Parry Palmer's murder? Was he one of the special people in touch with the Scott-Broughtons by satellite phone? Or was he already on his way to Cumbria? And when he found out about the murder, how would he react? Would he splash it all over social media to explain his own change of plans? That could certainly rock the Scott-Broughtons' boat. Suzy sensed that they wanted to control who knew what and when. While Suzy took all this in, PCSO Ro Watson put her head round the door to see if they were all right. She and DI Jed Jackson would be staying over too, though they had been given less opulent accommodation in an outbuilding.

Ro hovered at the door. 'I hear Edwin's much better.'

'Yes. Can you tell us anything more? Like why you're here? A PCSO?' Suzy asked.

'Well, I was at a school talk in Workhaven with Jed when he got the call and there's a vulnerable young person here.'

'Lily Martin?'

'Yes. She's not unknown to social services. Her mother has issues, shall we say. Mrs Armstrong will have heard all about that.'

Alex said sharply, 'Yes, I have. I don't think this is a great environment for a vulnerable teenager. And Parry Palmer isn't the only victim here. Have you got any more idea about who hit my husband? Are they still on the loose? Edwin could have been killed too . . . You should think about getting Lily to a safer place.'

Ro went on smoothly, 'Actually, Lily's OK with staying at the Hall. She says her mum's gone away for a few days. She's only sixteen. We can't send her home and she has no other relatives. The snow is an issue too. She's better off here.' Ro stopped and turned to Alex. 'You obviously get on well with the girl, Mrs Armstrong. I wondered if maybe you could look out for her? Lily says that she looks up to you. I think she relates to you as a mum.'

'I'm not a *mum*,' Alex snapped.

Ro paused, taken aback by the force of Alex's words. 'My apologies. I just meant that Lily told me herself that of all the people here, she felt most comfortable with you.'

But the atmosphere was tense. The talk of Lily was putting Alex on edge. It was another factor in the poisonous mix of power, personalities and danger. Alex got up, looking angry, and walked to the window.

Ro rolled her eyes at Suzy and shrugged. 'OK, well, I think that's all I can say. I'll be going now. See you in the morning.'

As soon as she had gone, Alex turned angrily to Suzy. 'Why do people always think I should be someone's mother?' She started to cry, tears rolling down her cheeks, as if she hardly knew what was happening to her face.

'Oh, Alex, I'm so sorry.'

'Suzy, the truth is that I'm wretched here. I wanted to come back to Cumbria. I thought maybe I might be pregnant here. At home. But it hasn't happened. You have no idea how much I wanted children of my own. You're so lucky with Jake and Molly.'

'You're right. I had no idea. Your life seems so . . . well, exciting and glamorous. Fulfilling!'

'But it's not complete. Edwin really wanted kids too. OK, I was nearly forty when we married, but we thought we could go for a managed pregnancy. And Edwin got that fantastic job in Philadelphia. We've tried IVF three times since then. The last time was this Christmas. That's Edwin's busiest period of the year, but time was running out. I should have known we had too much on our plate for all the treatment to work.'

'Do you always travel with him?'

'Yes, always. I don't really feel I belong anywhere now. I love Frankfurt but I don't want to stay there forever.'

'So what do you do? Write?'

Alex shook her head. 'Not anymore.' Alex had once had a career as a successful author of children's stories. 'I always thought I would write for my own children one day, but now that's not going to happen, and I don't want to write for other people's kids. I've changed careers. I developed an online sight-reading app for singers. It's pretty successful. Edwin's name helps, of course. I can work anywhere as long as I have my laptop. I don't feel anchored.'

Suzy thought about her own life and how much it was moored in one place however much she travelled. Such a different life from Alex's.

'I hope you don't mind me asking, but how did you know the latest IVF cycle had failed?'

'Oh, you know, the obvious way. You have a period. It's an unbelievable regime, Suzy — injections on time, pills — I'm booked in with a clinic in Manchester. I thought I could pop down there in the car a few times this week. I had no idea I'd be snowed in here. When this is over, I'll get it checked out. I'll need a negative pregnancy test to confirm it hasn't worked. But I know the signs. I've been there before.'

'I'm sorry, Alex.'

'Are you? I don't mean to be rude, Suzy, but don't pretend to empathize. Because you can't.'

Suzy paused. Alex was right. What did Suzy really know about Alex's pain? It was presumptuous to think she could say anything to help. Alex would have heard it all before, from well-meaning friends and from downright nosy parkers. Suzy should change the subject.

'OK, so let's get back to discussing the murder. It's what we do, after all!'

Alex smiled faintly. Seizing the moment, Suzy said, 'Now that you've given me the background to the Caldfell Chorus, tell me about Parry Palmer and why someone would want to kill him.'

'I'll tell you one thing for sure. The singers here all hated Parry. There were a few women he made up to, and that caused trouble. He had a reputation for being a bit of a sex pest. But Parry really liked needling weak men to amuse strong men. He would mock people to make Gervase laugh. Anyway, after just a few days I could see that, although Gervase thought Parry Palmer was a hoot, the ordinary blokes loathed him. Especially Gervase's scruffy cousin, Brigham.'

'Yes. The busker. I've seen him in Norbridge. Hardly a serious musician, although he has been known to play the flute on one leg like the guy from Jethro Tull. He does a nice rendition of that "North Country Girl" song.'

'By Joanie Cadiz. Yes, Edwin says Brigham has a good tenor voice when he puts himself out.'

'So Brigham's in the frame for murder, like half the male singers. And what about outsiders?'

'Well, there's the London connection. Parry Palmer, the murdered man, worked at the Academy of Voice under Professor Irene Przybylski. Irene's very well thought of in the music world and the Academy has gained a top reputation under her. Edwin rates her.'

'Does anyone else have a connection with Parry Palmer?'

'Well, one of the older sopranos is from Cumbria originally, but she works in the office at the Academy now. She's been dishing the dirt about him. She loathes Palmer. Apparently, they've had a particularly vitriolic complaint against him from two students.'

'Blimey. The busker, all the basses and tenors, two angry students. Popular bloke!'

Alex laughed but Suzy could see that she was suddenly flagging. 'That's given me a lot to chew on, Alex. Let's go to bed. I'm sure you'll sleep once you let yourself go. You must be shattered.'

They embraced. Alex said, 'I feel much better now. Yes, it was awful finding Palmer dead, and even more awful when Edwin disappeared. But he's back now, and you're here, Suzy.'

Suzy smiled. 'I do think if we stick together, with your insider knowledge and my nose for murders, we could find out who really had it in for Palmer.'

'And who attacked my husband, don't forget about that!
'I won't!'
'I'm so glad you're here, Suzy.'
'I'm glad too.'

But as she walked upstairs to her own room, Suzy wondered. It was great to see Alex again, and to rekindle their friendship. It was even rather exciting to have another murder to investigate. But the danger and the horror hadn't sunk in yet. It would before long. Murder wasn't a game, and you got involved at your peril. Literally.

* * *

Back in Tarnfield, after leaving Christopher Murray in the spare bedroom, once Jake's pit, Robert went back downstairs and into The Briars' big kitchen. He loved the quiet house at this time of night.

He thought back over the evening's conversation. It was a long, complicated story. But it wasn't impossible. Christopher might well have given a sperm sample in good faith, only to be cut out of the story. Robert remembered an item on one of Suzy's daytime TV shows a few years ago, about lesbian women being taken in by rogue sperm donors who just wanted the thrill of seducing a gay woman. It wasn't unknown.

Then Carly and her partner had split up and Carly had come home to Norbridge to have her child. Lily was clearly a talented young woman. Christopher Murray had no family. It must have been a consolation to him to treasure the possibility that the gifted Lily Martin was his child.

But then to be told that Carly had conceived her child with another man must have been deeply unsettling. And on top of that, to hear Carly's bizarre claim that she'd gone back to the snowbound Caldfell Hall and killed this man, after seventeen years. How could she have done that? Carly wasn't an organized person. Nor was she physically strong.

He wished Suzy was here so they could have talked about it. He just wished she was here anyway.

Outside the kitchen window large snowflakes were falling. He stood watching as he rang Suzy's number. Her cheery voicemail told him that she'd call back. But how could she, if there was no signal? Robert wondered how long this separation would last. He felt very alone without her.

CHAPTER SEVEN

Why should the name of our father be done away from among his family, because he hath no son? Numbers 27:4

Suzy Spencer had gone back to her own room in the servants' quarters at Caldfell Hall. The wi-fi was still dead. She lay on her bed looking at the white ceiling and the white walls, and then straight ahead through her window to the snow-filled fields dropping to the silver sea in the moonlight. It was a breathtaking view but she wanted to share it with Robert.

Now that the effect of her talk with Alex was starting to wear off, she felt isolated and anxious. For the first time she could remember, she was truly cut off. She had no phone signal, no laptop connection and no book to read. There was nothing to stop her mind wandering. Each time she started to drift off, her brain snapped back into action. Perhaps she was distracted by the silvery light outside, but she couldn't bring herself to close the curtains over such a wonderful view. She got up to sit on the narrow window seat and stare down at the sweeping Cumbrian coast.

Something was worrying her, but it wasn't Parry Palmer's murder. Not being able to talk to Robert that night had crystalized her concern. Since the autumn she had occasionally caught her husband looking distracted. It had happened several times when her son Jake and his girlfriend had come to visit. Mae was lovely, but she was rather superior with a strong French accent, and once or twice Robert had looked at her as if he couldn't remember who she was.

Then over Christmas, Jake and Mae had been joined at The Briars by Molly and her new boyfriend. He was a posh young man who talked in an affected mix of gangster rap and public-school drawl. Robert seemed to be baffled and had mooched off, leaving Suzy and the kids alone.

Suzy's mother had had Alzheimer's, and Suzy still remembered the sick feeling when her mum had looked at Molly, her granddaughter, and said, 'Who's that girl?' Robert's parents had died when he was in his thirties. He had a sister, but they only spoke two or three times a year. Suzy had no idea of Robert's family history. Was dementia in his genes too?

Family. That was another thing. She thought of Alex's torment. She had seen her friend's problem as a physical condition. Something to come to terms with. But Alex's childlessness was all-encompassing, and Alex felt it defined her. She was desperate for the touch and feel and love of a baby. She was experiencing grief and loss.

Had Robert ever longed for children of his own? Suzy didn't know. She had taken his childlessness for granted. If she were honest, it had been a relief to her because it meant he could give Jake and Molly all his attention. Robert's first wife, Mary, had been unable to have children, but Robert never talked of his own feelings.

Should Suzy have offered him the chance of a family of his own? It would have been possible. But she had never thought of it. A new family wasn't something she wanted. How selfish that seemed, in comparison to Alex, going through all that treatment, as much for Edwin as herself. So now Suzy was shaken by the idea that she might have deprived Robert of having his own children to love him. She thought of the years ahead, when he would be ageing and might feel frightened and alone, however loving she could be. Perhaps he would long for his own flesh and blood.

She sat up and took a deep breath. This introspection was pointless, the result of all the trauma of the day.

She needed to do something practical. As soon as she got back to Tarnfield she would call Robert's sister and ask her to come and stay. She was the only family Robert had left, and they should see more of her. She would tell Robert of her fears about his health. And she would ask him directly how he felt about the fact they had never had children together.

She lay down and drifted off to sleep, slipping into a dream where she was trying to find Robert. He was lost on the fells while they were trying to catch a plane to New York. It was not a restful dream. She woke several times, only to slip back into more and more bizarre scenarios.

When she finally woke in the morning, the shape of the fields outside the window had subtly changed. There had been another, deeper fall of snow with the coming of dawn. The last flakes, as big and floppy as wet tissues, were still drifting past her window.

* * *

Lauren Scott-Broughton had been awake most of the night. At times she seemed in a lot of distress. Pearl, her assistant, slept in a dressing room next door and came whenever Lauren called out.

'Are you sure you won't tell Gervase more about your illness?' Pearl asked.

'No, Pearl. You know we've decided not to involve him. And I have my medication.'

Pearl silently padded into Lauren's en-suite bathroom, emerging with a glass of water and an old-fashioned little pill box of black enamel. Lauren looked more arresting than ever, her steel-grey sweep of hair on one side against the white pillow. She stretched out her thin, pale arm, showing a white hand and perfect oval shellacked fingernails.

'Sit down on the bed and talk to me,' Lauren said. Unlike her husband's, her tone was soft and sweet. In the US, Lauren thought, Gervase behaved quite differently. Stateside, he was a charming English upper-class gentleman — and a ruthless businessman — smooth and impeccably dressed. In England, at Caldfell Hall, he was like something out of *Tom Jones* — an eighteenth-century landowner in tweedy clothes, red-faced with drink and inclined to shout orders.

And Brigham Broughton, his cousin, the country bumpkin, brought out the worst in Gervase. Lauren didn't know what to make of Brigham and kept her distance.

Lauren's bejewelled bedside clock showed that it was half past two. She would sleep a little and wake at around six o'clock when Pearl would make her some hot water with lemon. But that was three and a half hours away. She needed to fill the time till the medication gave her rest.

'So, what are people saying about who killed Parry?' she asked Pearl. 'Let's go over it.'

'Well, everyone thinks he upset someone who had an unstable personality. That person found him in the folly. Perhaps Parry said another of his horrible rude things and the killer snapped.'

'Yes. Plausible. But would the spontaneous killer have a penknife to hand? And why was Parry there? People must know he wasn't the sort of man to enjoy the *sensus numinis* by candlelight.'

'But it was perfectly possible that he went to the folly to think about the staging for the performance. Someone could have followed him.'

'True. That's a feasible explanation.'

Pearl allowed herself a small, tight smile.

Lauren went on, 'You know, I worry about Gervase. He was trying to blame me for employing Palmer, in front of Trent and Eva. I'm not happy about that. It must be made quite clear that employing Parry Palmer was not down to me.'

'Absolutely, Mrs S-B. Your husband made that decision.'

'Quite. All I did was agree. If Gervase wanted him, we could carry Palmer. With Gervase as impresario, and Edwin Armstrong as composer, we had enough heavyweights.'

'And there's Marcus Sotheby, of course . . .'

'Of course. He's certainly a major hire.' Lauren Scott-Broughton had been delighted with this choice. Yes, Marcus Sotheby was slightly over the hill, but he had recently been on the panel of a hit TV talent show and was a household name in the UK, with fees to match. He was due to arrive two days before the performance. Now he would have to be bought off and rebooked, if possible. *But that shouldn't be a problem*, Lauren thought. Sotheby's career needed this boost, and they had the money to keep him happy.

Lauren was feeling sleepy now. 'Close the curtains, Pearl. I'm sorry for keeping you up.'

'My pleasure, Mrs S-B.'

Pearl moved over to the window. Just for a moment she stopped and looked out. She saw a figure staggering up the hill, silhouetted against the snow in the moonlight. Pearl betrayed no emotion and moved to the left to see better. It was a man in dark clothing. He staggered and fell.

Behind Pearl, her beloved boss was already asleep. She shouldn't be disturbed. Pearl wasn't going to call out a search party.

She snapped the curtain shut on the scene outside.

* * *

A few hours earlier, in London, Marcus Sotheby, famous singer and TV celebrity, sat in the living room of Professor Irene Przybylski's spacious flat. He needed to talk to her about the Caldfell Chorus. He wished he'd never heard of it, never mind accepting their offer to sing there.

Irene's room was warm, sophisticated with deep taupe walls and golden curtains, open so they could look out at the cityscape. Marcus sighed. He didn't want to go to Cumbria.

Half an hour earlier, he'd rung the bell at the large front door of the mansion block.

'Irene,' he'd said on the intercom, 'can I come up? I need to talk to you.'

Irene was surprised. She and Marcus were close, but his agent ran a tight ship: Marcus wasn't allowed to go anywhere of his free will. He never just 'popped in'. He was too famous. So he must be very worried.

Marcus and Irene had been music students together thirty years earlier and had become firm friends. She had become an academic, and Marcus had become a struggling bass soloist. But Irene knew his potential. He had a great voice and was brilliant at interpretation. But there wasn't much scope for that when you were a jobbing singer, getting one-off gigs with choral societies or at festivals. He needed to be distinctive — to have a unique selling point.

Irene had advised him to release a CD of standard operatic arias, but to include one obscure piece which would catch the critics' ears. She had suggested 'Standing in the Need of Prayer' from the opera *Emperor Jones* by Louis Gruenberg. It was an original choice. The piece required sensitive re-imagining. Perfect for Marcus. That track was a critical success, and the rest of the album was a popular tour-de-force. Marcus's career went from strength to strength, peaking when he became a panellist on the hit TV show *Vocal Vote*.

Irene busied herself in the kitchen getting some snacks. Marcus settled himself on the sofa with a large glass of white wine. But he wasn't comfortable. When Irene joined him, he told her about the Scott-Broughtons' offer, and his impending trip to Caldfell Hall.

'It's supposed to be a big secret. I'm under contract not to reveal that it's me until two days before the performance. The strategy is to keep people guessing.'

Irene was surprised. She had no idea that Marcus Sotheby was the 'world-famous bass' the Scott-Broughtons had been touting on their website. And obviously Marcus believed the premiere would still happen. Did he not know Parry Palmer was dead? Did anyone? After Dave Oldcastle's call, Irene had hurried home and searched through everything she could find online. There was plenty about the terrible weather in Cumbria, but nothing about Parry Palmer's murder. Had Callum Oldcastle's father been hallucinating? Could Irene have misheard?

She thought not.

Now Marcus was staring into his glass.

Suddenly his whole posture changed. He went from being urbane and gracious to squirming, like something was on his mind.

'Fuck it, Irene, I need the Caldfell gig. But I don't want anything to do with that obnoxious clown Parry Palmer. I've never liked him. Years ago, when I was doing concerts with big amateur choirs, I saw how he treated his singers. And I know you don't like him either. I don't know why you put up with him.'

'He has important supporters. And you're working with him too . . . we all give in to him.'

'But not Ayesha. She never gives in. She's a rock.'

Ayesha was Marcus Sotheby's partner. After years of playing the field, to his friends' astonishment, Marcus had settled down. Ayesha Tomkins was gorgeous but totally down to earth. Now in her early forties, she was a music teacher in the minefield of inner London primary schools. She'd met Marcus when his agent had the idea of a TV project bringing classical music to disadvantaged kids. It had been a ghastly dog's dinner until Ayesha Tomkins took over. She was a superb organizer and a good musician with a gift for communicating. And she'd been more interested in the children than in Marcus, which put his nose out of joint. But eventually he'd been impressed.

And he fell for her like a ton of bricks. At first, she was amused. There was no way she could take him seriously. But as time went on and he kept in touch, she started to believe that he might be sincere. He was rich, famous and surprisingly nice. She was cool, in her comfort zone, and she brought him insight into real life. He met people living on housing estates, with tough lives. Ayesha gave him the sort of edginess he needed to stand out from other smooth singers. Thanks to her he'd landed the role on the panel of *Vocal Votes* because he understood what a diverse audience wanted.

But now Marcus looked agonized. 'Ayesha hates Parry Palmer. She says that if I work with him, she's leaving me.'

'That sounds a bit drastic.'

'She means it. Ayesha's a tough nut. You know that. You hired her to work on the Academy's outreach programme, after all. You know she doesn't stand for any nonsense. Has she contacted you? Because I haven't seen her for days. She just packed a bag and left, furious. I had no idea she felt so strongly about Palmer.'

'Do you know why she hates him so much?'

'No idea. I mean, no one likes him, but Ayesha was shaking with suppressed rage. She did say something about the way he treated her brother . . .'

Ayesha's much younger brother was a wheelchair user. Irene could imagine Parry making snide fun of a person with a disability, and that Ayesha would be appalled, but that seemed a slim reason for walking out on Marcus.

'So she threatened that unless you cancelled the contract with the Scott-Broughtons, she would leave you?'

'Yes. It was so extreme I couldn't believe it. I told her not to be silly and overreact. That didn't go down well.'

'No. I can see that.'

'But Ayesha's not a hysterical person. I just didn't realize it was a serious ultimatum.'

Irene took a deep breath. 'Marcus, I don't think you need to worry about it too much anyway. The Caldfell Chorus isn't going to happen. Not this week, anyway. For a start, Caldfell Hall's cut off by snow. And I've heard a rumour about Parry Palmer.'

'Really? Have the Scott-Broughtons sacked him? That would solve everything.'

'Not exactly. He's been attacked. In fact, I heard he was dead.'

'Dead? What do you mean, dead?'

'Expired. Not breathing. Passed away. In his case, murdered.'

'Murdered?' Marcus stood up suddenly, spilling his wine in a puddle on the glass tabletop. Irene resisted the urge to rush and get a cloth. Marcus was trembling. He sat down again, so fast that the remaining wine splashed onto his cashmere jumper.

'Oh my God, Irene, that's terrible news!'

'Well, I appreciate that you've lost a fat fee, but it will get you off the hook with Ayesha.'

'Off the hook? You're kidding. The last thing Ayesha said to me was that Parry Palmer deserved to die. She was shaking, Irene. She really meant it. If anyone was going to murder Parry Palmer, my money would be on Ayesha.'

CHAPTER EIGHT

Simeon came by the Spirit into the temple: and when the parents brought in the child Jesus, to do for him after the custom of the law, then took he him up in his arms, and blessed God.
Luke 2:27–28

Alex Armstrong woke from a very deep sleep. Like Suzy, she had left her curtains open, but the bed was a long way from the window. She climbed out and padded over to look out. Her view showed a hump of smooth white fellside, with the standing stones poking out of their snowy blanket.

Alex checked her phone. Still no wi-fi. She supposed that if anything had happened to Edwin in the night, someone would have come for her, but she was still anxious. She slipped on her warm clothes and Stutterheim raincoat. Alex was always stylish — unlike her husband. She sighed when she thought of his high street anorak. Most of the men on the course had something similar.

There was no one around in the Hall when she left to walk to the healthcare cottage. Everyone was in the refectory, a converted barn, having a huge breakfast.

Edwin was sitting up in a chair.

'I feel absolutely fine,' he said. 'I slept like a log. But they won't let me out of here until I've had every bit of me tested by that doctor. And I want Gervase to come and speak to me. I want to know what's going on.'

'Most of the chorus have gone for a huge fry-up despite everything. They're already institutionalized.'

'Oh, be fair, Alex. It's been pretty traumatic for people, and they can't escape from here. The wi-fi is down as well. People will cling together and do what they've been doing already. And there must be some folk in the chorus who are worried and desperate to contact home.'

'Maybe. But most'll be delighted to stick around and get compo from the S-Bs.'

'You're a cynic.' Edwin laughed. 'That's why I love you. Mrs Reality-Check!'

Alex laughed and kissed him on the forehead. 'Watch my blood pressure,' he said. 'You'd better go and get the latest on what's happening. I've already sent my compliments to Gervase and asked him to come over. I've got a proposition for him.'

Alex looked at him. 'Do you really want to carry on with this, Edwin?'

'Of course I do.'

'OK. I just needed to hear you say it.'

'Listen, Alex, I know you hate it here. I'm not so keen myself. But if the premiere is to be postponed rather than scrapped — and I can't see them scrapping it after all the hype — I think we should stay on and rent a place in Norbridge. I'd earmarked this spring for composing, not performing. We don't have to be in Frankfurt. Or Caldfell Hall for that matter. I can compose anywhere.'

'Oh, that's wonderful! I don't want to stay here a moment longer than necessary. It's not safe. Don't forget you got hit on the head.'

'But everyone thinks I was attacked by the person who killed Parry, leaving the scene. I was just in the wrong place at the wrong time.'

Alex shivered. 'But that means you were in contact with a killer. I think it's horrid here. People are just shrugging off a murder. At least I've got Suzy with me now. We're going to do a bit of digging together. She'll want to get at the truth, and so do I.'

'Be careful, Alex.'

'Of course. We've done this before, Edwin. Suzy knows what she's doing.'

'Well, maybe Suzy can help us find a house to rent in Norbridge for the spring.'

'But hang on, how can that work with the *Candlemas Oratorio*?' Alex asked. 'It's so time-specific. Candlemas is February the second.'

'I can make it work. The concussion must have cleared my brain. I'm going to write a new, bigger piece called *The Sacred Spring*.'

'*The Sacred Spring*? What's that about? And will Gervase buy it?'

'Absolutely he will! I can use what I've written already and build on it — it's back to front but it works. The Virgin Mary takes Jesus to the Temple at Candlemas; she and Joseph meet Simeon, who sings the *Nunc Dimittis*, about dying happy now he's seen the Lord. And in my new piece Mary looks back to when she visited her cousin Elizabeth, and the baby jumped in Elizabeth's womb. That's the Visitation on the thirty-first of May.'

'So the piece could be premiered later in the spring?'

'Exactly. Do you get it? Sacred Spring. When the baby jumped in Elizabeth's womb and Mary sang the *Magnificat* to her cousin. Praising God for choosing her, a lowly girl, to bear his Son.'

Alex nodded. 'After the Annunciation by the Angel. It always seemed far-fetched to me.'

'Oh, ye of little faith. But it's the trad *Mag* and *Nunc* combination. And it would give Gervase nearly three months to regroup and premiere the new piece then. And the music would have a much longer shelf life. At Easter every choir does the *Messiah*, or the Bach *Passions* — then there's nothing obvious till the *Requiem* season in the autumn. This would be the first great spring oratorio.'

'Well, if you say so.'

'I'm not being arrogant, Alex. I know I can do this. And we could still launch Lily as a star and use Marcus Sotheby if he's still available. It really works.'

Alex nodded. She was used to Edwin's enthusiasm, and it was her role to temper it. But this time he might be right. And it would give her more time with Suzy, but in a safer place. For the first time in days Alex began to feel more positive. Cumbria was her home, after all. If another IVF round was a no go, and if they were going to come back long-term, maybe they could think about adoption . . .

Edwin took her hand. 'Is it tactless of me to write about Elizabeth, the cousin of the Virgin, having a baby late in life?'

'Oh, Edwin. I'm Mrs Reality-Check, remember? My pain can't stop others' joy. What will be, will be. But right now, you need to have a plan before Gervase Scott-Broughton railroads you into something you don't want. And make sure you get an increased fee. They can afford it.'

'You're right. As always!' Edwin knew this new idea would work, and unlike the original commission, it wasn't just a response to the Scott-Broughtons' brief. It was all his own concept. Plus, he had found a better, bigger vehicle for Lily, who was his discovery, after all.

Alex got up to go. 'I'll pop back when I've heard Eva Delmondo's announcement to the troops. She's threatening to address everyone after breakfast. Good luck telling Gervase about your own idea. I hope he's big enough to buy it.'

But Alex never got back to hear Eva. As she entered by the front door of the Hall, she saw a slight figure standing by the window. Lily Martin was alone, looking out, crying silently. Without thinking, Alex went up and put her arms round the girl, letting Lily sob into her shoulder.

* * *

After she woke from her first restless night at Caldfell Hall, Suzy stayed in bed until the snow had died away and a weak sun was pushing through the clouds. Then she tried her phone again. No signal.

It was really frustrating and also rather suspicious, Suzy thought. It meant the Scott-Broughtons were the only people with access to the outside world. Alex had mentioned that they had satellite phones. Everyone else was dependent on the non-existent wi-fi. And Suzy wanted to talk to the outside world pretty desperately.

Her brain had been whirring since she woke up.

Alex had all the insider information, which was great. They were cut off now, but news of this murder was going to spread beyond Caldfell Hall as soon as the wi-fi was back up. And Suzy had had a brainwave. Apart from having a son who played the saxophone, and a husband who sang in a church choir, Suzy knew nothing about musicians. But lying in bed, she realized that her best friend in London might be able to help. Rachel Cohen was a top investigative journalist whose metropolitan base meant that she had been able to help Suzy in the past.

In the downtime between documentaries, Rachel taught at a London journalism college. Suzy had tried teaching there for a while, before she had come back to Tarnfield and become involved with the murder at the St Jane's women's hostel. Suzy had passed her freelance teaching on to Rachel. It suited Rachel much better.

But lately Rachel had been less happy. She had moaned to Suzy about the college being absorbed into the great maw of the University of North London. The big university had devoured smaller institutions, and Rachel had mentioned the Academy of Voice being another victim of the ruthless academic takeover.

Rachel was only a visiting lecturer, but Suzy wondered if she might know the renowned professor whose name had come up as Parry Palmer's boss.

If Suzy wrote a message to Rachel, it would reach her as soon as the wi-fi was working again.

Hi, Watson, it's me, Suzy wrote. *I'm snowed in at a stately home on the West Cumbrian coast. There's a choral course going on here, funded by the famous Scott-Broughtons. You'll have heard of them. But there's been a murder. A man called Parry Palmer has been killed. Do you know a Professor Irene something in music? He worked for her. If you get this, try and catch up with her. I need more info. Love from your favourite sleuth, Sherlock.*

Then Suzy got out of bed, in need of some breakfast.

* * *

Alex finally peeled Lily from her shoulder. She led the girl towards one of the sofas.

'We're going to be stuck here for weeks, aren't we?' Lily said loudly. Alex looked around to see if they were being overheard. But the big room was empty. Everyone else was eating heartily.

'I need to be back at sixth-form college to prepare for my mocks. I've been given time off and homework to do but that's going to run out. I love working with Edwin and the music's great, but I need to get back to my mam. And what about the premiere?'

'Well, we can't go ahead with it, can we? Everyone's too discombobulated. And it would be disrespectful now Parry's dead.'

Lily wailed, a visceral sound. 'But no one liked him. He wasn't even a good chorus director. Dave Oldcastle would have been better. Can't we just do it without him?'

'It's not that simple, Lily,' Alex said. 'Look, we need to wait to see what Gervase Scott-Broughton says. Eva is supposed to be making an announcement this morning.'

'Oh yeah, she came into breakfast — not that she ever eats — and told us all to be in this big room at ten o'clock. That's why I'm here. She said we could ask as many questions as we liked.'

'That will be helpful. But you're going to have to get used to the idea that we'll be stuck here for a few days at least.'

Lily suddenly wailed again. 'But what about my mam?'

'Oh, Lily, I'm sure Gervase and Lauren will get a message to her. She'll know you're all right.'

'Me? Of course I'm all right. It's not *me* I'm worried about, it's Mam. I'm her carer. She's hopeless without me.' Lily began to cry again, more noisily.

Alex stroked her shoulders. 'So you look after your mother?'

'Of course I do. Who else would? She's OK. She loves me in her own way. But she's not very responsible. And I left my birthday cash behind where she can find it. I didn't know I'd be stuck here for days. I don't know what Mam will do with money to spend. I really need to go home.'

Alex felt out of her depth. 'We'll find a way to check your mum's OK. Now, why don't you come to my room and have some coffee? Or hot chocolate or something? You can miss Eva's announcements. There's no reason for you to sit there with everyone else. I'll get Suzy to go to the briefing, then she can come up and tell us all about it. You deserve special treatment. You're the star of the show, after all.'

'Star of what show?' Lily said weakly. 'There's no show now, is there? Oh, that horrible Palmer man. He's ruined everything. And I'm not the star. I'm hopeless.' Again she started to wail.

'Stop there!' Alex said sharply. 'Edwin chose you, Lily, over dozens who auditioned. You had the best voice. No doubt about it! And Edwin has plans to carry on and make something even bigger than the *Candlemas Oratorio*. So get over it. Please.'

Whether it was relief or despair, Alex couldn't tell, but Lily sank back in the cushions and closed her eyes. There was no crying. Just a lot of dramatic heavy breathing.

But Alex must have done something right because Lily suddenly snapped out of it and grabbed her arm. 'OK, Alex. I'm sorry for losing it. I'm usually super sensible. I need to be, with a mam like mine. You can't have two loonies in one flat. I mustn't behave like a spoiled brat. But I shouldn't let myself be treated like a spare part either.'

'No. Quite right.'

'Parry Palmer was a right shit,' Lily went on. 'But he shouldn't have been killed. I get that. This morning I was tired and lonely and scared, after what I saw in the night. Really, really scared. But I feel much better thanks to you.'

Alex smiled, pleased. She shepherded Lily out through the door in the panelling and they walked together up the elegant staircase to Alex's room. Then, on the landing, Alex had a thought and stopped.

'Why were you really scared of something you saw in the night, Lily? Really, really scared you said. What did you see?'

Lily looked at her with huge hazel eyes. 'I got up in the night and I saw Parry's ghost. I honestly did. It was crawling up through the snow near the standing stones. In that skanky anorak of his with the hood up. I think he's come back as a zombie to make sure we don't carry on without him.'

Alex laughed. 'You probably saw a farmer looking for sheep buried in the snow. Or one of the security guards. Whatever you saw, it wasn't Parry Palmer's ghost.'

But Alex wondered what it might have been. Someone had been out there and had socked her husband on the back of the head. Was the assailant still prowling around?

And was that assailant Parry Palmer's murderer? Whoever had come to kill Palmer was probably still out there. There was a murderer at the Hall. However justified they felt, they were a killer. And killers had crossed a line. They were dangerous people.

CHAPTER NINE

As one whom his mother comforteth, so will I comfort you; and ye shall be comforted in Jerusalem. Isaiah 66:13

Suzy breakfasted in the refectory. She introduced herself to Dave Oldcastle, who looked as tired and stressed as she felt. Then she caught up briefly with Alex, but couldn't really talk because of Lily, who clung to Alex like a limpet. But Suzy agreed to attend Eva's briefing for them.

Suzy went back to the big main room. She stood behind the others and listened to Eva. The diminutive comms director could certainly capture the room.

Eva asked if everyone had managed to sleep despite the terrible events of the day before. People nodded blearily. The limitless booze plus the drama meant most members of the chorus looked stupefied.

Eva said that they were now in the middle of a police investigation and the worst weather crisis at Caldfell in living memory. It was a climate change issue, of course — and could she just remind everyone of something? It was the Scott-Broughtons' insistence on sustainability and helping the planet which meant they were safe and warm here, with the heat pumps and their own water supply.

Then Eva moved on to practicalities. She was the go-to person for any logistical queries. No fresh snow was forecast for that day, although more light showers were expected. But the storm would move east and weaken. A thaw was expected at the weekend. When the police were satisfied, people would be free to go.

There was nothing to worry about. There was plentiful food and drink. Everyone would be pleased to know that the S-Bs' technical team were working very hard to get the wi-fi restored and it should be back on in about an hour. They were pretty sure everyone would be safely home by Monday. If anyone desperately needed to go, that would be facilitated by helicopter, though anyone leaving would be expected to contribute to the cost. All those staying would receive a significant extra per-diem payment, which in Eva's view was very generous of Mr and Mrs S-B.

'So guys,' Eva finished, 'have some more coffee, stretch your legs as much as you can and come back here at eleven for Mr and Mrs S-B!'

She almost called for a drumroll.

Suzy left to rejoin Alex and Lily in Alex's bedroom, where the news was met with yet more wailing from Lily. Suzy had forgotten how self-dramatizing teenagers could be.

'So we're stuck here till Monday!' Lily sobbed.

'Lily, we must wait and see what Gervase tells us,' said Alex. 'I told you Edwin has an idea which might be even better for you.'

Lily put her head in her hands. 'No. It's all over. My big chance. And what about my mam? Has anyone got hold of her? Oh, I can't stand this stress . . .'

'Lily, pipe down,' Suzy said. 'Alex needs to go and see if Edwin has met with Mr Scott-Broughton. Let me take you to your room — you can get changed out of that tracksuit into something smarter. You need to hold your own at the next meeting when Gervase tells us what's going to happen about the music. It's not the place to be seen going to pieces. And as Alex said, there might be good news for you.'

Lily looked as if she wanted to sulk, but Suzy was having none of it and hustled her out of Alex's bedroom.

After they'd left, Alex went to the window and looked out before leaving. Had Lily really seen someone creeping around last night? And if so, where was that person now? They could have frozen to death. And was it the person who had attacked Edwin? Had Edwin seen anything of his attacker, perhaps out of the corner of his eye? Now he was better, she would push him a bit on this. The police seemed to have sidelined his attack, but eventually they would know from lab tests if it was Palmer's blood on Edwin's jacket.

Alex had never suspected her husband for a second, but it was good to know that no one else could either. He couldn't have killed Palmer and then knocked himself out with a blow to the back of the head. So Edwin was in the clear.

But everyone else was in the frame. Alex shuddered.

* * *

Rachel Cohen in London got Suzy's message as soon as the wi-fi was up and running again.

Rachel tried to read between the lines. As it happened, Suzy's instinct was right. Rachel did know Irene Przybylski. Rachel had Orthodox parents in Manchester; Irene had a Polish Jewish mother in Barnet. Irene had organized a Klezmer night for the university and Rachel had gone to hear the band. She had Irene's phone number. Rachel was working at the journalism college that day and sent Irene a message suggesting they meet for coffee. She mentioned that a friend was working at a choral course in Cumbria. It was a long shot, but when Rachel went into the coffee shop, Irene was already there. They moved to a quiet table by the big window.

Rachel cut to the chase. 'Nice to see you, Irene. I thought you might be interested to know, I've got a friend who makes podcasts up in Cumbria.'

Irene shuddered involuntarily. 'Another journalist?"

'Don't look like that,' said Rachel. 'My friend Suzy is one of the good guys, like me. Her podcasts are very successful. And she's a brilliant TV producer. Daytime, topical factual stuff. She developed Hiram King's famous show on Linkflex.'

'So?' Irene said. Rachel looked at her steadily without saying anything more until finally Irene said, 'This is to do with the Caldfell Chorus, isn't it? Has the news got out?'

'About Parry Palmer? I'm afraid it will soon, Irene. The whole set-up is going to get a lot of press attention. I must say I'm very surprised to hear that a couple of billionaires are running a course there. It's lovely, of course, but it's hardly Aldeburgh. I should think that most people in Norbridge think Billy Budd is a prize dahlia.'

'Not very funny. So why are you talking to me?'

'Well, you turned up pretty quickly, Irene, so you must be concerned . . .'

'How much do you know about the connection with the Academy?'

'Only what everyone will know once it's on social media.'

Irene closed her eyes momentarily. 'And your friend Suzy is on the case?'

'Looks like it.'

'Rachel, this has serious implications. For me professionally. I need to find out what's really going on in Cumbria. Yes, one of my staff, Parry Palmer, went up to Caldfell to be musical director on this course, and he's been attacked. Murdered.'

'It couldn't have happened to a nicer person. Yes, I know of Parry Palmer, Irene. He's a legend for inappropriate behaviour even in the journalism department. But if he's been killed, that's bad.'

Irene pursed her lips. 'Too true. What very few people know as yet is that two of our students threatened to kill him in front of several witnesses. And the partner of a friend of mine, who did some outreach work for me, is also off-piste after threatening to murder him. So that's three people with Academy connections who could be implicated in a murder of one of our staff.' Irene shut her eyes.

'My friend Suzy is trapped up there till the snow melts. But she's been involved in solving other murders in the past . . .'

'I'm not sure I want this solved if someone from the Academy has killed one of the lecturers.'

'You'd be better having one known perpetrator than three suspects, Irene. Let me hook you up with Suzy.'

Irene nodded. 'OK. I'll think about it. Let's talk. I like you, Rachel, and I think I can trust you. I'm going to need some damage limitation to say the least, and someone on the inside might help. I've got a meeting now which I'm already late for, but let's have lunch. Not here. Come to my flat. Here's the address. One o'clock. I'd really appreciate it.' Irene rose, straightening her tight black suit, and slipped away, clutching her leather music case.

Rachel sat and ruminated. Suzy's hunch had paid off as usual. Irene had certainly bitten. She was obviously desperate to know what was going on at Caldfell Hall. Rachel tried to call Suzy, but she didn't pick up, so Rachel left another message: *Hi, it's Lord Peter Wimsey here. I've just had an intriguing conversation with Irene Przybylski and I'm meeting her for lunch later. She's very rattled. No one liked Parry Palmer but no one wants to be in the frame for his death and there's a big reputational issue for Irene and the Academy of Voice. I'll keep you posted. Call me when you can. At this rate, we're going to run out of the names of famous sleuths. Are you up for Miss Marple? No, I thought not, Lots of love. Stay safe Suzy. Love R xxx*

* * *

That morning, Robert had got up and made tea and toast, woken Christopher Murray — fast asleep in Jake's bedroom — and called a taxi. They hiked up through the snow to the main road to meet the cab. Thankfully, the road had been gritted. Fifteen minutes later they were in Norbridge, unlocking the Advice Centre door and setting up the tables. They had areas of consultation: family finance, health, education.

But the weather meant the Advice Centre was quiet.

'Ro Watson isn't here to staff the community policing table. And there's no message.'

Robert nodded. 'We'll manage. I don't think we'll have many takers today. Even the regulars might be staying in.'

'I was hoping Carly might show up. If I had another chance to question her . . .'

'We talked about that, Christopher. You need to stop worrying. It's not realistic to think she could have reached the Hall in this weather and murdered someone, then come back to show off about it. The Hall is cut off. I can't even get a message to Suzy.'

As Robert spoke, his phone rang. 'Hey, that's her!'

'Take it. I'll wait here.'

Robert tucked himself into the tiny kitchenette at the back of the church hall.

'Suzy, thank goodness! How are you?'

'I'm so sorry, Robert, there's been no signal here since I arrived. The wi-fi's just come on again. And there's been a serious accident . . .'

Robert went cold. 'You're all right, aren't you?'

'Yes, but someone's been killed. The choral director. The police are involved. Ro and Jed. We're all stuck here.'

'So when will you be able to get home?'

'When the police have got statements and all that sort of thing. They're expecting a thaw this weekend, and I'm hoping to be home by Sunday as planned. Don't worry, everything here is very well organized.' She paused again. 'Too well organized really. It's all about logistics and keeping people happy. Even though someone's been brutally killed . . .'

There was the sound of voices in the background.

'Robert, I've got to go. I'm looking after that poor kid who was supposed to be singing the big part. Lily Martin.

She's just getting changed, so I had a chance to call you.' Suzy's voice was breaking up as Robert strained to hear.

'Suzy, I'm having trouble catching everything you say. Just tell me again: someone's been killed up at Caldfell?'

'Yes. The choral director has been knifed. I need to go, Robert. I'll call you later. Love you.'

Suzy was rarely sentimental. Robert knew that she must be rattled. He put the phone back in his jacket pocket. But he didn't rush back to Christopher, who would take the news of a murder at Caldfell Hall very badly. He would immediately assume Carly was the culprit. And he could be right.

Robert hoped against hope that Carly would come loping into the Centre with yet another money muddle, or an 'issue' with the council. But he had a horrible feeling that Carly Martin was AWOL after doing something dreadful. Could she really have gone to Caldfell to avenge herself on the man who had impregnated her seventeen years earlier? It seemed impossible. But she had boasted of a murder, and a murder had been done.

* * *

That morning, after a good night's sleep, Gervase Scott-Broughton felt better about life. They had put out a dignified communiqué with a tribute to Parry Palmer. Eva had addressed the plebs, as he thought of the chorus, and was now dealing with press enquiries. The police were tucked away in an outbuilding. He was sure that things would be tidied up in the next forty-eight hours. Eva Delmondo was holding up well. She was less obsequious than Trent, and less devoted than Pearl, but she was good with the troops, and she didn't panic.

He would make a dignified, well-thought-out announcement at eleven o'clock. And in the meantime, he'd had an excellent meeting with Edwin Armstrong in the health centre.

As he walked back to the main hall, Gervase found the crisp snow-covered environment invigorating. But he composed his features in case anyone could see him. Parry's murder was obviously a terrible blow, of course. But Gervase was loving his time at Caldfell Hall. He looked down at his walking boots, thick corduroy trousers and high-end waxed jacket. He would never dress like this anywhere else. He felt more at home here than in the USA, even though that was where he'd made all his money. Oh, NY was wonderful. And he loved California. But life there was so . . . manicured. Here, he felt his true self expand. He farted into the fresh air.

Gervase marched into the huge rustic hallway. It was crowded with people waiting for him. Trent and Pearl were standing discreetly to one side. They both moved towards him like large watchdogs, revealing behind them the breathtaking outline of Lauren Scott-Broughton. His wife was wearing an off-white sheath dress with huge black metallic buttons. She seemed even more skeletal than when they'd left the States to come to Cumbria, but thinness suited her.

'Morning, everybody,' Gervase called, and all heads turned to him.

'Right. Listen up. Eva's given you the logistics; now I'm giving you the future. I've talked to Edwin Armstrong and he's much better. We're cancelling Sunday's live stream of his *Candlemas Oratorio*. Instead, we'll be premiering a new work in May, using the material Edwin has already written. He's extending the piece to cover the biblical scenario of the Visitation with the *Magnificat*. This is an idea of pure genius. It will be called *The Sacred Spring*, which is a play on words. It will be twice as long as the original commission, and we'll engage the same soloists.'

For the first time, Gervase faltered slightly. He hadn't thought about confirming this with Lily Martin. She was at the back, and she looked rather better. More mature. She was wearing dark trousers with a neat beige sweater.

'Lily!' he said. 'Of course, you'll be the soloist in the new piece. And we're talking to Marcus Sotheby's agent today. Yes, Marcus Sotheby is the secret celebrity we engaged for the project, and we hope he'll be with us for the new premiere on the thirty-first of May, the feast of the Visitation.'

There were excited murmurs around the Hall. Sotheby was a big catch. This was new and thrilling news. People started to perk up. Suzy put a steadying hand on Lily's arm. She looked stunned. She would be starring in a new composition alongside a superstar. Marcus Sotheby was really famous, on the telly and all over social. Her mam would be ecstatic.

Gervase went on. 'We are, of course, trapped here while the police take statements and go on with their enquiries. We've set up an office for them in one of the buildings and they won't be tramping all over the Hall. We'll carry on each day as planned and run a concert just for ourselves on Saturday night, in Parry's memory.'

A communal shiver exposed this as Gervase's only false note. He hurried on. 'We'll need someone to lead us, and on Edwin's recommendation I'm going to ask Mr David Oldcastle to take over as informal choral conductor.'

To Gervase's surprise, there was a ripple of applause. Edwin's instinct had been right.

Dave murmured, 'I don't know what to say . . .'

So don't say anything, Gervase thought. Then he added a surprise of his own. 'And well-known folk artist Brigham Broughton will be arranging a Cumbrian folk song for us all to enjoy.'

This announcement was met with deafening silence.

'In the meantime, I believe the police will get to the bottom of this terrible tragedy quickly. And when the thaw comes, we shall all go home with something wonderful to look forward to here at Caldfell Hall in May. So, let's do it, everyone!'

'Brav-oh!' The voice was unmistakenly high class. Gervase turned to his wife and nodded his thanks.

'Eva.' Gervase waved her over while the audience erupted into excited chatter. 'We need to get our next press statement out pronto.'

'I'm on it, Mr S-B.'

The Scott-Broughton procession left the room, almost to applause. Most people were delighted, and a few hung round a flustered Dave Oldcastle. His life had changed completely in twenty-four hours.

But he wasn't the only one. Brigham Broughton watched the group with a grin of satisfaction. No one was crowding to congratulate him, but he didn't care.

* * *

Suzy and Lily were at the back and were first out of the door in the panelling and up the stairs to Lily's room. It was small, like Suzy's. It had a view showing the standing stones and Neolithic graves on the fellside.

There were plenty of ancient monuments in West Cumbria. But now, half covered by snow, these looked striking. The black stones stood out, while humps over the subterranean stone burial chambers were enlarged by their snow blankets.

Suzy said, 'So it's good news for you, Lily.'

'Yeah. S'pose so.' Lily was too much of a teenager to show wild enthusiasm now she was over the shock.

'Your life will change now, you know. This is a bigger challenge.'

'Yeah.' Lily looked out of the window rather wistfully. Now the thrill had worn off, she was feeling more anxious about the future. And thinking about the past. 'Look at those old stones in the snow. Me and Mam go walking up there in the summer. Folk gather by the graves. Hanging out, doing weed . . . drinking . . . being stupid.'

'Not your thing?'

'No. They pretend it's spiritual, but they just like getting pissed where no one can move them on. I usually like to get Mam home, but she always wants to stay and see the sunset.'

'Is she a bit of a hippy, your mum?'

'Yeah. It's not all her fault, though. She hated her stepdad when she was a teenager and ran away to London. Then she came home again when she was expecting me. He was dead by then and Nanna looked after me when I was little. But Nanna died when I was twelve. It's been tough for Mam.'

And for you too, Suzy thought. 'And how did you get into singing? Was it through the abbey?'

'Yes. That was my mam's idea. I really like singing in the abbey, and the bishop's very nice. I was the first girl in the abbey choir.'

'Hey, well done! Now, we'd better think about how you're going to spend the next few days. The wi-fi is back on, so you can try calling your mother or you can get hold of her through someone at the Advice Centre. You also need to think about what you'll be singing in the scratch concert. Do you have a singing coach here?'

'Yeah. She sings alto in the chorus. And sometimes Edwin comes to my lessons to go over tricky bits in his piece.' Lily blushed. *Aha*, thought Suzy. *Maybe there's a bit of a crush going on there.*

Alex knocked on the door and put her head round.

'Did you get to Gervase's eleven o'clock briefing?'

'Yeah . . .' said Lily.

'So you must know everything,' Alex replied. 'Edwin is really excited for you, Lily. He says you're to keep up the exercises and the work with your coach, and that when they let him get up, you're his number one priority.' Lily beamed, and Alex held out her arms. 'You're looking much better. Come on, I'll take you down to the practice room. We can talk about songs for the concert. See you at lunchtime, Suzy.'

Alex bustled round Lily with hardly a glance at Suzy. Suzy smiled to herself. This was all good. Lily was keeping her friend occupied. At some point she needed to fill Alex in with her brainwave about getting Rachel to track down Professor Przybylski. But Alex was concentrating on the singing prodigy.

Suzy watched Alex shepherd the teenager out of the room. She was certainly taking care of her, exactly as PCSO Ro Watson had suggested. Ro was right: Alex was good with Lily.

But thinking of Ro, Suzy felt troubled. Where were the police in all this? Physically they were in another outbuilding, well away from the Hall and the singers. Suzy suddenly felt that Jed and Ro themselves had been sidelined — outmanoeuvred even — by the Scott-Broughtons. That wasn't right. In fact, nothing about the situation was right . . .

She suddenly felt a deep distrust of the activities at Caldfell Hall. She sensed they were all being bought. The lavish food, the promise of entertainment and the limitless booze were blunting people's judgement. Bread and circuses. They were all being taken for mugs, and a little seed of anger was planted inside her. There was something patronizing about it and she didn't like it one bit.

CHAPTER TEN

For he that is mighty hath magnified me; and holy is his name. Luke 1:49

Suzy's best friend, Rachel Cohen, rang the bell of Professor Irene Przybylski's flat in Bloomsbury. Irene buzzed her into the building, and Rachel took the lift to Irene's top-floor landing. The other woman was waiting for her. She was dressed in elegant, flared ivory trousers, a white top and white crocs.

'Come in.'

Rachel followed her into the large corner living room. An impressive Tiffany lamp lit up the dark winter afternoon.

'Some white wine? And some nibbles?' Irene asked.

'That would be great. I've had a bad morning dealing with some students from hell.' Rachel sank into the luxurious sofa and looked out over the rooftops. Irene had a grand piano in the corner, and there were music sheets strewn about. Rachel could also see a cello case.

Rachel liked music as much as anyone and went to her fair share of concerts and opera, but she had no musical education and couldn't play a note. Her singing voice sounded like a mating magpie.

She stood up to look at the bookcases. At least she knew about books. Irene had just a few pristine volumes and much of the shelving was taken up with photographs, showing concerts and graduation ceremonies and family groups. But there was a series of worn snaps in incongruous heavy silver frames. In one, a young Irene had her arm around a girl with a pixie haircut, in skinny jeans. In another, the same two were laughing into the camera and pulling faces. A third just showed the girl, looking wistfully out of the shot. Was it her sister? A relative? A close friend?

Irene came back. 'I've thought about this. I really need your friend Suzy to help me, Rachel,' she said, pouring the wine and proffering the snacks. 'Like I said, I need to know what's going on up at Caldfell Hall. Information is coming out now, but it's all very sanitized. I might as well tell you: the friend of mine whose partner has stormed off, saying death was too good for Parry Palmer, is a very well-known person.'

'Oh yeah?' Rachel wasn't easily impressed. 'Why doesn't your A-lister just tell the police?'

'Because my friend is Marcus Sotheby. Mr Nice Guy of the panel show world. If his partner has so much as threatened a man who's subsequently been murdered, it's not going to play well in the tabloids.'

Rachel raised her eyebrows. 'Oh. Wow. Damaging. Even I've heard of Marcus Sotheby. And I'm not into music really.'

'Exactly. He's a household name. If it leaks out that Marcus's girlfriend has hightailed it to Cumbria to kill Parry Palmer for some weird personal reason, it would be quite a big story — and it wouldn't do Marcus any good with the billionaires. Worse still, from my point of view, she's done some work for the Academy in the past.'

'Why does this woman hate Parry Palmer so much?'

'Marcus has no idea. I mean, a lot of people have reasons to dislike him, but her level of hate is something else. It's baffling. She's a sensible woman. She's great at outreach work with kids in the community. She was a respected primary school teacher before she shacked up with Marcus. She's not the sort of hot-headed type who'd threaten to kill someone for the drama.'

Rachel had the greatest respect for anyone who taught in primary schools. 'It seems very odd,' she said.

'Very. And then there are the two students who accused Parry Palmer of pinching their work. Callum Oldcastle and Freddie Lamplugh. The Academy hasn't dealt with that well. The exam board didn't take it seriously enough. Callum and Freddie are both absent without leave.'

'So you need information from the inside. You want me to ask Suzy what's going on. For example, are the police questioning anyone? Is there a suspect? Have any strangers been seen lurking? Is there anyone in the vicinity who looks like the lover of a famous singer rather than a female sheep farmer?'

'I'm not being funny, Rachel. I really want you to find out.' Irene paused. 'Look, I don't think Marcus's partner Ayesha will have set out to murder Parry Palmer, but Parry had a bad reputation with women. Nothing too overt, just a sort of old-fashioned sleaziness. He could also be very provocative. But I'm not just worried about Ayesha.' Irene paused again. 'I think the Academy might have a lot to lose however this plays out. We've been sitting on the students' complaint against Palmer since Christmas. It's possible that Callum and Freddie got frustrated and acted unilaterally — and things got out of hand. It wasn't just because of the plagiarism row either. Palmer made fun of Freddie's sexuality as well. He was a bit of a homophobe, Parry. Not everyone in the arts is woke, you know.'

'It sounds like people were queuing up to get to Cumbria in a snowstorm and do him in.'

'He had a lot of enemies, yes.'

Rachel drank her wine, helping herself to some nibbles.

'This is delicious. Look, Irene, now I know what you're after, I'll certainly talk to Suzy as soon as I can. She knows her patch inside out. The odds are that she'll be across what's going on. I can call you as soon as I've spoken to her and got some inside info.'

'That would be great.' Irene smiled. 'Or you could come back in person.' She got up and went over to Rachel, letting her arm linger on Rachel's shoulder. 'Wouldn't you like that?' she said quietly.

Suddenly Rachel realized. The photographs of Irene with that young woman, going back decades. The clues were all there.

Oh dear. Rachel liked Irene, but not in that way.

'That's not my thing, Irene,' she said gently.

Irene moved away as if the touch had been totally accidental.

'Pity,' she said.

'Yes, I think so too.' Rachel smiled. 'Look, I'll certainly call Suzy, now lines of communication are back, and get the lowdown. I'll report back to you on the basis that anything you say to me will go straight to Suzy. Including the information about Marcus Sotheby's surprising girlfriend. What's her name by the way?'

'Ayesha Tomkins.'

'And do you think it remotely possible that Ms Tomkins might have knifed Parry Palmer in the snow in Cumbria?'

'Well, she certainly threatened it and she's gone missing. Marcus is in quite a state.'

'OK, Irene, it's a deal.'

* * *

In the practice room at Caldfell Hall, Alex suggested that Lily look for some music she might like to sing at Saturday's concert. While the girl started rifling through the sheet music on the piano, Alex moved to the window with her singing coach.

'The view is quite beautiful, isn't it?' said Alex. 'The scenery lured me outside yesterday afternoon. I could hear Lily singing then. It was a beautiful sound. You're doing wonders with her.'

'Thank you, Mrs Armstrong. She's a joy to work with.' The coach paused. 'But you can't have heard Lily singing yesterday afternoon.'

'Really? I was sure I could.'

'Not yesterday. Lily said she had a bad headache, and she went to bed.'

Alex wondered if the shock of finding Parry Palmer's body had affected her memory. But of course it hadn't. She recalled vividly walking around the Hall on the outside path. She'd reached the corner and was wondering where to go when she heard Lily singing. She wasn't wrong.

But she wasn't going to make an issue of it. 'I must have been thinking of another afternoon.'

Lily came over to them, her eyes sparkling. 'I would love to try this one,' she said, holding out a copy of 'L'hiver a cessé' by Fauré.

'If your French is good enough . . .' advised the coach.

'My French is very good,' said Lily. 'This is about hope for the spring. It's perfect.'

'It's not an easy song,' said Alex.

'Of course not.' Lily laughed. 'I want to do something which challenges me. And shows people how good I really am. I'm not stupid. I know Eva wanted a photogenic little boy and thanks to Edwin they got me. So I've got a lot to prove.'

She turned away, back to the piano.

The girl is complex, Alex thought. She acted in a childish way to preserve the illusion that she was the kid and her mother the grown-up. But it was the other way round.

And Lily kept her intellect under wraps. Being brainy wouldn't suit Carly. Brainy kids got ideas and left home. Carly would whisk her out of the abbey choir in a nanosecond if she thought Lily was getting too independent. So Lily played dumb. But she was certainly intelligent, and a dab hand at camouflage.

Camouflage. So where had the real Lily been the afternoon before? Alex knew she had heard her singing. But the lesson had been cancelled. So where was Lily at the time

Parry Palmer had been murdered? And why was she pretending to have been having a lesson?

For a moment Alex thought she would just ask. But Lily was getting her confidence back. Any hint of suspicion or distrust might derail her. And surely the girl couldn't be involved in murder.

But someone was, of course. Despite the Scott-Broughtons' pep talk, and Eva's hard sell, they were still in a snowbound house with an unsolved killing. Edwin had been attacked. And Lily had seen someone walking on the fells in the night. Alex shuddered, and then surrendered herself to Lily's beautiful rendition of 'L'hiver a cessé' — 'Winter is over'. Though it wasn't, by any means.

* * *

At lunchtime, Alex and Lily were absorbed into a group talking music, while Suzy ate alone. Realizing that Alex would be staying with Lily until rehearsal time, Suzy went off in search of Eva Delmondo. In the slick operation led by the Scott-Broughtons, nothing had been said about Suzy's own role. Of course, she was just a bit player, but she still needed to find out what was expected of her now. A podcast about the candlelit murder at the Caldfell Chorus would be fascinating, but she reckoned the Scott-Broughtons would lock her in a barn if she even suggested it.

She wondered where the police had been housed. Their huge car was parked outside, but she hadn't seen either them or any other officers. The Scott-Broughtons had been clever: out of sight, out of mind. DI Jed Jackson wouldn't like that, but he obeyed orders. His boss was inclined to placate the powers that be. And those powers were the Scott-Broughtons.

Suzy looked down at her phone and saw that Rachel had called. Great. She shelved the idea of looking for the police and went back up to her room in the servants' quarters. The wi-fi was fine. She lay on the bed listening to Rachel's voicemail, before ringing back.

'Rache, it's me. I don't mind being Miss Marple.'

'OK, I'm Maigret. *Comment vas-tu?* How's the weather up there? It's finally made the national news.'

'The weather is the least of our problems.' Suzy started to give Rachel a full briefing on Parry Palmer's murder, but Rachel interrupted. 'I know all about it. And there's stuff you should know in return.'

Rachel explained that Irene had identified three people who had threatened Parry, and that she was very worried. They could all mean trouble for the Academy of Voice. One was the lover of Marcus Sotheby, the famous singer. The other two were disgruntled young students who had accused Parry Palmer of stealing their compositions. In public they had said they would like to kill him, especially as the authorities were doing nothing about their complaint.

This was really interesting stuff. Suzy felt her interest perking up. Suddenly she didn't feel quite so passive. She had independent information to go on. Now, she wasn't just in the hands of the S-Bs.

Suzy told Rachel in turn that the police were up at Caldfell and that they were questioning people. But she could add that she herself had been on her way to Caldfell Hall at the time Parry Palmer had been murdered. There had been no other vehicles on the road. Suzy had seen no one on foot — walking would have been impossible in the snowdrifts. Heavy snow had fallen that morning and fell again in the evening after Suzy had arrived. If someone from outside had killed Parry, Suzy was sure it would have been almost impossible for them to escape. Unless they knew another route, and in that weather it would mean intensive local knowledge.

On the other hand, the Caldfell property was big and rambling; perhaps someone could be hiding in an outbuilding. On balance, in Suzy's view the killer had to still be there.

'I don't know how you do it, Suzy,' Rachel said. 'You're always around when these things happen.'

'I must have a nose for it. But it's also very scary when you come across a murder. Although the funny thing about this set-up is that it's not scary at all. It's actually all rather comfy. Lovely and warm with great catering. With a killer on the loose, you'd think everyone would be terrified, but people are having rather a good time. The general view is that Parry got what he deserved and that whoever did it has been and gone. But that's so improbable . . .'

'Well, here's hoping it wasn't Marcus Sotheby's lover. Or the unhappy students.'

'I should tell DI Jackson about them. But I can't find him. We're all on a tight rein here.'

'Weird.'

'I know. I get the sense we're all being played. I don't like it.'

'Well, let me be your spy on the outside. I can tell you that Marcus Sotheby's lover is called Ayesha Tomkins and she's rather a stunner on a lot of levels. She'd certainly stand out in Norbridge. And the students are called Freddie Lamplugh and Callum Oldcastle.'

'Oldcastle?'

'Yep.'

That's interesting, Suzy thought. Was Callum Oldcastle related to Dave Oldcastle who sang bass in the chorus? It wasn't such a common name. And Dave knew Robert through church choirs, she was sure of it. Maybe she should find Dave Oldcastle and talk to him.

She rang off, promising to call Rachel later. Feeling invigorated, she grabbed her anorak and put on her wellies. She really did need to speak to the police now, to pass on what she knew to DI Jackson.

But when she went out, she found that security guards were discreetly stationed around the Hall, keeping people on the cleared paths. She asked where the police were based, and the answer was a vague wave. 'I'd like to speak to them,' she said.

'We're only letting people through when they're called. It's a difficult path down to the police office. Possibly dangerous to the public. If you really want to speak to them, you can. But Mr Scott-Broughton's team is making appointments. Health and safety. You need to go through them.'

Suzy felt furious. This place was getting more like North Korea every minute. Was she the only person who thought a killer was roaming free at Caldfell? Everyone else seemed perfectly happy. Relieved, even. Relying on Big Brother. Perhaps they had all conspired to kill Parry Palmer, like in *Murder on the Orient Express*.

But that was ridiculous. Palmer had been a horrible man, but he'd had a right to live. His killer had done an evil thing. And in Suzy's experience, murder being once done . . . It could happen again. It probably would.

So why wasn't everyone else as worried as she was?

CHAPTER ELEVEN

A feast is made for laughter, and wine maketh merry; but money answereth all things. Ecclesiastes 10:19

Eva Delmondo was renowned for her energy but now she was pooped. She lay on her bed, hoping for a nap after a shattering morning, but she was frustrated by the sound of Lily Martin's warbling downstairs in what sounded like French or some goddam poncey language. Same bit over and over. Lily was in the big spacious practice room, twice the size of Eva's little pad, on the floor below. It made Eva want to throw something at the wall, but as the nearest thing was her laptop, she didn't.

'Shit, shittery, shit!' she moaned. It was all right for the chorus, who would be getting more spondulicks and a free trip home by Monday. But Gervase had made it quite clear Eva was to stay on till everything was sorted. Of course, she had a hugely increased 'honorarium'. But she still felt she had been demoted.

She had put her absolute best into the press release and had handled calls from the States and London, which poured in once the wi-fi was back. She guessed the outage had something to do with the slimy Trent. He was so far up Gervase's butt he could lick his tonsils. He'd do anything to buy the S-Bs enough time to get the story under their belt.

The wi-fi outage had also meant Eva was cut off from her life support. Just after lunch, she had finally contacted the agency doing the launch of the male fragrance which should have been her next project. But she hadn't delivered on time, so they had gone ahead with someone else. Life was crap.

The only good thing was that the podcast woman had managed to get through the snow when most people would have turned back; Eva was developing a sneaking admiration for Suzy. She wasn't a Scott-Broughton worshipper, and she didn't seem quite as gullible as the other punters. Eva had noticed her at the back of the briefings, one eyebrow slightly raised. And it was good that Suzy and Alex Armstrong had taken over caring for the hormonal Lily Martin. The podcast idea would have to be binned, which was a shame, but Gervase should offer Suzy Spencer a big handout. In Eva's opinion, Suzy deserved it for not fussing.

Though she might be too far beneath Gervase's radar.

But he was sloshing money around everywhere else. Suzy should get a cut. It would help keep her quiet. Eva reluctantly got off the bed, changed out of her leisurewear into her suit, and trotted off in her signature bootees to speak to the boss.

In the Scott-Broughtons' suite, Pearl was on guard at a desk by the door.

'Hi, Pearl!' chirruped Eva. 'I have a quick query for Mr S-B.'

'Go through Trent.'

'Is he around?'

'I don't know.'

Eva hid a sigh. Pearl was one of the most obstructive people she had ever come across. But Trent, alert to being sidelined, came sidling out of the sitting room.

'Oh, it's you, Eva. Whaddya want?'

'I need to see Gervase about something.'

'I'll tell him, if you tell me.'

'OK, but it's a bit of a problem.'

Trent backed off. He didn't like problems. He did solutions. He motioned with his head for Eva to follow him and she found herself in The Presence.

Gervase was seated in a deep armchair. He was ensconced with his cousin, Brigham, who was wearing ragged jeans and nasty sandals over smelly socks. His hand flopped over the arm of the chair, holding a large glass of liquid. Eva could smell whisky but was unsure whether it was the drink or Brigham's breath.

Brigham couldn't see her. But she could hear him. 'Well, Gerry lad,' Brigham said, 'that's your problem. You're the one who can get me what I'm owed.'

'Sorry to interrupt, Mr S-B,' Eva began.

'Yes?' he snapped.

'It's about the podcast woman.'

'Oh Christ. Why are you coming to me? She was your idea. What's the problem?'

'Actually, no problem. Au contraire. She's gone out of her way to look after Lily. Plus she's keeping Alex Armstrong calm. We owe her. So what's the deal?'

Eva suddenly realized that she had challenged Gervase Scott-Broughton. It was only a minor thing, but she felt an adrenaline rush. It was exciting. She'd started to lose respect for him once she'd sussed that dodge with the wi-fi outage. And seeing this nasty little set-up, with Pearl and Trent acting like stooges, she realized she didn't want to be one.

Gervase thought for a moment. 'Tell the podcast woman no recording, or I'll sue her arse off. But if she's saving the kid from meltdown and keeping the Armstrong diva quiet, that's good enough for me. Is that it?'

'Will you pay her an honorarium as well as the podcast fee?'

'Why would I do that?'

'Because she's a local journalist. She's been around other murders. She's nosy. And there's no harm in keeping her sweet.'

Gervase flapped an irritated hand. 'Point taken. Pay her the pre-arranged fee times two. If she can keep Mrs Armstrong away from me, she's worth it.'

Brigham laughed, an ugly sound.

Eva said brightly, 'Thank you *so* much, Gervase. In my opinion, you've made a good call.' No one talked like that to Gervase Scott-Broughton. It amused Eva to see Trent's jaw drop.

Gervase actually laughed. 'I'm glad I meet with your approval, Miss Delmondo.'

'My pleasure.' She turned on her Dior heels, leaving Trent and Pearl staring after her. In the corridor she congratulated herself on her chutzpah. Only then did she wonder — what was Brigham Broughton talking about? What was he owed? And what could Gervase possibly need to do for him? Wasn't it the other way round?

* * *

David Oldcastle came back in a daze from the first rehearsal for the scratch concert. It had gone better than he could have hoped. He'd pulled out the 'Libera Me' from Fauré's *Requiem*, suggesting the bass solo be sung by all the men. It made a big, affirming noise. Add to that something clever from Lily, then a couple of familiar old chestnuts, and the programme was complete. Except for Brigham's contribution. If it ever materialized.

Dave lay on the bed, thinking about his son Callum again. There had been no reply to his last three calls.

Callum had been an arsey teenager with a charmless manner. But he'd been good at music. Then Dave and his wife had split up. She'd met someone whose idea of classics was Abba's *Greatest Hits*, and Callum had gone to live with his mother down south. Dave had stayed in Norbridge, sticking at his day job managing a farm shop and thrown himself into music as a gifted amateur. Callum took after hi but wanted to be a professional, and gained a place at university to read music. While a student, he had written a few songs which had been published. After graduating with a first, and gaining confidence, Callum enrolled for an MA at the Academy of

Voice — it was a one-year course, and he'd teamed up with Freddie Lamplugh.

By this time Callum had grown closer to his father because they had music in common. He told Dave all about his problems with Parry Palmer. For their MA final project, Callum and Freddie were working on a book of re-arranged madrigals for community choirs. They had a music publisher lined up, who liked their simple but tuneful arrangements. It was designed for easy singing, but with strong, interesting chords at regular intervals, which meant amateur choirs could sound exciting.

Then their tutor, Parry Palmer, published his own songbook entitled *My Madrigal Guide: Madrigals Made Simple*. Callum and Freddie knew Parry had pinched some of their arrangements. His songbook certainly lacked the grit of Callum and Freddie's superior work, but the market couldn't take two similar projects, and their publisher pulled the plug.

Callum and Freddie immediately took legal advice, which cost them a bomb, only to find that there was nothing they could do. Palmer argued that they had been discussing madrigals as a possible dissertation subject when he was already working on his songbook. Madrigals weren't an obscure area. It was possible they were working on the same thing simultaneously.

Having got nowhere with the law, Callum and Freddie made a formal complaint to the university, and they knew this time it was compelling. No tutor should put themselves in a position where they could ever be accused of stealing a student's work.

But Parry Palmer had laughed it off. He'd sauntered across to them in the university café just after Christmas.

'Happy New Year, lads. If lads is the right word. Maybe you've got fancy pronouns now, like ems or zirs. Zirs for queers, is that it? Anyway, here's some *straight* talking. I've been informed of your formal complaint about me and I'm going to fight it. And win.'

Parry had stooped to be on a level with Freddie Lamplugh, who was sitting down. The young man turned away, trying to ignore him, but Parry was right in his face. 'No one in the music business will touch anything by you after I've finished with you. So you can take your formal complaint and shove it up your tight little bum. And don't be too sure of getting your MA either. If I prove you took *your* ideas from *me*, you might be out on your arse.' Freddie had stood up suddenly, provoked and holding his arms out as if to push Palmer away, and Callum had aimed a fist at him. But . Professor Przybylski had seen them from across the café, and they froze. Parry waved jauntily at her and moved off, laughing.

Callum had told his father all about it, in detail. 'The man's a complete shit, Dad. It's bad enough losing out on the songbook, but we shouldn't have to take abuse and worry about our exam results as well. We could have killed him.'

When Dave Oldcastle had applied to come to the Caldfell Chorus, the musical director hadn't been appointed. When he found out that it was Parry Palmer, Dave had dithered over telling his son. Dave loved Callum but Callum had a temper, and Dave didn't want to be on the receiving end. Callum's adolescence had coincided with the end of Dave's marriage. Dave remembered a lot of shouting, slammed doors and Callum racing around the street furiously on his bike. Once, Callum had thrown some of Dave's clothes into the garden, and another time his son had vandalized his garden shed. Callum could become very angry.

So Dave had said nothing about taking part in the Caldfell Chorus or working with Palmer. But he knew how much Callum hated the man and he also knew Callum could lash out.

Could Callum be there, at Caldfell Hall — could he have posed as a caterer or a delivery boy or something? Had he done something stupid? Like murder a man with a penknife? Dave shuddered. He was thrilled to be leading the Caldfell Chorus, but it would give him no pleasure until he had proved his son and his son's friend were in the clear.

Dave had only met Freddie once. Callum was a big, ungainly lad, but Freddie was small, thin and very intense. And he had been verbally abused by Palmer. Was Callum so fond of Freddie that he would channel all that anger and stab Parry Palmer in the neck? Or could Freddie do it for himself?

But there was nothing more Dave could do for now. Callum wasn't answering his phone. Dave had to think about the music for the concert and hope and pray that, by the weekend, the police had found the culprit. And that it wasn't Callum.

* * *

After her little triumph over Gervase, Eva went to find Suzy Spencer to tell her the good news about her money. The obvious place to look was in Alex Armstrong's suite. The Hall was quiet. It was ten past four and the afternoon rehearsal had started. The singers were all in the barn where they practised.

Alex was alone in her room, reading what looked like medical reports, which she pushed under her laptop.

'Hi, Eva, can I help you?'

'Yeah. Where's Suzy the podcaster?'

'I haven't seen Suzy since earlier this morning. Lily and I have been tied up with music. I think she must have gone for a walk.'

'A walk? You mean outside? Where to?'

'I don't know, Eva. She'd been looking for you and I think she wanted to clear her head.'

'Why?'

'Well, there's been a lot happening in the last twenty-four hours.'

'OK. I need to find her too.' Eva wanted to tell Suzy about the extra dosh before Gervase thought more about it. He could be nasty if challenged and his amusement might turn to rage.

Eva looked at Alex's feet.

'What size shoe do you take?'

'Pardon?'

'What size. Shoe. You.'

'A six.'

'What's that in real sizes?'

'USA, you mean? It's about an eight.'

'OK, it's a bit big for me but maybe you can lend me some hose as well?'

'As well as what?'

Eva looked at Alex in wonderment. 'As well as some outdoor shoes. I can't go schlepping round trying to find your bestie in my Diors.'

'So you want to borrow my walking boots and some socks. OK — you only had to say please.'

'And?' Eva was genuinely baffled.

'Oh, never mind. Sit on the bed and I'll get them. You'll need a warm anorak as well. You can't go out in that little jacket.'

Alex found the boots and helped Eva get into them; then with a sigh she lent her the posh waterproof that she really liked. It swamped the doll-like American, but Eva swaggered in front of the mirror and decided she looked rather cute. Then off she clomped in her unfamiliar footwear to try and find Suzy.

Alex looked at the details of her IVF treatment again and the clinic number in Manchester. She could call them now the wi-fi was back and make an appointment for next week. But suddenly she couldn't be bothered. It was all too obvious that the treatment hadn't worked. And if she was honest, she wanted to stay in Norbridge and be close to Lily. And to Suzy . . .

They had caught up very briefly. Suzy had said she might have a contact with the Academy of Voice. Alex wasn't sure where that would lead. She had also said she wanted to speak to the police. Alex was sure Suzy would blag her way in to see Jed Jackson and Ro Watson somehow or other. She would be out, looking for a way to get to them.

* * *

But Suzy had gone back to her room having given up on finding Eva. She tried calling Robert again just to say hello, but he was obviously busy at the Advice Centre. On a whim she tried Rachel again. There was something at the back of her mind. Rachel was between tutorials at the journalism school and took the call.

'Hello again, Harriet Vane.'

'Hmm. Lord Peter, I've been thinking. I've been involved in quite a few murders . . .'

'You're famous for it.'

'But I've never come across a victim as universally disliked as Parry Palmer. What's your take on him? Did you ever meet him? You work in the same place.'

'I've seen him around and I knew him by repute. He's one of those people who knows where the bodies are buried and everyone knows he knows.' Rachel paused. 'I've been thinking about him too. He's worked at the Academy of Voice for thirty years. Man and boy. He lives in Islington, not far from me. He's a local man. I saw him about sometimes.'

'What did he look like?'

'In his sixties. Not unattractive. Longish hair. Thin. Tall.'

A bit like Edwin, Suzy thought. 'Did *anyone* like him?' she asked.

'Well, he was useful to some people, I guess. You know the sort of person I mean. Good at making other men laugh. I suppose he was an extreme example of the sort of bloke you used to find in every office. The wind-up merchant.'

That's helpful, Suzy thought. So Parry was a bit of a lad. A posh lad. The taunt who'd gone too far and ended up with a knife in his neck. With three very clear suspects.

Suzy decided she would go for a walk again and this time would insist on seeing DI Jackson. He needed to know what she'd heard from Rachel. She kitted herself up, went downstairs and braved the bitterly cold air.

CHAPTER TWELVE

He hath filled the hungry with good things, and the rich he hath sent empty away. Luke 1:53

At the Advice Centre in Norbridge, Robert found Christopher Murray in the kitchen listening to Radio Cumbria.

By lunchtime the news was everywhere, and it was clear that Parry Palmer had been killed by stabbing.

Christopher said, 'It must have been Carly. She said she'd killed someone and now someone is dead. And she's gone missing.'

'Did she mention a knife?'

'No. I was too gobsmacked to ask her how she'd done it.'

'But if she knifed someone at Caldfell Hall and then got back to Norbridge in time to meet you at around five thirty, she'd still have been covered in blood. Look, Christopher, Carly came into Norbridge last night to tell you what she'd done. Why do you think she did that?'

'Because it was cathartic, and she was proud of it.'

'Exactly. She wanted to boast about it and that's the Carly we know. But we also know she fantasizes. She might be making herself the centre of someone else's actions. And what's the point of you going to the police right now with what might be a delusion? According to the radio, Palmer was stabbed in the neck. His carotid artery was probably severed. That takes skill. It's not Carly's way of operating. If Carly hasn't appeared by tomorrow then it will be a different story. But for now, there's only her overactive imagination to go on.'

'But if she's killed someone and we don't report it . . .'

'Report what? Hearsay in the pub? Wait till tomorrow. Look, Christopher, come back to The Briars with me again tonight. Your car's still there. You've had too many shocks to be by yourself, going over it all. And for now, we've got customers at the Advice Centre. Let's just get on with the job.'

Robert went back to his table and the dribble of people who had come in on this dark, dreary afternoon. Two of Robert's afternoon clients at the Centre had remarked with wide eyes about the Caldfell murder.

'Old Fred won't like a murder in his village,' the woman said with spiteful satisfaction. 'Having the po-lis tramp over 'is land.'

'I don't know how much tramping they'll be doing in the snowdrifts.'

'Mark my word, lad, po-lis always mek a mess of stuff. They did my place over, looking for me great-grandson's stash.'

Robert laughed out loud. He wondered whether the police had found it. The Advice Centre was full of drama but a great-granny hoarding drugs was a new one.

Maybe he shouldn't be surprised. When he thought about it, the woman wasn't much older than he was. When Robert caught sight of himself reflected in shop windows, he was shocked by the old man who looked back. He wondered how Suzy felt about it. She never seemed to age at all. But maybe he was biased. He loved her so much — her energy, and the way she constantly surprised him with her crazy ideas. Except they weren't always crazy.

At the end of the day, Christopher was calmer, and the two men had a companionable pint in the pub, ignoring the elephant in the room, which was Carly's weird confession. Then they ventured out to get a cab back to The Briars. There was just one, on the town's only rank. The air was already damper, and the snow was melting when they were dropped at the lane down to the house. When they reached home, Robert defrosted one of Suzy's intriguing casseroles. He hoped Christopher wouldn't mind one of her original concoctions. This was labelled Cumbrian lamb tagine with apricots. Worth a try.

He opened a bottle of red wine. The stew was good. They gossiped gently about the Advice Centre. And they were both tired.

By ten o'clock Robert felt ready for bed. He was surprised Suzy hadn't called. He wanted to try and get hold of her again before turning in, and he already felt like dropping off.

'I think I'm going to bed, Christopher,' he said. 'If you want to sit down here, the kitchen stays warm.'

'No, I'll go up too. Thanks for this, Robert. This is a tough time for me, and you've been very kind.' He yawned.

A sudden banging had Robert jumping out of his chair and shouting, 'What the hell!' Someone was hammering on the kitchen door. Robert rushed over to the door and looked through the small square windowpane. A ghastly white face was peering in.

'What in God's name is that?'

Christopher turned to him. 'You'd better let her in, Robert. I think it's Carly.'

* * *

In London, Marcus Sotheby was back at Irene's flat for the second day running. The news of Parry Palmer's murder was out. But media response was muted. Palmer was virtually unknown outside North London. The Scott-Broughtons were big news, of course. But they'd issued a dignified press release with all bases covered and then receded behind the snowdrifts.

Gervase's factotum, Trent, had contacted Marcus's agent. They'd agreed Marcus would still be available and be at Caldfell to sing in the premiere of Edwin's new work in May. It was to be a bigger and, if Marcus's instinct was right, much more significant performance. The fee had risen more than proportionally. It wasn't just a good gig: it was now a great gig. It could mean a career step change, from national treasure to international phenomenon. Marcus just could not say no. And why should he, if Parry Palmer was no longer involved? Surely Ayesha couldn't object now?

But he couldn't find her. He could hardly confide in his agent, and since his fame had increased, he had ceased to confide in people, except for Irene. He was at his wits' end, but he still had a concert to perform the next day at the Wigmore Hall. Marcus had taken a brief time out from rehearsals to google Parry Palmer's murder on the internet — he had been stabbed with a small penknife. It seemed ridiculous to suspect someone he loved so much of a horrible crime like murder. Of course he didn't think Ayesha Tomkins had done it . . .

But stabbings were part of her everyday life. There were about fifteen thousand stabbings in London each year, many by kids. Ayesha had dealt with children who brought knives to school. Had she been tempted? But he was being ridiculous.

He went over and over all he knew about his partner's life. He had been warmly welcomed by her mother, sister and disabled younger brother. They were all musical — the brother was now in a Pentecostal choir, though he had been a young offender in the past.

When Marcus and Ayesha had met, Marcus wasn't the national celebrity he later became. It was easy for him to visit the Tomkins family. They lived in a council flat in one of Islington's more notorious projects. Ayesha's sister worked in a supermarket. It was an utterly different world for Marcus but the music was a link. And he wanted to understand more about the close-knit extended family — the aunties, who were usually not relations at all, and cousins, step-kids and godchildren, all living locally.

Marcus had been desperately sexually attracted to Ayesha, but in the context of her home, he started to love her. She had been brilliant at music from an early age and had found herself at Cambridge taking a degree, thanks to perceptive teachers at the local girls' comprehensive. But she had decided against high flying and come home to roost. She had done her teaching training and gone on to working in local schools. She was beautiful and special, and was wary of men. Marcus had had a lot of girlfriends, most of them blonde and skinny and in the music business. He was a promiscuous womanizer attracted to promiscuous women. His new-found passion in his fifties for this luscious but restrained Black woman with a strict moral code astonished both him and the people he knew. But they couldn't deny that it worked.

It had taken him months to convince her. But he had taken her to a concert at the Festival Hall, and she had cried at the beauty of the music. Afterwards they had walked along the embankment and talked for hours about her life, not his.

It was totally uncharacteristic for Ayesha to flounce out. She didn't do histrionics. And she would never cause Marcus pain like this if there weren't something seriously wrong.

Irene listened to Marcus's agonizing.

'You've tried her family?'

'I didn't want to worry her mother. She's in her eighties. But her sister said they hadn't heard from her. I'm going out of my mind, Irene. There's no point in anything if Ayesha doesn't come back. What could Palmer have done that would upset her so much?'

'You don't think Ayesha could have killed him.'

'I did wonder. She's a passionate person. I could imagine her grabbing a kitchen knife and using it in self-defence. But butchering someone in that way wouldn't be her style. Although I did have this crazy thought . . .'

'What?'

'Well, say she knew someone else who wanted Parry Palmer dead? I could imagine her sympathizing and getting involved with someone else who had a grudge and being sucked into some sort of plot.'

It was a possibility, Irene thought. Ayesha could easily have met Callum Oldcastle or Freddie Lamplugh at the Academy. The outreach organizers were always looking for student ambassadors for events.

Irene wondered. Parry Palmer's goading, provocative as it was, was hardly the incentive for an opportunist knife attack. Whoever had stabbed him had been prepared and knew what they were doing. This was coldblooded murder. Callum. Freddie. Ayesha. Were any of them capable of that? Or — crazy thought — all of them?

* * *

Robert opened the kitchen door of The Briars and Carly Martin fell in. Despite the cold and damp, she brought with her the choking smell of weed and alcohol. Robert stepped back. She was soaked. She was wearing her skin-tight leggings and a parka, plus the inevitable baseball cap over her stringy hair.

'Got any drink?' she mumbled. 'It's a bleedin' long walk down that lane.' It was about a hundred yards, but Carly looked incapable of putting one foot in front of another. She lurched onto a kitchen chair.

'You're frozen, Carly,' said Christopher.

'I'll get a towel,' said Robert. 'Have a hot shower. I'll get you something warm to put on.'

'I was hoping for a wee dram.'

'Get dry first.'

Robert found a large towel in the washing basket in the utility room. He flung it at her, pointing to the downstairs shower room. He was furious. And concerned. How had Carly known where he lived, and that Christopher was here? Then he remembered their cheery chat with the barman in the pub. Carly only had to ask around and she would soon discover where to find Christopher. Most taxi drivers in Norbridge would know The Briars. She might even have come in the same cab which dropped them off earlier.

But was she expecting to stay? He was horrified. Carly Martin holed up in The Briars with two men was a scenario he didn't want to contemplate. She could make any sort of accusation.

'Get dry, Carly, and then come and sit by the stove. I'll make tea.'

'I don't want tea.'

'That's what you're having.'

'Have you got soya milk?'

Robert was so irritated he couldn't answer. He pulled the door shut on Carly and found her a large jumper and tracksuit bottoms. He put the clothes on the floor outside the bathroom.

'Put these on when you've finished, Carly. Leave your wet ones in there. I'll deal with them later.'

'All right. No need to shout.' But there was. She was running the hot water full tilt.

Robert went back into the kitchen. 'What's her visit in aid of?' he asked Christopher, who was sitting at the table.

'I've no idea. I'm so sorry. What should we do?'

Robert looked out of the window. The snowstorm had weakened in its journey east, but there was still heavy sleet coming down. 'I don't know, Christopher, but I don't like it. I'd better make her some tea. And no, I don't have soya milk.'

After a few minutes Carly came shambling out. She looked surprisingly young and fresh: the hot water had given her a pink flush and the floppy clothes covered her painful skinniness.

'I need to talk to you guys,' she said.

'What is it, Carly?' As always, Christopher sounded calm and understanding. Robert wondered where he found the patience.

'It's that Caldfell stuff. Where Lily is. You know how brilliant she is. She's goin' to be the next Maddie Prior.' Carly smiled, showing that she had lost another tooth.

'Well, I imagine she's been worried about you, like all of us. Where have you been?' Robert knew he sounded snappy, but he felt snappy.

'Oh yeah. I went to Workhaven. To my boyfriend's. I needed a break after what happened.'

'And what did happen?'

'You know, I went to Caldfell by myself. And I killed that bloke. Parry Palmer. I smacked him over the head wi' a bit of a plank. He went down like a sack of tatties. But then I heard on Radio Cumbria that he'd been stabbed. I don't get it. I'm all confused.'

She looked desperately from Robert to Christopher. 'So I came to find you. I *did* kill him, didn't I? I said I'd do it, and I did it. Tell me I killed him. The bastard had it coming. I don't care if they come for me and lock me up. Because I did for him. Bang! On the head.'

Carly made a sweeping movement with her arm, just missing the teapot, and collapsed with her head on the kitchen table.

CHAPTER THIRTEEN

Fear not them which kill the body, but are not able to kill the soul. Matthew 10:28

Eva Delmondo found Alex's walking boots clunky but strangely liberating. And the big raincoat was something to hide in. No one stopped her. The rehearsal had wound up, and there were few people about. As she walked through the big reception room to the back door, she saw Brigham Broughton sitting by himself, with another glass of whisky. He was a lush, for sure. She couldn't see why a power figure like Gervase put up with him for a nanosecond.

There was a large cloakroom before the back door. Lots of people left their coats there, but now all that was left were two anonymous, average male anoraks. Both dark blue. *Standard boring British menswear*, she thought contemptuously.

To her surprise, as she walked towards the back door, it opened, and Trent came in, dressed as if for the ski slopes at Aspen.

'Hey — Eva! I didn't recognize you. Are you going outside? Those boots look scary!'

'Yeah. I find them good for getting through snow and other crap. Talking of which, if you'll excuse me, Trent.'

'Sure. But you need to know that no one talks to Mr S-B the way you did this afternoon. You need to watch your step, especially in those giant boots.'

'Don't worry about me, Trent. I'm not up his ass like you.'

'I admire you, Eva. I really do. The brave way you face penury and humiliation. Have a nice walk. Don't go wandering around, though. We don't want to find your icy body in the morning.'

'My body ain't icy, Trent. See ya later.'

Outside the Hall, Eva realized it was getting darker. She looked around for Suzy Spencer and saw her in the distance, coming back along the path from the folly.

Suzy squinted at the diminutive figure swathed in Alex's high-end waterproof. 'Eva, I hardly recognized you.'

'No, well I don't go outside if I can help it. I want to save the planet and everything, but I'd rather do it in a warm office. I wanted to catch you, Mrs Spencer . . .'

'That's nice, Eva. Shall we walk along? If we stand here, we'll freeze. I wanted to talk to the police, but the heavies still won't let me in.'

'No. Gervase doesn't want people bothering the cops. Look, Suzy, I need to talk to you about money. I saw Gervase' . . .'

Their conversation was interrupted by a male voice. It was Dave Oldcastle. He had come outside, avoiding the chorus members. The afternoon rehearsal had gone well, but his worry about Callum was gnawing at him. He didn't want to be nobbled by any of the singers.

But Suzy Spencer was different. Reassuring. Not from the choir. He'd met her before with her husband. He desperately needed to talk to someone.

Dave said, 'Hello, Suzy. Are you out for some fresh air too?'

Then he realized Suzy had been talking to someone else, and he nodded distractedly at Eva, whom he didn't recognize. She turned away and kicked, disgruntled, at the snow.

Dave took the opportunity and blurted, 'I'd like to talk to you. Suzy. Please. Away from the Hall.'

Suzy glanced back at Eva, who wasn't going away. 'OK. Why don't we all walk up towards the standing stones?'

She started to stride out; Dave followed her, and Eva clomped behind in her borrowed boots, not wanting to be left out. It was annoying that Suzy had been ambushed by Dave, but Eva could see the dude was seriously agitated. Intriguing. She trotted behind him, and after a few yards, she realized she was enjoying the walk. It was a strange sensation. Then she nearly collided with Dave's back. He had stopped suddenly.

'What's that?' Dave said, pointing up to the fell. It looked like a black rag on the hillside.

'Someone has dumped one of those boring men's jackets,' said Eva.

For a moment, Suzy and Dave were both silent. Suzy said quietly, 'No. I don't think it's that.'

'Well, what is it?'

'Eva, stay here,' Suzy said firmly. The comms director stopped. Suddenly they were all aware that darkness was falling. The strange mess of clothes on the hill looked pitch black against the snow.

Dave moved forward. 'Suzy, I'll go.'

Dave clambered up the snowdrift. Suzy knew what he was going to say. She held her breath.

'What's going on?' Eva squeaked, her voice high-pitched with alarm.

'Just wait, Eva. I think Dave's found something . . .'

'What? Why are we standing here? Why are you holding on to my arm?'

But Suzy said nothing. Her eyes were fixed on Dave as he stood over the mess of dark clothing in the snow.

Then he shouted back to them. 'There's a dead man here!'

Eva gasped, then started shouting, 'What? What is it?'

'It's a body,' said Suzy. 'Who is it?' she called to Dave.

He called back. 'No one from the course.' He paused. 'But I know who it is.'

Dave turned away from them and Suzy heard him vomiting. He was bent over. After a moment he stood up. In the freezing-cold still air Suzy could suddenly hear him clearly. 'It's someone I've met. Just once. It's a friend of my son's. His name's Freddie Lamplugh.'

Suzy's brain was in overdrive. She thought about what Rachel had told her. Freddie Lamplugh. He was a student. At the Academy of Voice. Two students had accused Parry Palmer of stealing their material and now one of them was dead.

'Don't touch him, Dave.'

But Dave was incapable of movement. He had collapsed onto the snow and was sitting there, immobile. Suzy turned, pushing Eva ahead of her, stumbling down the snow-covered path, finding handholds in the frozen snowdrifts on either side as she rushed back towards the Hall.

A security man had appeared at the foot of the path. 'Ladies, where are you going . . . ?'

'There's a dead man up there! We need to get to the police. Get out of my way.' Taking Eva by the hand, Suzy pushed past the astonished guard, who stood back involuntarily. She started to run, making for the building where DI Jed Jackson and PCSO Ro Watson would be. There was no stopping her this time.

* * *

About an hour later, Pearl took Mrs S-B some hot water and lemon. Lauren clutched with clawlike hands at the neck of her thermal nightdress. It was designer wear, of course, from Bon Nuit in LA, a rich grey flannel.

'Where's Gervase?'

'He's with the police, Mrs S-B.'

'So, tell me the latest.'

Pearl took a deep breath. 'Apparently, Eva Delmondo was with some guy who found the body.'

'Eva? Did she know who the dead person was? Can I talk to her?'

'I can try and find her. But that would mean leaving you alone.'

'I don't mind that, Pearl. What I mind is not knowing what's happening.'

'I'll go and find Eva. I'll be back in ten minutes.'

Pearl hurried out of the inner sanctum, along the corridor and into the area where the admin people had rooms. Their names were on the doors. She rapped on Eva's.

'Hey! Who is it?' Eva shouted.

'It's Pearl. Mrs S-B wants you. She should be in the loop.'

Eva opened the door and motioned Pearl in. There was another woman in the room.

'This is Suzy Spencer,' said Eva. 'She came to Caldfell to make a podcast and found a dead body. It's a speciality of hers.'

Pearl was uncomprehending, but she only wanted one thing. 'Mrs S-B needs to talk to you, Eva, because you found the body. She wants you to come up to her suite. Pronto.'

'Ghoul!' Eva did a dramatic shudder.

Pearl reacted as sharply as she could with her impassive features. 'Mrs S-B is no ghoul! She just wants to know what happened.'

'Then she can ask her husband,' Eva snapped. 'He was down at the police office faster than a rat up a drainpipe. Along with creepy Trent.'

Pearl said with heavy formality, 'I can inform you that Mr Scott-Broughton is busy organizing the police and keeping the chorus members from overreacting.'

Jed Jackson had responded immediately to Suzy's news about the body on the hill. He had told her and Eva to go back to the Hall, stay by themselves, and he would call for her. Getting the body out of the snow and into an outbuilding would take time. Not to mention dealing with Gervase Scott-Broughton.

But now Suzy felt that she and Eva had been hanging around a long time. She said, 'While we wait for the police, I wouldn't mind going to see Lauren Scott-Broughton with you Eva. I'd like to meet her. She'll be the soul of discretion,

I'm sure. And we could do with a change of scene until we get to see Jed.'

'Jed?' Pearl looked confused. 'Who's that? Will that mean anything to Mrs S-B?'

Suzy said, 'Jed's the detective inspector leading the investigation into Parry Palmer's death. And presumably into this new death too.'

Uninterested in the British police, Pearl turned to Eva. 'Will you come and see Mrs S-B or not? She's your boss. She has every right to want to talk to you.'

Eva said, 'OK, but if I come, Suzy comes too. I'm not going to be caught between Gervase and his zombie bride. I need a witness and back-up.'

Pearl took an inward gasp of breath but decided to ignore Eva's cheek. She could deliver two witnesses to Mrs S-B for the price of one. 'Come with me, both of you. I'll need to buzz you in.'

* * *

Suzy followed Eva, fascinated, as they walked behind Pearl downstairs to the first floor, back along the corridor and through security. They were ushered into a French-style bedroom fit for Marie Antoinette. Ahead of them, Lauren Scott-Broughton rested her chiselled face against a mountain of snowy pillows, her curtain of grey hair sweeping over one side of her face. On the other side the cut was razor short. Her face was waxy with creams.

'Sit.'

Suzy and Eva perched obediently on the side of the huge four-poster bed.

Suddenly, Lauren Scott-Broughton smiled. When she spoke, her voice was softer and pleasanter than Suzy expected.

'Goodness, you must feel as if you're at the Grande Levee.' Suzy laughed and felt herself warm towards the skeletal figure in the bed.

Lauren murmured, 'Please don't mind me. I've been a little under the weather lately and the terrible business with Parry knocked me sideways. Now I hear that someone else has died. Pearl tells me you two gals were at the scene. Is that correct?'

'Yes, ma'am,' said Eva.

'And you are?' Lauren looked at Suzy.

'My name's Suzy Spencer, Mrs Scott-Broughton. I came here to make a podcast about the chorus.'

'Ah, yes. I've heard about you. Eva suggested we use you, and I thought it was an excellent idea. I've done some digging. You're the showrunner for Hiram King's production on Linkflex, aren't you?'

Suzy was rarely impressed by the great and the good, but this time was an exception. Lauren knew her stuff. 'Yes, that's right. That show has been a surprise success. I devised it and my role was development.'

'But I hope you get your share of the proceeds.'

Suzy smiled. 'Enough to mean I can afford to make my local podcasts. They seem to work well.'

'Not surprising, if your production record is anything to go by.'

'Thank you.'

'I always research interesting local people when we change locations, and of course, Caldfell is particularly fascinating because of Gervase's ancestry. Pearl, bring Eva and Suzy a drink. What would you like?'

'A wine would be good,' said Suzy. 'We were waiting to see the police, but I think they forgot about us. When we found the body we had a man with us, David Oldcastle. He's the one the police really want to talk to. Because he went up close.'

Lauren leaned forward from her pillows. 'And who was it? One of the chorus?'

Suzy took a deep breath. She had heard Dave say quite clearly who he thought it was. It wasn't confirmed, as far as Suzy knew, but Dave had been certain.

'We think it was a young man called Freddie Lamplugh. He's a postgrad student at the Academy of Voice. A friend of Dave Oldcastle's son, apparently. Dave saw that he had an empty whisky bottle with him, and some blister packs of pills. He wasn't a pretty sight. Dave was sick.'

Lauren leaned back on her pillows, looking drained. 'I've not heard of this Freddie Lamplugh. I know the Academy well,' she murmured. 'Gervase and I have been patrons for years. That's how we knew Parry Palmer. He was on the list when we started looking for a choral director for the project here. He checked out as being very experienced, so Gervase wanted him. This is quite dreadful.' She seemed to have gone paler. 'It's appalling that someone seems to have come here to take his own life. Drink, drugs and then possibly frozen to death. Quite horrible.' She seemed genuinely distressed.

Suzy said, 'Dave Oldcastle thinks Freddie may have killed Parry Palmer, then hidden away in the outbuildings and killed himself in the snow. Freddie had a grudge against Palmer. He thought Palmer had stolen some of his work.'

Mrs Scott-Broughton closed her eyes. 'Oh, how terrible. Sometimes I think it would have been better if we'd never come here at all.'

'Don't say that, Mrs S-B,' Pearl said tersely. 'It's still a truly wonderful project. You know the new date for the premiere in May works well. And people say the new piece of music will be even better.'

Pearl turned to Eva and Suzy. 'You should go now.'

Lauren Scott-Broughton opened her eyes. 'Thank you, Suzy,' she said. 'I really appreciate your sharing.' Then she sank back, exhausted.

* * *

Suzy and Eva went back to Alex's suite. Lily was there too, plus the traditional sandwiches and snacks. The girl sat on the window seat, eating heartily.

Alex and Suzy drank a little of their tea, ate nothing, and talked.

Alex asked, 'Do you think the dead man must have been on the site for some time?

'You mean, did he kill Palmer and hide in the outbuildings?'

'And then did he see my husband and attack him? Why would he do that?'

'He could have thought Edwin had seen him and might go back and tell people. So he clobbered him. That ties everything up neatly here.'

'You're right,' Alex murmured.

Suzy thought some more. 'But it's not neat at the London end. The Academy of Voice will be in trouble. A student murdering his tutor is going to be nightmare for them when people find out. And Gervase and his team haven't tried to stem the gossip on this one!'

By the time of the evening meal, everyone knew that the body was Freddie Lamplugh, a student at the Academy of Voice. And that he'd held a grudge against Parry Palmer. People were saying that he'd had a lot of dried blood on his jacket and that tests would reveal it was obviously Palmer's. Those with more local knowledge of Caldfell started speculating that Freddie Lamplugh was the grandson of the old farmer who had the land around the Hall. It explained where the murderer might have been staying. There was reputedly a shortcut over the fell between old Fred Lamplugh's farm and the folly. It was in a sheltered cleft, and the heavy snow hadn't penetrated. Freddie could easily have come and gone, up to the farm.

It also explained the ghost-like figure Lily had seen in the night. That would have been this poor young bloke wandering around in the snow, in the dark, before he took his own life. Tragic as this was, it seemed a clear and simple explanation. There was nothing supernatural about it.

Alex took the girl up to her bedroom and made sure she was OK, waiting till Lily's eyes were closing before leaving the room and going back to Eva and Suzy.

Eva had opened another bottle of wine. 'So that's it then, gals,' she said, mimicking Lauren Scott-Broughton. Then in her usual New York accent she said, 'So this is the story. The stiff who's now laid out in the barn was lurking around after knifing Parry Palmer. He got totally wasted and died in the snow. From a distance he just looked like another rock sticking out, but we walked further than other people and found him. So that's it.'

At that point, Suzy's phone rang. It was Robert. She took the call in the corner of Alex's huge suite, and was on the phone for some time.

When she came back, she said, 'I've just heard something from Robert which upsets your theory, Eva. It alters everything. Robert has got Lily's mother with him at The Briars. Carly's in a bit of a state. She thought she'd killed Parry Palmer by hitting him with a chunk of wood. But it looks as if she attacked Edwin instead. They were a similar build and had the same type of anorak.'

Alex gasped. But Eva raised her glass. 'I knew all those crummy jackets would play into this somehow!'

'I don't get it,' Alex said sharply. 'Carly Martin hit Edwin? Why on earth would she do that?'

'Apparently she mistook him for Palmer.'

'But why would Carly want to attack the musical director of the Caldfell Chorus?'

'Well, here's the thing...' Suzy tried to explain the story of Lily's conception as simply as she could. 'Robert says Carly identified Parry Palmer as Lily's natural father. He showed her my hard copy of the Caldfell Chorus prospectus. Like a lot of these portraits, it's quite out of date. So the picture of Parry Palmer looked like the man who seduced her seventeen years ago.'

'I can't believe Lily's father was a first-rate shit like Palmer,' Alex said.

'Good kids can have bad dads.'

'But what do we tell Lily?' Alex went on. 'And what will happen to her if her mother's arrested for assault?'

'All we know is that Carly has only told Robert and Christopher that she attacked someone. We don't need to report her confession to the police.'

'Then we say nothing,' said Alex. 'The police will probably think the obvious, that it was Freddie Lamplugh who attacked my husband after killing Palmer and trying to get away. If they think about it at all. I know Edwin will agree with me when I tell him. We don't want Lily brought into this.'

'And Carly insists she'll just say she was making it all up if we go to the police,' Suzy added. 'Robert hasn't told her that it was Edwin she hit. She'd be devastated if she thought she'd injured Lily's mentor. That might mean goodbye to Lily's chances of fame and fortune.'

'Edwin would never drop Lily,' Alex protested.

'But it's better if Carly thinks she just hit some random bloke.'

'Agreed. There's no need for her to know it was Edwin,' Alex said. 'And we want to keep Lily out of all this. It's bad enough already, for her to be exposed to two awful deaths, the victim and the suicidal perp . . .'

'Yes. The suicidal perp. Don't you think it's a bit too neat? The Freddie solution?' Suzy mused. 'And it's very good news for the Scott-Broughtons. Bang on time as well.'

'Oh, what the shit?' Eva took a gulp of wine. 'If it ain't broke, don't fix it. This means we can all go home. Whoopee!'

CHAPTER FOURTEEN

For in the time of trouble he shall hide me. Psalm 27:5

Ayesha Tomkins sat on the bed in her Norbridge hotel room. It was cold. She pulled her ankle-length leather coat round her shoulders. On her phone she was looking up trains back to London. There was one in an hour, the first one south that day, because of the weather. She needed to be on it, but she suspected it might be mobbed.

She didn't know much about Norbridge, but she knew she would stand out. Her trip to the Crown and Thistle at lunchtime that day suggested that her skin tone, her cornrows, her height and her curves would turn heads.

But she had to get out of this place. She had been hiding in the hotel room for twenty-four hours, eating from the vending machine, watching mindless television, sleeping. And crying, endlessly going over how she could get out of this mess.

Ayesha did not usually act hastily. It had been breakfast time the day before, when Marcus had told her he'd signed up for the Caldfell Chorus. She'd been at Norbridge by two o'clock in the afternoon. It had all happened so quickly.

Marcus had smiled over his coffee and looked at his watch. 'I can tell you now, Ayshe,' he'd said. 'I've got an absolutely brilliant booking for the next few days.' And he'd told her he was the secret weapon at the world-famous Scott-Broughtons' new music initiative, the Caldfell Chorus. She'd been delighted for him and chuckled. Her rich, rare laugh always made Marcus smile.

'I'm under contract not to tell anyone until two days before I arrive,' he'd said. 'But exactly forty-eight hours from now I'm due to burst onto the scene at Caldfell Hall in West Cumbria, in time to rehearse a new piece by Edwin Armstrong.'

'Edwin Armstrong! That's classy.'

'Absolutely. They're streaming it live on Saturday. Money no object. Edwin Armstrong has been sending me the work in progress each day. It's very good.'

'Sounds like a bit of a stunt — in a good way. And just what you need. It's fun and a bit crazy. Everyone will love it, and you'll have a great story to tell when it's over — working in secret, getting up to the North of England in terrible weather. You'll be in the arts supplements. It's good.'

'I knew you'd get it. Armstrong is brilliant and the Scott-Broughtons can make anything happen. The musical director is a bit of a let-down though. It's that pain from the Academy. Parry Palmer.'

Ayesha had felt her knees turn to water. This wasn't possible. Marcus was in a totally different class to Parry Palmer. They should never even have met.

'You can't go,' she'd said. 'You mustn't work with that man.'

Marcus had told her not to be ridiculous. She could tell from the pain in his voice how much he wanted this gig.

Then she'd said some things about Parry Palmer which she regretted. But Marcus hadn't responded. She knew his stubborn look when he disagreed with conductors or producers. Now he'd turned that look on her. She went into their room to pack a small bag, leaving the apartment while Marcus was taking a call from his agent. She got a cab to Euston.

There had been a train to Glasgow via Norbridge leaving in twenty minutes. She caught it. On the train she rang

Parry Palmer's number. It was years since she'd used it, but he answered in seconds.

'Hello, Ayesha,' he'd said, with his silly giggling laugh. 'I wondered how long it would take you to get in touch, once the cat was out of the bag about Marcus. I expect you want to talk to me, don't you?'

They'd agreed to meet in a pub in the middle of Norbridge, mercifully quiet because of the impending snow. Meeting Palmer again made her feel ill. She'd begged him to say nothing to Marcus about their history, but he'd laughed at her and suggested they go back to her hotel room 'for a bit of fun for old times' sake'.

She'd walked out of the pub in a rage.

She couldn't bear to think what had happened next, but whenever she stopped watching the bright flickering TV screen, she saw Parry Palmer after she'd attacked him, his face frozen in shock and his eyes wide with surprise.

She'd managed to find her way back to her hotel, a cheap place with no reception desk and everything done by card. She saw no one. Then she'd lain on the bed.

There had only been one time as bad as this in her life. As a golden girl from a comprehensive school, she'd gone to Cambridge, where she was a novelty. She'd been unable to believe any so-called friends wanted her for herself. After the warmth of her family and the support and praise of her school, she'd been desperately lonely but unable to voice it. Marcus was only the third man Ayesha had slept with. Her married tutor was the first. She found she was pregnant just before finals, and she failed to get the First everyone predicted. She was the one who was supposed to break the mould but now she was just another girl in trouble. So she'd gone home. Her family closed ranks. It had all been sorted.

That was what she would do this time. The only thing she could do. She would go home to her family.

* * *

Things at Caldfell settled back into routine remarkably quickly after Freddie's death and the tying up of the Parry Palmer murder. The scratch concert went ahead and was a great success. The choral pieces were sung with gusto. Dave's way of conducting paid off — he encouraged people and used entertaining metaphors to get the best out of the singers. Even Brigham Broughton's contribution, which looked on the face of it like an uninspiring version of 'D'ye Ken John Peel', worked very well, helped by Dave's direction. Brigham, of course, sang the verses, but he had all the high voices yelping like hounds and the low voices booming like horns in the chorus. *It would be a great fun piece for a community choir*, Dave thought. Brigham also gave them a version of 'North Country Girl', the song made famous by the American folk-singer Joanie Cadiz. He did it quite well. And he thanked Dave for encouraging him, which was surprisingly gracious.

Of course, Dave was still upset about Freddie's death. And finding the body had been traumatic. But if Freddie had killed Palmer, then it couldn't have been Callum. There was no suggestion that Freddie had had an accomplice. Callum was missing but there was no sign he was implicated. He could be anywhere. That was enough of a relief for now. Dave could park his worries about his son until the course was over.

Gervase was delighted by the concert and made a little, light speech about how music heals. Mrs Scott-Broughton presided regally, supported by half a dozen cushions on a throne-like chair, with Pearl in attendance. She gave a bottle of vintage champagne to Dave 'as a token of our thanks and looking forward to seeing you in May'. It was hinted that Dave might get the full choral director's job in the spring.

Edwin was well enough to be there, in the audience, and Lily's version of Fauré's 'L'hiver a cessé' went down well. It was a bit obscure for some tastes and lacked the rowdiness of 'John Peel' or the massive swell of Fauré's 'Libera me', but it was certainly an accomplished performance.

So, a good night was had by all. It was a blessing for Suzy not to have to record it. It would have been a technical headache. Looking back, she realized that the whole podcast idea had been fraught with bear traps. The Scott-Broughtons were charming with her now — Lauren even made sure they had a few words together at the concert and Gervase had smiled in her direction more than once. But it could all have been very different. Gervase was exacting and controlling. They could easily have come to blows.

On Sunday after lunch it was announced that the police enquiries were finished, and they could all go home. There would be formalities but essentially it was all wrapped up.

Alex and Edwin checked into a real country house hotel. The thaw was underway and the driveway down to the road from Caldfell Hall was slowly revealing itself as a pleasant but unremarkable gravel sweep. The Armstrongs were taking Lily back to Pelliter, the estate on the outskirts of Norbridge where the Martins lived. Carly was home now. No more had been said about her attack on Edwin. Carly was in the clear, but before Suzy left Caldfell Hall to go back to Tanfield, she'd had a much longer phone conversation with Robert about Carly's alarming arrival at The Briars.

Carly had slept in Molly's bedroom and on Friday morning had gone back to Norbridge with Christopher Murray. She seemed to have already rationalized what had happened at Caldfell. She didn't know the real name of her victim, and in any case, she couldn't be expected to remember after all these years. After she'd contacted the sperm door, and he'd demanded sex, she'd just wanted to get it over with and get him out of the flat before Renee came back from some job she was doing somewhere or other. Renee had some fancy career. Carly couldn't remember much about that either. But when Renee came home, all Carly's plans were torpedoed.

Now, though, Carly was weirdly satisfied. As far as she was concerned she had taken action and walloped someone. So it was the wrong man. So what? They were all bastards, she told Robert.

Robert thought that no one could have been less of a bastard than Edwin Armstrong, but he wasn't going to argue.

He agreed with Suzy that, if the police were blaming the attack on a fleeing Freddie Lamplugh, then they should let it be.

But after Suzy arrived home and they sat over a cup of tea at The Briars, they both felt there was something unsatisfactory about it all.

'There's the question of the blood,' said Suzy. 'I've spoken to Ro Watson on the phone. She told me the lab identified the blood on Edwin as being from Parry Palmer.'

'That would give weight to the police's idea that Lamplugh hit Edwin while he was escaping from the scene.'

'But as *we* know, it wasn't Lamplugh who hit Edwin, it was Carly, so how did he get Parry's blood on him?'

'Good point. Maybe Lamplugh fell over Edwin after she'd hit him, as he tried to get from the folly to the outbuildings.'

'Yeah, right. He'd have to practically embrace Edwin to get blood all over his jacket. You know, Robert, this case is full of holes. How did Carly get back to Caldfell? Was there someone helping her?'

'All she says is that she got a taxi back up to the Hall after spending a night in London getting psyched up. It could only go so far because of the snow and she hiked the remaining distance up the hill. She hid in a storage shed until dusk when she saw the man who looked like Lily's father, and then she hit him.'

'I don't believe it. Security was so tight there. And she'd have been frozen. No drugs or drink would have taken the edge off that freezing weather. And how did she get home? Take the bus?'

'I know it sounds odd. But let's not get involved, Suzy.'

But as he said it, Robert knew this was a forlorn hope.

* * *

On Monday, after Suzy had unpacked and checked in with the Manchester TV producers she worked with, she and Robert went to their favourite pub, the Plough on Tarnfield

Green, for supper. The Plough was regularly refurbished. 'They're tarting it up again,' Robert said. The latest version had dispensed with the sticky multi-coloured carpet; instead there were brightly varnished wooden floorboards. On the main wall, the fake panelling and wallpaper had gone, revealing beautiful stone walls. They sat at their usual table.

Suzy suddenly saw that Robert was looking vacantly at her.

'What is it, Robert?'

'Nothing. Oh, well, to be honest I can't follow you. Something about . . . oh dear, I seem to have forgotten what you were saying.'

He started to study the menu even though he knew it by heart. Or did he? Had he forgotten that too? Robert looked up at her and smiled, but Suzy found she had nothing to say. They had been apart for five days, and she had forgotten how alarming his vagueness could be.

'I'll have the lamb shank,' said Robert. 'I'd forgotten they had that.'

'That was what you had last time.'

'Was it? Great. I really like it.'

Suzy said nothing more but made a mental note to take Robert to see their GP.

'What are you having?' Robert asked her. 'You usually have the sea bass.'

'Yes. It's less calorific.'

But Robert looked bemused. Now Suzy felt sick. 'I'm not so hungry,' she said, and took a large gulp of her wine. Robert, unconcerned, sipped his beer and smiled at her over the glass.

'But you usually have the sea bass,' he said again.

This is awful. He's in a fool's paradise, Suzy thought. It had never been hard to talk to him before. She wondered what an earth she would do if she couldn't discuss things with Robert. It didn't bear thinking about, but it happened to thousands of people each month. Some weren't even lucky enough to get a diagnosis and lived in limbo. If Robert was sinking into dementia she would rather know. They would have to face up to it.

'Cheer up,' said Robert. 'It might never happen.'

But say it already had?

* * *

Monday was a bad day for DI Jed Jackson and PCSO Ro Watson. They were an unusual partnership. Jed had teamed up with Ro years ago, when a teacher had been killed in Pelliter, a sink estate on the outside of Norbridge. Jed had been a very serious-minded young Christian, inclined to be rather self-righteous. Ro had been a cynical single mother with a disabled child and a difficult history. But they had formed a good relationship, both ending up in the Workhaven sub-branch.

As time had gone on and the safeguarding of children and vulnerable people had come more to the fore, Ro had blossomed. Jed relied on her judgement. He appreciated his team of officers, but he was very much in charge and needed to keep his distance from them. It was easier for him to talk to Ro when he wanted to brainstorm. Or just offload.

'So the boss says it's all over bar the shouting now. The Caldfell business.'

'They must have found some corroborating evidence in London.'

'Yes. It confirmed Freddie Lamplugh's handwriting. He had a handwritten plan in his overcoat pocket; the doodles established that it was his work. He went up to Caldfell to kill Parry Palmer. He'd obviously scoped it all out in advance and arrived before the snow came. They're not looking anywhere else. I have to say . . .' Jed paused.

Ro shook her head. 'Well, this suits the Scott-Broughtons very nicely. They're big fish, bringing a lot of money into West Cumbria.'

'Which doesn't mean there's anything fishy about it in turn. OK, you and I might both have our doubts, but remember what happened when that dead woman was found in the wheelie bin in Norbridge? The Super insisted it was a Merseyside gangland thing. We had to fight to be allowed to investigate.'

'Yes, and we won.'

'But I don't think the boss ever got over being wrong-footed. He won't let us do it again without cast-iron evidence.'

'I guess you're right. Anyway, I've been away from home too much lately, thanks to Caldfell Hall.' Ro had recently moved in with Phil Dixon, a local farmer, and she was missing him.

Jed missed his home too. He cleared his desk and decided on an early night with his wife and kids. He was sure there weren't going to be any new developments in the Caldfell case anytime soon. If ever.

CHAPTER FIFTEEN

For behold, from henceforth, all generations shall call me blessed. Luke 1:48

The train from Norbridge to London Euston was delayed, overcrowded, sometimes hot, sometimes freezing. Ayesha Tomkins spent the first half of the journey in the corridor, hunkered down on the floor outside the toilet. Then she got a seat and huddled in a corner, her face plastered to the window and her back to the crowd. When she arrived in London she took a taxi straight to the flat in Islington that her mother shared with her sister and brother. Her sister opened the door. The familiar smell of beans and rice made her want to cry. The flat was warm, cluttered, full of family knick-knacks. It looked like heaven to Ayesha.

'What the feck are you wearin'?' her sister said.

'I paid the cleaner in my hotel fifty pounds for this parka. And gave her my Burberry Leather. I didn't want to be recognized.'

'No problem there,' said her sister. 'You might have been taken for a bag lady though.'

'Yeah, well I ditched the Louis Vuitton bag for a couple of Sainsbury's I found in a bin. Can I come in?'

'OK. But that coat's a bit whiffy. Seriously, we've all been worried sick about you.'

'Not least your man,' her mother said drily. Mrs Tomkins was in her eighties, heavy, arthritic. But she had heaved herself up from her chair and staggered into the little lobby to meet her daughter and hold her close.

'Mummy!' Ayesha was choked. 'What do you mean, not least my man?'

'Marcus is here,' her mother said. 'He's been waitin' for you for hours. We knew you would come here. Once the trains were running.'

'I can't face him, Mummy. I really can't.'

'You have no choice. He won't go away till you speak to him and you have nowhere from here to go to. And anyway, Ayesha, it doesn't matter anymore. I've told Marcus everything.'

'Mummy . . .'

'He needed to know, Ayshe. You try too hard to be perfect, girl. It's not possible. You're a poor sinner like all of us.'

'But it's worse than you think, Mummy.'

'And that's bad enough.'

Marcus came through from the tiny living room. 'Just tell me everything from your own lips, Ayesha. Did you kill Parry Palmer? Or were you involved with someone who killed him? Tell me.'

She looked back at him defiantly. But before she said anything else, he added, 'Even if you did kill him, Ayesha, I will still love you. Always. You're more important than my career and more important than anything. You're the love of my life.'

He walked towards her and Ayesha stumbled into his arms.

But it was Monday before she finally cracked and told him the whole unpalatable truth.

* * *

That Monday, Callum Oldcastle had left London and driven straight up to Norbridge in his car club Mini. He didn't want to hang round waiting for the trains. They had been all over the place with the weather.

His father had called him as soon as the police had established Freddie Lamplugh's guilt and allowed them all to go home from Caldfell Hall. That same evening, Callum and Dave were sitting in the Crown and Thistle in Norbridge. Dave was secretly chuffed that Callum had stayed in Cumbria and dossed down at his father's flat. And it was nice to go out together. There was something matey about a father–son chinwag in a pub. They had never done anything like it before. But Callum still looked awful — white, drawn and edgy.

Obviously he was distressed about Freddie's death but Dave was still uneasily aware of that undercurrent of anger in his son. The slammed doors, the furious bike riding . . . There was a lot of rage in Callum. Even the impatient way he snapped at the barman, tapping his bank card on the bar while he waited for his beer, and the angry glances he threw at a group of girls with high-pitched voices . . . Callum had always been a bit of a loose cannon.

'I shouldn't really be here. I should be working on my MA project,' said Callum bitterly. 'But I'm going to have to get an extension on the deadline. Extenuating circumstances. They can't get more extenuating than your co-worker freezing to death. Poor old Freddie, he really was a lovely bloke. But he took things to heart.'

'Obviously,' said Dave a little tersely.

'You don't get it, Dad. Freddie was impulsive, mercurial. He took action. But he didn't brood. I don't think he killed himself.'

'Suicide isn't an issue of personality type, Callum. Anyone can be driven to it. If Freddie killed Palmer then regretted it, don't you think he would have been suicidal?'

'No, I don't. That's what I wanted to talk to you about. I want to tell you what happened. You see, I knew Freddie really well.'

'So you were both . . . ?' Dave left the question hanging. He didn't know what he wanted the answer to be.

'Oh, for God's sake, Dad. Did you think I was gay?' Callum laughed, but it was an aggressive sort of braying. His nostrils flared. 'Just because I don't like football, and I like classical music? Bach sired twenty children. And there's always *Carmina Burana*.'

'OK, OK. So do you have a . . . a girlfriend?' Dave asked tentatively.

'Not at the moment. But I have had. And I'm not a virgin. Everything works in that department.'

Involuntarily, Dave put up his hand to stave off any more intimate revelations.

Callum suddenly seemed to calm down. 'Oh, Dad, that's you all over,' he said ruefully. 'You never wanted to really know what was going on in my head, did you? Remember when I threw your clothes out, and messed up your shed? You never pried, but perhaps you should have. You were always frightened of hearing the worse. Your imagination ran away with you like it's doing now. I'm not gay, Dad. And I'm not violent. I was an awful, withdrawn teenager, full of angst and misery. My parents were splitting up, for God's sake! I hated it when you and Mum divorced. I went down south with her when she moved, because she was my mum and she wanted me, but I always knew that you and I had more in common.'

Callum sipped his pint. Dave thought, *You have no idea how significant that throwaway remark is to me.* But he was too wise to say so. He felt a weight lift from him.

'I'm sorry about the past, Callum.'

They sat in silence. Just two blokes in the pub not given to talking about feelings. Except that Callum clearly had more to say about Freddie.

Dave said quietly, 'So you were going to tell me about Freddie when we got sidelined. He was just a mate? A colleague?'

'Absolutely. A close colleague and a good mate. Straight guys and gay guys can be friends. Freddie had a sort of crazed plot to find Parry Palmer and force him to come clean about pinching our work. Freddie had some great evidence — an essay of his that Palmer had marked — with musical examples

133

which reappeared in Palmer's book. We submitted it as part of our complaint to the Academy, but nothing happened.'

'So where were you when Palmer was killed? I know you weren't at college, Callum. I rang your professor.'

'You shouldn't have done that, Dad. It was none of your business.' Callum's voice rose, the old short fuse smouldering as he twisted in his seat.

'But I needed to know . . .'

'Don't push me. I know you mean well. But can't you just trust me? I didn't have anything to do with Parry Palmer's death and I'm sure Freddie didn't either. But I can't give you proof.'

Dave thought for a while. Callum could have been more implicated in Palmer's murder than he was admitting. But he was Dave's son, and Dave was going to believe what he said. This was a make-or-break moment for their relationship.

Then Dave thought of something Suzy Spencer had said to him just before they all left Caldfell Hall: 'It's a bit too neat this, isn't it, Dave? And your son must be feeling terrible. Maybe they'll find that it wasn't his friend who murdered Parry Palmer after all. There are things which don't add up.'

Dave said, 'Callum, I believe you. I think there's someone we should contact. She's been involved with a few murders in Cumbria and she's helped the police solve them. You'd like her. Stay up here with me for a while. You can still work on your project for the Academy. And we'll try and get to see Suzy Spencer.'

* * *

On Monday evening Ayesha Tomkins sat in the modern, super-comfortable apartment she shared with Marcus. They had spent Sunday pottering round, going for a walk and having lunch at a pub in Wapping with plenty of dark private corners. In the evening Marcus looked at a draft of the new music Edwin Armstrong was writing. It was good. The bass role was now expanded to cover Elizabeth's husband

Zachariah, as well as Simeon. There would be plenty for Marcus to do.

Ayesha sat on the chesterfield, looking out of the window down to the Thames. She liked the flat. Her mother had visited and been horrified at the space — so much to heat. But Marcus was well off, and Ayesha was savvy with money. They had nothing to worry about. Marcus had even suggested getting married, but she'd laughed it off. She knew she hadn't been honest with him about her past. Thinking about that was painful, so she rarely did it. And when she succumbed to remembering, she left out chunks of the grim bits.

But that afternoon she went over it all. Ayesha had gone into teaching after coming home from university, and eventually she'd also started singing again, beginning with an evening class at the Academy of Voice. Her little brother was a good singer too and she'd taken him along to the kids' choir, organized by Parry Palmer. Parry had made a big fuss of the pair of them. They'd upped the diversity quotient in his classes by about twenty per cent just by enrolling, but Ayesha didn't see Parry as cynical. She thought he was great. Anyway, it was the one thing her brother enjoyed. He had no interest in schooling.

Boys like him were easily exploited. It was the start of the 'county lines' scheme where drug gangs expanded into the countryside. They recruited schoolkids to deliver the goods, and her brother had fallen for it. At the same time, Ayesha had fallen for Parry Palmer. As class tutor, he had charisma. And power. She started to see him after the sessions. And on other evenings.

Then she'd been asked to look after her little brother in the evenings. Her mother was working nights at the hospital.

She hardly noticed when Parry Palmer started to rack up his demands, wanting to see her at inconvenient times when she ought to be babysitting. He had a beautiful flat in a Georgian street just on the other side of the tracks from where they were both brought up. Like her, Parry was clever and, unlike her, he'd moved on.

She was completely infatuated. But looking back, she could see he'd been messing with her, putting pressure on, having fun playing her and pulling her away from her family — forcing her to make choices. And she had chosen Parry.

One night when she should have been with her brother, she came home to find the police at the door. A stolen car had hit an elderly woman. Car crashes were more common in North London than stabbings and took more young lives. Her brother had been a passenger, and he'd lived, but he was seriously injured. The woman was killed.

Ayesha was distraught. She still thought of Parry Palmer as her dearest friend. Her brother was lucky to escape a sentence, and when he came home from hospital he was depressed and started self-harming. Music was his one great love and a way to rebuild a life despite his disability. But Parry had dropped them both like a stone.

He said to Ayesha: 'Look, it's a competitive world out there. I like you, Ayshe, and the kid is smart. But there's no way I can promote him now. He can stay in my class, we've got a ramp and disabled loos. But no one in the business wants to cope with a wheelchair. So I can't do more for him. Get it? No can do.'

'But you just live round the corner. Couldn't you even come and see him? Give him some advice?'

'No way, Ayshe. Your life might be screwed because of your brother but that's not my problem. Anyway, you screwed up at Cambridge first. Maybe you're all just losers in your family.'

Ayesha had been cut to the quick. After that she had occasionally seen Parry around in the neighbourhood, but eventually she had to work with him in the Academy's outreach programme. She just blanked him when she could. She had started to build a reputation, and to command a decent salary. She did everything she could for her brother. Things were looking better, and then one day Parry Palmer caught her in the corridor.

'So you're making a little niche for yourself,' Parry had said. 'But be careful. Community work can be difficult. You have to say all the right wokey things to the plebs. If you don't, it can be reported back to Irene. So watch out.'

It was a threat to keep off his turf.

Ayesha continued to ignore or avoid Parry Palmer and eventually built a reputation for herself. When Marcus Sotheby's project to bring music to schoolkids looked as if it would hit the buffers, she'd been drafted in. When she met Marcus, she knew he admired her sexual restraint and her dedication to her work. She never told him about the affair at Cambridge, or the baby. She never told him about her brother and the drugs either. Or that it had been her fault he went out that night in the stolen car. She'd bitterly regretted confiding all that to Parry Palmer.

When Marcus had said he was going to Caldfell Hall to work with Palmer, she'd cracked. She knew Palmer would love making mischief. He was bound to tell Marcus about her past and she had to stop him. So she'd gone to try and reason with him.

Thinking of all this, Ayesha began to sob. Marcus moved over to the sofa and put his arm around her. Softly, stumbling at times, she told Marcus the whole story.

'So you slept with a real shit, Ayesha. You're not the only one. Don't cry,' he said. 'Palmer was a first-class bastard.'

'I know, Marcus. And I thought I could persuade him not to talk to you about me. But he just laughed. And he stood outside that pub in Norbridge, with the snow falling, and suggested I sleep with him that afternoon. To make beautiful babies, he said. He said you would never know it wasn't yours. And it would have more brains than the rest of my family. That was what I couldn't take. So I hit him in the face and scratched him and ran. I went to the station but the snow meant there were no trains to London. So I went back to the hotel. It was there I saw on the TV news that Parry was dead. I thought the police might come after me because of the scratches on his face. I could have been seen attacking Parry. That's why I left Norbridge dressed like a bag lady.'

'The police think Palmer was killed by a student called Freddie Lamplugh who accused him of plagiarism.'

'Freddie Lamplugh? From the Academy? But that's crazy. Freddie wouldn't kill anyone. He was student ambassador on a few of my courses. He was lovely.'

'Freddie killed himself, Ayesha.'

'Oh no! That's terrible.'

'It could be proof he murdered Parry Palmer.'

'I don't believe it. Palmer was knifed, wasn't he? Freddie couldn't have done that. Have you ever heard the story of the composer who stabbed himself in the foot with his baton? And died? Jean-Baptiste Lully. Some of the teenagers on one of our courses were laughing about it and I thought Freddie was going to faint. He hated knives. He'd never stab anyone.'

'But that's just your feeling,' Marcus said gently. 'Not proof of anything.'

'But Marcus, we've got some time, haven't we, now the gig is postponed? Let's go back to Norbridge. I want this sorted. I'll tell the police about the scratches.'

Marcus thought for a moment. 'Maybe you shouldn't do that, Ayesha. Not the police. But Irene says there are other people who think Freddie was innocent. There's a journalist who's unhappy about it all. Maybe we should see her first. Her name's Suzy Spencer.'

CHAPTER SIXTEEN

And I heard a voice from heaven, as the voice of many waters. Revelation 14:2

Suzy and Robert walked home from the pub in what would have been a companionable silence, except that Suzy was furious.

Just as they had finished supper, she had suggested that they should invite Alex and Edwin to join them at the Plough on Thursday.

'Why Thursday and not the weekend?' Robert had said.

'Because Jake and Mae are coming at the weekend.'

'Are they? That's a shame. I'm away next weekend.'

'You're what?'

'I'm away next weekend. On the parish weekend trip. The vicar arranged it months ago. I told you.'

'No, you didn't.'

'Oh, Suzy, I'm sorry. Maybe I forgot. They're relying on me.'

'But I told you before I went to Caldfell Hall that Jake wanted to come over from Durham to see us. And you said OK, that will be nice.'

She could remember the scene clearly. Jake had WhatsApped her to say he and Mae would like to have supper with Robert and Suzy on the Saturday. She remembered the whole scene. She'd just put some washing in and had noticed her phone was in the washing basket by accident, so she'd taken it out and looked at messages. Her heart had leaped a little at the message from Jake. Since he'd met his girlfriend, Suzy felt he was a little more distant. It was inevitable, of course. What was the old saying? *Your son is your son till he gets him a wife but your daughter's your daughter the whole of her life*. She'd told Robert.

Robert had had the vacant look she dreaded these days; then he seemed to snap out of it and said, 'Righto. That'll be nice.' No mention of his parish weekend away.

She ordered a malt whisky with her coffee at the Plough — and was so upset she downed it in two gulps.

'How could you have forgotten Jake coming to see us, Rob? I must admit I haven't thought about it much with all that business at Caldfell, but now I'm home I'm really looking forward to us all being together at the weekend. And now you blithely tell me that you'll be away. And Jake said he wanted to talk to us. Perhaps they're getting married. Oh, Robert, how could you be away for that? You'll have to cancel the parish weekend.'

'I'm sorry, Suzy, I can't.' Robert looked decisive. 'I do vaguely remember you saying something about Jake coming but I never thought any more about it. I can't possibly cancel.'

'But don't you want to see Jake?'

'Of course I do. But he can come another time. This church meeting is important.'

Suzy had a sudden sick feeling. Would Robert forget about Jake's visit if Jake were his own child? The wobble she had felt at Caldfell came back. She had expected Robert to be a father to her children, but it could never be the same. And she had never even considered giving him a child of his own.

As they undressed later, Robert broke the silence. 'Suzy, we can go over to Durham to see Jake and Mae whenever you like.'

But how could she explain to him that visiting Jake wouldn't be the same as Jake visiting them — of his own volition. It meant so much that Jake wanted to come. *I still need to know that my kids think I matter*, she thought.

And she had definitely told Robert about Jake's proposed visit. Robert hadn't mentioned the parish weekend. Another cold little worm insinuated itself into her mind. Had Robert forgotten something so important because he really was losing it? That vacant face . . .

The whisky was keeping her awake, and she tossed and turned. Annoyingly, Robert had flopped into bed and was fast asleep. He looked good. He didn't snore or dribble. He had nice features, and a cowlick of brown hair flecked with grey. He didn't look his age.

But he *was* his age; she mustn't forget that. And she was ten years younger. He couldn't have just forgotten about Jake's visit. There had to be more to it.

Suzy couldn't sleep. In the dead of the night, she wondered how all this was affecting Irene Przybylski. That was one thread she hadn't really followed up. She got up and went to her computer in the attic.

She googled her. Professor Irene Przybylski was a graduate of Oxford University and had gone on to study at the Royal Academy of Classical Music. She had impeccable credentials as a musician and performer, and academically she was first-rate.

There was nothing about her private life.

Suzy also googled the Academy of Voice. It had been a middle-of-the-road institution until the turn of the twenty-first century, when several donors had come forward. They were following the Scott-Broughtons, who had given a sizeable sum for a new studio.

So why had the Scott-Broughtons chosen to support the Academy of Voice? There could be all sorts of reasons. But Suzy knew that what most charitable donors wanted was to support people like themselves. So most donors would be alums.

As soon as it was a decent time to call in the morning, Suzy rang Rachel. 'Rache, can you do me another favour?'

'Why not? It isn't as if I haven't got a job to do. I'm marking two dozen dissertations, if you must know.'

'I'm sorry. Look, I don't know if it's possible, but does the uni have records for the students at the Academy of Voice?'

'Going back how long?'

Suzy took a guess. Gervase Scott-Broughton was in his sixties. 'Forty years, I suppose.'

'Well, we certainly have them in the journalism department. How else do you think we know who to milk for money?'

'Exactly!' Suzy said 'So can you get someone to check some names for me?'

'OK. But it will cost you. I'll think of something.'

'Anything.'

'Will you do some marking for me?'

'If you want them all to fail.'

'OK. Too dangerous. I'll think of something else to ask for. Leave it with me.' Rachel rang off.

Rachel was friendly with one of the administrators at the university. They liked her because she often volunteered to sit on disciplinary panels, a job most academics hated. She took a punt on calling him.

'As a matter of fact, we do have records of alumni from the Academy of Voice. But if I shared them with you, I'd have to kill you.'

'I'd die happy.'

'Before you do, you're in the department of journalism, aren't you? Do you happen to know anyone who might come and do a session for engineers about media interviews?'

'As a matter of fact, I do. When would you want her?'

'Oh, not till the summer term. We're just trying to put the programme together.'

'I know just the person. I can vouch for her. She's a close friend of mine. A TV producer.'

'Great. And what was it you wanted?'

'A list of alumni from the Academy of Voice, back in the 1980s.'

'Send me your friend's details, and the list will be with you in an hour.'

'Deal.'

Rachel smiled. So Suzy was following a hunch. Only a hunch. But her hunches often paid off. And a lecture to the Engineering Department was a small price to pay!

* * *

That same evening, Alex and Edwin Armstrong were enjoying dinner in the elegant dining room of the Norbridge Glen Hotel.

'It's a change from sandwiches in the room at Caldfell,' said Alex.

'At least you had that. And you got a drink. I was stuck in that awful sickbay having soup and toast.'

'But you had your head scanned and there were medical professionals on hand.'

'Yeah. But I didn't rate that doctor, he was absolutely terrified of the Scott-Broughtons.'

'Wasn't everyone? Except you, of course, Edwin.'

'Why are people scared of them? Just 'cos they're rich?'

'Oh, darling, sometimes you're so naive. You have total confidence in your own ability. For most of us it's not like that. People like the Scott-Broughtons have power over us because we're insecure. And anyway, it's a human trait to gravitate to power.'

'What about rebels?'

'Well, there are always exceptions. But even rebellious people get caught up in the magnetism of the mighty.'

'But the mighty don't last. Remember that verse in the *Magnificat*: *He hath put down the mighty from their seat and hath exalted the humble and meek.*'

'I think the truth is in the word "exalted". The Virgin Mary wasn't a doormat, you know. She was enjoying her new status.'

Edwin smiled. He always enjoyed Alex's take on things.

Alex went on, 'You know, it's a funny thing about the *Magnificat*. Well, not the canticle itself, but me hearing it and thinking about it. I was walking around the Hall after the first big snowfall. The day I found Parry Palmer's body. Before that I could hear Lily singing part of the Bach *Magnificat*. The same few phrases over and over. It was enchantingly beautiful. But then her singing teacher told me there had been no lesson that afternoon. Lily had a headache and had gone back to her room. It's been puzzling me.'

'That sounds like a dodge a lot of students pull.'

'What dodge?'

'You record something on your phone during a normal lesson, and then you book a rehearsal cubicle. Then you leave your phone playing on a loop while you go to the bar or meet a mate or something.'

'So where do you think Lily was, Edwin?'

'Not hanging round me, before you ask. Who knows? Maybe she wanted some time to herself.'

'Or maybe she was at the folly. Oh, Edwin, maybe Lily killed Parry Palmer!'

'But the killer was that poor student from the Academy, Freddie Lamplugh.'

'I've never been happy about that.'

'No.' Edwin was thoughtful. 'You're right, as usual. There are still a lot of questions no one else has answered. Like, how did Palmer's blood get on the front of my jacket? I was hit from behind, by Carly Martin.'

Alex thought hard. 'You're right. No one's come up with any realistic explanation for that blood. It's another thing we should be looking at.'

'I know what you're going to say, Alex. We need to talk to Suzy.'

* * *

On Tuesday morning, Robert lay in bed listening to Suzy downstairs. The Briars had thick walls, but years of experience had taught him the sounds of Suzy getting up and making tea in the kitchen. He closed his eyes. Being a senior lecturer was not the sinecure so many people thought, but the hours weren't regular, and Suzy often went out before him. And now that he was retired, he always stayed a little longer in bed.

He liked to listen to her clattering about and getting ready while he lay there thinking. Robert needed to sort everything in his mind before facing the day ahead, whereas Suzy was up and doing as soon as she was awake. He mused about their conversation the evening before. Their dispute about Jake's visit had not been resolved. He'd been tired and had crashed before she was undressed and in bed.

He racked his brains. He understood how important these visits were to her. He was always pleased to see his stepson. But he found Jake's girlfriend, Mae, a little more difficult. Her accent was hard to follow, which surprised him because he had always been good at languages, particularly French. But Mae was from Strasbourg. Perhaps the inflections were different.

Anyway, he needed to think about getting up. He was due at the Advice Centre at ten o'clock as usual. He let his mind wander over what Suzy had told him about the murder at Caldfell Hall. He wished she wasn't part of it. He recognized that she was brilliant at pulling threads together, and that she had an ability to engage very different people and get them to talk.

But she put herself, and others, in danger sometimes. He didn't like the sound of the killer by candlelight at Caldfell. Nor did he like the idea of Suzy messing around with billionaires. Robert had run a very successful postgraduate course at the University of Mid-Cumbria, attracting a wealthy international cohort. But he had never come across people as rich as the Scott-Broughtons. Their purchasing power worried him. They could buy people as well as things. He shuddered and decided to get up.

By the time he was downstairs, Suzy had gone out and left him a note. 'Gone to Workhaven for coffee with Ro

Watson. Need to know the latest on the candlelight killer case. Back for lunch. Suzy.'

No, Suzy, he thought, *you don't need to know the latest. The police have identified a murderer. Let it alone.*

CHAPTER SEVENTEEN

A talebearer revealeth secrets: but he that is of a faithful spirit concealeth the matter. Proverbs 11:13

Robert drove into Norbridge along the newly gritted road. The snow was over. Now it would just be a long grey wait for spring.

At about eleven, he finished advising a student about a landlord problem and looked up to see Christopher greeting a tall, fair-haired man. When he turned, Robert realized it was Edwin Armstrong.

'Robert! Good to see you after all this time!'

'And it's great to see you again, Edwin. We've followed your illustrious career.'

'Well, nowadays my fame seems limited to the Caldfell Chorus murder by candlelight. Although the police seem to think that's tied up.'

'So what can we do for you?'

'I'm looking for a practice room here in Norbridge. I need a piano. And a room with a door that can be left open, with people around. I'm going to be working with a young person, so I want to be visible from the corridor. I heard that you have rooms to let, and a piano?'

'It's only an upright,' Christopher said. 'But it's been tuned recently and it's in good nick.' He looked at Edwin curiously. 'Will you be working here with Lily Martin?'

'Yes. The prodigy. But that makes her sound freaky, and she's a very normal young woman. Intelligent. But not peculiar. And she has a sublime voice. Do you know her?'

'We know her mother.'

'Ah, yes. Her mother is problematic, I think.' Edwin rubbed the back of his neck.

Robert felt uncomfortable. 'I think we all know what we're talking about here. Forgive me for being blunt, but Carly Martin attacked you, Edwin. Do you really want her to be hanging around?'

Edwin smiled. 'We're in Norbridge now, not out on the lonely hillside. Anyway, from all accounts, Carly Martin seems to be away with the fairies most of the time, and she certainly didn't attack me because she knew who I was. On the contrary, I understand from Alex that she thought I was someone else.'

Quickly, Robert said, 'I think it's a good idea for you to practise here, Edwin. Alex is very welcome too. Carly will probably be around, but we're used to that. I don't think she knows or cares who she hit, but the police believe it was Freddie Lamplugh who did the hitting. We've made a decision not to shop Carly.'

'And I don't want to do anything which would destabilize Lily,' said Edwin. 'I got a nasty bang on the head, but the Scott-Broughtons have superb medical facilities, and it didn't take me long to recover.'

'As long as practising here would work well for Lily,' said Christopher. 'Of course, it's a familiar space for her and not intimidating.'

'Exactly!' said Edwin. 'It will be nice to work here. I don't want to commute to Caldfell every day and it will be good to be away from the place, to be honest.'

Edwin went with Christopher to look at the practice room and Robert checked his phone. He couldn't believe it. There was a message from the vicar at his parish church.

She had Covid. The away weekend was postponed. Robert breathed a sigh of relief. Now he would be at The Briars for Jake's visit. But he still had no memory at all of Suzy telling him about the arrangement. He felt a shiver of concern.

He shook his head and concentrated on texting Suzy to say everything was all right after all. He would be home that weekend.

* * *

Suzy met Ro at the coffee house in Workhaven's shopping centre. It was a typical 1960s concrete structure with empty retail units. Workhaven had at least one attractive eighteenth-century square, harking back to its buccaneering days, but the heavy industry of the nineteenth century and its decline in the twentieth gave much of the town a depressing air.

'So what's latest on Caldfell?' Suzy asked Ro.

'We're finishing the paperwork on the case today if we can. The Scott-Broughtons want closure. They've gone back to New York. Mrs Scott-Broughton has some mystery illness. Could be cancer, I suppose. She's seeing consultants there, and then they're going to their estate in Florida, before coming back in May. We have full contact details for them.'

'And what about the blood on Edwin's jacket?'

'I've told you, it was Parry Palmer's. It adds to the evidence that Freddie Lamplugh hit Edwin.'

Ro added in a more conciliatory voice, 'Look, they found a signed, handwritten note in Freddie Lamplugh's pocket outlining his grudge against Palmer, with his doodling all over it, and a clear intent to kill him. That and the blood makes it an open-and-shut case. Jed and the DS are adamant.'

Suzy sighed. 'Yes, I can see that.'

'So what's making you query it, Suzy?'

'I suppose because I think that if Freddie Lamplugh had killed Parry Palmer, he must have had some help from the inside. You were there, Ro. You know how tight the security was and how bad the snowdrifts were.'

'Freddie's grandfather owns the village farm; he was staying there. He didn't have far to walk to the folly, even in the snow. He didn't need inside help.'

Suzy sighed. Ro knew how the weather had been. Freddie would have had to walk over and take his chances that Parry was going down to the folly — unless he had inside help, either to set Parry up to go there or to tip Freddie off that he was there already. And what about the fact that Freddie or someone like him had been seen wandering through the grounds of the Hall at three o'clock in the morning after the murder? Why wasn't he back at his cosy quarters if that was where he was holed up?

'Look, Suzy' — Ro leaned forward — 'only yesterday I was telling Jed I thought we needed to look deeper into this. I don't like the way it's worked out so neatly for the Scott-Broughtons either. I can see why you think it's all too convenient. But I honestly cannot fault the conclusion that Freddie Lamplugh killed Parry Palmer. If not him, who?'

Suzy had to admit she didn't have any idea who the murderer might have been if it wasn't Freddie.

Ro went on, 'I was happy to talk to you this morning because I respect your judgement and your ability to see the bigger picture. But on reflection, in this case I think you're wrong.'

'OK.' Suzy sat back in her chair. 'I respect your judgement too. Anyway, there isn't much I can do about it. The other murders I've been involved in were Norbridge-centred, maybe with a London connection, like a lot of things. But this time I take your point. When I was snowbound at Caldfell it all seemed very localized. But when I got home and talked to Robert, I realized that there were too many threads all over the place. Caldfell, Norbridge, London, New York, and before long, the Scott-Broughtons in Florida . . . The circle gets wider and wider and there's no way I could ever bring it all together.'

'So go home to Robert, Suzy. Chasing crime is a dangerous business and you've been lucky so far. Leave this one alone.'

Suzy smiled and paid for the coffee.

Outside, Ro strode away towards the police station. She was a good friend even though she could be brusque. Suzy wondered whether her own doubts about this case were only because she wanted something to work on to bring her and Robert closer together. But this case was just too big, and too vague, and anyway she had other things on her plate. There was Jake's visit. And Robert's strange behaviour. A murder involving national singing stars and billionaires wasn't her bag. She didn't have the time or resources to deal with it, and no way could she get all the relevant people together.

Looking at her phone, she saw a WhatsApp from Jake: *Mum, I'm sorry. Mae isn't very well. Nothing serious, but she's really knocked out. We've cancelled the Cumbria trip.*

There was a WhatsApp from Robert too: *Suzy, just to say, the PCC away weekend is postponed. The vicar has Covid. So it will be great to see Jake.*

Then there were three text messages. Rachel wrote: *Suzy, I've been working on some interesting information. Call me. I think you need to talk to all your other informants and cross-reference.*

Astonishingly, another said: *Hello, you don't know me but my name's Marcus Sotheby. My partner and I are on the way to Cumbria. Can we talk?*

And there was one from Dave Oldcastle asking if she could meet him and his son Callum, who was visiting from London.

All of sudden, she had time for this after all. She had been momentarily defeated by Ro's lack of support. And it was true that she had no idea who the murderer could have been. But that was no reason for taking the soft option. She took a deep breath and put her shoulders back. She wasn't going to be put off.

The weekend was now free. She texted Robert: *Jake has cancelled. So Saturday is free. Why don't we do what we used to do, and get as many people as we can round our kitchen table to try to thrash out what really happened at Caldfell Hall?*

At the Advice Centre, Robert read her message. He looked at it and re-read it. Suddenly, to his own surprise, he felt happy. This was Suzy doing what she liked to do. He had been wrong to try and stop her. OK, there were dangers. But Suzy needed to do this. And if she wanted him to be part of it, he couldn't be so old, doddery and confused after all.

He texted back: *Excellent idea. Let's invite the lot of them and see what happens.*

* * *

Alex looked at her watch, a present from Edwin on their tenth anniversary. She never imagined she could be so happy. They had taken a huge risk when they were first together. After a successful concert at Norbridge Abbey, Edwin had applied for a job at a City church in London. He'd been successful but it was hardly well paid. Alex had been his adviser, confidante and business partner. They also depended on her capital from selling her mother's bungalow, plus the dwindling royalties from her children's books.

Then she perfected and marketed their sight-reading app and it went well. They were happy and mutually dependent.

But now Edwin was most certainly the breadwinner, and it was bread with butter on. Alex enjoyed the vicarious fame and attention that came with his success. It would have been the perfect time to have a baby, but that wasn't to be. But she was coming to terms with it and Lily Martin was helping her do it. Lily was taking up a lot of her time.

It was eleven o'clock on Wednesday morning in the week after they had left Caldfell Hall. Alex had two major jobs for the day. First, she had to pick up Lily in Pelliter. Then, after Lily's lesson with Edwin, she planned to take the girl to lunch in Norbridge. Lily had assured Alex that she didn't need to go to sixth-form college on a Wednesday. Lily could help her, looking in estate agents' windows for a house to rent till they returned to Germany. It would be fun and a complete change for them both.

Alex was finding Lily easier to deal with now she understood the girl's relationship with her mother. Lily was complex but she was also caring. Her mam was her priority. A recent incident had revealed this to Alex. Coming home from Caldfell, they'd had a long wait outside the Martins' flat because Lily had forgotten her key and Carly wasn't in. Carly had obviously been mixed up about when her daughter was coming back and had gone off somewhere. Lily wasn't fazed. She just sat on the doorstep and waited. She'd spent a lot of her young life waiting on the doorstep.

But Alex was appalled. She was determined to be reliable for Lily. So this Wednesday morning, Alex had a cab waiting outside Lily's home to pick her up for her singing session with Edwin. Their flat occupied the ground floor of a grimy building. The door opened and Alex peeped inside. There were bags piled under the stairs, and the tiny living room straight ahead was dark, filled with stuff blocking the windows. A cheap scented candle was flickering in a lurid pink glass holder and there was a sickly smell. The general impression was foetid, and Alex marvelled at how Lily always managed to be so clean and neat. Carly was chaotic, that much was obvious.

Lily came running out. 'Hi, Alex! Thanks for this. Wow, a taxi. I hope the neighbours can't see. They'll think we're really up ourselves.'

'You'd better blow that candle out.'

'Oh, it'll just burn down. We have them all over the place. Mam likes scented candles. She thinks they cover up the damp smell.' Lily smiled, indulgent and apologetic, as if she were the mother and Carly a wayward teenager.

'OK. Get in the cab, Lily.'

'Oh, thank you so much Alex. This is amazing!'

After that warm welcome, Alex decided she would pick up Lily every day for her lesson with Edwin. She believed the girl would blossom under the right sort of attention. But Alex never criticized Carly and kept quiet when Lily said things like 'Mam's good today' or 'Mam's not so well today.' Or 'Mam's upset — one of her mates has done a bunk.' It was the casualness of the throwaway remarks which made Alex understand how manic life was with Carly Martin.

Occasionally she still wondered what Lily had been doing when she left that recording on a loop in the practice room at Caldfell Hall. But it was amazing to hear her voice soar under Edwin's direction and Alex soon dismissed her suspicions about the day of Parry Palmer's murder. It was incredible that such an awful home life had produced such a lovely creature. Caring for Lily was making Alex feel almost fulfilled. Maybe coming to Caldfell had not been such a bad idea after all.

CHAPTER EIGHTEEN

Behold, I have prepared my dinner: my oxen and my fatlings are killed, and all things are ready. Matthew 22:4

Robert and Suzy had decided to host Saturday night's supper at The Briars for anyone who had doubts about Freddie's guilt. It promised to be a bit disorderly and they were taking a risk. Two risks. People might disagree and conflict. Or they might have nothing useful to say.

Suzy called Alex to tell her about the plan for the Saturday night meal. It all depended on Alex's buy-in. Suzy was sure her friend would approve, but she needed to hear her say so.

'That's an amazing idea,' Alex said. 'I love it. You can count on us being there, Suzy. It'll be great to see The Briars again. And you're great at creating an atmosphere where people open up. We both know there's more to all this, don't we? That blood on Edwin's anorak . . .'

On Thursday Suzy heard from Alex that Marcus Sotheby and Ayesha Tomkins had arrived at the Norbridge Glen Hotel and would be delighted to come to supper. Suzy's cuisine couldn't compare with the Michelin-starred chef at the Glen, but her guests weren't coming to The Briars for the food. Suzy had emailed Marcus telling him there would be a group of people present. Alex and Edwin would be there, of course, plus Dave Oldcastle and his son Callum, who had asked to meet with her.

On Thursday evening Robert was at a meeting of the church council standing committee at the vicarage, so Suzy was alone at home preparing. She would need to do a big shop in Norbridge the next day.

On Friday she took the car into the town and managed to get a space in the car park just off the market square. She did the shopping in two loads and then decided she hadn't bought enough cream for the pollo pesto she had decided to make — with a veggie version as well if required. Catering for people she didn't know was a challenge. And she was unsure what she expected to get out of this big meeting. There would be nine of them round the table. It would be crowded, but they could pull out the leaf on the old kitchen table. Her head was full of logistics.

In the square it was market day, pleasantly buzzing with traders and shoppers, but it felt different. Then she realized that for once she couldn't hear Brigham Broughton's yowling delivery of Bob Dylan.

An elderly man came and stood next to her. 'You miss 'im when 'e's not 'ere, don't you?'

No, Suzy thought, but she didn't like to say so. She nodded.

'I hear 'e's still up at Caldfell Hall. Minding the place while 'is rich relatives go sunning themselves in Florida.' The man spoke as if Florida were one of the circles of hell. 'Allus too big for their boots, them Scotts. Anyway, Brig's fallen on his feet now. Not that 'e did too bad for a busker afore. 'E's got one o' them studio flats in the Ginnels.'

'Has he?' That was a surprise to Suzy. The Ginnels development wasn't cheap.

'Aye. 'E must 'ave come into money somehow. Not many people know that. I only know because I used to be a postie. I delivered to 'im. G. Broughton. You'd be surprised 'ow some people round 'ere live. You'd think they've got nowt and they're as rich as Croesus. Like old Fred Lamplugh up at Caldfell.'

'*Old* Fred Lamplugh?'

'Yeah, owns half of Caldfell, where the old stones are. Well, lass, I canna keep on wi' this crack when ah've got to gan yam for me bait.'

Suzy nodded as the man walked off jauntily for his lunch. She stood thinking, and then realized that if she didn't hurry, her parking would run out. But all the way home she was wondering about Brigham and his surprising affluence, and Freddie Lamplugh's grandfather owning the standing stones. And there had been something else in the man's gossip that had struck her, but she couldn't remember what it was. I'm getting like Robert, she thought, forgetting things. But Robert had seemed livelier since they decided to have their Saturday supper. He was out getting some wine that morning. He hadn't wanted another Suzy Spencer investigation, but now that it was happening, he was enlivened. Maybe it was just retirement that had slowed him down.

But then she remembered his vacant face when she'd reminded him about Jake's visit. That wasn't like Robert at all — but she didn't want to think about it. She made herself concentrate on Saturday night.

How well did she know these people? Not at all, in the case of Marcus Sotheby and Ayesha Tomkins. Having a national treasure at your kitchen table would be daunting. And Callum Oldcastle was a new face.

But whatever, it would be good to have The Briars full again. She'd never had so many people involved in chatting about a case. Though that might be a problem. With a smaller group you were sure that everyone round the table was in the clear. But with nine of them . . . could she be certain everyone was as innocent as she was?

There had to be an insider involved in the murder of Parry. And why was Marcus so keen to bring Ayesha to talk to her? Obviously they had heard about Suzy's interest in local murders from Irene Przybylski. But what was their connection to an ongoing case? Wouldn't it be in their interest to have it closed down? Could they have asked to meet up with Suzy in order to throw her off the scent in some way?

And then there was Callum Oldcastle. He was Freddie's mate — he might know more about what Freddie's plans had been, and about who was helping him from the inside. And where had Callum been when Freddie was at Caldfell, allegedly murdering Parry Palmer?

And what about Christopher Murray? Robert had insisted on inviting him too. Christopher was suspiciously supportive of Carly Martin. She must have had inside help to attack Edwin, even if she hit the wrong man. Could that help have come from Christopher? Christopher might well have wanted to get rid of Parry Palmer, if what he had told Robert about Lily's parentage was true.

Even Alex was behaving oddly. Suzy's friend was becoming a little bit besotted with Lily, a girl who had conned people that she was having a singing lesson when she wasn't. Could Lily have been at the folly with a penknife? Would Alex cover up for her? Was Alex becoming too protective of a surrogate daughter?

A group of nine was a lot for a confidential chat. Maybe it wasn't just Suzy who wanted to find out what was going on. If there was a killer on the loose, or a killer's accomplice, they would want to be at Suzy's Saturday meeting.

Perhaps she had bitten off more than she could chew this time. But it was too late to cancel now.

* * *

On Friday afternoon, Robert was at the Advice Centre as usual while Suzy did some work on her TV projects. She checked a few queries to do with Hiram King's hit show on Linkflex, and she pottered around the internet. She tried phoning Jake and got his voicemail. On Friday night, she and Robert went round to supper with their neighbours.

On Saturday she woke early and did basic things like sorting out the cutlery and crockery for nine people and doing some rudimentary cleaning of the kitchen. Robert went into Norbridge because he'd forgotten to get tonic water. It was late morning when the phone rang: it was Rachel.

'Hello, Maigret. Don't you go to the synagogue on Saturdays?'

'Not every Saturday. Actually, I'm trying to avoid someone who's got their sights on me. A widower who plays in a Klezmer band. I seem to have been propositioned a lot lately. First Irene and then this guy. It must be my late flowering. Anyway I've been busy on your latest project. The killer by candlelight. Why do you think the murder was done by candlelight? Presumably with all the tech stuff the Scott-Broughtons have at their disposal, there would have been electric light for the killer to work by?'

'I don't know, Rache. That's a good point. I suppose the candles made it more like a sort of ritual killing.'

'Yuk!' Rachel said. 'Anyway, I have some new info for you. The stuff you asked for. I got the lists of students for the Academy of Voice, between thirty-five and forty-five years ago.'

'It had better be good now you've set me up for that lecture to the engineers.'

'It is, actually. Back then the Academy only took twenty-five students a year. I thought maybe Gervase Scott-Broughton was an alum, but I couldn't find his name anywhere. I'll tell you what I did find, though. Two names which might interest you. One was Parry Palmer. Of course we all knew he was an Academy lifer who came as a student and never left. But there's another name you mentioned, in the same year.'

'What was that?'

'Broughton. Not a double-barrelled name, just Broughton. The first name was Gordon. Gordon Broughton. And because I'm very thorough I also looked up all the alums. Gordon Broughton didn't graduate.'

'You mean he dropped out?'

'Looks like it.'

'That's really weird, Rachel. Yesterday I met an old bloke in town who referred to a G. Broughton. I didn't really clock it at the time. But maybe Brigham Broughton's proper name is Gordon. And Rache, there's something else. The same old bloke was talking about Gervase, but he said that the Scotts were too big for their boots. Not the Scott-Broughtons. Just the Scotts. Could you have another look and see if there was anyone called Gervase Scott?'

'I checked all the first names. There was no Gervase, not in the whole ten years. Let's face it, Suzy, that's a name you'd remember.'

'But say he wasn't always Gervase? Say he was just called, I don't know, Ian or Neil, something ordinary, and came up with Gervase later when he became a fancy music producer.'

'OK, I'll look and see if there's any Scotts who might fit. But you owe me.'

'Anything you ask. Except another guest lecture to the engineers.'

'Well, If I have to escape from the widower, I might need a bolthole in Norbridge.'

'Anytime, sister. But don't turn your nose up at a widower. It worked for me.'

'Yes but . . .'

'But what?'

'You probably got the best of the bunch.'

Suzy was smiling when she put the phone down. Yes, she did get the best of the bunch. Even if his memory was failing, Robert was still a great bloke, and she shouldn't forget it. When he came back, she flung her arms round him and kissed him.

'It's only tonic water, Suzy.'

'But at least you remembered you'd forgotten it!'

* * *

They were all organized for their guests by six thirty. Alex and Edwin came first, as arranged.

'How are we going to play this?' asked Alex.

'By ear, largely,' Suzy said. 'But I think we need to ask everyone to come clean about their role in this scenario. We should have a rule that everyone at this supper party has to tell the truth, the whole truth and nothing but the truth. Of course they won't — but they may get nearer to it. And when one person confesses to something, others tend to pile in. It's a cathartic activity once someone opens the floodgates. Anyway, I'm more worried about the catering at this stage. I've got some nibbles, and some gin and wine. When we've broken the ice, I'm serving up supper. And then we'll get the conversation going while we eat and see what people have to say.'

Alex looked wary. 'Suzy, I've been thinking. What if . . . ?'

'I know what you're going to say. I've been thinking that too. What if the killer — or the killer's accomplice — is here tonight?'

'Exactly. It seemed a great idea to get everyone together for a brainstorm, like we did all those years ago. But then there were just four of us, and we knew we were all innocent.'

'Yes. This is different. But I've thought it over. Except for Ayesha Tomkins, no one except Dave Oldcastle and myself was anywhere near Caldfell, and Ayesha was apparently staying at a hotel in Norbridge. Without a car. And when it comes to the Oldcastles, I really don't think Dave is a likely killer. We need to know where Callum was, of course. And then when it comes to you and Edwin . . .'

Alex looked momentarily alarmed.

Suzy laughed. 'Only joking. I totally trust you and Edwin. Though perhaps . . .'

'Perhaps what?'

'You're very protective of Lily. But you told me she left a recording running and bunked off from her lesson.'

'I know.' Alex sighed. 'But I don't think she's strong enough to have murdered Parry Palmer. I'll find out what was going on with her. But not yet. I don't want to rock her boat.'

Suzy nodded. 'OK. That makes sense.'

'Anyway, Suzy, you've got skin in the game too. What about Robert's mate, Christopher Murray? Why have you invited him?'

'Because of Carly's blundering attempt to kill Palmer. She confessed to Christopher. And Robert trusts him.'

Alex nodded. 'OK, Robert's judgement is good enough for me. You've reassured me. Just as well, because now your doorbell's ringing. There's no going back, Suzy. The show's on the road.'

Suzy nodded, hurrying to answer the bell. But it wasn't the show she was expecting. On her doorstep was Eva Delmondo.

CHAPTER NINETEEN

Remember, I pray thee, who ever perished, being innocent?
Job 4:7

Eva had been stuck at Caldfell since the chorus all went home. Gervase had made it clear he expected her to stay on at his beck and call, regardless of any plans she had made.

Which was fitting because her plans had collapsed. She'd lost the launch of the new fragrance she was supposed to be promoting, thanks to all the work for the Scott-Broughtons. Gervase and Lauren had flown back to the States midweek with Pearl, leaving Eva behind. She was to field any press enquiries and kick out any journalists who dared to try and gain entry to the Hall.

She was also to ensure that every chorus member had signed a non-disclosure agreement drawn up by Trent. Only if they did so would they qualify for the enhanced pay and the contract for the new gig in May. The NDAs were vital to the Scott-Broughtons. They didn't want to see any lurid online details, crazy comments on social, or newspaper articles about 'My Time at the Music Murder'.

Eva had hoped to get away from Caldfell Hall asap. But Gervase had made it clear that if she left the Hall before everything was neatly tied up, she'd be heaving her own luggage onto trains rather than travelling in a limousine all the way to London and getting fast-tracked through Heathrow.

Trent was staying behind as well, to 'legal' everything.

'It's just you and me, Eva — and these four-poster beds!'

'That's inappropriate, Trent. I could report you to Mr S-B.'

'I mean that all that bedlinen must be laundered. That's not in my job description.'

'Mine neither.'

'Really? You report to me now, and you do everything I reasonably ask. That could include a little light cleaning of the johns if you don't watch out.' Trent had laughed. He sounded like a cross between a donkey and a robot. 'And you've got to look after Mr Brigham as well, Eva. He'll want you to serve his whisky on a silver tray, wearing a backless maid's outfit. You'd find it hard to say no, Eva. He's the new boss now.'

Trent's mechanical laughter had followed her down the corridor.

It was true that Brigham Broughton wanted to be waited on hand and foot. He had nothing to do but check up on her and Trent and watch from his armchair as the brigade of caterers and cleaners packed up the Hall. Brigham had his takeaway food delivered from Norbridge, and two local women to clean his suite — he had taken over Gervase's sumptuous bedroom — but he was still gross and unkempt. His long snakes of hair, in dreadlocks of gingery grey, looked greasier than ever, and he sat in the main hall each afternoon, drinking whisky, strumming his guitar and singing in a loud whiney voice.

On Saturday he'd ambushed Eva when she had no choice but to walk past him.

'Eva!' Brigham had called drunkenly. 'Join me for a drink.'

She'd had no option. In any case, she liked Jack Daniels. She got herself a tumbler, took the bottle from the bar and sat opposite him. He was drinking from his Super Blend bottle.

'You missin' Gervase?' she'd asked.

'Nah. He's OK, my cuz, but it's more relaxed without him and I kinda like being in the ancestral home, y'know.'

'So why is it Gervase's place and not yours?'

'Now, that's a story.' Brigham wriggled into his chair and took a slurp of his drink. 'My great-granda and his great-granda were bros. But Gervy's great-granda inherited the pile. Mine was a bad lad. So my grandaddy got nowt from the family and had to go to work in t'mill. But he never forgot he was a Scott. He only had daughters, and my nan married a Brigham from Cockermouth. Then my mam married a Broughton. That's how I got the name Brigham Broughton. I used to be . . . oh, never mind. I think Brigham Broughton sounds great.'

Eva had lost the thread by now. 'So how come you and Gervase are so close?'

'We kicked about together a bit as kids. And I met up with Gerry in London. When I was still into poncey music. But that went tits up and I came back home where I belong.' To prove it, he'd burst into a yowling rendition of 'Take Me Home, Country Roads'.

'Why do you drink that stuff, Brig?' Eva had indicated his half-empty bottle of cheap Super Blend. No one else had drunk Brigham's poison while there were malts on offer. Brigham had got through several bottles of Super Blend, labelled with his name, kept behind the bar.

'I like it. It suits my guts. I've got dodgy guts. That stuff wouldn't do me insides any good. Too rich. I'll be getting the runs. I'm pretty loose already . . .'

Yuk. To change the subject, Eva had asked, 'Hey, Brigham, do you know Tarnfield? Is that far from here?'

'Maybe forty minutes. It's a small place. Why?'

'It's where Suzy Spencer lives. I've got her address on her contract. She left without signing her NDA.'

Eva had a vague idea that she would like to see Suzy again. But Suzy had a husband and kids and a busy life. She wouldn't want to be reminded about Eva or Caldfell.

However, Eva had nearly finished her drink and it had been a big tumbler. She felt disinhibited, thinking: *Why don't I just go down to Tarndale or whatever it's called and see Suzy? If she's out, so be it. But if she's in, I can get her to sign the NDA. I like her. I'm bored here. There's no one to talk to except Brigham, or Trent, and they're equally awful in totally different ways.*

No time like the present. She'd left Brigham lurching into sleep, called a cab, and an hour later was on Suzy's doorstep.

When Suzy opened the door Eva saw her shocked face. But Eva also saw the Armstrongs behind her, in the hall. And another cab was offloading David Oldcastle and a rather nice-looking young man in the lane. Then she saw, walking towards the house, someone she thought was Marcus Sotheby. Jesus, it *was* Marcus Sotheby! With some sort of dusky supermodel.

'Eva!' Suzy Spencer looked stunned. 'You'd better come in.'

Oho. What's going on here? thought Eva. So, Ms Spencer was doing some private investigating. Eva guessed Suzy had never been happy with the Freddie Lamplugh solution. What had she said? 'It's too neat.' So now all the key players were here. It was like something out of those Hercule Poirot films on PBS.

Eva sashayed into The Briars. This was something she couldn't miss. It was so crazy British. Eva just had to stay and watch the fun.

* * *

Suzy stared at all the faces in her living room. Robert was serving drinks; most people were standing round, making conversation as if it were an ordinary party.

Marcus Sotheby and Dave Oldcastle had hit it off. Dave was a keen if discerning fan of Marcus's and was delighted to meet him. Dave had feared he would be overwhelmed by Marcus's celebrity but in the living room at The Briars it was easy to chat.

Callum Oldcastle had goggled at Ayesha Tomkins; then he remembered where he had seen her before. She did some outreach work with kids for the Academy of Voice. And she wasn't as aloof as she looked. They were soon gossiping, though neither mentioned Parry Palmer. Or Freddie Lamplugh.

Christopher Murray had immediately become a metropolitan charmer, talking animatedly to Eva Delmondo about New York versus London.

Alex was helping Suzy dish nibbles, and Robert was talking to Edwin. It was almost cosy. *This is ludicrous*, thought Suzy. *In a moment I'm going to ask them all to come and sit down in my kitchen and talk about murder over a chicken pasta bake. What have I been thinking?* Yet they were all here. Beneath the burble of civilized chat, they all had their reasons.

Eventually she shepherded people in. When everyone had sat down and been served, she said, 'Thanks for coming, everyone. We all know why we're here. We want to talk about Parry Palmer's murder. Was it Freddie Lamplugh who killed him? It seems so plausible. But I've always had my doubts, and I guess you've all got in touch with me because you have doubts too. I think I'm right in assuming we all feel that blaming Freddie is an injustice?'

'Absolutely!' said Callum Oldcastle.

'But feeling isn't proving, OK?' said Suzy. 'You kick off, Alex. You found Palmer dead.'

Alex described leaving the Hall through the cloakroom, where several similar men's jackets were hanging. She remembered feeling irritated because Edwin had brought his old shabby anorak with him, like a lot of the men on the course. She had been nagging him to get a better brand. Everyone laughed. Then she described walking to the folly and finding Parry dead. A knife had been sticking out of Parry's neck. There were lurid scratches on his face. And a lot of blood.

People stopped laughing.

Edwin went next, describing how he had gone out to find Alex, and had been attacked by someone who had knocked him out. His anorak had been covered in Parry's blood. He knew his assailant, as it turned out. That person could not have killed Parry. So where had the blood come from?

Edwin added, 'I've been racking my brains, and I think I did see a figure down near the folly. A small person, in a dark anorak. Could that have been Freddie?'

Or Lily, Suzy thought. She caught Alex's eye. Alex looked away.

There was a lull in the conversation. It was a timely reminder of Freddie's tragic death. Ayesha Tomkins looked at Marcus and took a deep breath.

'You must be wondering why I'm here. It's because I've known Parry Palmer longer than anyone here. We were very briefly lovers.' There was a slight gasp. She looked evenly at everyone around the table. Then there was silence.

'I'm a teacher in London. But I've been to classes at the Academy of Voice on and off all my life. And lately I've been working on the Academy's outreach programme for schoolkids, with Professor Przybylski. That's how I met Marcus. But I have a brother who's in a wheelchair. He got involved in drugs and was in a bad car crash. He's very musical and I had hoped Parry Palmer would help him. I told Parry private stuff . . . when I was desperate. So Parry knew things about me' — she stumbled slightly — 'including how I'd let my brother down. I could have stopped him going in that stolen car but I didn't. I was in bed with Parry Palmer. So an innocent pedestrian was killed. I can never forgive myself and I thought Marcus would be unable to forgive me if he knew. So I was desperate to stop Marcus meeting Parry Palmer. Parry would enjoy telling him I had feet of clay.'

She was clearly struggling. Around the table you could hear a pin drop. Ayesha breathed deeply and went on. 'I called Parry and came to Norbridge. I wanted to persuade him not to tell Marcus about . . . about my past. We met in a pub in the town. Parry said some terrible things. We left together, but I was so upset I . . .'

'Yes?' Suzy asked.

'I hit him, hard. In the face. I scratched his cheek.'

'So that's where the scratches came from,' Suzy said.

'Yes. It was me. He fell against the wall, and I ran back to my hotel.'

Suzy nodded. 'But why are you telling us this?'

'Because I was worried that if anyone had seen me attack Parry, or if there was some way the scratches could be traced, then I might be questioned. And because of Marcus it would be all over the press and social media. And then the truth about my brother might come out.'

Callum Oldcastle looked sceptical. 'How would that affect Marcus's reputation? After all, you're not your brother's keeper.'

There was another silence. Everyone waited for Ayesha's response.

'But he's not my brother,' she said. 'He's my son. But he doesn't know. No one ever knew. Except my mother. And Parry Palmer.' She looked over their heads.

'And me, darling,' said Marcus. 'Your mother told me.'

Ayesha grasped his hand. 'I'm so sorry, Marcus. But now I've told you the whole truth. You'll just have to trust me. I have no proof that I was alone in my hotel room when Parry Palmer died. There's no one to give me an alibi. It would suit me to believe Freddie Lamplugh killed him. But I just can't do that. I'm sure Freddie's innocent.'

Marcus said, 'So we're here because we want you to find out what really happened, Suzy.'

CHAPTER TWENTY

Confess your faults one to another, and pray for one another, that ye may be healed. James 5:16

'OK, if we're all in the truth-telling game, you might as well know it was me who drove Freddie up to Cumbria,' Callum Oldcastle said loudly. 'He wanted to stay with his grandfather because he'd found out that Parry Palmer was to be at a prestigious music course right next door to the farm. The Caldfell Chorus. Freddie couldn't believe his luck. He had a plan to get to Palmer in a public setting and make him confess to stealing our work. He thought it would be great to accuse him in front of some of the musical great and good, including you, Dad. Freddie had found one of his early essays, written for Palmer, and it included a bit of our composition which turned up in Palmer's madrigal book. It was incontrovertible evidence, but we were getting nowhere with our complaint to the Academy.'

Dave said quickly, 'The Academy dragged its feet because the Scott-Broughtons were donors to the Academy and big Parry Palmer fans.'

Callum went on, 'Exactly. We were being fobbed off. I wasn't sure it was a good plan to out Palmer as a cheat at the

Caldfell Chorus but Freddie felt it was all meant to be — it was such a coincidence Palmer turning up next door to his grandad's farm. But I got cold feet. I told Freddie I didn't want to be involved anymore, then dropped him off and went to an Airbnb in Norbridge. I stayed there, by myself, for two days because of the weather. Then I saw on social media that Palmer had been murdered. I fled the scene, to be honest. But I wanted to talk it over with someone who would understand, so I called my dad. That's why I'm here.'

Suzy stayed silent. If anything, this substantiated the idea of Freddie's guilt. But most people were still processing Ayesha's revelations as well. If Freddie was guilty, she could easily be implicated too. She worked with Freddie and they both hated Palmer.

This supper party was just throwing up more suspects. People splintered into little groups, talking to each other. It was getting nowhere.

Then Eva Delmondo spoke up.

'Oho, listen up, folks,' Eva said. 'I think you might be on to something. Not that it's in my interest to spill the tea. But you've all made good points. Never forget, the Scott-Broughtons are mega wealthy and these days right is right. You need to go back to the beginning. These people are seriously powerful. And Gervase has been a lot more cheerful since Palmer died. Plus, they had a plan B ready and waiting. So I truly think there's more to this than meets the eye. But if any of you ever quote me . . .'

'I think we've all agreed that we're not going to repeat anything said here,' Suzy said.

'So can I add something that chimes with what Eva has said?' Callum Oldcastle said. 'This is really significant, but it never struck me before. I know that Freddie wrote to the Scott-Broughtons telling them about Palmer's plagiarism and saying he wanted to speak to them. The Scott-Broughtons knew Freddie would be at Caldfell.'

'That's awesome news,' Eva breathed. 'You sure?'

Callum nodded.

'If that was the case,' said Suzy, 'you would think, when Palmer was found dead, the Scott-Broughtons would tell DI Jackson to go to the farm and question Freddie straight away.'

'And something else,' Callum added. 'Freddie hated knives. I'm not saying he had a phobia or anything, but he was really uncomfortable about sharp objects. He never ate steak because he hated the knives. And when I went to his bedsit, he'd eat with a spoon.'

'That's true,' said Ayesha. 'I remember that about him.' She repeated the story of the conductor who stabbed his own foot with his baton, and Freddie blanching.

While they'd been talking, Suzy had cleared the table.

Now she felt it was time to pull things together with the coffee. She said slowly, 'Can I give you my take on what you've all said? Let's start with the victim. Parry Palmer was a taunt, a manipulator and an exploiter. Eva's right, we need to go back to the beginning. Why did Palmer get the job as choral director for Gervase Scott-Broughton's vanity project? That's something which needs explaining, especially given Palmer's reputation for pinching other people's work, and the complaint against him at the Academy of Voice. That complaint was brought by you, Callum, and Freddie Lamplugh. Freddie concocted a vague plan to make Palmer confess to the plagiarism. But this is really crucial, and to me it blows holes in the police evidence. If Parry was dead, Parry couldn't confess, so why would Freddie kill him? A confession was all important to Freddie.'

'Yeah, you're right,' said Callum. 'Spot on.'

Suzy continued, 'The police say they have written evidence of a plan by Freddie to kill Parry. I have no explanation for that either, but scribbles aren't conclusive in a court of law. And a plan isn't a crime.' Suzy paused. 'But of course there'll never be a court of law to decide Freddie's guilt or innocence because the case will be wrapped up. There'll be no one to clear Freddie's name except us. And there are other things. We've had an explanation for the scratches on

Palmer's face, that was Ayesha, but we have no explanation for his blood on Edwin's jacket, given that we know someone else attacked him, not Freddie. Plus, there's Freddie's fear of knives. So I believe someone else killed Parry Palmer for some other reason and engineered an amazingly ingenious and evil cover-up including putting Parry's blood all over Edwin.'

'Yes, I agree,' Edwin Armstrong said. 'I was hit from behind. The blood was all over the front of my jacket.'

Robert said, 'So, Suzy, I think it's the view of the meeting that you should have another go at Jed Jackson. We don't have any hard evidence, but maybe we have enough to cast doubt on their conclusions. I'm not sure we'll get anywhere with the police, but if anyone can, it's you.'

* * *

'No. I'm not listening to this, Suzy.'

Jed Jackson was having a bad time. He'd agreed to see Suzy on Monday morning because he'd known her a long time.

'Suzy, just because you were right about the gardener in the graveyard case, it doesn't mean you're right again this time. Sometimes the obvious answer is the answer. Occam's razor. Freddie Lamplugh, poor sod, killed Parry Palmer in anger because he believed Palmer had stolen his material. Then he drank a bottle of whisky and took a packet of temazepam, fell over in a snowdrift and died. He had a plan on paper in his pocket, accusing Palmer of being a thief. He wanted to kill him. Not conclusive, I grant you, but it was in his handwriting with his doodles all over it. It's cut and dried.'

'But it was counterproductive for Freddie to kill Palmer. He wanted him to publicly confess to stealing his material. He wrote to the Scott-Broughtons telling them that. You need to find that email . . .'

'What you're saying doesn't mean anything, Suzy. You've talked to a few people who are all involved in this mess, but you don't have a scrap of evidence.'

'What about the fact that two people say he hated knives?'

'Oh, come off it, Suzy. That's the same as saying two people thought he was a nice guy. Yes, Parry Palmer was butchered. But Freddie Lamplugh came from generations of Cumbrian farmers. Don't tell me he was a complete stranger to butchering.'

Suzy could see that Jed was worked up. No doubt the DS in Norbridge was on his back too. The last thing Jed needed was Suzy's theories. There was no point pushing any further; that would just make Jed more stubborn.

'OK,' she said. 'I'll go. See you around.'

Walking to the car, she thought over what had been said at the supper party on Saturday night. It had all seemed so compelling at the time. And she thought about Eva's point. Why was Palmer at Caldfell Hall in the first place? All the other musicians were top class. There was something odd about his appointment. And about the whole relationship between the Scott-Broughtons and the Academy of Voice. But how had that led to murder?

Jed was right. It was all terribly flimsy. Maybe she had made a fool of herself.

Suzy drove home slowly. She wondered if she should put all this behind her. In the end, no one would be much worse off if she did nothing. Ayesha Tomkins had reached her own personal catharsis and had gone home happy. No one had reported her attack on Parry Palmer. Jed was hardly likely to be interested in the fact that Ayesha had known Freddie Lamplugh. There was nothing to link her to the scratches on Palmer's face. Ayesha and Marcus had turned up at her supper party to find some sort of closure of their own. And Callum wanted to believe his academic partner was innocent. Of course Eva had made a good point about the Scott-Broughtons coping so efficiently, and suspiciously, with Palmer's death. But perhaps the rich and famous always coped efficiently with nuisances.

And on top of her disillusionment with her own efforts in the murder case, Suzy was worried about something else. That morning Robert had said that he was thinking of going to see his sister. He saw her once in a blue moon. What was that about? He hadn't given Suzy an explanation and had dashed out to the Advice Centre.

She parked her car outside The Briars and went in. The house seemed cold and dark, as if it was annoyed with her for wasting time on sleuthing when she should have been dusting the bedrooms.

As she sat in the kitchen with a cup of tea, looking out at the grey garden, her phone rang. It was Rachel in London.

'Hello. This is Lord Peter Wimsey again.'

'And I'm Miss Marple. Or not.'

'Well, if you are, could you knit me a disguise, please? This widower from the schul is still trying to track me down.'

'Lucky you. I'm feeling really low, Rache. I think my investigating is going nowhere.'

'Well, that's a shame, because I've got something interesting for you. You were right to ask for lists of alums from the Academy of Voice. The same year as Gordon Broughton and Parry Palmer were at the Academy, there was a Gerry Scott. Could that be your Gervase? He graduated with a distinction.'

'Yes! I suppose it could be!'

'Well if so, Gervase Scott-Broughton and his relative Brigham were both students at the same time. Along with Parry Palmer. So all three go back a long way.'

'Yes, but I'm inclined to say — so what?'

'Suzy, what's wrong? You sound terrible.'

'Oh, it's everything, Rachel. I'm really worried about Robert. Now our case has hit the buffers, he's talking about going away for a few days to see his sister in Manchester and I don't know why. And I'm tired of this grey weather, and the house seems grimy . . .'

'You need a break, Suzy. If Robert's going to Manchester, why don't you come down to London for a few days and stay over with me?'

Suddenly the thought of getting away was irresistible. 'I'll have a word with Robert. If he's serious about going to see his sister I'd love to spend a few days with you.'

'Brilliant! The bright lights of London await you!'

* * *

Robert came home from the Advice Centre at five o'clock. He and Suzy sat in the kitchen, each with a glass of wine, but the conversation didn't flow as much as the booze. Always a bad sign.

'Robert, if you're serious about going to see your sister, I'd like to go and spend a couple of nights with Rachel in London. Work is quiet now and the weather is getting me down.'

'Well, I can see you're at a low ebb with the candlelight case going nowhere.'

'And I'm a bit confused about you suddenly wanting to go and see your sister. Is she OK?'

'Yes, she's fine. I had a chat with her earlier today. It's just that I need to check out some family stuff.'

'Family stuff? Is it about money?'

'Not exactly. Just a couple of questions that have been bugging me. You've always been in contact with your family. But I've lost touch with sis. And there are things you can only talk over with blood relatives.'

Suzy stepped back. They were standing in the kitchen, and for a moment she felt slightly faint, grabbing the edge of the kitchen table. Robert had never spoken like this before. She thought of her wobble at Caldfell Hall when she wondered if they should have had children together. Was Robert now feeling that blood was thicker than water?

The doorbell rang, interrupting her thoughts, and Robert went to answer it.

'Suzy!' he called. 'I need to go round to the vicarage.' Suzy thought she could hear relief in his voice. He was always being called to the vicar's house because of church crises. He had an excuse to be away for a while.

'OK,' Suzy called back. 'I'll leave your supper in the microwave.'

When Robert had gone, Suzy took a deep breath. He clearly didn't want to tell her any more about the reasons for his trip to Manchester. She wasn't going to interrogate him about why he suddenly wanted to see his sister. She needed to think carefully about how to handle his sudden desire for family contact. She wouldn't just rush at it and say the first thing that came into her head, not this time. It was all too sensitive.

Maybe they needed a break from each other too. She decided that she would take up Rachel's offer. Although she loved Norbridge, there was always the attraction of the bustle, the gossip, the people in London. The feeling of being a player.

And perhaps it would be good to draw a line in the sand after the murder at Caldfell Hall.

But as she decided, her phone rang. It was Eva Delmondo. As always the comms director launched straight in. Eva didn't waste time with small talk.

'Hey, Suzy, I've been thinking, and I realized I never told you what it was that made Gervase Scott-Broughton so rich.'

'No, you didn't. Does it matter?'

'I don't know. But it's interesting. I can't believe you don't know this. You guys are old enough to remember that hit song, "North Country Girl" by Joanie Cadiz. On the lines of "Scarborough Fair" by Simon and Garfunkel. Well, it was arranged and produced by Gervase Scott-Broughton. That's how he got started. From then on, he had his fingers all over the music business.'

'"North Country Girl" — yes, I know it. It's got a flute solo. Like Gerry Rafferty's "Baker Street" with the wailing sax. The only decent song Brigham Broughton could perform in the market square.'

'Exactly,' said Eva. 'And it fills in some background for you. You need to know everything you can about the suspects, don't you? Gervase Scott-Broughton never looked back after writing that song. Everything he touched turned to gold. But he never wrote anything else either. He wasn't a creative. Gervase Scott-Broughton produced other people's material brilliantly, but he never composed himself.'

'Yes. Well, thanks, Eva. I'll park that.'

'You never know when the information might come in handy. I could ask Brigham a bit more about it. I might have to have a drink with him later.'

'Rather you than me,' said Suzy.

Eva chuckled. 'We'll keep in touch won't we, Suzy? Even when I'm back Stateside?'

Suzy honestly didn't know. She said a subdued goodbye and concentrated instead on a trip to London. Hopefully the big city would take her mind off the killer by candlelight for good. And when she and Robert were back home, she would make sure that the atmosphere was right for a heart-to-heart.

But for now, there was nothing she could do. She ate her supper alone.

CHAPTER TWENTY-ONE

Hear counsel, and receive instruction, that thou mayest be wise in thy latter end. Proverbs 19:20

The next morning, Christopher Murray opened the Advice Centre on his own. Robert had texted to say he was going to Manchester and would be back later in the week.

Christopher wanted to have another chat with Carly Martin.

He knew where the Martins lived but he didn't want to go there. He could imagine Carly making allegations against him if he were alone with her in the flat. He always kept his texts to her brief and formal. He wrote to her again that morning: *Hi Carly, it would be useful to meet. We might be able to review your Personal Independence Payments.* That would bring Carly to the Advice Centre for sure.

He constantly thought about the idea that Carly had had inside help at Caldfell. It made sense. There was no way she could have taken a taxi, disembarked where the road was blocked, hiked to the Hall through the snow, and lain in wait for the man she thought was Lily's father, all without help.

Yet Christopher believed her when she said that she'd whacked Edwin with a piece of wood. She might have bigged up her part in an attack launched on Edwin with someone else, but there was no doubt the attack had happened. Christopher was sure that when she'd put her head down on the kitchen table in The Briars and told them she was confused about who she'd whacked with the wood, she was telling the truth.

So who had helped her? And might the person who successfully killed Parry Palmer be the same person who helped Carly Martin in a separate attempt? Then Carly botched things — and that person would not be pleased. Now, Carly herself might be in danger.

He set up the tables at the Advice Centre and welcomed the other volunteers. Ro Watson was back on the community policing table.

'You're no longer at Caldfell Hall, Ro?'

'No, that all seems done and dusted. I know Suzy isn't happy, but she can't argue against the evidence, much as she would like to.'

Christopher nodded, waving to Alex and Lily who had just come in. Alex had brought Christopher a coffee — the cappuccino he liked from the café next door. He looked sideways at Lily. *She's becoming very beautiful*, he thought. Her long coppery hair still reminded him of his own mother. He thought about his treasured fantasy that he was her father. He was pathetic, he told himself. As much of a fantasist as Carly.

And it wasn't long before Carly came loping into the Centre wearing her usual outfit. She stopped to hear her daughter singing.

'Luverly!' she said to Christopher. 'She's gonna be a star. And them Armstrongs can't do enough for her. Good, eh?' She smiled, sly and toothless. Christopher wondered whether the Armstrongs knew what they were doing. Helping Lily was one thing, but the burden of Carly would be something else.

'Good to see you, Carly. Let's go over your benefits schedule,' he said. 'But first I want to ask you a few questions.'

Carly rolled her eyes. But she couldn't have one without the other.

'OK,' she said listlessly.

* * *

Suzy caught the London train the next morning. Pushing her laptop to one side, she wanted to think. Robert had seemed pre-occupied before going to Manchester. They had last seen his sister before the pandemic, and since then she had moved house. He was consulting maps and printing them out. Suzy had kissed the top of his head.

'Give Eileen my love. We should see her more often.'

'Yes, we should. That would be nice.'

Since making the decision to come to London, she had forced herself to forget about the murder. She hadn't wanted to talk to anyone about it, not even Robert. Her embarrassing interview with Jed Jackson, and the depression which had followed, were unlike her. But lying in bed, unable to sleep at the witching hour of three o'clock in the morning, she had started to think about Rachel's new information.

Say there was something from the past — in their days at the Academy of Voice, for example — which meant that Parry Palmer's death wasn't as tragic for Gervase Scott-Broughton as it might appear? Gervase couldn't have killed Parry himself because he was in the Hall at the time it happened. But Gervase had minions. What about the creepy Trent? He'd do anything to make his master happy, according to Eva.

And the Scott-Broughtons had an effective security operation, so how could two people like Carly Martin and Freddie Lamplugh slip under the net? Unless it was meant to happen . . .

She thought about the London connection. Brigham Broughton, aka Gordon Broughton, had been accepted at the same college in London as Gerry Scott and Parry Palmer.

Gervase was an Oxford graduate, and Parry had gone to the University of London. That was stressed in the high-end Caldfell online brochure. Brigham Broughton hardly had A levels, according to Dave Oldcastle. How could they all be studying together? She needed to know more about how the Academy of Voice operated.

As the train sped through the Midlands, Suzy mused about Irene Przybylski. What little she had found out about her on the internet confirmed that she had gone to work at the Academy fifteen years earlier, first as a visiting lecturer, then securing a staff post and rising to become a professor and head of department. She had successfully raised funds for better facilities, and she had gradually found good people to replace mediocre teachers — apart from Parry Palmer, who had somehow managed to cling on. Irene didn't have much of an online profile. She wasn't on X or Facebook. There was a highly creative, arty shot of her which appeared several times, with her face half in shadow and her hair a shiny, unnatural black. It was the sort of photo popular with professional musicians and not a real likeness at all.

The train drew into Euston sooner than Suzy had expected. She took the Tube up to Islington where Rachel lived and was there in time for supper. She and Rachel walked to Upper Street, home to dozens of little eateries, and settled down in Suzy's favourite, an unassuming French brasserie.

'It's good to be here,' she said, 'with the lights and the people. I love Cumbria, but this spring has been hard with the snow, and the endless grey thaw.'

'I know you're disappointed about your murder case, Suzy . . .'

'And I'm worried about Robert too, Rache. He seems, well, so detached sometimes. As if things are confusing him. And now this sudden need to go and see his sister. I wonder if he's thinking about the importance of family. Eileen is his only blood relative. Maybe he feels alone.'

'But there's you, Suzy. And Jake and Molly.'

'But they're not his children,' Suzy said gloomily.

'Oh, for heaven's sake! Snap out of it. This isn't like you, Suzy. These days the world is full of perfectly happy childless people, either by accident or design. If you ask me, childbirth is a cast-iron case for atheism — what sort of God could have dreamed up that torture?'

Suzy laughed despite herself. 'Don't be provocative! You know I'm a churchgoer, Rachel. I believe in God. I need someone to forgive my sins. But I take your point about childbirth. Having children isn't the be all and end all . . . Maybe I'm just overreacting to whatever is wrong with Robert.'

'And I'll bet you another dinner at this place that whatever's wrong with Robert has nothing to do with longing for children in his old age. He's hardly Mick Jagger, is he? I mean, he wasn't that young when you met and it's too late now. If he'd wanted kids, he would have found someone daft enough to have them with. Thinking the way you've been thinking is a bit of an insult to him. And to other childless but happy people. Like me, for example. Or Irene Przybylski.'

'I'm sorry, Rachel. You're right. I just got to thinking about it after hearing what Alex was going through to have a baby. And I'd like to meet Irene. She sounds interesting.'

'Good, because you're having lunch with her tomorrow at her gorgeous flat in Bloomsbury. I fixed it for you. I guessed you'd want to meet her. It's not the sort of place that would work for children, by the way. Way too smart and glitzy. Irene lives alone. But there's some rather touching pictures of her with a younger woman. She's obviously had lovers, but I don't think having kids was ever on the cards for Irene.'

'But you don't know that, Rachel. Now it's you who's making assumptions. Gay couples have kids all the time these days.'

'Fair point. I stand corrected. Now, as neither of us needs to go home to the kids, let's have some more wine!'

* * *

The following day Rachel went to work at the Academy, and Suzy travelled on her own for lunch at Irene's address in Bloomsbury, near the British Museum.

Suzy pushed a brass button and gave her name. The art deco glass front door opened, and she went up to the top floor in the vintage lift. A stylish woman in her fifties was waiting for her.

'Suzy. So good to meet you. Do come in.'

Irene had lunch set out on the dining table. She also had her laptop. Suzy took in the elegant surroundings and spotted the pictures Rachel had mentioned of a younger Irene and a much younger woman. Intriguing.

Irene didn't bother with too much small talk. 'Rachel tells me you want to know about a cohort of students which included Parry Palmer.'

'Absolutely. I'm not sure if it will lead to anything but you should know that I'm representing a group of us who don't believe in Freddie Lamplugh's guilt.'

'It's causing terrible shock waves through the Academy,' said Irene. 'I'm coming in for a lot of flak. If Freddie could be exonerated it would be a great relief.'

'The police have tied up Parry's murder very neatly,' Suzy said.

'Neatly, yes. But it looks bad for the Academy. A member of staff murdered by a student. The fallout is going to get worse.'

'Of course, you knew Freddie . . .'

'Yes. He was a delightful student, very imaginative and creative. He had great passions. But I can't see him killing someone with a penknife. And that's not just because I want to protect the Academy's reputation. Freddie was, I'm sure, capable of lashing out, but a premeditated killing with a knife doesn't wash with me. So, how can I help you? I've got all the information we need on my laptop.'

'I've lost my mojo with this case in the last few days, and I don't really know what I'm looking for,' Suzi said. 'But I want to know as much as I can about the past, the time when

Gerry Scott, Gordon Broughton and Parry Palmer were all here. And about why the Scott-Broughtons are so financially supportive of the Academy.'

'Well, the last question is the easiest. Gervase has more money than he knows what to do with. He wanted to support us for completely altruistic reasons.'

'And Lauren?'

Irene looked surprised. 'To be honest, she didn't take much interest. I mean, she comes to concerts sometimes. But it's Gervase's baby really.'

'So how much can you tell me?'

'Perhaps this is interesting. Gerry Scott changed his name while he was here. He came as Gerry Scott and left as Gervase Scott-Broughton. We get that sort of thing quite often these days. Students marry and take a double-barrelled name. Or their parents remarry. Back then it was less usual, but Gervase certainly changed his name during his year here.'

Irene was also able to confirm that it was while he was at the Academy that Gervase had arranged the traditional folksong 'North Country Maid', which hit the charts as 'North Country Girl'. There was a short piece congratulating him in the Academy newsletter of the time.

On the other hand, his cousin Brigham had left without qualifying. He had been a dud. There was no record of him after his second term.

Suzy thought about it. 'So the student called Gerry Scott wrote the song. But it was published under the name of Gervase Scott-Broughton.'

'No, just G. Scott-Broughton, as far as I can see. "North Country Girl" was quite a success. There's only one recording and that's by Joanie Cadiz. She was a big star. Gervase would have made quite a bit of money out of it.'

Suzy said, 'Apparently he never did anything else creative. He was a good producer but it was always using other people's material.' She thought for a moment. And then she had another brainwave.

CHAPTER TWENTY-TWO

Woe unto them that are mighty to drink wine, and men of strength to mingle strong drink. Isaiah 5:22

'Irene, presumably the students played musical instruments.'

'Of course.'

'So what did Gerry Scott play? Would it be on his application?'

'Yes, and we have an online version of that. All the paper applications were scanned and filed when we started fundraising. Gerry Scott . . . Yes, here we are. He had grade eight in piano, but he wasn't studying an instrument here. Technical production was his main subject.'

'But on the song, it's the flute solo which really made it stand out, isn't it?'

'It certainly helped.' Irene fiddled with her phone and then the sound of Scott-Broughton's hit, sung by Joanie Cadiz, stopped them talking. It was a beautiful song with a lovely melody. The flute solo was filled with yearning.

'Do you have any information about Gordon Broughton?' asked Suzy.

'Yes, here he is. In those days the Academy did both postgraduate and diploma courses, taught by the same tutors.'

'So the Academy was one of the few places where Brigham and his cousin Gervase could study together? Maybe that was why the Oxford graduate Gervase chose the obscure music college. To be with his cousin?'

'That's right. Gordon Broughton wasn't well qualified academically, but he was musically gifted. He had grade eight piano and flute. But he dropped out, as you know.'

Suzy's brain was bouncing from idea to idea. 'On another tack, Irene,' she asked, 'is there anyone still working at the Academy who might have been there when Parry Palmer was a student? Someone who maybe followed his career? At the Caldfell course my friend Alex Armstrong mentioned a woman who works in your admin offices. She took time off to be in the Caldfell Chorus. Could I talk to her?'

'Oh, I know who you mean. She's a lovely lady in our admin office. From Cumbria originally. Still has the accent. A very good amateur singer. Coming up to retirement. I'll call her and see if she's around after work and can see you.'

'Thanks so much,' said Suzy. 'You've been an enormous help.'

But why is Irene bothering? Suzy wondered.

Irene went into another room to call the administrator to ask if she might have time to meet with Suzy. In the meantime, Suzy managed to get a peek at the photos of Irene and a younger woman that Rachel had mentioned. There was something about the scenes which reminded Suzy of Cumbria. In one they were standing in front of a low whitewashed house with the merest shadow of a North Country fell behind them. In another, the young woman seemed to be on the shore of a lake. Suzy was always making imaginative leaps. Sometimes they fell flat, but occasionally they led to the solution to a case. Irene. Renee. Suzy had a flash of inspiration. Could that former partner be Carly Martin? The girl's face was slightly in shadow in all the pictures. Identifying her might be hard, and in any case Suzy had never met Carly. It was probably a ridiculous conjecture. But stranger things had happened. Suzy thanked Irene, leaving her swish apartment to meet the Cumbrian admin assistant in a pub near the university.

* * *

The smart, smiling middle-aged woman was waiting for her. She recognized Suzy straight away.

'You're the podcast lady from the Caldfell Chorus. Whoa — it's tricky seeing people out of context. I need to get my breath back! And Professor Przybylski said you wanted to know about Parry Palmer back in the day. How long have you got?'

'It's more about how long *you've* got.'

'Well, not long, to be truthful. I'm babysitting my granddaughter tonight,' the woman said with a touch of pride.

'Can I start by asking how long you knew Parry Palmer?'

'Decades. I've worked in admin at the Academy all my working life, except when I had maternity leave. I've got two daughters and four grandchildren.' She beamed. 'I started the same year as Palmer, and I was a bit unsophisticated then, just down from Cumbria. He tried to chat me up more than once, but I think he was more attracted to my confidential files than my figure. He was one of the nastiest people I ever worked with, both as student and a lecturer, and that's saying something. He was quite unscrupulous.'

'And was he friends with Gerry Scott?'

'Gerry Scott — it's years since I've heard that name. Of course, he goes as Gervase Scott-Broughton now. He didn't recognize me at all at Caldfell and I never said anything to him. He probably never even noticed me. He was pompous enough all those years ago, and he's ten times worse now! We didn't get many Oxford graduates at the Academy in those days. Now, you're falling over them.'

'So if you didn't get many, or any, Oxbridge people, why did Gervase pick the Academy?'

'Oh, I suppose because his cousin was coming here, doing the diploma. I saw Brigham as well when I went up to Cumbria for the course, swanning around like a white Bob Marley. Brigham hadn't a clue who I was when I turned up either, but then he was drunk most of the time. I wasn't surprised to see him. He and Gervase were thick as thieves when they first came to the Academy.'

'But Palmer would know you?'

'Oh yes. And he didn't like me being at Caldfell Hall. It was Edwin Armstrong who picked my audition application. They had to go along with whatever Edwin said. But Parry was horrible to me. Kept hinting I was too old to sing first soprano. But my top Cs are as good as anyone's.'

'Was Palmer always like that?'

'Absolutely. He was a complete toad. I'm not surprised someone murdered him. As for Gerry, he was just arrogant and entitled, even then. Even Palmer couldn't deflate Gerry, so instead he sucked up to him. Brig was a different matter. Palmer made Brig's life a misery by teasing him and mimicking his accent. Brig couldn't take the strain, so he left the Academy and just went downhill.'

'You certainly didn't like Parry Palmer.'

'No one did. Pity he hasn't lived to see that complaint about him come home to roost. The one brought by poor Freddie Lamplugh. It was looking ugly for Parry.'

'I can see that,' Suzy said. 'Would you like another white wine?'

'Oh, no thanks. Like I said, I've got my eldest granddaughter coming round tonight. Her mummy's going to her book club. Would you like to see a picture?'

Suzy dutifully cooed over a plump little girl in a Peppa Pig top.

'Thanks so much for talking to me.'

'My pleasure. It was good to get it off my chest. They say you mustn't speak ill of the dead but there wasn't anything else to say about Parry Palmer.'

***

Suzy walked back to Rachel's flat in Islington. That evening Rachel was cooking and Suzy stood with yet more wine in the big open-plan kitchen/diner/sitting room on the top floor of a converted warehouse.

Suzy thought for a while before saying, 'Rache, I've been wondering. Don't you think it's much more likely that "North Country Girl" was composed by Brigham Broughton than by Gervase? He played the flute. Gervase didn't.'

'Maybe they collaborated? They were supposed to be close friends, weren't they?'

'Till Parry Palmer came between them.' Suzy grimaced. 'And Parry became well known for stealing other people's material. Maybe Parry put Gervase up to pinching the rights.'

'What? You think Gervase stole the work from his own cousin?'

'I wouldn't put anything past Gervase Scott-Broughton. Even murder. And if he did turn on Parry Palmer and kill him — for whatever reason — he wouldn't have the slightest qualm about pinning it on a poor innocent like Freddie Lamplugh.'

* * *

At Caldfell Hall, Eva Delmondo had just had a very interesting chat with Brigham Broughton. Which was surprising because he'd lost the art of conversation years ago. Few people talked to him or stuck around long enough to listen. That afternoon, Brigham had been finishing off one of his personally labelled bottles of Super Blend whisky. Eva had joined him, but once again, she had a Jack Daniels.

'Hey, Brig, tell all. Who was the creative one. You or Gervase?'

'Oh, we worked together back in the day, yer kna'. I'm not supposed to talk about it, but it's different now. She's dead.'

'Who's dead?' Eva asked sharply. 'There isn't another body here, is there?'

'Nah, cloth ears. *She's* dead.' He looked round conspiratorially. 'Joanie. And when she died, I thought, well, maybe now's my turn to get the big bucks. I don't really understand all that legal bollocks but if she's dead, does the agreement stand? I dunno.'

'I have no idea what you're talking about, Brigham.'

'The agreement.'

'Tell me more.'

Brigham Broughton grimaced. 'No can do, Eva. That's the agreement.' He shut his eyes.

'Whatever.' Eva looked at her phone. Time was getting on. She was flying home tomorrow having finally persuaded Gervase Scott-Broughton that everything was sorted at the Hall to his satisfaction. And he didn't just mean the cleaning and the dust sheets. He needed to know that there would be no more investigation into Parry Palmer's murder or Freddie Lamplugh's death. Eva had thought briefly about Suzy Spencer's supper party, but she didn't mention it. Anyway, it had gone quiet. She had done her bit and now she would be out of the picture. Leave the digging to Suzy and forget about it. What more could a girl do?

'We're all done here,' she had told Trent. 'I need to get home.' She was booked on a flight for the following day and needed to check in online. She certainly wasn't coming back for the re-run of the Caldfell Chorus. She stretched. She couldn't wait to touch down in LaGuardia.

'I have to go,' she said to Brigham.

'Okey-dokey. Just pass me that new bottle.'

'You're a wino, Brigham. You shouldn't hit the sauce like this.'

Brigham laughed and burped disgustingly. On a whim, Eva picked up his half-finished bottle of Super Blend, plugged the neck and put it straight in the bottle bin behind the bar. She replaced it with Gervase's Jack Daniels Single Barrel 100 Proof.

'Drink that, Brigham. It's much better stuff.' Brigham looked too exhausted to argue. He sighed and opened the Jack Daniels. Eva got up and looked down at him. He was pathetic.

'Goodbye, Brig. And good luck.'

He waved at her, his mind, what was left of it, already somewhere else.

Half an hour later, having checked in and finished her packing, there was a manic knocking at Eva's door. She opened it to see Trent, his face rigid with shock.

'Eva, come downstairs with me. Brigham's in the hall. He's dead.'

* * *

The Scott-Broughtons flew back for Brigham's funeral a month later. Lauren was reportedly very weak, but her illness wasn't mentioned in any official communiqués composed by Eva. There was a press release expressing shock and grief, which was circulated locally. A short paragraph was also posted on the Caldfell Chorus website.

And there was the announcement of a fund, set up by Gervase, for a music scholarship in Brigham's name, for a local child who played well.

There was no suggestion that the May premiere of *The Sacred Spring* might be postponed. Brigham's death was uncontroversial. Natural causes, self-inflicted. No need for plans to be derailed.

Lauren was installed back in her fabulous Madame de Pompadour bedroom. She had declined noticeably, so said the women drafted in to clean and cook — though cooking was hardly the word for it. They unpacked and heated food from the catering company, delivered in containers from London. Lauren was reportedly eating only specialized plant-based stuff and the occasional piece of fruit. Everything that was sent up to her room was vetted by Pearl, whom the other women resented for her brusque manner. But Pearl was impervious to any criticism.

Gervase was short-tempered and unapproachable. He spent a long time closeted with Trent.

The atmosphere at the Hall was bleak. Alex and Edwin visited to have lunch with Gervase, but it was an austere affair, with only basic logistics about the new composition discussed, and Gervase left after an hour to do a breakfast Zoom with California.

Alex and Edwin had checked out of the Norbridge Glen Hotel and were renting Tarnfield House, near Suzy and Robert. Lily still practised in the Advice Centre and was improving every day — Alex believed she was going to be a spectacular success. Carly told anyone who would listen that Lily was going to make millions and, when she did, it would be goodbye to this dump.

Suzy had been told of Brigham's death the night she was staying at Rachel's in London. Eva had been the one to call her and break the news. Suzy had been due home in Tarnfield the next day anyway, and Eva started phoning her for help even when she was still on the train. Eva had been ordered by Gervase Scott-Broughton to cancel her flight and see to all the arrangements for Brigham's funeral. There was nothing she could do but stay on. Without Gervase's funds she had no money for a return flight. She was trapped.

But she seriously needed help navigating the local procedures; Suzy was her life-saver.

And Suzy didn't mind. She was getting to like Eva; helping her with the funeral kept her ticking over. She couldn't quite let Caldfell go from her mind . . .

So Eva and Suzy met several times once Suzy was home from London. Suzy helped Eva through the post-mortem, the coroner's court and the funeral arrangements. The Scott-Broughtons arrived the day before the funeral, planning to stay on for the foreseeable future, for the regrouping of the Caldfell Chorus and the premiere of Edwin's new work.

After the shock of finding Brigham dead, Trent soon made it clear to Eva that though they were stuck at the Hall together, he was in charge and his role was purely the business side. Eva could deal with the tedious local logistics of a sudden death.

But Brigham's death was uncontentious. He had already been seeing his doctor but had been in denial about his health. The doctor confirmed that previous tests had shown that Brigham was in an advanced stage of cirrhosis. He might have lived for a few more years but the post-mortem showed he had died from heart failure. It was to be expected in his sort of case. So that was that.

Without saying much, Suzy did wonder. And when she met Alex Armstrong for coffee at the Tarnfield bakery, she voiced her suspicions.

'If Brigham really wrote "North Country Girl", then Gervase would want him out of the way.'

Alex said reasonably, 'But Eva says he's very upset about Brigham's death.'

'The two things aren't mutually exclusive,' Suzy answered.

Alex sighed. 'I thought I was Mrs Reality-Check but you're Mrs Cynical. Forget it, Suzy. Brigham drank himself to death. End of story.' Even Alex seemed to want to give up on the killer by candlelight case.

CHAPTER TWENTY-THREE

Lord, now lettest thou thy servant depart in peace, according to thy word. Luke 2:29

In the time between Brigham's death and his funeral, Suzy also met PCSO Ro Watson. It was her last chance to rekindle interest in the case. Suzy and Ro used to have lunch or coffee together at least once a month, but the killer by candlelight had put a damper on their friendship. In the past, it had been Ro who had encouraged Suzy and supported her ideas, but this time Ro wanted nothing to do with them.

But Suzy persisted. She started by outlining her meeting with Irene Przybylski, and Rachel's digging through the archives, discovering that the three men, Gervase, Brigham and Parry, had all been at the Academy of Voice together.

Ro sighed. 'But surely that was hardly a secret. You found it easily enough.'

'Well, we had to dig.'

'OK. Carry on.'

But Ro clearly had difficulty keeping up. 'Stop!' she said eventually. 'Hold it there. You're losing me. So, Gervase's surname was originally just Scott, and he called himself Gerry.

Gerry Scott. Well, why not? I suppose Gervase was rather a poncey name for a trendy student back then.'

'Absolutely. And Brigham's first name was Gordon. Not a very trendy name either. But both men had G as an initial. G. Scott and G. Broughton. Now, you must have heard of Joanie Cadiz.'

'Yes. Famous American folk singer.'

'And do you know a song called "North Country Girl"?'

Ro thought for a moment. 'With a flutey bit?'

'Yes! Well, that was written by Gervase Scott-Broughton. Allegedly.'

'Great! Good for him, I say.'

'Ro, listen. My theory is that Joanie Cadiz was originally approached, *not* by Gervase but by Gordon Broughton — the man everyone knew as Brigham. Lots of famous singers get sent songs by wannabee songwriters. Brigham's a much more likely songwriter than Gervase. And in this case it paid off. Joanie probably never met Brigham. But she loved the song, her people started talking megabucks, and Brigham went back to his cousin with the good news.'

'His cousin being Gerry Scott?'

'Yes! A much sharper business brain. So Gerry Scott took over. He changed his name to Scott-Broughton because Joanie was already dealing with a G. Broughton, and the insertion of a middle name wouldn't cause any comment. And he kept the initial G. Then he finalized the deal with Joanie Cadiz as Gervase Scott-Broughton and pocketed the money. Brigham was a brilliant musician but not very clever and his cousin did the dirty on him.'

'And where do you think Parry Palmer came into all this?'

'Maybe Gervase used Parry Palmer's bullying to see off his weaker cousin. The admin woman we met confirmed that Parry had been horrible to Brigham.'

'Oh, Suzy, this is all so complicated,' Ro said wearily.

'But life is complicated,' said Suzy. 'And it's the perfect explanation for why Gervase changed his name from plain old Scott to Scott-Broughton. And it totally fits the psychological profile of all three men.'

'What? Gervase the evil business brain, Parry the sidekick manipulator, and poor old Brig the naive creative genius?'

'Exactly — not so complicated after all. The trouble is that the only person who could prove this is Joanie Cadiz. But she died last year, in her eighties. Though I suppose we could try tracing her manager or agent from that time.'

'No, we couldn't, Suzy. It sounds vaguely plausible but it's just conjecture. It's all too flimsy. And even if all this rigmarole about who wrote the song is true, what would it have to do with Parry's murder?'

'Well,' Suzy began, 'it could be that—'

'Suzy, stop now. You're just speculating. I know you've had some amazing success with local crime. No one can touch you for your combination of local knowledge and an imagination the size of the planet. But back off on this one. Please. Jed is harassed enough with inquests and reports and the DS on his back. And there isn't a shred of evidence for any of this.'

'OK. But I'm going to keep looking. It's only fair to Freddie Lamplugh.'

Ro shrugged. 'I can't stop you. But this time I think you're telling yourself what you want to hear.'

Suzy knew when to stop. Only this time perhaps she had gone too far. She said goodbye to Ro feeling that she had made a fool of herself again, and their relationship had suffered.

But it had been a fraught time, and her friendship with Ro Watson was just one more casualty in her messy life.

To start with, she desperately needed some quality time with Robert. They had a lot of things to talk about, not just the case of the killer by candlelight. But when she came back from London she had immediately been caught up with poor Eva Delmondo, who was trying to find her way round Norbridge funeral parlours. There was a surprising number of people who were Brigham fans, and his funeral was going to be a major local event.

Then Suzy had a worrying time trying to get in touch with Jake, who kept leaving brief messages saying he and Mae were trying to fix a date to come over, after cancelling a few weeks earlier. And her daughter Molly turned up from university in York for a few days. She had finished with her posh boyfriend, and she mooched round The Briars wearing brightly coloured vintage pyjamas and talking on her phone until she felt fit to face the world again. There was also a problem with the indie television company Suzy worked for, trying to sell the rights to the Hiram King show to the USA. Suzy was busy.

On Suzy and Robert's only free night for a fortnight, they had dinner with Edwin and Alex. Suzy was desperate to catch up with Alex, and still sore about her friend's dismissal of her theories. Alex and Edwin's new house was lovely. And at least the Armstrongs listened intently to Suzy's news from London.

To her surprise, Edwin agreed with her.

'It all adds up,' Edwin said. 'Gervase isn't a composer or arranger. He's a producer. And you're right, he never mentioned the success of that song. People usually boast about their successes, but Gervase never mentioned it. Brigham was a pain, but he was the better musician. And a flautist. It makes complete sense to think he was the G. Broughton who first took the song to Joanie Cadiz.'

'And so do you think there might be a motive in there, somewhere, to kill Parry?' Alex asked. 'I was unsure about that but now I wonder. Maybe Gervase wanted rid of Parry because he knew too much. But what can you do about it now, Suzy?'

'Not much. I've a feeling it's significant that Joanie Cadiz died only last year, but I don't know enough about copyright.'

'I do,' said Edwin. 'But there are all sorts of different deals. I would think the ownership of the song passed to Joanie's estate when she died, so there'd be no real change.'

There was a pause. No one seemed to have any other suggestions. So Suzy changed the subject. 'How's Lily doing?'

'Oh, she's wonderful!' Alex glowed. 'She's made great progress. She's growing up too. It's marvellous to see her develop. She's definitely university material.'

'Yes,' agreed Edwin. 'She's good.'

But at some point the Armstrongs would leave Cumbria to go back to Frankfurt. They couldn't take Lily with them. There was a danger that they would build her up, then leave her to confront her mother with her new ambitions.

On the walk home from Tarnfield House after their dinner with the Armstrongs, Suzy thought about talking to Robert about all the things jangling about in her mind. But the time wasn't right, and she still hadn't clarified her thoughts. And as so often happened these days, he seemed pre-occupied. He was never cold or disengaged. He was just as affectionate. But he was very thoughtful. He was also out of the house a lot more.

It was all unsettling and unsatisfying. They still hadn't caught up with Jake. And then there was a problem with the sale of rights to Hiram King's Linkflex programme. And underneath it all was the nagging worry about Robert's health. Nothing had gone right since Suzy had gone to Caldfell Hall. And in her heart she knew a killer was still out there.

***

And suddenly, here they were at Brigham Broughton's funeral. It was packed. Callum Oldcastle was there to support his father, who had known Brigham from school. He was taller than Dave and looked over him to see Suzy and Robert at the back of the abbey. Callum smiled and said something to his father, who turned and nodded. He and his father chatted quietly as they moved into their seats. Callum seemed calmer now. Less of an angry young man. Christopher Murray brought Carly Martin, who wore a huge black fake fur coat and the all-too-familiar baseball cap. She cried loudly all through the service at Norbridge Abbey. In the street, as the hearse drew away, she was heard calling out,

'He was a good gadgie. I love you, Brigham!' Christopher steered Carly away into the pub, away from the other mourners. The wake was to be at Caldfell Hall. Not a good place for Carly to revisit.

Suzy kept at the back in the funeral service. Eva was very much in evidence, ushering the Scott-Broughtons — protected by the ever-present Trent and Pearl — to the front as chief mourners. The abbey was heaving. Some people genuinely mourned Brigham Broughton. But some rubberneckers had just come to see the mega-rich couple and their hangers-on.

When it was over and the Scott-Broughtons were safely in the huge Merc with its darkened windows, Suzy and Eva grabbed a quick word. Suzy had told Eva all about her theories. Eva was one of the few people who was genuinely impressed.

'Keep going, Suzy, you're onto something. I'm here until Gervase lets me off the leash. But we should keep talking. I'm gonna keep on searching and you should do the same. Funny, I think Mr S-B is genuinely upset about Brigham. He's doing things on autopilot, and he ain't enjoying his power like he used to.'

'His wife's very ill as well. That can't be easy.'

'Hmm. I dunno. She's probably one of these invalids who lasts for years.'

Suzy was surprised at Eva's cynicism.

'And look at those two,' said Eva. 'Trent and Pearl. Vultures, in completely different ways. I tell you what, Suzy, despite the long faces, they're both delighted that Brigham Broughton is no longer. A rival has departed.'

'Lucky for them.'

'Yeah, but I wonder how much luck had to do with it.'

* * *

Inside the Mercedes, Gervase Scott-Broughton looked out at the people milling around. Brigham had certainly had a following. Beside him, Lauren shivered in her furs. Her grey hair was swept up under a little 1950s hat with a spotted net veil hiding her face. She had tottered into the church and up to the front row on Pearl's arm. Pearl's squat figure made Lauren look even taller, more striking, and totally out of place. But at least she was there.

'I'm glad you made the effort to come,' Gervase said.

'I know you loved him in your own way. And you had history.' Lauren settled back into the heated seat and shut her eyes. She looked exhausted.

'Yes. Yes, we did.'

Gervase turned away from his wife and looked out of the window. He saw Eva Delmondo talking to that podcast woman. He had heard about Suzy's experience with murder. Brigham had mentioned it, and Trent had researched it. She had been responsible for exposing several killers over the last two decades. Gervase grimaced. He didn't want the woman anywhere near his operation anymore.

He wasn't happy to see Suzy talking to Eva. Something would have to be done about that.

* * *

Carly Martin sat opposite Christopher Murray in the Crown and Thistle. She was still sobbing. In front of her was a double vodka and tonic.

'I didn't know you knew Brigham,' said Christopher.

'You know nowt, you. I swear to God I don't know what it is yer want. I thought yer might be after Lily, one o' them paedos, like.' She laughed hoarsely.

'Don't be disgusting, Carly. I'm gay and had a partner for years until he died. I'm certainly not sexually interested in Lily, and you'd better not suggest that again. And I'm not sexually interested in you either.'

'So why are you here?'

'Because I want to know why you're so upset about Brigham Broughton.'

Carly was looking at him, and suddenly Christopher saw that her eyes were clear and wide open, alive with humour and perhaps affection. The slyness had gone. He could imagine her as a girl, maybe with a bit of a drug habit, maybe with an eye for the main chance, but attractive, with a perky air and a refreshingly direct approach.

And now, for some reason, she had decided to talk. Maybe because it had finally sunk home that Brigham Broughton was dead. There could be no harm in the truth now.

Carly said clearly, without her usual affected accent, 'When I came back to Norbridge, I was pregnant. Mam helped me. But she wanted me to stay in all the time and I liked a bit of life. I met Brig in a bar. We had a little fling, but he couldn't really get it up. Even back then. But we stayed friends. I've had boyfriends since. And girlfriends. But Brig was my best friend.'

'And when you went to Caldfell Hall that day with Lily, you knew Brigham was there?'

'Yeah. He told me he was going to go and stay at Caldfell Hall, and that his posh cousin was going to do something for him, moneywise. We'd planned to meet when I went up with Lily. It was before the bad snow. I got out of the cab and met him in the buildings at the back of the Hall. I'd seen that bastard who screwed me, and I'd gone all to pieces.'

'So, did you tell Brigham?'

'Too right I did! I described him to Brig. He knew him.'

'What was Brigham's reaction?'

'He was delighted. He said he hated that bastard too. I wanted to kill him, and Brig wanted to kill him as well. So he said that if I did it, I could share in his dosh.'

'So he was going to pay you to attack Parry Palmer?'

'Yeah. Just like you say. Brig said I should come back on Wednesday. He'd meet me on the road and get me to the Hall. Brig was familiar with all the old paths and grave walks and the like. So I went as far as I could in a cab, and then he guided me up there on some paths which weren't snowed over. I waited in a store at the back of the kitchens. Brig knew Caldfell Hall like the back of his hand. He'd been there as a kid, when he was allowed to play with Gervase.

And he'd been well in with the builders doing the refurb too. He brought me a blanket and some food and a piece of wood. And a bottle of whisky. And a bit of the class A. He said that the man I wanted to whack would be sure to be walking over to the practice room that afternoon, ten minutes before anyone else. He said I would know him. So I waited. And I leaped out and socked him.'

Brigham Broughton and Carly Martin. The least likely people to hatch a successful plot and pull it off. Poor Edwin Armstrong, looking just a bit like Palmer, in the same sort of anorak, getting the brunt of Carly's rage.

'How did you get away from Caldfell afterwards?'

'I went back to the storeroom and got pissed and wired and waited till it had stopped snowing. Brig had left me a man's jacket and some new boots. He'd already arranged with that cab driver to come back to the crossroads and keep his mouth shut. I walked down through the secret route and met the cab on the main road. The booze kept me warm. And then I fetched up at the Crown and Thistle with you. It was exciting, Chris. Thwacking that man gave me a real high. I needed to tell someone, and you're such a good listener.'

'Did you see Brigham again?'

'No. That's why I came to see you that night in Tarnfield, after I heard about the man being stabbed. Maybe Brig done it after all. He wasn't a strong bloke, though, wasn't Brigham. Too much substance abuse, as they say. That's why he wanted me to do it. But maybe he found the strength and killed that bastard himself. Suits me.'

She looked sharp, vicious and old again. 'Anyway, Brig never gave me nowt, 'cos I'd socked the wrong bloke. I never got my dosh.' She took another gulp and carried on crying loudly. But Christopher couldn't tell whether her sobs were for Brigham — or for the money he never gave her.

CHAPTER TWENTY-FOUR

Thou shalt not curse the deaf, nor put a stumbling block before the blind. Leviticus 19:14

Suzy and Robert walked slowly back to Robert's car after the funeral. 'Rob, I don't want to go up to Caldfell Hall for drinks,' Suzi said. 'I hardly knew Brigham, and Eva is going to be run off her feet looking after local worthies.'

Robert breathed an audible sigh of relief. 'I agree. We could have some time at home for once. I'd like that.'

'Would you?' Suzy raised her eyebrows.

'Don't sound so surprised. Being at home with you is one of my favourite things.'

'But I feel as if I've hardly seen you since you went to Eileen's.'

'Well, in fairness, Molly came to stay. And you went back to Manchester a few times.'

'True enough. But there were things I needed to do — I didn't have any option. But you just seemed to disappear, off to the Advice Centre, or drinking with Christopher, or just going out.'

'Well, let's make up for it now.'

He drove them home. It was a grey, miserable March day. The lane to The Briars was muddy, and the front garden was brown and messy with uncleared winter debris. Spring came late in Cumbria and was often cold, wet and windy, more so than in most of England. The house looked cosy, but there were water marks beside the drainpipes and some of the paint round the windows was peeling again. They went in through the front door, which was sticking. Suzy hung up her dark raincoat and Robert followed her into the kitchen, loosening his tie. He rarely wore one these days, but a funeral was a funeral.

'I suppose that went off OK,' he said.

'Oh, Rob, what a cliché! That's what everyone says. But I suppose a funeral does bring a form of closure.'

'Well, that's true, even given how weird it was. Those Scott-Broughtons in their fantastic clothes — and their hangers-on looking like robots.'

'Trent and Pearl?'

'Was Pearl the mannish-looking woman in the smart coat? With the woman who was obviously Lauren Scott-Broughton? In that sumptuous black fur, and that hat with the little net veil? You don't see many of them in Norbridge.'

'Yes, it was rather a bizarre outfit, but very Lauren.'

'Lauren! So you're her best friend now, Suzy?'

'Of course not!' Suzy hit her husband playfully on the arm. 'But I have been in her bedroom. I rather like her. She was very complimentary about me.'

'Was she? Don't be taken in. The Scott-Broughtons are something else. I do wonder what Gervase Scott-Broughton has really been up to. I mean, the whole Caldfell Chorus thing could be a front, couldn't it?'

'What, for murder?'

'Why not? That's what you were thinking, weren't you?'

'I'm not sure anymore.'

Suzy got up to put the kettle on, but Robert had gone to get the whisky bottle out of the cupboard. 'Forget the tea.

We're home now. Let's have a wee dram. It's traditional after funerals. And it sort of goes with discussing murder.'

'OK. I'll just put the tumble dryer on. We left it earlier and there's so much wet washing in this weather.'

Suzy set the machine off and sat down.

'Oh, by the way, Molly rang earlier,' she said. The tumble dryer started its familiar domestic throb. 'She said she's got to pick her dissertation subject.'

Suzy smiled at Robert but then she saw that blank look on his face. He was staring at her. He had no idea what she was talking about. And then he suddenly leaped up, marched to the back of the kitchen, turned the tumble dryer off and kicked it.

He turned to Suzy and said, 'So Molly's got sick and missed her station? Is she coming over by train? We aren't expecting her, are we?'

Suzy looked at him in horror. 'Robert — I said Molly has got to pick her dissertation.'

'Oh God.' Robert put his head in his hands. 'It's happened again!'

'Robert, tell me what it is. But my darling, whatever it is, it doesn't matter.' Suzy got up and came to his side of the table and put her arms round him. She kissed the top of his head. 'I don't mind, Robert. We'll cope together. For better or worse, remember. And whatever happens, it's so much better with you than anyone else.'

Robert twisted around and looked up at her. Then he smiled. And even laughed.

'What are you laughing at, Rob? This is terrible!'

'Oh, Suzy,' he said. 'Did you think I was going mad? Well, it might happen. But not yet. I'm not losing my mind. I'm losing my hearing, Suzy. That's what it is.'

Deaf. She went back to her chair. Robert was going deaf. It was bad but it wasn't dementia. She felt relief wash up from her knees.

'Oh, Robert, we can cope with that. Loads of people have hearing loss. You just need to get a hearing aid. Is that all?'

'All? It's not great for me. It's infuriating. I never know when the deafness is going to kick in. It's like a sudden dropout on the soundtrack of life. That bloody tumble drier . . .'

'Of course, the background noise. Like in the Plough with the new minimalist décor and ambient sound bouncing off the walls.'

'Yes. Exactly.'

'And I said the sea bass was less calorific and you just looked blank . . .'

'I thought you said it was horrific. I couldn't understand what you were talking about!'

'Oh, Robert, it must be awful.'

'It is. At first, I wasn't sure what the problem was, which is why I took the opportunity of going to see Eileen. I've always felt guilty about leaving her to cope with our parents, but life wasn't easy for me with my first wife, as you know. And I didn't want to talk to Eileen on the phone because sometimes I can't hear what people are saying.'

'So you wanted to know about your family's health history?'

'Yes. Exactly. And only Eileen could tell me. She said that Dad lost his hearing twenty years before he died and really struggled. It wasn't very reassuring, but that was nearly forty years ago. Hearing aids were very different then. I've been trying out different shops in Norbridge.'

'So that's where you've been sloping off to. But why on earth didn't you tell me?'

'When? You've not been here half the time, and when you have, you've been thinking about Molly, or Jake, or the killer by candlelight.' He paused. 'And to be honest, I worried that you would start to treat me like an old man, a deaf old git.'

'Rob, that's ridiculous. I don't mind you being an old man. But we were going to have to talk about what was going wrong, sooner rather than later.'

'It feels like later, to me. I thought you were just irritated with me.'

'I'm so sorry if I've seemed impatient. But now we know. I suppose, when I told you Jake and Mae were coming . . .'

'I heard it as "Jake may come". I didn't think it was a proper arrangement. The bloody washing machine was going then.'

Suddenly Suzy began to laugh. 'I know it's not funny, Robert, but it's such a relief. I should be honest too. I think I put off talking to you because I was scared. But that was weak and stupid of me because thousands of people every month have to cope with a dementia diagnosis.'

'And we still may. My mother suffered from dementia in her eighties. But Eileen made me promise to get my hearing checked before worrying about Alzheimer's. And she was right, hearing was the problem. But in the future . . .'

'We must make a vow, Robert. A serious vow. We must never, ever brush old age under the carpet. It's going to happen, maybe sooner than we think. We're not invincible. And we're lucky to be in it together. Whatever happens, I do really love you.'

'Yes, I like stew as well. Have we got any in the freezer?'

Suzy looked at him anxiously. Then she saw his mouth twitching.

'You horrible man! You heard me perfectly well, didn't you? It's not funny. I can't believe you're all smiles.'

'You can't believe I've got piles?'

Suzy leaped up and attacked him with the dishcloth.

'I'm serious,' she said.

'Yes, I know. I'm just so happy we're back on our usual terms. I promise I won't make a joke of it. At least, not all the time. And I agree: we must face up to the future. I love you — and I love your stews. Even the more original ones.'

And then because they had absolutely nothing else planned, and no one to disturb them, they left the whisky and went upstairs to bed.

'Old people need a nap after funerals,' said Robert.

As they undressed, Suzy decided it was time to completely clear the air. 'Robert, there's something else. I'm being serious now.'

'I'm all ears.'

'Robert, please don't joke. I've been listening to Alex Armstrong about her struggles to have a baby for Edwin. She's been through such a lot of invasive treatment, and it hasn't worked. She felt that Edwin really wanted it, and so did she. But I wondered if this business of going to see Eileen and getting to know more about your family was because you didn't have children of your own. You said something about blood relatives . . .'

'Oh, Suzy. I just meant that blood relatives know about genetics. For heaven's sake. I married Mary and she couldn't have children, so I got used to the idea. Then you came along with a ready-made family, and Jake and Molly have brought so much into my life. Of course they're not my children, but I love them in a different, amazing way. I don't yearn for fatherhood like . . .'

'Like Christopher Murray?'

'Yes, like poor Christopher. I had no hankering for a child of my own. And to be blunt about it, we couldn't have afforded cycles of expensive treatment like Alex and Edwin. Anyway, it never occurred to me. So put it out of your mind. In fact, put everything out of your mind. We don't get many opportunities like this.' As he put his arm around her and held her close, Suzy's phone rang. They lay there for a moment before she said, 'I need to answer that.'

As if in sympathy, Robert's phone gave a little cheep, which meant he had a message. They both looked at each other and laughed.

'To be continued,' said Robert.

They consulted their screens. Suzy's call was from Eva and Robert's text was from Christopher.

'Looks like today wasn't any form of closure at all,' said Suzy.

* * *

Eva's message to Suzy was hurried and sounded whispered.

'Where are you, Suzy? I thought you were coming to the drinks. I've got to talk to you. That old farmer hillbilly turned up here in a suit out of the ark. He told me something weird. I can't stop, I'm going down to the — what d'you call it? — the cellar now, getting more whisky up. These locals can certainly put it away. Then I'm going to see that old farmer. Can you get here? I need you. I really need you, Suzy.'

It would be over an hour's drive from Tarnfield to Caldfell, but Suzy dressed quickly, grabbed her anorak and set off. She was wearing her black trousers and rollneck sweater, so she'd blend in with the remaining mourners — if there were any left. She thought of Alex; it was over a week since they'd met. Eva's problems and Suzy's work difficulties had got in the way. And Alex was so wrapped up in Lily. But Suzy knew Alex would be there for her when she needed her.

She texted her: *I've had a message from Eva and I'm going over to Caldfell. If you're still at the wake, can you hang on for me?*

In less than a heartbeat Alex wrote back: *Of course.*

Suzy went out to the car. At least it wasn't raining. It was just a dim, heavy, overcast afternoon. Suzy had associated March with dreary wet days, early darkness and nothing to look forward to. But once she was living at The Briars, she had started to celebrate the first new shoots and to look forward to the same patch of snowdrops poking through each year, followed by the daffodils along the lane and the forsythia blossom by the famous fence. It wasn't showing yet. Everything was grey.

But she felt somehow that she was on the edge of a breakthrough. The last few weeks with no progress on the case now seemed less a period of disillusion and more a time of waiting. Something was about to break; she was sure of it. And she wanted Alex with her when it happened.

CHAPTER TWENTY-FIVE

Blessed are they that mourn, for they shall be comforted.
Matthew 5:4

Suzy drove quickly and skilfully around Workhaven and up the road to Caldfell Hall. It looked quite different now the snow was completely gone.

There were still some cars parked outside, but most people had left the wake. At the door was a bouncer with an earpiece on. He held his hand up in front of Suzy.

'Name?'

'Suzy Spencer. I'm so sorry I'm late. I had to go home first.'

The bouncer said her name into his lip mic and then nodded her in. 'It's pretty much over now,' he said. 'You've missed the speeches.'

'I'll just pop in and pay my respects.'

She walked into the huge reception hall. Remembering the first time she had been there, she thought about the flashing blue lights on the snow, the Scott-Broughtons with their mask-like faces, and Alex's terror about Edwin going missing. Now she looked back outside and saw the grounds looking beautiful, cosmetic and stylish as the drive swept up from the road. Caldfell Hall was still stunning. But without the white cloak which had turned it into a mysterious world of its own, the Hall was just a beautiful, well-maintained country house.

'Suzy!' Lily Martin bounced up to her. Alex was just behind.

Alex said, 'I can't find Eva.'

'That's odd. Are you sure she isn't here?'

'Nowhere to be seen.'

Suzy thought for a moment. 'Alex, I think I know where she's gone. Could you come with me? I need to drive into the village.'

'But what about Lily? Her mother's not here. And Christopher Murray hasn't turned up. I brought Lily and I need to take her home.'

'Could Edwin take her?'

Alex turned away and went towards her husband, standing by the open fireplace. Alex leaned in and spoke to him. Then she came back.

'Edwin will take Lily back to Pelliter. If Carly's gone missing again, Lily can come back to Tarnfield House with him. I'll go with you.'

Suzy was keen to leave. Eva's message was urgent and suggested she would be at Fred Lamplugh's farm. Suzy motioned Alex to follow her outside. The bouncer was still on the step.

Suzy said, 'I think Eva's gone to see old Fred Lamplugh, the farmer. She left a voicemail, saying he'd turned up today and told her something weird. She really wanted to speak to me. I can't think where else she could have gone.'

'Do you know where the farm is?'

'I think so.'

Suzy manoeuvred out of the car park space and slowly drove down to the road. She turned right into the little row of houses that formed the tiny village. Caldfell Farm was in the middle, the farmhouse flush to the road in the Cumbrian style. She parked outside; she and Alex emerged into the dank air and made for the huge wooden front door. As was often the case in old-fashioned hamlets, the door just pushed open.

'Mr Lamplugh?' Suzy called. 'Are you there? We're looking for someone.'

The farmer lurched forward from the back of the house. He was wearing a ragged green jumper over the trousers of an ancient tweed suit. He stared at Suzy.

'I ken who you are. You're that television woman. And you' — he waggled a finger at Alex Armstrong — 'you're married to that composer, but I know your kin. The Gibsons at Fellside. Am I right?'

'Yes, you are.' Alex looked surprised but she shouldn't have been, Suzy thought. It was a small world in Cumbria and the farming community was even smaller.

'I haven't any visitors,' Fred said. 'It's just me. Come in t'parlour.'

He looked in his late eighties, Suzy thought. His brown, weatherbeaten face had eyes like currants. But he hadn't shaved, and his face had a pallor underneath. He must have been hit hard by his grandson's death. She looked around the oak-panelled hall and up the staircase with its candy twist bannisters. The old house was beautiful.

She and Alex followed him into a living room which appeared to have been untouched for fifty years. There was a big lumpy sofa with a blanket on it, where a sheepdog opened one blue eye, then one brown eye, and started to bare its teeth.

'I keep 'im in t'house these days. Safety. Quiet down, Rags.'

In here, too, the walls were panelled for the first three feet, but with dark vertical planks. Above, there was some tired brown wallpaper. There was an antique TV on a low table, a standard lamp with a flowered and tasselled shade, and a worn grey rug on the huge stone flags. The room was dark but not gloomy. There were two very small casements looking out onto the street. The house faced due west and there was still a trace of the dim sunset through the tiny panes.

'Sit down,' the farmer said. Suzy edged into a protesting old armchair. Alex, despite her glitzy life, had been brought up in the country and was more used to Cumbrian farms.

She managed to sit alongside the dog. It looked balefully at her from its unmatched eyes.

'We're looking for a woman called Eva Delmondo,' said Suzy. 'She's the press officer up at the Caldfell Chorus.'

The farmer made a noise and motion as if to spit. 'Them lot are nothing but trouble,' he said. 'Look what they did to me grandson. Poor young 'un were a queer but that din't bother me. Teks all sorts. I was fond of t'lad. Lal Freddie used to come up here in t'summer. Clever bairn. These music people ruined him.' The farmer's eyes were watering. Then Suzi realized he was crying.

'It's truly tragic what happened to Freddie.'

'Aye. And Freddie would never have killed anyone, especially with a knife. He was soft as butter himself. He might tek a swing at yer, but he'd never stab anyone in cold blood. He couldn't even kill a chicken! He was staying here wi' me. Police came and looked round. Found nowt.'

'And you were telling all this to Eva up at the Hall? She phoned me and told me.'

'Yon Yank? Glamour-puss? Aye, I was. She said she din't believe Freddie had killed anyone. I was grateful. I was shunned up there, but I had every right to go to Brigham Broughton's wake. I knew his mother. I own all the land around here. Me fayther bought it off the Scotts. Brig was a Scott on his mam's side.'

Suzy wondered about asking the old man what he had said to Eva which was so important to her, but she faltered. He might not know that what he had said was significant.

'Aye,' Fred Lamplugh was saying. 'She was alreet, yon Eva. Not like t'other one who fetched up here.'

As he spoke, the light outside the windows suddenly darkened, and Suzy turned to look. A huge Land Cruiser had pulled up right outside the farmhouse, blocking the last of the light.

Gervase Scott-Broughton and his faithful factotum Trent were getting out.

* * *

Fifteen minutes earlier, the bouncer had reported Suzy's name back to Trent via his lip mic. Trent was at the other end of the connection, checking the guests against his list.

'Suzy Spencer's arrived,' Trent had said to Gervase, who was standing in the office with a glass of the best malt.

'Shit. I thought we'd seen the last of her,' Gervase growled. 'I don't like that stuff you dug up on her while I was away, Trent.'

'Yeah. True crime in a place with more sheep than people. England's answer to Nancy Drew. She's a nosy bitch. And Eva was talking to her outside the abbey.'

'I know. We don't want anyone rocking the boat now things are straightened out.'

'And we don't want Eva knowing more than she needs to either.'

'I rate Eva. She's got balls,' Gervase grunted. 'But that doesn't mean I trust her. And I certainly don't trust the podcaster woman. Get your man to let us know when she's leaving.'

'She's leaving now. Shit. I can hear her on his mic. Oh my God, she's going to the farm.'

'Lamplugh's farm?'

'Yes.'

'Christ, that's all we need.'

'I'm on it, Mr S-B. I'll see you at the Land Cruiser.'

Gervase nodded. This was turning into a serious problem. But not for long. The Gulfstream was at Manchester, ready to go when he snapped his fingers. He just needed to sort out Suzy Spencer, and he would be out of this bloody mess.

* * *

In the farmhouse, Suzy stood up abruptly. The dog curled round and yapped, showing his teeth.

'Steady, Rags,' said the old man.

Gervase and Trent were already in the hallway. 'Can we come in?' Gervase's voice boomed in the small space. He didn't wait to be asked but strode into the parlour, pushing past Fred Lamplugh.

'Mrs Spencer. Oh, and Mrs Armstrong. How interesting to find you here.'

Fred Lamplugh had backed towards the door. 'What're you two after?'

'Just a quick chat, Mr Lamplugh. With these ladies maybe. Have you got a brew on?'

'Yer want tea?'

'Why not? Do you mind?' Gervase smiled in an oily way. Trent was hovering behind him and managed a rictus grin in the old man's direction.

'We've both suffered a sad loss, Fred,' Gervase went on. 'And a funeral is a strain. As you may well know.'

'If you're talking about Freddie, he's not buried yet. Or whatever they'll do w'im down south. Very handy for you, wasn't it? The poor lad dyin' in t'snow.'

'What do you mean, Fred?' Gervase moved forward in the small, crowded room.

'Don't "Fred" me. I'm Mr Lamplugh to you. I remember when you were a toffee-nosed little snot in a school blazer, paying yer visits once a year to check over yer birthright. I don't want yer here but I'm not throwing yer out. Tea's what yer want, is it?' The farmer brushed past them. 'Stay, Rags.'

Gervase looked nervously at the dog, who stared back venomously.

'Sit down, then,' Mr Lamplugh said. 'But I can't say dog won't bite yez.' He laughed, a croaky, bitter sound.

When he'd gone to put the kettle on, Gervase sat and relaxed into the sofa. He smiled, Trent squeezing in beside him.

Alex was standing by Suzy's battered armchair.

'So, what's going on, Mrs Spencer?' Gervase asked nicely. She was beneath his rage threshold, he implied, as he wriggled his large bottom on the old shiny leather cushions. Really very small fry.

'We're looking for Eva.'

'Eva? Well, you won't find her here.' Gervase laughed. His tone was patronizing and confident. 'Look, I think it's time we came to an arrangement. You've been causing a ridiculous amount of trouble for me. I know you've been trying to get the police to look further than sad little Freddie Lamplugh. They won't. The case is over. You' — he pointed at Suzy as his anger rose — 'you stuck your nose in to get more publicity for your cosy country podcasts. Oh yes, Trent knows all about your visits to the local police.'

Trent smirked. 'One of our security men is an ex-cop. He has his ear to the ground for us.'

'So we knew you were stirring things up,' Gervase finished triumphantly. 'But you won't be making capital out of the Caldfell Chorus.'

He smiled confidently at Suzy, and for the first time she felt scared of him. But then his eyeline shifted.

'Gervase!' Trent screamed. Gervase twisted his head away from Suzy.

Standing at the door, Fred Lamplugh looked a different man. Taller, straighter, focussed. And Gervase was looking down the barrel of an ancient shotgun.

'Get on your feet!' Fred said to the two men. 'Now, kneel down. On the flags.'

'Oh, for goodness' sake . . .' Gervase started to laugh.

The sound of the shot was deafening. The pellets ripped through the panelling and into the wall. In the dust and noise, Suzy saw Fred load another cartridge.

'The next one is for you!' he yelled at Gervase. 'I mean it. I want to kill you. And I don't care what happens to me. Freddie was my only grandson. He would have inherited the farm. You ruined that. My life's work, you bastard. Go, Rags!'

The dog lurched forward and sank his teeth into Gervase's leg. Gervase howled, dropping onto his knees. Trent followed.

Fred Lamplugh shouted, 'You can tell us the truth, and the podcast woman can record it! On her phone. I'm old but I'm not daft.' He levelled the shotgun at Gervase's head. 'These pellets will either kill yer or leave yer wishing you were dead. And the dog will see to *you*' — he laughed in Trent's terrified face — 'while I get another cartridge into the barrel. Pump action.'

'Now,' he said to Suzy, 'yer going to interview 'im. Go on. Let's find out the truth. You 'eard what I said. Pump action!'

CHAPTER TWENTY-SIX

I acknowledged my sin unto thee, and mine iniquity have I not hid. Psalm 32:5

Earlier that afternoon, as the mourners streamed out of Norbridge and up to Caldfell, Christopher Murray and Carly Martin had been sipping their drinks in the Crown and Thistle. Carly had stopped crying, and in her mercurial way, she was suddenly smiling and laughing. 'Oh well,' she said, 'Brig's gone. Good luck to 'im singing with the angels. Can I have another?'

If it keeps her happy, Christopher thought. He went to the bar, but when he came back, Carly was looking at her phone and hyperventilating noisily. She was breathing like a horse, rolling her eyes and taking useless breaths too quickly.

'What is it, Carly?'

Carly started screaming, little squeals at first, then louder wailing. But it didn't stop her grabbing the vodka out of Christopher's hand and pouring it down her throat. Then the noise started drawing more attention. Christopher heaved her to her feet and bundled her out into the street. Carly doubled up and screamed.

'What is it, Carly? Tell me.'

Now Carly was shrieking, and passers-by were looking concerned. Christopher pushed her into the alley at the side of the pub.

'Tell me what it is, Carly!'

'It's 'er. 'E's found 'er!'

'What? Who?'

'My mate in London. 'E's found 'er. Bloody fucking Renee! I'm gonna kill 'er too!'

It was then that Christopher called Robert. He needed back-up, fast.

* * *

At Fred Lamplugh's farmhouse, Suzy thought quickly about what to do. Gervase and Trent were both kneeling on the stone flagged floor. Fred Lamplugh had tied their hands behind them. Unlike at Caldfell Hall, the floor was icy cold. Suzy shivered. The dog was small and wiry enough to circle round them, snarling. Gervase's tweed trouser leg was ripped on the calf and Suzy could see the puncture marks from the dog's teeth in his plump, suntanned skin.

She was unsure how long it would be before either Gervase or Trent heaved themselves up in the crowded sitting room and attacked the farmer. In the fracas, any of them could be injured by shotgun pellets. She could hear Alex breathing loudly. So far she seemed calm, but Suzy had no idea how long that would last.

Suzy took control. She clicked her voice record app on the phone and put it on the coffee table. There was a strange, high-pitched sort of noise which showed up on the screen. She realized it was Trent, whining. He was terrified.

'This won't take long, Trent, if you answer my questions,' she said. He was weaker than Gervase, but his anxiety was catching. The whining noise dropped a semitone but was still there.

Suzy said calmly, 'You'd better do as Mr Lamplugh says, both of you. I'll make this as quick as I can, because I can see you must be very uncomfortable. That leg needs looking at, Gervase. Will you talk to me?'

There was no answer but no bluster either.

'Let's go back to the beginning, Gervase. Why did you go to the Academy of Voice to do your postgraduate studies after Oxford? It was hardly a top establishment in those days.'

Gervase had been looking at the floor but now turned his big head up to her, his immaculate hair covered in dust and his eyes bloodshot in the white, plaster-powdered skin. 'Why on earth are you asking that?'

'Just answer, lad.' Old Fred Lamplugh lurched a little on his feet but positioned himself comfortably against the sitting room's ancient wallpaper. He was old but he was strong. The shotgun barrel never wavered. Gervase shook more dust out of his eyes.

'I went there because it was the only college where my cousin Brigham could get a place. He was only doing a diploma. He was great musically but a bit thick about everything else.'

'Why did you want to be with him?'

'I liked him. Loved him, even. We'd played together as kids . . .'

'And you thought you could exploit his musical talent?'

'No . . . no. Not exactly. I thought we could work together.'

'And Brigham wrote a beautiful piece of music, "North Country Girl".'

Gervase's head snapped up. 'How the fuck did you know that?'

'I didn't,' said Suzy. 'But I do now. You found out he'd already contacted Joanie Cadiz and amazingly she'd bitten. So you took over negotiations but changed your name from Scott to Scott-Broughton.'

'I changed my name. That's not a crime.'

'But why did you do it at that point in time, Gervase? Tell me the truth. It's not hard to guess.'

For the first time, Gervase dropped his eyes and Suzy felt him weakening. He was a horrible man, she was sure of that.

But he had loved his cousin. 'OK. I'm not confessing to any wrongdoing. But . . .'

'You'll feel bad about this, Gervase, if you don't tell the truth now.'

'It was for Brig's benefit! Brig couldn't negotiate his way out of a paper bag. Joanie's management were tough people, of course, you'd expect nothing less. But she was lovely. I could deal with her and see off the lawyers. It was meat and drink to me. If we'd left it to Brig he'd have got tuppence-halfpenny and put it all up his nose.'

'Ah,' Suzy murmured, 'so you pretended it was you who'd written the song, and you did a deal with Joanie Cadiz for one big sum of money. Didn't you?'

'Christ.' Gervase looked disgusted but for the first time he was also professionally wary, narrowing his eyes. 'I'm not saying any more.'

'Yer not? Rags!' Fred Lamplugh had been taking this all in. The dog unwound from the hearth rug. Its maw was level with Gervase's face.

'OK, yes!' Gervase almost shouted. 'Yes. You're right.'

'And did you give Brig what he was owed from this one-off deal?' asked Suzy. 'Eighty per cent, maybe? No, I thought not. And then last year Joanie died, and Brig thought the rights would come back to the both of you and there was new money to be made? So you needed Brigham out of the way.'

'No! No, I never wanted Brigham hurt.'

Trent Packard was crying now. 'Oh God, please don't bully Mr S-B anymore. It was me who thought Brigham would be better out of the way and I told Parry. Everything I did, I only did it for you, Mr S-B.'

'Shut up,' Gervase snarled. 'Brigham died of natural causes. He was an alcoholic with multiple conditions.'

Suzy said, 'So did Palmer know about your conning Brigham out of his money?'

Gervase said, 'Of course he did. We were best mates. And Parry had no scruples.'

'But recently Brigham started to make a fuss, didn't he? Ownership of music is big news these days. So you went to your old accomplice Parry Palmer. He'd been your sidekick for years. He knew all about the deal with Joanie Cadiz and how you kept the money. Did Parry want more too? Was your best friend turning on you? Did you kill him?'

Gervase Scott-Broughton looked up at Suzy icily. 'You won't believe me. But I swear to God I had absolutely nothing to do with Parry Palmer's death. Palmer had been my friend for years. I supported the Academy because of him.'

'And that helped keep him quiet.'

'Yes.' Gervase spoke simply and clearly, all pomposity gone. 'Exactly. My sponsorship of the Academy kept Parry Palmer onside. It could be called blackmail, or it could be called synergy. Actually, I rated his chutzpah and his nerve. Palmer said and did what he liked. Big fish in a small pond, of course, but he claimed the pond. I wasn't sorry when he was killed, it suited me, but I had been close to him once.'

Suzy waited. There was something compelling about the reduced and drained Scott-Broughton telling the truth. She felt sure it *was* the truth.

He went on, 'I thought Palmer was a real man. I thought it was amusing how he behaved with women. I couldn't do it. I was repressed. You all talk about toxic masculinity, but it's just plain masculinity. Parry Palmer did what he liked. He kept women in their place and laughed at gays. I respected that. I would never have killed him or colluded in his killing.'

'And what about Freddie Lamplugh?'

Suzy was aware of the old farmer straightening up. This was the moment where things could get very nasty.

Gervase smiled. He was coming through this ordeal. 'I never had anything to do with Freddie Lamplugh's death either. He emailed me with his moaning threats to Parry Palmer, and of course I couldn't let Palmer down or he'd tell the truth about the song. I steered the Academy away from finding Parry guilty and I just ignored Lamplugh's emails.

I never believed he would come up to Caldfell. Not that I cared. But his death was very convenient and got the police out of our hair. I want to say now, for the record: I didn't kill Parry. It probably *was* Freddie, stupid incompetent little twat. And no one killed Brigham.'

Trent said suddenly, 'But that's not true. You really wanted Brig dead, didn't you?' Trent was pleading. 'Please say you wanted Brigham dead. Brigham was a real problem. So Parry killed him. I asked him to.'

Gervase's head snapped round to his henchman. 'How could Parry have killed Brigham? Parry was already dead.'

But Trent was vomiting onto the flagged floor. He groaned.

Fred Lamplugh said suddenly, 'Let 'em go. They're pathetic buggers.'

Suzy thought for a few minutes. Gervase was swaying on his knees. It had been a physical ordeal for him.

'What are you planning to do now?' she asked.

He said, gasping, 'Trent and I are flying out of here tonight. That's always been the plan.'

'So why were you so bothered about us coming to the farm?'

'Because Freddie Lamplugh's involvement suits us very well. If you start digging around, God knows what you'll find. Leave well alone, Ms Spencer.'

'So if I publish this recording . . .'

Gervase stopped laughing. 'Don't do that. My wife is a woman of tremendous integrity and high standards. And she's ill. I don't want her to know I stole Brigham's work. It would break Lauren's heart to know the truth. You could never prove that I made a real confession anyway. Not with a shotgun in my face. You know the truth. Now just let us go.'

Fred Lamplugh called his dog; with Rags' teeth bared, he untied Gervase and Trent.

'Get out of 'ere,' Fred said. 'But listen. This 'ere woman will find out who killed Freddie and blamed a murder on 'im.'

Gervase looked levelly at Suzy. 'Maybe you will. I hope not. And whether it was Freddie who killed him or someone else, Parry Palmer is dead and a lot of people are relieved. Me included. I'm sad but I'm not sorry. When all this has died down, I'll be back for the revamped Caldfell Chorus. I'll be welcomed with open arms. We're in a new world now, where the rich get the respect they deserve. Publish if you like, though it would kill my wife. I'll take my chance.'

Then he and his sidekick sidled out of the door, rounded up like sheep by the vigilant Rags. Within minutes the Land Cruiser had gone.

Suzy, Alex and Fred Lamplugh sat down on the creaking furniture.

'What a shit,' said Alex.

'Thanks for all that, Mr Lamplugh,' said Suzy. 'It doesn't seem much, but in a process of elimination, we can rule out Gervase Scott-Broughton. He's unprincipled and selfish, but I believe him when he says he didn't organize the deaths of Palmer or Freddie.'

'Maybe he didn't have to,' Alex said. 'Maybe someone else did it for him. Power attracts subservience and lackeys need to prove themselves. So maybe we're nearer the truth.'

'We may be nearer to the truth,' said Suzy, 'but we're no nearer to finding Eva Delmondo. We need to go back to Caldfell Hall.'

CHAPTER TWENTY-SEVEN

Avenge not yourselves, but rather give place unto wrath: for it is written, vengeance is mine; I will repay, saith the Lord.
Romans 12:19

The Advice Centre looked strange by night. Christopher had unlocked the door and pushed the hysterical Carly Martin inside. For the time being it was neutral ground, private, without alcohol to hand. And Robert was on his way. Christopher propped Carly on a chair and went into the kitchen to make hot, strong tea with sugar.

'Drink this,' he said to Carly. Snuffling, she drank deeply and grabbed a biscuit.

Robert arrived very quickly. Christopher said quietly, 'Carly's heard from a friend in London from the old days. She's been trying to trace her ex-partner Renee, though I'm not sure why.'

Carly looked up. 'I'm not deaf!' she shouted. 'I heard that. If you want to know, as soon as Lily got chosen for this big part, and there was stuff in the papers, I thought I ought to trace Renee. I didn't want her getting wind of this without me knowing.'

'But what if she did?' Robert asked. 'She has no claim on you or your daughter.'

'But I've got a claim on her, the cow. And I worried she might muscle in on the action, if she saw Lily was a star. She knew Lily's name and birthday because I was stupid enough to send her a letter about it when Lily was born. I thought there might be money in it for us. It's not easy being a single mother.'

'Nobody's doubting that,' said Christopher. 'But I thought Renee walked out on you.'

'Yes, she did. But babbies soften people up. Lily was a lovely babby. Anyway, I never heard from the selfish cow. But when Lily got famous, I thought that might flush her out.'

'So you asked a friend to try and trace her,' Robert said, 'and today you heard from him. What did he say?'

Carly fumbled with her phone and pushed it at Christopher. He moved next to Robert so they could both read the screen.

hi carly babe thnx for the gear you don't change you space cadet you Renee in the music world now big cheese at academy of voice no less d' you want to put the screws on or me do it for you?

Christopher and Robert looked at each other.

Christopher said, 'Good grief. This must be the woman Suzy was talking about. Irene Przybylski. Of course: Irene, Renee — same name.'

'And Suzy said there were pictures of Irene and a younger woman, taken somewhere which looked like the Lakes.'

Christopher stooped down, putting his face close to Carly's.

'If your friend is right, and bear in mind that we don't know where he got his information, then we probably know where Renee is now. But it would be wrong for you to do anything about it. Renee has no obligations to you or Lily.'

'What?' Carly's face twisted angrily. 'No obligation? She talked me into having a baby, then walked out on me. She owes me. And I'm going to see she pays up, the cow. Wait till people know. It'll be all over the net.'

'Carly,' Christopher said calmly, 'I don't think there's any way legally you would get any money out of Renee for Lily. And I hope you're not talking blackmail.'

'It's not blackmail.' Carly searched for the words. 'It's . . . it's justice.'

'Oh, Carly, be fair.' Christopher sighed. 'It would be very hard to prove that Renee owed you anything. You went back on the arrangement, after all.'

'Only because the stuff in the turkey baster turned out to be just piss! Pathetic. She chose the wrong man, and I found a real one.'

Robert could see the hurt on Christopher's face. Christopher said, 'You don't know that, Carly. The first sample might have been fine, and it just didn't take, that's all . . .'

Robert looked at him warningly.

'Anyway,' Christopher went on, 'that's not the point. The point is that there's nothing to be gained from you pursuing Renee now.'

'Oh no?' Carly turned her face to Christopher's, so the spittle hit him on the chin. 'Listen, I'm going to go down to London as soon as I have the dosh and I'm going to find Renee at her poncey Academy. And I'm going to make her pay for the way she deserted us. What did you say her name was now?'

Robert and Christopher looked at each other and said nothing.

'Don't you worry,' Carly snarled. 'I'll find out. There can't be that many academies of poncey whatever in London. Now, I want another drink.'

'I think a taxi might be more sensible,' said Robert. They stood up and walked to the door, with Carly loping and lurching between them, almost incapable of walking. They found a cab and when they opened the door she went in meekly enough. Christopher gave the driver the address in Pelliter.

Robert and Christopher walked on to the pub without speaking. Once seated, Christopher said, 'Well, maybe Irene Przybylski is Renee. Let's see if there's a picture on the web.' He used his phone, and squinted at an arty picture of the music professor.

'I can't be sure,' he said. 'She's about the same age. But this is a glamour shot and that's not how I remember Renee. She was a heavy woman, with brown hair. Nothing remarkable to look at but a remarkable character. People change a lot in sixteen years of midlife. I could get in touch. It makes sense. Maybe I should go to London and see for myself if Irene Przybylski is the Renee I remember.'

Robert thought about it, looking into his pint. 'That's not a bad idea.' It would give Christopher something to do. 'Why don't I give you Rachel's number? That's Suzy's friend who came up with the inside information about the Academy of Voice. She can help you to see the professor.'

'Thanks.' Christopher brightened. 'I'll think seriously about a trip to London. Carly isn't the only one who was deceived by Renee. I'd like to tackle her too.'

* * *

At the farm, Alex and Suzy looked at each other. Then Suzy glanced at her phone. It was over an hour since she had left Caldfell Hall and there was no message from Eva. 'Mr Lamplugh, we need to leave. We're worried about Eva.'

'Aye, yon Spanish-looking lass. You'd better go. Rags and I will be alreet. Ye'll come again?'

'Of course. And we'll do everything we can to find out what really happened to Freddie.'

'Aye. You do that. I won't have it that he killed himself. Or anyone else.'

'I promise you, Mr Lamplugh. But forgive us, we need to go.'

The old man nodded. 'Aye. Best do. It's getting late.'

In the car, Alex said, 'Any idea where Eva could be?'

'No. We need to go back to the Hall and see if any of the staff know where she is. Gervase and Trent have got half an hour on us. I think they'll have done a fast turnaround and left the place. They said they were all organized to leave tonight. They won't have had time to do anything to Eva, and why would they want to? They just wanted to keep her away from us till they left. They won't be there now.'

Suzy pulled up in front of the Hall and checked her phone. 'Last thing Eva said was that she was going into the cellar.'

'Well, she could easily have been trapped there. That's the first place to look,' said Alex.

The door of the Hall was firmly shut, though there were lights on the first floor.

'Mrs S-B is still here,' Suzy said. 'And Pearl. They must have staff. Someone will come to the door.'

She was right. The bouncer from earlier opened it to their knocking.

'I'm so sorry,' said Alex. 'I'm Alex Armstrong, the composer's wife. I've left something here. Can we come in?'

The man looked at her and then recognized her. 'Yeah, OK.' He wasn't wearing his lip mic; he looked tired.

'The funeral's all over?' Alex asked brightly.

'Yeah. The boss has left as well, in a hell of a hurry. But the wife is still here with her people.'

'I see, thanks. I think I left my tote bag in the kitchen area. I went in for some non-alcoholic wine. They weren't serving it on the trays, and I was dying of thirst. I think non-alcoholic drinks are de rigueur these days and I'm surprised the S-Bs were so slow delivering the Nozeco. Sorry, the kitchen's this way, isn't it? Don't mind us if you've got somewhere else you want to be.'

The bouncer looked dazed. Too much information. He wanted to escape. 'We'll be fine,' Alex was saying. 'We'll just pop in and look. Don't worry about us.'

'OK. Let me know when you want to be let out.'

'Sure, no trouble.'

The man smiled wearily and then receded into the back of the house where the staff hung out.

'That was brilliant, Alex. Two older women,' Suzy murmured. 'No threat there, then.'

They walked into the kitchen area. It was spotlessly clean with no evidence of Brigham's wake. Suzy closed the door behind them.

'Where can the cellar be?' Suzy asked.

'This bit of the Hall is an old Cumbrian farmhouse, basically,' said Alex. 'I've visited more than one with my parents in the past. The cellar will be downstairs past a large wooden door. I doubt they've bothered refurbing that. We're not going to be dealing with panic rooms or high security when it comes to kitchen supplies.' She went around the kitchen perimeter, carefully tapping on the walls.

And then they heard it. The tapping coming back. Alex moved quickly. It took her just seconds to locate a door in the still room off the kitchen.

'Thank goodness the key's still in the lock,' said Alex. 'If you want to trap someone in the cellar, it's much easier just to turn it and skedaddle.'

It took her quite an effort to turn the key. Eventually, the door flew open.

It was floodlit inside, so bright they both recoiled. Eva Delmondo was standing on the inside step.

'OMG, it's you, at last!' she snapped.' I've been stuck in here for a coupla hours. Luckily, I found an old comforter waiting for the garbage or I'd have frozen to death. What kept you? I need the john.' Eva sped past them, shouting over her shoulder, 'Don't go. You need to see something.'

'Is that half a bottle of whisky she has in her hand?' asked Alex.

'Looked like it. Maybe she's drunk the other half. She seems pretty wired. I wonder what happened.'

Eva was back almost immediately. 'Jeez, I needed that. You asked what happened? That shit Trent locked me in. He told me to go down there to check supplies and then he shut the door on me. I know it was him because he followed me a bit too close and as soon as I went down the steps the door slammed, and I heard the key rasping away.'

'Why did he want you locked in here?'

'He didn't want you talking to me. He thinks between us we're going to find some dirt on his precious boss.'

'He's right,' Suzy said. 'We have.' Suzy told her about Gervase Scott-Broughton's confession that he had conned his cousin.

'I knew there was something dodgy about that song business.'

'But it doesn't get us any nearer Parry's murderer.'

'Never mind that . . .' Eva sat at the kitchen table and motioned them to sit with her. She put the half-drunk bottle of Super Blend whisky on the table in front of her.

'Get this. The S-Bs as you know are crazy about recycling. But the bottles and other recyclable garbage are only collected every few weeks by specialists. Can you guess how many empty bottles of Super Blend there were down there in that basement — sorry, cellar?'

'A couple of thousand?'

'Very funny, Suzy. There were twenty-three. Brigham Broughton was the only Super Blend drinker. The bottles had his name on, just stuck on with a sticky label, but labelled, for sure. They were right at the back. I had to clear my way through about three hundred bottles to get to them.'

'But why did you bother?' Alex asked.

'A hunch. Hear me out, won't you?'

Alex smiled and nodded. Mollified, Eva went on, 'OK. On the day he died, Brigham Broughton was drinking whisky from his bottle. It smelled like a douchebag, so I swapped it for Jack Daniels. I thought if he was drinking himself comatose he might as well do it in style. I dumped his labelled bottle into the glass recycling behind the bar to save him from himself.'

'So the bottle he was drinking from got mixed up with all the other used bottles? And the bottle he had his last drink from wasn't the bottle he'd been enjoying all afternoon?' Suzy said.

'Exactly. Brigham normally drained a bottle of Super Blend at a sitting. There weren't any dregs. But this time — hey, here's half a bottle. The bottle I dropped into the bin.'

Eva paused and then leaned close to them, saying quietly, 'I don't know if the police looked at what Brigham was drinking. If they did, the bottle they would have tested would just have been pure bourbon. But the bottle he was really drinking from most of that afternoon went into the recycling, half full. That bottle could have been polluted. Tonight I was in there with nothing to do and hundreds of bottles. So I just put in a bit of time going through them all. And hey! I found this one. With Brigham Broughton's name on it. The only half-full bottle of Super Blend.'

'And what exactly do we do with it?' Alex asked.

'We get it tested!' said Eva triumphantly. 'I think it's been poisoned. It smells even worse than the usual British shit.'

Suzy said suddenly, 'Alex, do you remember something Trent said tonight which sounded delusional? He said that Parry Palmer had killed Brigham Broughton.'

'And we all ignored him because Palmer couldn't have killed Brigham. Palmer died first.'

'Yes, on the face of it,' Suzy said. 'But say Palmer put something in one of the Super Blend bottles and just waited to see what happened. Brigham didn't drink them in any order. He would have just got to the poisoned bottle eventually. Palmer must have known that Brigham would be installed at the Hall for a long time, drinking a bottle a day. Brigham might have only got to the poisoned bottle after Parry was dead.'

'So you think Parry Palmer and Trent got together to kill Brigham? Because they thought that was what Gervase wanted?' Eva asked.

'Something like that.'

'I think you might be right, Suzy. As usual.'

CHAPTER TWENTY-EIGHT

My son, give me thine heart, and let thine eyes observe my ways. Proverbs 23:26

It was one o'clock in the morning when Suzy came home. Robert was still up, prowling round the kitchen, on edge. Suzy had called him briefly before leaving Caldfell, but he'd heard nothing since. At her end, Suzy had seen Eva off to bed at the Hall, clutching the bottle of Super Blend, and then dropped Alex off at Tarnfield House.

When she finally walked into the kitchen, Robert jumped back.

'Suzy! You look awful!'

'Well, that's a nice welcome home!'

'But your face — it's all covered in white dust.'

Suzy went into the downstairs loo and looked in the mirror. It was true. The plaster dust from Fred Lamplugh's sitting room still clung to her face.

'It's from when I got caught up in a shotgun incident . . .'

'What?'

'It was OK. I wasn't in the line of fire.'

'And I thought I'd had a dramatic time! But you look done in. Would you like a nightcap? A little whisky?'

Suzy turned greenish under the dust. 'No! I don't think I could face whisky after what I've heard. You can make us a cup of tea and bring it to me in the bath. Then I'm crawling into bed. And you're going to join me and I'm going tell you about an incredible evening.'

'You and me both,' said Robert.

* * *

Despite the bath and the tea and the warmth, it was impossible for either of them to sleep.

'You go first,' said Suzy.

'OK. There's been a big scene tonight with Carly Martin. She finally told Christopher that she was helped at Caldfell Hall by Brigham Broughton.'

'Aha. So he was her inside man.'

'Yes. She had plans to meet him up at Caldfell. They've been friends for years. Carly wasn't welcome anywhere near the Hall, thanks to Eva. But Carly always has an eye for the main chance, so she'd arranged to see Brigham anyway, when she went up with Lily in the free cab.'

'And that's when she also saw the man she thought was Lily's natural father. Parry Palmer.'

'Yes. After that, Carly came straight back to Norbridge and hightailed it to London. She put a mate onto finding Renee, then she came back home. The next day she took a cab using Lily's cash and got as close to the Hall as she could, despite the first snowfall, before the big dump. She met Brigham on the road. He's known the area like the back of his hand since childhood. There's a shortcut from the road that no one else at the course knew about. They hiked a mile or so, through the snow, though apparently it wasn't so bad in the lee of the fell.'

'And I suppose drink and drugs fuelled them up.'

'Yes, I should think so. They managed the walk anyway. Back at the Hall, Brigham found her somewhere to hide in a storeroom and gave her the weapon. She was supposed to hit

Parry Palmer. It seems that Brigham was someone else who wanted Palmer dead, so he set her up to do it. He was going to pay her with money he thought he had coming.'

'Ah, I know what that might be about, but I'll tell you later.'

'Anyway,' Robert went on, 'Carly wanted revenge on Palmer, of course.'

Suzy nodded. She thought about what Gervase Scott-Broughton had said: that Parry Palmer treated women as a commodity. Toys. She thought of Ayesha Tomkins' experience. It fitted. Parry Palmer would have found it both challenging and funny to coerce lesbians into sex.

'But listen, Suzy. There's more. Carly has been trying to find her ex-partner, Renee. Some cockeyed idea about getting money out of her now Lily's becoming famous. Anyway, Carly's contact in London has identified Renee. You're not going to believe this. Apparently, Renee is a big cheese at the Academy of Voice—'

'It's Irene Przybylski, isn't it?'

'It certainly all adds up. Irene went to Oxford and hung out in the London gay scene around twenty years ago. She had a younger lover, and according to you and Rachel there are pictures of what looks like the two of them in the Lake District.'

'But if Irene is Renee, surely she would have recognized Palmer as the man who seduced Carly as soon as she started work at the Academy. She'd met the man, hadn't she? And kicked him out?'

'That only took a few minutes. And it was in a very different context.'

'Carly recognized him.'

'Yes, but she spent the night with him.'

'Christopher knew Renee well. Why can't he just identify Irene?'

'Because we can't find any suitable pictures of Irene online for Christopher to see! So Christopher is thinking of going down to London to face her.'

'Well, it would certainly solve part of this mystery. But wait till you hear about my night!'

Suzy told him about Fred Lamplugh and the shotgun, and Gervase's confession to defrauding his cousin, plus Eva's discovery of the half-full whisky bottle with the strange smell.

At about three in the morning, they were finally talked out.

But as Robert put out the bedside light, the last thing he heard was Suzy saying, 'Robert . . .'

'What?'

'We still don't know who killed Parry Palmer.'

* * *

In the morning, they sat over coffee in the kitchen, bleary-eyed. Suzy went back to bed when Robert left for the Advice Centre. She was exhausted, but she kept going over it all in her head. However much she turned it round, she still had no idea who could have murdered Parry Palmer. It was someone who skilfully wielded a penknife, strong enough to overpower him and cut the carotid artery. Someone who hated him enough to want him dead. How many of the people who were originally in the frame should go back on the suspect list? Ayesha, Callum . . . she needed to rethink them all. And what about Dave? Maybe his concern for his son led him to murder. And he hated Parry anyway, he was fit enough and strong enough, he worked as the manager of a farm shop. He would know about butchering . . .

Her phone rang. It was Jake. 'Hi, Mum.'

'Hi, Jake.'

'Mum, I'm sorry we've been messing you around, but Mae and I really do want to come over. How does a week on Saturday sound?'

'I think that's OK. I'll just check.'

'Cool.'

Keep calm, thought Suzy, though she would have cancelled a date with George Clooney for her son. She didn't ask whether Jake meant lunch, or supper, or a flying visit for a cup of coffee on the way to other friends. Anything would do.

'Yes, next Saturday would be all right.'

'Can we do lunch, Mum?'

'Yes, sure.'

'That's great. We'll be there about twelve. Oh, is Molly going to be around?'

'I'm not sure. I could ask her. She might like to come back this weekend. She's finished with that new boy, and I think her old boyfriend from the village might be back on the scene.'

'Mum, that's her business.'

Suzy felt like snapping: *Well, you wanted to know if she was around.* But instead she said evenly, 'I'll see.'

'OK, but don't fuss about it.'

A few years earlier, Suzy would have told her son not to be so rude. But these days she walked on eggshells. She had no idea how Mae felt about Jake's family. The last thing she wanted to do was create a chance for a rift. Mae was always pleasant, but there was something elite about her. She was certainly very sophisticated. Jake had been such a happy-go-lucky, affectionate boy. Now he was always slightly curt, as if his mother was a bit of an embarrassment. There was something serious going on. Maybe they really were getting married. Her heart lurched. If Mae was to be her daughter-in-law, she would have to love her, whatever.

'OK, Jake, see you a week on Saturday. Lunchtime, you said?'

'Yep, that would be OK. We want to get back home in the afternoon.' And Jake was gone. Home now for Jake was his flat with Mae in Durham. Of course. That was how things went.

Suzy snapped out of a reverie about time passing and started thinking about what she might cook for their visit. Lasagne or something like that would be too everyday. A roast would be too formal. Was Mae a vegetarian? She wasn't even sure about Molly anymore, though she remembered the smell of bacon wafting through the house when Molly had visited to mend her broken heart a week ago. Of course, bacon might be justifiable when you were suffering, but an outrage when you bounced back. The young could always justify themselves.

And should they eat in the dining room, which was a bit posh, or the kitchen, which was a bit routine? They couldn't go outside. Spring might be round the corner, but from where Suzy was lying, looking out of her bedroom window at the grey unyielding sky, it was still out of sight.

Still, Jake was coming to visit. And Robert would be at home. Perhaps he would have a new hearing aid by Saturday and be able to hear everything Mae said. The thought made Suzy smile.

She got up and decided to polish the copper pans hanging in the kitchen. They had been there for decades, inherited by Mary and passed on to Robert. They needed cleaning. And it was about time she did the kitchen floor as well. If spring were to peep over the windowsill, it would recoil in horror. It was a mistake to treat lunch with Jake as a royal visit. But she still wanted The Briars to look its best. She should tackle the winter grime. Sometimes a menial job left your subconscious free to work. And Suzy was still worried by the candlelight killer. Who could it be, and why? She felt that the answer was somewhere in all the bits they had pulled together. But the picture wouldn't come clear. The kitchen floor was a different matter. She found the mop and bucket.

* * *

The next few days passed quietly. Suzy caught up with work from Manchester as well as with spring cleaning. Robert went to the Advice Centre as usual. Christopher had started to worry because Carly hadn't been back. Lily didn't turn up either. Because Edwin wasn't around, she wasn't practising at the Advice Centre. He and Alex had flown back to Frankfurt for a few days to sort out their apartment.

Christopher was relieved to get a text message from Carly after two days.

'I've heard from Carly,' he said to Robert. 'I think she and Lily might have gone away, maybe to London. I'll forward you her message and see what you make of it.'

Robert read the message that pinged into his phone. It was enigmatic and garbled but typical Carly: *Found frenetic too messy at all back soon. C and L.*

'Looks unintelligible but I get the drift,' Robert said. It says she'll be back soon. And when Edwin gets back from Germany, he and Lily will need to start rehearsing again. Carly will get Lily back to Caldfell for that. Lily's performance is worth big money.'

'True,' said Christopher. 'But I hate to think of Lily sofa surfing with Carly's mates. Like I said, I'm seriously thinking of going down to London myself and tackling Irene Przybylski. She could so easily be Renee. Same age, same sort of basic look. If Carly is trying to trace Renee, I'd like to get in first. If I go for the next few days, would you cover for me?'

'Of course I would.'

'It will probably take me mere seconds to establish whether Irene is Renee. I just need to see her in person. I appreciate it won't help much in Suzy's search for Parry Palmer's killer, but it's possible this Przybylski woman is more involved than we think. Maybe she's known about Palmer impregnating Carly for years but then finally found a way to get rid of him, through Freddie Lamplugh. Who knows?'

'But if you do find Carly in London, don't do anything rash, Christopher. Leave your armour and your white horse in Norbridge.'

Christopher laughed. 'I just want to know if Irene is Renee. Remember, Renee owes me an explanation. She never told me that Carly's baby wasn't mine, and she just sidelined me. I was betrayed too.'

* * *

In Norbridge, in the same week, Dave Oldcastle went back to work at the farm shop. The strain of Parry Palmer's murder, then his worry that his son Callum might be implicated, then finding Freddie Lamplugh's body, had all upset and disoriented him. It was offset by his success as the chorus director for Gervase's scratch concert, but he still found it hard to get back into his routine. One good thing was that he and Callum were speaking regularly. He had the crisis at Caldfell to thank for that.

Marcus Sotheby had taken Ayesha Tomkins on holiday to the Maldives. Ayesha was still upset about Freddie's death. But as the sun sank over the Indian Ocean, winter in Cumbria was receding. Ayesha had told her son the truth, and he had not been surprised. His life was looking up. Now Parry Palmer wasn't taking the evening classes at the Academy of Voice, he had been taken up by the new tutor and persuaded to audition successfully for a diversity choir that had gigs booked throughout London. Marcus had his big concerts too, not least the *Sacred Spring* premiere in May. Things were looking good.

In London, a new term had started at the Academy of Voice. It had been easy to replace Parry Palmer with a quality lecturer. On one level the whole atmosphere was better. But the University of North London had ordered an enquiry. Irene was still at her desk, but she could sense the blame game gaining momentum. It was no good saying the authorities had dragged their feet over Freddie Lamplugh's complaint because Gervase had nobbled them. The uni didn't want to know. It was easier for them to accuse Irene of mishandling things — creating an environment where a distressed student could commit murder and suicide.

Alex flew back from Frankfurt midweek. Edwin remained for a few days, wrapping up his German commitments now that they were staying on in Cumbria. Tarnfield House felt more like home. Alex noticed the daffodils in the large, well-stocked garden, coming through with their bulging spear tips, the sign of flowers to come. There was a bank of spindly, fragile snowdrops dusting the green lawn. The apartment in Frankfurt had a lovely balcony but it wasn't the same as having your own earth. She rang Suzy.

'Hi, I'm back in Cumbria. How are you fixed this week? Should we go and see how Eva's doing? And old Fred Lamplugh? We said we'd go back.'

'That would be good.'

'I'll drive us to Caldfell,' Alex said. 'You did the chauffeuring last time. Will you call Eva? I can't wait to see Lily again.'

'Robert says Carly and Lily have gone away. But they've heard from Carly, and she says they'll be back soon.'

'Yes, I know. Edwin wrote to Lily saying she could have this week off and then start again next Monday. Lily said she was looking forward to it.'

'You've been very involved with her.'

'Too involved? That's what you think, isn't it? I'm not stupid, Suzy. I know I need to back off a bit. But until the premiere of *The Sacred Spring*, I'm going to see she practises until she can't put a foot wrong. And if it's the success we hope, she's going to need guidance in the music business. Guidance which I could give. I've been thinking about this. I could make it work with Carly too. She'd be crazy to turn down my help.'

Carly is crazy, Suzy thought. But all she said was, 'I'm glad you've thought it through. See you tomorrow?'

'I'll pick you up at ten.'

CHAPTER TWENTY-NINE

And they came unto the brook of Eshcol and cut down from thence a branch with one cluster of grapes. Numbers 13:23

Suzy enjoyed the drive back to Caldfell. It would be nice to see it in the spring. As a passenger in Alex's luxurious car, she could appreciate the scenery. It was a clear grey day, with high cloud and a fresh wind, but the breeze was softer, and it wasn't raining. The car cruised round Norbridge and along the coast to the road to Workhaven, then cut inland towards Caldfell. The clumps of windblown trees were tinted with green. Soon there would be lambs.

The driveway up to Caldfell Hall was punctuated by large tubs of flowers — forced daffodils and fat hyacinths ahead of season, brought in by landscape stylists from Manchester. *It's beautiful but bizarre*, Suzy thought. Alex parked outside, next to a pink van with the logo 'Cleaning Perfection'. They saw that the Hall door was open. Inside the big room, four women in gingham overalls were polishing and wiping busily as a man scoured the huge fireplace. Next to him was a huge arrangement of orchids and palms, presumably to fill the hearth. Whatever was happening outside, spring had come to Caldfell Hall — and been paid for.

Eva came sashaying over towards them. 'Hi, guys! I saw the car come up the drive.' She was wearing a blue cotton boilersuit and a scarf knotted around her head, with two black kiss-curls protruding. 'We're setting the place up for the new season. Gervase will be back for the *Sacred Spring* premier, but he's not staying. Even so, he wants this place kept running as a family seat. He's masterminding all this from the States. Mrs S-B has stayed here. She didn't want to travel. She's not well.'

'Rosie the Riveter meets Leonard Bernstein,' murmured Alex drily as they followed Eva through to the stairway.

'I've got your old room now,' Eva said to Alex. 'Fantastic, isn't it? Though those creepy old stones out the window give me the willies.'

'Really? I always found them comforting. Evidence of human resilience.'

'Yeah well, we've got that in here as well. Mrs S-B is hanging on upstairs. Her staff are a nightmare. Pearl's in charge, of course, but I'm supervising the seasonal changeover across the premises. Gervase is calling me regularly. Trent's off the scene. He must have done something to upset Gervase.'

'Like colluding with Parry Palmer to poison Brigham,' Suzy proffered.

'Could be. Gervase wouldn't like that.'

As they reached the landing, Pearl was coming downstairs. Eva stopped.

'Hi, Pearl. Everything OK in the royal suite? You remember Mrs Armstrong, of course. And Suzy Spencer, who was supposed to make the podcast.'

Pearl's impassive face swivelled between the two visitors. She nodded. 'I remember you two. You came to tell Mrs S-B about that boy's body. Freddie Lamplugh.'

'Yes,' said Suzy. 'And Mrs S-B was very nice about my work. Please give her my best.' Pearl nodded and went on down the stairs.

Eva ushered them into the huge bedroom which now doubled as her office. She seemed to be in command. 'I've ordered some coffee and lunch for us in here. The food is delicious, I must say. I've put on a coupla pounds. But it'll soon come off when I'm home.'

'When do you fly back?'

'Next week, I hope. I'm hoping to go back in the Gulfstream if Gervase will sign off on it. I could get used to living like this.'

Suzy smiled. 'And what about Brigham's Super Blend bottle?'

'It's already at the lab. All paid for by Gervase, though he doesn't know it.' Eva laughed.

'Have you seen old Fred?' Suzy asked.

'I called by. He's not in a good place.'

'We're thinking of dropping in this afternoon.'

There was a rapping at the door. Eva opened it and Pearl stood on the threshold.

'Hey, Eva. Mrs S-B would like your visitors to come up and see her.' Pearl indicated Suzy with a head movement. 'She likes you.'

'And whatever Mrs S-B wants, Mrs S-B gets,' Eva said tetchily. 'There goes our gossipy lunch. Guys, report back to me on your way down.'

'Follow me,' said Pearl brusquely. Suzy and Alex did as they were told.

* * *

Lauren Scott-Broughton was lying in her French-style bedroom on a mountain of white pillows. Her shiny, steel-grey hair swept down in a smooth curtain over her right cheekbone. On the left side it was just a soft fuzz, revealing a perfect ear with plain metal studs in four piercings. Her skin was white and smooth, pulled tight over her skull. Her eyes were set in deep wrinkles, but when she opened them, they were almond-shaped slits of glittering pale blue, looking out through the pain.

'Here they are,' said Pearl gruffly.

'Suzy and Alex,' Lauren said in her soft voice. Then she smiled. Her lips still had some colour and her teeth were perfect.

'Come sit on the bed, Suzy — and Alex, you take the chair. It is *so* lovely to see different faces. How is Edwin's work going, Alex?'

'He's very pleased with it. He thinks it's the perfect vehicle for Marcus Sotheby and Lily Martin.'

'Ah yes. A star is born. Clever combination. And how are you, Suzy? I've been watching some of your work while I've been confined to bed. I very much enjoyed *Living Lies*. I got it on catch-up TV.'

Living Lies was a show Suzy had devised before the pandemic. It was about people who were literally living a lie. It had hardly been an international hit but it had done well in the UK. Suzy was astonished that Lauren had found it.

Lauren went on, 'The programme shows such compassion for the deceivers, but at the same time a ruthless search for the truth. Non-judgemental. Very clever.' That was exactly Suzy's aim. Lauren Scott-Broughton was perceptive. People rarely discussed Suzy's work except in terms of ratings or sponsorship potential. It was exhilarating to hear it talked about with insight.

'And, of course, there's Hiram King's excellent exposé of scams and scammers, on Linkflex, which we discussed before. So very much in the present. Now, gals, would you like a drink? Some fruit?'

She closed her eyes as her head dropped back, nodding towards the bedside table. On it was a silver bowl with nectarines and grapes.

'Have some grapes,' Pearl said. 'They're Californian. Ordered specially. Cut them off the bunch.'

Suzy glanced at the bed. Lauren seemed to have sunk into a doze.

'These are beautiful,' said Suzy, picking up the some tiny, light, fragile fruit scissors. 'Such detail, and pearl-handled.'

Lauren seemed to speak in her sleep. 'Yes, pearl-handled . . .' Then she snapped awake. 'You're very clever, Suzy. How did you know?'

'I suppose I must have seen something like it on the *Antiques Roadshow*.'

'Another very good British TV programme.' Lauren laughed, but weaker now. Her voice sounded tired and distant. Then she seemed to rally, and fixed Suzy with a sudden widening of her pale blue eyes. 'But I've been interested in your production record, Suzy. In fact, it occurred to me that you might like to develop some ideas for me.'

'Really?' Suzy felt a little flicker of excitement.

'Absolutely. Nothing to do with Gervase, of course. I have my own media company and I'm looking for something new. I may be very ill, but I have some time left. I want to leave a legacy of good ideas, from women particularly. I think I might like to fly you over to the States to meet some people.'

'Goodness, thank you.' Suzy's voice sounded rather hoarse. She was rarely short of something to say, but that was all she could manage.

'You should go now,' Pearl intoned in her expressionless voice. 'Mrs S-B is very tired.' The woman in the bed looked as if she were comatose. Suzy wondered if she should ask her to repeat what she said. But Lauren was clearly exhausted. Alex and Suzy tiptoed away.

'That was interesting,' said Alex. 'She seems very taken with you, Suzy.'

'Well, she's certainly researched me. It's nice to be taken seriously. I'm glad we went to see her again.'

* * *

But Eva was cross when they were back in her room.

'Typical of Mrs S-B, grabbing all your time. And Pearl waits on her hand and foot. They've sent the other staff away.'

Suzy had a thought. 'How do they get Mrs S-B in and out of a place like this now she's bedridden?'

'Oh, there's the elevator for her exclusive use. Takes a deluxe wheelchair.'

'And where does it come out?'

'Search me. I've never seen it. I just heard Pearl referring to it. Mrs S-B was still walking about until after Brigham's funeral. It was after that she went downhill. When Gervase skedaddled back to the States in a hurry.'

Alex was staring out of the window at the standing stones. 'It's getting a bit murky out there. If we want to go and see old Fred, we'd better get a move on, Suzy. No time for lunch now.'

Eva hugged Suzy emotionally. 'Hey, sister, it's been great working with you. I loved your Poirot-style supper party. I'll do all I can to get over to Tarnside before I go home.'

'Tarnfield.'

'Whatever. And so long, Mrs Armstrong. Give my love to hubby. And your little red-haired protégée. Silly Lily. But she coped all right in the end, hey?'

Alex just smiled but Suzy could see what she was thinking: *No thanks to you, Eva.*

But Eva looked genuinely sorry to see them go.

On the way to the car, Alex said, 'So was Mrs S-B really offering you some work? Did I actually hear her mention a trip to New York?'

'That was the impression I got. Though she seems very ill. It would have to be soon, I think.'

'Mmm. Well, I hope she's sincere.'

'Why shouldn't she be? Are you saying that rich billionaires would want to sponsor Edwin's classical music, obviously, but not my TV programming?'

'Oops! That's a bit touchy. Very unlike you, Suzy. Of course I didn't mean that. Anyway, never mind. Let's go and see Fred Lamplugh.'

But when they reached the farm, the front door was tight shut. Fred Lamplugh wasn't at home. Suzy frowned, disappointed. She liked the old farmer and felt for him. They got back in the car and left the village.

Alex drove carefully back through the dusk. They didn't talk. Lauren Scott-Broughton's astonishing invitation had distracted Suzy. She was looking out of the window at the fells, and seeing herself walking down Fifth Avenue after pitching brilliant ideas to wealthy American media moguls. But when they arrived in Tarnfield, Suzy felt a little guilty for being waspish with her friend. There was a slight coolness between them.

'Thanks for driving, Alex. I'm not sure we'll see Eva again, despite her good intentions. She can't even remember the name of the village.'

'I'm sure she's desperate to be back home in the States. You were the only person in the whole Caldfell scenario that she seemed to warm to, Suzy.'

They were parked at The Briars, and Suzy felt bad. She'd been touchy that afternoon because Lauren had unsettled her. She wanted to reconnect with Alex. Her friend's involvement with Lily, Suzy's own work worries, plus concern about Robert and worry over Jake had kept them apart lately. But Alex had been there for her that day.

In a rush, she told Alex all about her nervousness over Jake's visit and what he might want to tell her. She and Alex had been at their closest when Jake was in his teens, playing in a jazz band. Alex had known Jake a long time.

'Never forget, Suzy, you have two lovely children — and Jake still wants to come and see you,' Alex said. 'If he's getting married, he's probably far more anxious than you are about having to break the news. You're very lucky compared with so many of us.'

That was true. Alex still longed to be a mother and here was Suzy moaning about it. 'Forgive me, Alex. Something's got to me this afternoon.'

'I've been tense too,' said Alex. 'I'm really anxious about Carly and Lily. Edwin seems sure that they'll be back next week when Lily starts rehearsals again. But I'm worried. Say something has happened to them in London?'

'Yes, you're right. It's odd they've gone away like that. But let's see what happens. There isn't much we can do.' Suzy kissed her friend. 'Let's go to the Plough for dinner on Saturday night,' she said. 'As long as Robert has got himself a hearing aid.'

Alex laughed. 'Done!'

CHAPTER THIRTY

The beginning of strife is as when one letteth out water: therefore leave off contention, before it be meddled with.
Proverbs 17:14

In Bloomsbury, Rachel Cohen and Christopher Murray sat opposite Irene Przybylski in her elegant top-floor apartment. The customary cold white wine was on the glass-topped table.

'I'm glad you came,' Irene said. 'And I'm sorry to disappoint you.'

'You don't disappoint me,' answered Christopher. 'Now I've met you I'd be sorry if you were Renee. But there's really no resemblance.'

'But there are similarities, I can see that. Both in our late fifties, both on the gay scene. Both with a younger lover at one stage, with connections to the north. My girlfriend hated my fame, small though it was. She was horrified when I got trolled and abused online.'

'Maybe Parry Palmer was targeting you. He could troll you anonymously. And he certainly seems to have been a misogynist. But there's one other thing to check on. Carly Martin's mate in London is a bloke on the edge of the music scene. He was looking for Renee for her. He said Renee was at the Academy of Voice. Do you have any other teachers or alums who might fit the bill?'

'So they would need to be between fifty and sixty, female, gay. There could be dozens of people fitting that description with Academy connections. You must have known Renee's surname in the past.'

'You know, I can't remember, which seems crazy. Anyway, names change.'

'Absolutely. Look at Gerry Scott and Gordon Broughton. So Renee could be called anything now. But there must be pictures.'

Christopher said, 'I've gone through all my old emails and social media accounts. Funnily enough there isn't even a photograph of Renee. Carly, her ex-partner, practically lives on social media, but she hasn't got any pictures or posts of the past either.'

'Well, a gay woman wanting a child might keep her head down. You can get a lot of hate online for something like that.'

Rachel stood up. 'Thanks so much for seeing us, Irene. If by any chance Carly Martin makes the same wrong deduction and comes after you, at least you're warned. You don't want to be hit over the head with a piece of wood like poor Edwin Armstrong.'

'Don't worry.' Irene laughed. 'I'll be watching out. Seriously, if this woman does try to contact me, I'll let you know straight away.'

On the steps outside the art deco building, Rachel asked Christopher if he was going to stay any longer in London.

'I think I'll go back tomorrow,' he said. 'I have no idea how to find Carly and Lily, and I'm not going to try asking round the druggy corners of London.'

Rachel smiled. 'Why don't you come out for a meal tonight with me and some friends? You'd like my friend Howard. He's in a Klezmer band.'

'I'm not too sure about Klezmer — I'm more of a Mozart man.'

'Well, that's handy. Howard's brother is coming. He's a violinist with the London Symphony Orchestra.' Rachel looked at Christopher appraisingly. 'He's gay and he likes walking in the Lakes. You might have a lot in common. You're not Jewish, are you?'

'No. I'm an Anglican, I'm afraid.'

'Pity.' Rachel laughed. 'Come to supper anyway.'

'I'd love to. But I should call Robert first. He needs to know that we haven't found Renee.'

* * *

When Suzy got home from Caldfell, Robert was busy in the kitchen. He turned round and smiled. 'I'm defrosting a Suzy Spencer special. Cumberland sausage in onion and apple gravy. How was Eva? There's some red wine opened. I've got a PCC meeting at the church tonight. But we can have a nice supper first and you can tell me about your trip.'

'Great. And have you heard from Christopher?'

'Yes. I don't know whether it's good or bad news, but Irene Przybylski isn't the infamous Renee. You were right about her having a lover from the north, though. They split up because she couldn't stand the pressure from social media when Irene did well. That's why Irene's presence online is rather muted.'

'Oh, well that's that.' Suzy felt suddenly flat and disappointed.

So Irene wasn't Renee. And, frankly, did it matter? This murder case was at a dead end. Literally. She had given it three goes with Jed and Ro, embarrassing herself every time, but she was still getting nowhere. Maybe she should do what they said and let it be.

And Suzy was also distracted. She was still thinking about Lauren Scott-Broughton's astonishing offer. Of course, it could just have been flattery — or a sort of power play. But it had lit a little spark of ambition inside Suzy. Even if Lauren was crazed with illness, or just toying with her, she was a contact in the global world of media.

There was an alert and Suzy looked at her phone. A garbled text message from her daughter. Molly was in York; Jake was in Durham. Molly could make it for lunch with Jake and Mae as long as Suzy or Robert could get her back to Norbridge for a train to York in the afternoon. *Nice of Molly to condescend to join her mother*, Suzy thought angrily.

Suzy was tired, scratchy and low. Why did everyone take her for granted? She had to beg just to get her family together. How would Jake and his smart girlfriend have reacted if she'd said, 'No can do for your lunch — I've got a meeting in Manhattan'?

She turned to Robert. 'I've had a mangled message from Molly about coming to lunch a week on Saturday with Jake and Mae. I think it means yes, but she'll need a lift to the station in the afternoon.' She held up the phone for Robert to see. He read: *In hurry yes to lunch will need lifting rain Norbridge ration spk soon Molls.*

He laughed. 'Predictive text. Bloody nightmare. It knows better than you every time!'

'True.' Suzy sipped her wine and then sat up straight — something had struck her.

'Robert, why don't you let me see Carly's text to Christopher? You said it was a bit garbled. Maybe that was mangled by predictive text as well.'

'Interesting thought.' Robert left off peeling potatoes and found his phone. He read out the message to Suzy, who then looked at it: *Found frenetic too messy at all back soon. C and L.*

'I suppose it makes more sense than *lifting rain Norbridge ration*. But "frenetic" doesn't seem like a Carly sort of word.'

'But that's the trouble with Carly. She's not totally stupid. She'll say something smart even though she seems like a complete ignoramus. She did once tell me she was a fan of Hiram King, your latest media star.'

'Thanks.' Suzy was used to people disparaging her programmes, but it sounded harsh from Robert. So, watching Hiram King proved Carly was an idiot, did it? It made her doubly grateful for the appreciation from Lauren

Scott-Broughton. Then she thought — there's no time like the present. Go for it.

'Rob, how would you feel if I got some work in the States?'

'Pardon? Did I hear that correctly? I still haven't got a hearing aid fitted.'

Suzy shouted irritably, 'I said, how would you feel if I got some work in the States? The USA. I had a meeting with Lauren Scott-Broughton today at Caldfell Hall. She was really complimentary about my shows. She says she'll be in touch about possible development work for her own company. Nothing to do with Gervase.'

'But I thought you were cutting down on big projects and could afford to work more locally now? Anyway, are you sure she was serious?'

Why is it so surprising? Suzy thought. Robert was reacting just like Alex. She said angrily, 'Why shouldn't Lauren Scott-Broughton appreciate my TV work? And I resent the implication that Carly Martin likes my programmes because she's dumb.'

'Suzy! That's not what I meant. I meant the exact opposite. I meant Carly was bright enough to enjoy them.'

'Really? It didn't sound like that. It's set me wondering, Robert. Maybe you want me at home in Tarnfield so I don't embarrass you by making daytime television. And maybe that's what's embarrassing Jake in front of Mae. She probably only respects people who loll around reading Marcel bloody Proust.'

'Suzy!'

'And if you say calm down, I'll throw these plates at you.'

'Of course I won't say calm down. But you got my remark completely wrong, and you know you did. But, if I'm absolutely honest, I don't want you getting more involved with the Scott-Broughtons. And I certainly don't want you going to the States.'

'There are direct flights to New York from Newcastle.'

'Suzy, please, this isn't what we planned for our future together.' Robert put the supper on the table.

'Well, what we planned might have suited you more than it suited me. You've never been very ambitious.'

Her remark stung and she knew it. They ate in silence. Then Robert said, 'I can't talk about this now, Suzy. I've got to go to this PCC meeting at the church. Please don't agree to anything with Mrs Scott-Broughton till we've discussed it.'

'There isn't anything to discuss. Yet. It was just something she threw out. She said she'd be in touch. I have no idea what it might lead to. But if it happens, Robert, I want to do it. It's exciting.'

Robert finished his supper and got up. He said coldly, 'It's the exact opposite of what we've talked about for our future, Suzy. I think this is because you don't want to live the life that we planned. Not with me, an old man going deaf. And maybe worse. If that's how you feel, you can go to America.'

Robert rarely lost his temper. His coldness was worse. Suzy felt a sudden shiver. But she wasn't going to give in. She watched him stride out of the kitchen and heard him banging up the stairs. He went out to his church meeting without saying goodbye.

Suzy sat and drank the rest of the wine.

* * *

By nine o'clock Suzy felt tired and drained, sick of trying to watch TV. There was no point waiting for Robert to come back to start round two of their fight. She went upstairs to bed. About an hour later she woke to hear Robert going into the spare room. Well, if that was how he felt, sod him. She settled into an uneasy sleep. At three o'clock in the morning, the witching hour again, she woke alone. She got up and went to her desk in the attic. It was cold. She wrapped herself in a blanket and made herself think.

And then she found herself doodling. That was interesting. What was it that convinced Jed Jackson that Freddie had meant to kill Parry Palmer? A handwritten note — his plan.

But it would be so easy to write something on top of a messy handwritten note, if you could get hold of one.

Something old Fred Lamplugh had said nagged at her. It was very important.

Suddenly she remembered. Yes. When they had talked about Eva, he'd said she was 'a glamour-puss, not like the other one'. Who was 'the other one'? Had someone else from Caldfell Hall turned up — to get a sample of Freddie's writing?

Gervase Scott-Broughton had counted himself out as the murderer, and Suzy believed him. A process of elimination. She should stop agonizing about who had motive, because everyone did. She should just start eliminating people on the grounds of practicality. Who could have done it, if you looked at absolutely everyone.

She started to go over all the people she had come across in this, the strangest of her cases. She studied all of them, one by one, all over again, however unlikely. Slowly, a theory started to form. It was crazy but it was possible.

Suzy looked back at Carly's text message. She was right: 'frenetic' wasn't a Carly word. *Found frenetic too messy at all back soon. C and L.* But what if the words Carly had tried to type in a hurry were something else? Like Molly's *lifting rain Norbridge ration*. Bloody predictive text, as Robert had said.

And then she knew. It all clicked into place, and she was suddenly very cold and very certain. And very angry.

It was six o'clock in the morning. Every bone in Suzy's body wanted to run to Robert in the spare room and tell him what she had suddenly deduced.

But what if he was still angry? He rarely went so cold on her that she feared waking him. And he had been right in his reaction to her dreams of going to America. She had indulged in the idea of going back on their plans and becoming a player in the world of media. She felt too ashamed and too proud to go to him and tell him she was sorry.

Now, she wanted to go back to Caldfell and find out if her theory was correct — if it was, it changed everything. She needed to go now. But not on her own. She wasn't safe to drive with her mind on fire and a bottle of wine still sloshing round her system.

Alex was an early riser and Edwin was away. Suzy picked up her phone. 'Alex. Thank goodness you answered. I really need you. You've got to listen to me.'

There was silence. Then Alex said, 'OK . . .'

Suzy knew she was babbling. 'Alex, we go back a long way. We've worked on a murder together before. I'm so sorry I snapped at you yesterday. You were right. I was making a silly mistake. Look, I need you now. We must go back to Caldfell Hall. I want you to come with me. We can be there by eight o'clock if we set off right away. I think I know what's been going on. It seems incredible but I think I'm right. I can tell you in the car. Can you pick me up?'

'Suzy, you must be mad.'

'Maybe. But not as mad as the murderer. Please, Alex.'

Alex said slowly, 'We do go back a long way. I owe you. Without you I wouldn't have Edwin. And I trust you. I'm sorry I was insensitive yesterday. OK, if you want to go to Caldfell, we'll go. I'll meet you at the top of the lane in fifteen minutes.'

'Thank you, Alex. You're a good mate. Thank you so much.'

Before she left, Suzy grabbed a pen and scrawled a note to Robert.

Robert,
I'm so sorry. I've been a total idiot, but I get it all now. I'm going to Caldfell to make sure I'm right. Alex is driving. Text me if you still love me.
Suzy

She left the note on the kitchen table and ran up the lane to meet her friend.

CHAPTER THIRTY-ONE

The driving is like the driving of Jehu the son of Nimshi; for he driveth furiously. 2 Kings 9:20

The journey to the west coast wasn't easy. It started raining — a fierce spattering shower coming full on to the windscreen. Alex was a skilful driver, but farm vehicles seemed to lurch out of hidden gateways without warning and there was congestion in Norbridge. Suzy had imagined telling Alex all her theories, but Alex was concentrating and driving as fast as she could without aquaplaning on the road.

And anyway, although Suzy was now certain of the basic facts, she wanted to tie up every loophole. She was convinced that Carly and Lily were in danger. Anything she said to Alex might alarm her.

Suzy had to decide what to do first. As they turned onto the road leading to Caldfell, Alex seemed relaxed at the wheel for the first time.

'So what's this all about, Suzy?'
'I think Carly and Lily might be at Caldfell Hall.'
'At the Hall?'
'Alex, I think I've sorted out the whole story in my head — but when I try to explain, it just seems so crazy.'

As they turned through the village, they saw the Hall looming above them on the ridge. For the first time it made Suzy shiver. The soft, magic whiteness in February and then the touch of soft spring a few days earlier had masked the Hall's other aspect — austere and forbidding on the crest of the hill. Behind, in the distance, the standing stones rose up like big, black bones. The driveway still had the same expensive flower tubs as the day before, but they looked ridiculous, wind-battered and broken. There was a dusting of winter sticks and windblown debris whirling on the lawn. Suzy shuddered. 'It looks empty,' she said.

They parked, and walked in the fierce easterly wind to the massive front door. It was tightly shut.

'Have you called Eva?' asked Alex.

'She's not answering,' Suzy said. Alex looked at her. 'You don't think Eva's involved in all this, do you?'

Suzy didn't answer. She was banging on the door as if her life depended on it. Eventually it was opened by the same bouncer who had been in charge at the funeral.

'Is anyone here?' Suzy asked.

'What's it got to do with you?'

Suzy pulled down her hood, shaking her hair free in the rain so he could see her. 'You remember us from Brigham's wake. Alex Armstrong and Suzy Spencer. We came to visit Eva Delmondo yesterday. And then we went to see Pearl and Mrs Scott-Broughton.' If she quoted important names, Suzy thought, he would be more likely to let them in.

'We're closed up now,' he said, more civilly.

'But we need to speak to someone.'

'I said there's no one here.'

'Where's Mrs Scott-Broughton?'

'She was taken to hospital in the night. That's all I know.'

'Which hospital? Workhaven? Norbridge? Newcastle?'

'Nothing to do with me, mate. That yank bird sorted it all out.'

'Eva?'

'Well, she's not here either. She must have gone with them. I don't have nuthin' to do with upstairs. Look, you'd better clear off the premises. We've got a new security company starting at nine o'clock. With dogs. This place is going to be locked up tighter than Dartmoor.'

This was new. Only the day before, fresh plants had been delivered; cleaners had been preparing the place for the new season. Eva had said Gervase wanted the place kept beautifully until he came back for *The Sacred Spring*.

Suzy turned into the wind and rain. She motioned to Alex, and they ploughed through the downpour to the car.

'Where now?' Alex asked.

'Old Fred's. He knows more than he realizes. If Carly and Lily aren't here, they must be somewhere nearby. Although this hospital thing — and the place being shut up — I don't get that.' Suzy shook her head. She hadn't expected this.

To her relief, the door at Fred Lamplugh's was open. She went inside. 'Fred? Are you home?' There was a reassuring smell of frying bacon.

The old farmer came into the hall. 'Aye, 'ow do?'

'Fred, I need to talk to you.'

'Come into t'kitchen. Tea? It's a bit brewed.'

'No, thanks. Fred, when we talked about Eva, you mentioned another one coming here. Another what?'

'Aye, so I did. I didn't know it mattered. All wrapped up in winter gear with a scarf round their head. I thought it were a lass but it could have been a gadgie. Wearing one of those anoraks everyone wears.'

'And what did they want? When did they come?'

'They came the day that Freddie went missing. He'd left here, and I never saw him again. They said they was helping Freddie get an interview with that Scott-Broughton bastard and Freddie'd left something in his room. They took some papers of his but just ones with scribbles on. I dunno what it was about.'

'Did you tell the police about it?'

'They never asked. They had it all cut and dried. Anyway, what difference would it make?'

'The police used doodles from Freddie's London flat to prove the confession was his. Are there any others here?'

Fred said gruffly. 'I'll go and look.' He lumbered out of the door.

'Don't you see, Alex?' Suzy said as the door swung behind him. 'Someone came and took paper that Freddie had scrawled on. Then they turned it into a suicide note. They could write some blather — like, I WANT TO KILL HIM — in upper case or felt tip — something hard to identify as handwriting. It would look like a confession of murder. If we can get other doodles of Freddie's we can show how it was done.'

'But who was it who came here?'

'I'm pretty sure I know. Someone who could disguise themselves. But more important is finding Carly and Lily. Look at this, Alex. It's the text from Carly to Christopher. Robert showed it to me. *Found frenetic too messy at all back soon. C and L.* But Carly would never say frenetic. I think this message was mangled by typos and predictive text. Carly didn't check it — she just pinged it off. We've all done that.'

'But you can't work backwards to find out what she wrote.'

'Oh, but you can try. Look.'

Suzy wrote: *Found rene tic tok message at hall back soon*.

'Oh my God!' said Alex. 'So Carly found Renee through a TikTok message and now she's at the Hall. Who sent the message?'

'I think I know that too. I was sure Carly and Lily would be at the Hall. But as it's all locked up, how can we find out? Say they're trapped in there? Or have they been taken away?'

Old Fred came back in. 'There's these scraps of paper. Freddie was a great one for scribblin'.'

'Fred, can you put them in an envelope, and in a safe place. The police might need them. You know about Lily Martin, the girl from Norbridge who's the singing star? We think she and her mother have been abducted. I think someone could be hiding Lily and her mother in the outbuildings.'

The old farmer looked at her. 'I was out lambing in the night. I thought I saw something . . .'

'Where, Fred?'

'Get yer togs back on and follow me. We're going out the back way.'

Suzy and Alex wrapped up to follow Fred, who grabbed his ancient waterproof and, without thinking about it, a loop of lambing rope from the peg. Then he set off at a pace which astonished Suzy, but not towards the Hall.

'Where are we going, Fred?' she called to him through the rain.

Fred started to climb.

'This is madness, Suzy.' Alex was out of breath. 'They can't be out on the fells.'

'He knows what he's doing,' said Suzy. 'I think I understand where we're going.' Fred suddenly turned off on a path to their left.

'Look,' she said to Alex. 'We're above the Hall.'

Alex gasped. 'We're going to the standing stones.'

'Yes. Of course. I get it now . . .'

'Get what, Suzy?'

'Where they are and what's happening. Come on, Alex, you're the local. Your forebears carried coffins over hills like this. Keep walking. It's not far now.'

Suddenly the standing stones were right in front of them. Fred motioned them to stand still.

'Listen,' he said. Very faintly, from out of the earth, they could hear someone singing.

* * *

Robert woke up at The Briars at eight in the morning, unhappy. Then he remembered. He and Suzy had had a serious row. After he'd come home, he'd looked in their bedroom and she was lying on her back snoring. He'd seen the wine bottle on the draining board. So he went to the spare room.

This was the sign of things to come. She was asserting her independence and her relative youth and energy. Even if this mad idea about working with Lauren Scott-Broughton in the US was just a fantasy, it was a fantasy she was enjoying. If that was what Suzy really wanted, then the life they had been planning was just a sham. He wondered how he could face her in the light of morning.

His mind started working madly. It was astonishing how, at times of terrible crisis, you started thinking about things like who would get the copper pans when they split up. Would Suzy want to have her own place in Manchester or Newcastle? She'd put a lot of money into renovating The Briars after her divorce. He couldn't afford to buy her out. He would have to move too.

For goodness' sake, he told himself. *You're a long way from splitting up. Maybe you could compromise.* He shouldn't have been so hasty. He should have tried to understand that there would still be a flicker of ambition burning inside Suzy, and a powerful woman like Lauren Scott-Broughton could ignite it.

I'll just go into our bedroom and see if she's awake. He longed to put his arms around her. He walked onto the landing and found himself knocking at his own bedroom door. Ridiculous. There was no answer. She must still be asleep after all that wine.

He went back to the spare room and dressed in yesterday's clothes. He felt tired and slightly nauseous. The trendy artisan bakery in the village opened early. He would walk up there and get fresh croissants, bring them back and put coffee on for when Suzy woke up.

He went out of the front door, not seeing Suzy's note on the kitchen table.

* * *

'Can you hear it? The singing?' Suzy whispered through the rain. Alex nodded. 'They're in the graves.' Old Fred had hung back. 'Fred, how do we get in?'

'There's a doorway. I put a big stone in front of it but in the night I saw it had gone. There was a light. Candles. I thought the hippies were back.'

'I'm going in there,' said Suzy.

'I'm coming with you,' Alex called after her.

Suzy could see the entrance clearly. It was high enough for her to go in if she stooped, but harder for Alex, who was taller. There was a passageway ahead with a corner, then it turned and opened out into a first chamber. She'd visited other graves like this in Scotland.

But this wasn't like anything she'd seen before. As she entered the chamber, Suzy saw it was full of candles. Scented candles. And it was furnished. There was a sofa made of stone slabs covered with thick animal skins. But the cold was intense.

Suzy shouted into the darkness beyond, 'Come out. Come out now!'

Alex watched over her shoulder, mesmerized by the lights.

A figure came from the chamber beyond. It was ghostly, skeletal, in black.

'I know it's you, Lauren,' Suzy shouted. 'Where's Lily?'

Lauren Scott-Broughton sashayed almost jauntily from the second inner chamber. She had no trouble walking now, erect and elegant. She even laughed as she passed Suzy, and sneered with a raised eyebrow at Alex. She then stood with her back to the passageway where they had come in, blocking their exit.

'So you worked it out in the end, Suzy Spencer,' she said. 'It took you long enough. But now we hold all the cards.'

'Oh my God!' Alex screamed. 'You've got Lily.'

Alex rushed in fury at the elongated figure and brought her crashing to the floor, cracking her head on the side of the stone-built sofa. At the same time, Suzy became aware of a trussed-up body in the corner of the chamber with some sort of sack over its head. It writhed and moaned.

'Eva,' said Suzy. 'It's OK, we're here. Fred, untie her and get her out, the way we came in.' Fred went to Eva and began to drag her away.

'Watch out for Pearl!' Alex yelled.

Pearl had followed her beloved boss out of the inner chamber. She was carrying a burning candle in one hand

and a plastic container in the other. She said in her flat voice, 'Where's Mrs S-B?'

'On the floor over there,' said Suzy. Pearl gasped and moved towards her boss. Alex didn't try to stop her.

'You've hurt Mrs S-B. You'll pay. This is kerosene I've got here.'

Suzy thought of her note to Robert. Would he understand where she was? Would he come after her?

'Lauren is out cold, Pearl,' Alex said. 'But she'll come round. It's no worse than what happened to my husband . . .'

Pearl turned slowly towards her. 'No, actually. Someone else hit your man. We found him in the snow and smeared some of Palmer's blood on him. We hadn't planned it but it seemed a good idea. No harm in muddying the waters.'

Alex advanced on Pearl and pushed her onto the sofa.

Suzy said, 'Let's start at the beginning, Pearl. Lauren used to be called Renee, didn't she? And Carly was her lover. But Carly was Parry Palmer's lover too, if only for one night. Did you kill Parry Palmer to avenge Mrs Scott-Broughton?'

Pearl laughed. 'We did it together. It was wonderful; I just held him down. Mrs S-B put the knife in like I told her to. I'm not American. I'm Canadian. From the Northwest Territories. I know about snow. And butchering. I'm a farmer's daughter, used to killing pigs. We kept some blood as it spurted out. I'd brought a container.'

'And you put the blood on Edwin?'

'Yeah. We found him lying in the snow. We thought he might get blamed for Parry if there was blood on him. But we really planned to pin it on Freddie. When it was his turn, we soaked him in the stuff. We had to keep the blood warm all day, which wasn't easy. But that blood on his coat proved to your dopey British police that he'd killed Parry Palmer. Little idiot. He was asking to be blamed.'

Pearl put her head back and laughed.

CHAPTER THIRTY-TWO

He hath showed strength with his arm; he hath scattered the proud in the imagination of their hearts. Luke 1:51

'So explain about Freddie?' Suzy asked, when Pearl had stopped laughing and became impassive again.

'He made trouble. He wrote to both the S-Bs making a case against Parry Palmer for stealing his silly little madrigal. Gervase ignored him, of course. But Mrs S-B could see how we could use him. She replied, and told him she would like to meet him at Caldfell. But I went instead of her. I told him to go back to the farm and write out how much of a shit Parry Palmer had been. I took a chance on the boy not having a printer up here and writing it out by hand and I was right.'

'You went to the farm!' Suzy said. 'You were the other one. You wanted some writing of Freddie's!'

'Yes, I needed to pick up his scribbling. I just wrote over it in big letters, *I WILL KILL HIM*. Then later I put it in his pocket. The police loved that.'

'And what happened then? After you'd killed Parry Palmer?'

'I met the boy again. He thought I was going to take him into the Hall for an audience with Mrs S-B but I kept him locked up in the buildings. I needed to kill him in the night, once Palmer was good and dead. I forced the drink and drugs down Freddie, then let him out into the freezing night, up there by the stones. It didn't take long for him to die, but it took you a while to find him.'

Alex whispered, 'That was the man in the night, the one Lily saw.' Suzy nodded. But she kept her eyes on Pearl.

'And you managed all this, traipsing about in the snow?'

'Yes. It was a godsend. I'd brought the snowshoes in case. I had a pair for me and for Mrs S-B.'

'So you handled things for Mrs S-B, didn't you? She said so yesterday. I said the scissors had pearl handles and she thought I said, "Pearl handled it." Do you keep her drugged up most of the time, Pearl? Or is she the one pulling the strings?'

Pearl waved the candle around. The light flickered off her distorted face.

'Mrs S-B is a wonderful person. I help her when she needs rest. But this was all her plan. She has an amazing brain. And she's not really an invalid. But she made everyone think she was. In fact, she's unbelievably tough.'

As if in proof of this, Lauren Scott-Broughton suddenly uncoiled herself from the floor and stood up, all in one movement, a black snake-like figure with a huge shadow highlighted by the scented candles, like some sort of evil angel. Suzy was sure she was drugged.

Lauren moved to where Pearl was sitting on the stone couch and put her arms around her. She towered over Pearl and lovingly kissed the top of her head. Pearl shuddered with pleasure.

'Let me tell you more,' Lauren said in a conversational tone. 'We're all going to die here today. But you should die knowing what you've been dealing with. You have to understand,' she said softly, 'that I've done everything from the highest moral principles. I was in a terrible marriage. Oh, Gervase loved me. Desperately. But that wasn't the deal. For me it was a business arrangement and that is perfectly respectable until one partner asks too much. It was meant to be a sensible match — money, prestige, opportunity. After Carol, I knew there could never be anyone else for me, so I married Gervase for commercial reasons. When it comes to taste' — she sniggered lasciviously — 'I prefer women.' She stroked Pearl's shoulder again. Pearl still held the candle and the kerosene but leaned her head back against Lauren's thin chest.

Suzy had to keep them talking.

'And Carly Martin?' she asked.

'*Carol* Martin,' Lauren corrected her. 'Carol was the love of my life. Love and hate. Twin feelings. Carol betrayed me. I could never forgive her, but I could never forget her either. *You* might think of Carol as a lightweight but to me she was light itself, a free spirit. But she had a common soul, and she lied to me. And she got pregnant by a loathsome man. Not the father I had chosen so carefully for our baby. She was unfaithful. As I said, I have very high moral standards.'

That was what Gervase said too, Suzy thought. *My wife has very high standards.*

'And of course,' Lauren went on chattily now, enjoying an audience at last, 'in the fulness of time I discovered that Gervase had betrayed me too. Granted, he didn't know it. But he never told me the truth about his relationship with the ghastly Parry Palmer. He talked me into giving our money to that Mickey Mouse outfit, the Academy of Voice. But as soon as I saw Palmer, I recognized him. All along, Gervase had been best friends with the man who ruined my life — Parry Palmer.'

Pearl said softly, 'Everyone betrayed Mrs S-B, poor sweetheart. Everyone but me!' She waved the kerosene can.

Suzy had to keep the dialogue going.

'But how come Parry Palmer didn't recognize you in turn, Lauren?'

'No chance,' Pearl piped up gleefully. 'He'd only met Mrs S-B once, and believe me she looks totally different now. Gorgeous. But when she was with Carol Martin, she was overweight. Her hair was just brown. Messy. She didn't look anything special till I came to work for her. I made her beautiful.'

'How did you meet Carol, Lauren?' But Pearl answered for her boss.

'My wonderful Mrs S-B was in London for a year after Oxford, on the fringes of the music scene, and she fell in love. It was her chance to have a baby. Mrs S-B was desperate for a child. A mini me.'

Suzy was suddenly aware of movement in the passage behind the two women. Now was the time to ask the most important question.

'So where are Carly and Lily now? Was that Lily we could hear singing? And what's the point of all this set dressing?'

Lauren looked around. 'It's beautiful, isn't it? Carol liked scented candles. She had them all round the bed when we lived together.'

'And you re-created the love nest?'

'Exactly! You're not as stupid as I thought, Suzy, although you fell totally for my ludicrous suggestion that you come to New York. Everyone can be bought, can't they? That put you right off the scent, didn't it?' Lauren started to laugh more harshly, her thin chest heaving under the black, slinky fabric.

Pearl cut in, 'Stay calm, Mrs S-B. You mustn't get hyper.'

'So is Lauren ill or what?' said Suzy. She needed to know but she also needed to keep these two women talking. In a minute Fred Lamplugh would come back from releasing Eva. His entry into the chamber was behind Lauren and Pearl. Suzy hoped against hope that he had heard what was happening and would creep down in the shadows to attack them from behind. But he was an old man: even if he thought of it, would he be able to do it?

'Oh, Mrs S-B's ill, all right,' Pearl said. 'But not in the way you thought. That was another of her brilliant ideas. No one suspects a cancer patient. My darling Mrs S-B is the most brilliant woman you can imagine but . . .'

'I'll tell them, Pearl. Yes, I do have an outstanding intellect. But with that comes depression. Terrible suicidal, wretched depression and fear. I'm ill. Very ill. That is my illness. After I lost Carol — or rather she lost me — I could never get her out of my mind and it ate away at me. Oh, I tried to beat it . . .'

'Yes,' Pearl said. 'Look at her beautiful hair. She lost one side of it when she had the NMD.'

'The what?'

'Neurosurgery for mental disorder. A hole in the skull. She had it done privately back home. But it didn't work.'

'I let everyone think I was terminally ill,' Lauren said. 'And I was. I wanted to terminate my own life. But my plan for Carol kept me alive. It gave me something to live for, a planned death not just for me but for the woman who deceived me — and her unwanted child.'

Pearl said, 'Exactly. We've been planning this for over a year. Mrs S-B never lost track of Carol Martin. She had a letter from her when the child was born and she paid private detectives to track her down. It suited us perfectly to persuade Gervase to come back to his ancestral home.'

'Yes.' Lauren's voice was soft now. 'I couldn't believe how it all came together for us. And just one TikTok message had Carol racing back to me when we were ready. It was meant to be.'

Pearl added, 'So Mrs S-B wants to die now, in peace. We both want to die. And we want Carol to die with us. And that warbling child of hers. We were going to use pills but now it will be fire. Because you have to go too . . .'

'Yes.' Lauren sounded almost dreamy. 'How odd that the misbegotten child turned out to be just the sort of daughter I would have wanted. But it was impossible. Her parentage was disgusting and her singing voice was an aberration. I just want all the moral misfits to die with me. So we killed Parry Palmer first. Freddie Lamplugh was a nobody, collateral damage. Now the rest of us will die together.'

'So Carly and Lily are here?' Suzy asked.

'Of course,' Pearl laughed. 'In the next chamber. Isn't it perfect? We scoped these graves months ago. It has atmosphere.'

'It's a burial chamber.'

'Exactly! Perfect,' said Lauren. 'Though now it will be a cremation, not a burial. But it will be death. That's all that matters.'

Suzy looked levelly at Pearl. The candle she was holding was burning lower.

'Put that candle out, Pearl. You don't really want to die, do you?'

'We're all going to die. My life is over when Mrs S-B goes.'

Suzy felt cold in her bones. 'But not like this, Pearl, in a fire. Dying from burns will be excruciating both for you and for Mrs S-B. Does she know how agonizing it will be? And it won't be a quick conflagration because we will fight you. Mrs S-B will get horrible injuries. Do you want that?'

Pearl wavered. Suzy tried to hold her stare. They locked eyes. But Suzy could see movement on the floor.

Eva Delmondo and Fred Lamplugh had both come back into the cave and had crawled in the shadows down the passage to the burial chamber. As Suzy held Pearl's eyes, and Lauren shut hers in an ecstasy of self-fulfilment, Eva and Fred rushed forward.

Pearl went down. The open kerosene can flew through the air and landed inches away from the scented candles. The fuel slowly began to drip out.

'Where's Lily?' Alex screamed.

'We're here!' Lily shrieked back from the furthest chamber.

Suzy thought fast. Fred had used these caves for his lambing ewes. 'Is there another way out?'

'Yon hole at the back!' Fred Lamplugh shouted.

'I can't see it!' Lily screamed.

'There's a big stone over it,' old Fred shouted. 'Just push it and crawl out.'

'You go, Alex!' Suzy called. 'Go and get Lily and Carly out at the other end. I'll be OK. Fred, can you tie Pearl up? And Eva, can you hold Lauren down?'

'My pleasure!' yelled Eva Delmondo.

Alex had already run through to the furthest chamber. Fred dragged the writhing Pearl, arms fastened by the lambing rope, and scrambled after Alex, who was pulling Lily and Carly towards the stone at the exit of the cave. Suzy and Eva followed, pushing a crazed, writhing Lauren.

The first flame suddenly shot towards the roof, making hellish shadows. Suzy pushed one final time, the fear of the flames giving her courage. She didn't dare let go of Lauren's flailing legs, while Eva pulled the wriggling woman by the arms. Suddenly they burst through the adjoining low doorway and into the second chamber. At the end Suzy could see light. Behind her, flames were licking the domed ceiling and there was a sickening smell of burning sheepskin.

Then there was a watery grey light. A crude hole had been cleared in the side of the second tomb. Alex, Lily and Carly had wriggled out, with Fred heaving Pearl after them. Eva followed, dragging Lauren, and Suzy came last, pushing Lauren's resistant body forward as she kicked back at Suzy's arms and face. Then suddenly Lauren slumped — passed out again. She was a dead weight now, but she wasn't kicking.

Behind them the fire crackled at the rugs. Suzy pushed Lauren's body with all her strength to the daylight at the end of the hole and then followed her out, falling behind her onto a ledge at the side of the sweeping fell. Fred, Carly, Lily and Alex were already sitting, retching, trying to get the scorched smell out of their lungs, balanced precariously on a lip of land below the exit from the burial chambers.

They relaxed too soon. With a mad, primeval roar, Pearl stood up and lurched her bound body head first back into the chamber. There was nothing they could do. They heard her screams as she went into the fire.

Suzy lay there, looking down to the Irish Sea and the sweep of the West Cumbria coast. Dawn was coming over the fells behind her to the east and a flash of cold sun hit the silvery water below.

She didn't know what hit her when Lauren Scott-Broughton, screaming wildly, cannoned into her from behind and went to her death, crashing down on to the rocks below and taking Suzy with her. The last thing Suzy saw as she fell was the blue light of the police car winding up the road towards the Hall.

* * *

Robert had arrived home from the bakery and seen Suzy's note on the kitchen table. He groaned, 'No!' and phoned Ro Watson.

'Ro, please, you've got to help me. Suzy has gone to Caldfell Hall. She must have left hours ago. I think there's going to be some sort of confrontation. Can you and Jed get up there and see? I may be wrong but I don't think so.'

Ro sounded sleepy. 'What?' she said.

'Please, Ro. For the sake of the times when you and Suzy have solved murders. Whether she's on the right or wrong track, you owe it to her to go after her. Goodness knows what she's stirred up but please, please go to Caldfell Hall!'

* * *

Ro was first on the scene. She tried some basic first aid, but she could see that Suzy was unconscious and in a strange, twisted position at the foot of the ridge. She called an ambulance, cursing herself for not getting there sooner. Suzy was in a bad way.

She was taken to Workhaven Infirmary with concussion and a fractured vertebra. The vertebra was snapped but still connected. The treatment was complete bed rest, lying on her back, for at least three weeks.

When Robert came to see her, he explained to her what had happened after she had been knocked unconscious by her fall.

'It seems Lauren was full of drugs. There was a stash of cocaine in the chamber, but in her body there was other stuff too.'

'And Eva?'

'She's bounced back. She's still at the Hall, back in great form, wearing that boiler suit and dealing with everything. She says Gervase Scott-Broughton is a mess over in the States. He really had no idea about his wife. He thought Trent had set up Freddie Lamplugh. He realized that it was all too neat, and he knew someone had used Freddie as a scapegoat. But like a lot of rich and powerful people, he just assumed some lackey had sorted out his problem for him. Although there was something Gervase couldn't forgive Trent . . .'

'Brigham's death?'

'Yes. Gervase told Eva that Trent confessed to helping Parry Palmer poison Brigham Broughton's whisky. But there was a post-mortem on Brigham which showed he died from heart failure, so Brigham was cremated. And we'll never know for sure how he died.'

'But Trent thought by asking Parry Palmer to see Brigham off, he was doing Gervase a favour.'

'Yep, but he got it wrong. And he got the sack.'

* * *

After three days, Alex was allowed to come and see Suzy. She looked awful, Suzy thought. Pale and drawn.

'Are you OK, Alex? You don't look too good. We went through a lot up there on the fell. I'm not the only one who had a tough time.'

'I'm all right.' Alex smiled. 'In fact, I'm very all right. I'm pregnant!'

'Oh, Alex, that's incredible. How wonderful. I'd sit up and kiss you if I wasn't pinned to this bed. But I thought you said . . .'

'Yes. I started what I thought was a period when we were at Caldfell. But it was just a bleed. I didn't really think about the fact it had stopped. Let's be honest, there was a lot going on.'

'So the IVF had worked after all.'

'Yes. I went to the clinic the day after . . . the day after that terrible business. It really was a miracle.'

'And then you got so involved with Lily.'

'Yes. Maybe having Lily to love helped somehow. And something else, Suzy. I've tried very hard with Carly. I think all that shock has changed her. Of course, she's got deep-seated mental health and addiction problems but she's clean now. And she's getting proper therapy.' Alex coloured slightly and Suzy wondered who was paying for it.

Suzy felt warm, and suddenly contented. Then she frowned. 'But Alex, why did Lily mock up that singing lesson? Where was she?'

'I've asked her that. When Carly refused to get out of the cab and meet the rich and famous S-Bs at the Hall, it was totally uncharacteristic. Lily constantly called her mother and knew she'd gone to London, but suddenly, on the day Palmer died, Carly stopped answering. Lily reckoned she was plotting something. She faked her singing lesson to go out just after the snowfall because she thought her mother had come back. She was right, of course. Carly was there, in the storeroom, with Brigham's supplies, getting ready to smack Parry Palmer with a piece of wood. But he had already been killed by Lauren and Pearl. Lily was the little figure that Edwin saw, and who he presumed was Freddie Lamplugh.'

'But why didn't Lily see Lauren and Pearl coming back from the Gothic folly?'

'They walked round the top, via the graves, on their snowshoes. I realize now that I had seen strange patterns on the floor in the folly. They must have been from the snowshoes.'

Suzy lay back exhausted. It was all sorted now. Messy. Not nearly as neat as the police's solution — but it was the right solution.

Just as she was leaving, Alex turned and said, 'Oh, and Eva wants to come and see you. Apparently, Gervase is talking about turning the Hall into a centre for young musicians and he needs a manager. She may be staying around and she'll need friends.'

'Wow, that's a big change. Cumbrian's answer to Jennifer Lopez.'

Alex smiled. 'Maybe not so much. You remember me saying that I thought Eva was about as Puerto Rican as I am? Well, I was almost right. She confided to me that she's really Eve Desmond, a nice middle-class girl from the burbs. But she knows how to make an impression. And she did have a Puerto Rican grandfather on her mother's side. But he wasn't a Jet or a Shark. He was an accountant.'

CHAPTER THIRTY-THREE

He hath shewed strength with his arm; he hath scattered the proud in the imagination of their hearts. Luke 1:51

Suzy had another visitor, this one totally unexpected. She was an inconspicuous woman in her seventies. Parry Palmer's sister.

'Thank you for seeing me.'

'I'm sorry for your loss.'

'Really?'

'Yes. Your brother didn't deserve to be knifed, whatever he did. How did you know about me?'

'Mrs Tomkins, Ayesha's mum, told me. We're neighbours. We didn't live too far from the Tomkins when we were children. Parry went up in the world, but he stayed in the same neighbourhood. My brother was a funny mix. He seemed so confident, but he was uncomfortable away from his manor.'

'And he lived and worked in Islington all his life.'

'That's right. I know a lot of people didn't like him. And I can see why. He was even horrible to me sometimes, the mocking and the meanness. I came to see you because I wanted you to know why he was like that.'

Suzy was intrigued. 'Tell me.'

'Parry was the youngest boy. We had two older brothers. People were brought up in areas like ours to be tough and hold their own, back in the old days. You had to survive and carve out your place and you did it by putting other people down. Even in your own family. My dad was a taunt and a bully. And Parry got the worst of it. He was skinny and liked posh music and sang in the church choir. They were merciless with him. Dad thought it would toughen him up. And I suppose in a way it did.'

Suzy said, 'I wondered why he behaved as he did. Thanks for helping me understand.'

'Oh, there are other people still bearing the scars of that sort of upbringing. And they don't all go bad like Parry. But it was worse for him. They made fun of the fact he had a condition.'

'A condition?'

'Yes. He had to have an operation for it. Testicular torsion. Twisted balls, to put it bluntly. He was only twelve. Poor Parry. It was the source of endless jokes at home. I loved him, you know. I think I'm the only person who did.'

After she had gone, Suzy lay in bed and thought about Parry Palmer. She felt as if she knew him better now. And she was glad she understood why he had been as he was. It was no excuse. But it was an explanation of sorts.

And then she wondered. She googled his 'condition' and found that it could have affected his fertility. It would be his biggest laugh. Tell them you could make them pregnant, make them come back for more, and all along know there was no chance.

Or maybe he never knew he was firing blanks.

She thought about Alex being pregnant all along, despite having had a period, a slight one. Maybe the same thing had happened to Carly. The slightest show of blood would have panicked her into trying again with someone else. She was scared of Renee. Renee wanted her to be pregnant by Christopher Murray.

But perhaps she was. He should get that DNA test after all.

* * *

At the weekend Jake and Mae turned up at the hospital. Jake was sheepish and Mae looked completely overwhelmed. She grabbed Suzy by the hand.

'You look so vulnerable in here,' she said. 'It would have been a tragedy for us if you had been killed.'

'It wouldn't have been so good for me, either.'

For a minute, Mae looked blank, and then she burst into laughter. 'But you are funny! And I have been so scared of you.'

Really? Suzy thought. *Scared of me?*

'Anyway,' Jake said gruffly, 'we had some news until you got all the attention.'

Mae blushed. 'You are going to be a grand-mère.'

Suzy thought the world was spinning around her bed. 'Pardon?'

Jake said, 'Mum, Mae is having a baby. And we're moving back to Cumbria, so you can help with the childcare. Robert said you were thinking of going to America. You'd better think again.'

* * *

That evening Robert came back. 'Actually, Suzy, I didn't know when to tell you this. Your company has sold Linkflex a concept. A podcast with video called *Country Crime with Suzy Spencer*. That's only the working title, of course. But they want six what they call 'beautifully crafted gems'. True crime but cosy. To be made in Norbridge and marketed globally. What do you think?'

So much had happened that Suzy just held his hand.

Eventually she said, 'Babies. Alex and Mae. A new media venture based in Norbridge. It's all too much. I don't suppose you managed to get the right hearing aids, just to make things great.'

'Bake things date? Date and walnut. One of my favourites.'

'Robert . . .' Suzy flapped at him with her arms from her prone position. He was laughing.

'Yes, Suzy, I really did hear you clearly now I have super-discreet hearing aids. But listen to me. This true crime series is for six episodes. No more. It's a finite deal. It works because people can just about believe that you were involved in six country murders in twenty years. Any more and you're in the realm of fiction. Untrue crime. So this investigation has to be the last. Do you understand?'

'I hear you loud and clear.'

'It's mutual!'

* * *

A few weeks later, the doctors gave Suzy the OK to sit up. Robert and Molly came to help. It was the most peculiar sensation she had ever felt. She didn't know what to expect, but as they raised her up to a sitting position, she felt all her internal organs shift and fall softly. The fragility of her own body suddenly overwhelmed her. Robert was right. There would be no more crazy risks. That period of her life was over.

And Molly said, 'Jake isn't the only one coming back to Cumbria. My friend Becky and I are thinking of opening a vintage clothes shop. You know I've always liked off-beat fashion, Mum. I've got my day job photographing weddings and commercial shoots. The clothes will be fun. And I'm back with my old boyfriend, Rafi.'

'He's coming back to Cumbria too?'

Molly smiled. 'Yes. We're all coming home. Don't worry, not to The Briars. But close enough to mind the place while you and Robert go to New York to promote *Cumbrian Crime*.'

'Best of both worlds.' Suzy smiled, exhausted with sitting up.

'Best of *all* worlds,' said Robert, and kissed her lightly on the head. Suzy wriggled. It had been so odd, feeling her insides shift. But now she was sure that her heart was back in the right place.

* * *

The Sacred Spring was a big success. Lily was on the path to stardom, supervised by Alex, who swore she would still have time for Lily when her own twins were born. Tom Finch, a wonderful young tenor whom Suzy had met during a murder case years before, came back with his wife Poppy to sing the part of Joseph to Lily's Mary. Callum Oldcastle was entranced by Lily's performance, his father noted. Dave Oldcastle was the choral director and did a sterling job. Marcus Sotheby was outstanding as Simeon and Zachariah, and Ayesha was there with all her family. Irene Przybylski was in the audience, along with Rachel, and Howard, the Klezmer-playing widower she was seeing. And Christopher Murray looked extremely proud, sitting next to Howard's brother, the violinist he had met in London. Old Fred Lamplugh came, with Freddie's parents. Freddie's mother had decided to move back to Cumbria and take over the farm. They left Rags the sheepdog in the Land Rover during the performance.

And Alexandra Armstrong, an outstanding contralto herself, sang the poignant song of Elizabeth when her baby sprang in her womb.

* * *

Suzy took her time getting well. And when the summer sun shone through the trees and there was a sense of drowsy peace, she sat up suddenly in her garden chair. She was overwhelmed by a vivid memory of winter, triggered by the sunlight on the thick white roses draped over the wall. For a second it looked like snow, and she was transported back to that day in February when it all began . . . It had been her strangest case, her most dangerous, and her last.

It was high summer now. And her days of sleuthing were over. She settled back in her chair and let the sunshine play on her face till Robert came out and kissed her on the lips.

THE END

MUSIC FOR *THE SACRED SPRING*

At the start of this story, Edwin Armstrong is composing a piece of choral music for Candlemas, 2 February, a church festival also known as 'The Presentation of Christ in the Temple' or 'The Purification of the Blessed Virgin Mary'. It marks an event described in the Bible in Luke 2:22–39.

According to Jewish law (in Leviticus 12), a firstborn child should be presented and dedicated to the Lord forty days after the birth. (Candlemas falls forty days after Christmas Day.) Mary and Joseph took the baby Jesus to the temple in Jerusalem — only about five miles from Bethlehem — in order to offer a sacrifice to God. If the parents could not afford a lamb for sacrifice, a pair of doves or young pigeons would be an acceptable alternative, and it seems that this was what happened here.

Luke tells us that at the temple they met a man called Simeon. It had been revealed to him that he would not die until he had seen 'the Lord's Christ' — the Messiah. He took Jesus in his arms and spoke the words which came to be known as the *Nunc Dimittis*, starting with 'Lord, now lettest thou thy servant depart in peace.' In the Anglican church, the *Nunc Dimittis* is always sung during the evening service, and is often used at funerals. The family also met a devout eighty-four-year-old widow called Anna, described as a prophetess. She realized who Jesus was, praised God, and spoke about him to everyone she met.

From about the year 1000, 2 February became a major feast requiring attendance at church. Parishioners had a duty to bring a gift of candles which would be blessed with incense and sprinkled with holy water, and so in England it became known as Candlemas. As they processed with their candles, they were making a reference to Simeon's description of Jesus as 'a light to lighten the Gentiles'. Candlemas processions were discontinued in England with the Reformation in the sixteenth century.

In this story, Edwin Armstrong goes on to compose a piece for the postponed concert. This includes his original Candlemas music, and adds material for another date in the Church calendar: the Visitation on 31 May. This marks an event described in Luke 1:39–55.

The Virgin Mary, while pregnant with Jesus, travelled to the hill country to visit her cousin Elizabeth, who was pregnant with a child that would become John the Baptist. When they met, Elizabeth's baby leaped in her womb (the 'spring'). Elizabeth blessed Mary and her child, and Mary responded with the words which became the *Magnificat*, starting 'My soul doth magnify the Lord.' As with the *Nunc Dimittis*, the *Magnificat* is always included in the evening service in Anglican churches.

THE JOFFE BOOKS STORY

We began in 2014 when Jasper agreed to publish his mum's much-rejected romance novel and it became a bestseller.

Since then we've grown into the largest independent publisher in the UK. We're extremely proud to publish some of the very best writers in the world, including Joy Ellis, Faith Martin, Caro Ramsay, Helen Forrester, Simon Brett and Robert Goddard. Everyone at Joffe Books loves reading and we never forget that it all begins with the magic of an author telling a story.

We are proud to publish talented first-time authors, as well as established writers whose books we love introducing to a new generation of readers.

We won Trade Publisher of the Year at the Independent Publishing Awards in 2023 and Best Publisher Award in 2024 at the People's Book Prize. We have been shortlisted for Independent Publisher of the Year at the British Book Awards for the last five years, and were shortlisted for the Diversity and Inclusivity Award at the 2022 Independent Publishing Awards. In 2023 we were shortlisted for Publisher of the Year at the RNA Industry Awards, and in 2024 we were shortlisted at the CWA Daggers for the Best Crime and Mystery Publisher.

We built this company with your help, and we love to hear from you, so please email us about absolutely anything bookish at feedback@joffebooks.com.

If you want to receive free books every Friday and hear about all our new releases, join our mailing list here: www.joffebooks.com/freebooks.

And when you tell your friends about us, just remember: it's pronounced Joffe as in coffee or toffee!

www.ingramcontent.com/pod-product-compliance
Ingram Content Group UK Ltd.
Pitfield, Milton Keynes, MK11 3LW, UK
UKHW011150300625
6641UKWH00026B/132